# SHADES OF HATE

JACKY LEON BOOK FIVE

K.N. BANET

Copyright © 2021 by K.N. Banet

All rights reserved.

No part of this book may be reproduced in any form or by any electronic or mechanical means, including information storage and retrieval systems, without written permission from the author, except for the use of brief quotations in a book review.

This is a work of fiction. Names, characters, businesses, places, events, locales, and incidents are either the products of the author's imagination or used in a fictitious manner. Any resemblance to actual persons, living or dead, or actual events is purely coincidental.

# CHAPTER ONE
## MARCH 20, 2021

I walked out of my house with a smile, ready to get through another day of work. The sun was going down, the bar was open, and the spring night still had a little chill to it. I just needed to get to Kick Shot, but I wasn't in any sort of rush because I didn't open anymore. I didn't do anything, really. I showed up as the owner and talked to the patrons, then disappeared into the office to go over the finances with Oliver if needed. Honestly, it was boring work, but it was my job now. Kick Shot had been overrun by overachievers, handed off to me by my own family.

I was getting used to it. Every day, I got a little better at standing to the side and letting Oliver make the important decisions. He was good at hiring the right people, better at managing the finances, and he excelled at keeping the customers happy, both new and old. There were a lot of new customers. We were beginning to attract a younger crowd, exactly as Oliver wanted. College students from Tyler were now coming down to Kick Shot to stretch their legs. It wasn't the most exciting bar, my Kick Shot, but it was finally in the black, making money instead of bleeding it. Dirk was the same way but in a much grumpier fashion. He knew how to keep the place exciting, how to listen to the customers, and how to give them what they wanted. He knew how to blend in and be one of them in a way I never quite achieved. He also made sure the other bartenders stayed in line, and was now technically the assistant manager to help Oliver.

All I had to do was stay out of the way—me, Jacky Leon, the *owner* of the bar, had to stay out of the way. The werecat who ruled the territory around Jacksonville, Texas, not that any of the humans knew that. I was the daughter of Hasan, ruler of the werecats, yet I couldn't work in my own bar anymore.

Some part of me was still a little upset, but another part of me, one growing larger by the day, knew it was for the best for moving on with life. One day, I would have had to shut it down because I was hiding. Not all supernatural species hid from humanity, but werecats certainly did. Humans believed I was one of them, even if a small handful had their suspicions to the contrary. If I let others run my little bar, I would never have to shut it down to hide what I was. One day, I could become the owner who never came around while Oliver and Dirk trained their replacements. So, while I was upset with the radical change in my life, I also could finally step back and see the bigger picture.

Things were better in this new normal.

*My new normal. It took months to get here, but it's nice.*

I couldn't stop smiling as I walked down the trail

toward the bar. I was still resistant to putting in a sidewalk or a driveway to my home. Until I had no other choice, I was keeping the trail, and no one could convince me otherwise. Although people tried.

I passed my little car, parked behind Kick Shot, and entered through the back door. Only one step in, one of the new employees saw me and smiled.

"Boss is here!" he called out.

I smiled in return and kept my feelings about his announcement to myself. They all did it now, except Oliver.

*One day, I'm going to kill Dirk for starting it.*

As the young man disappeared, I could smell something in the kitchen from where I stood. I had let Oliver put in the kitchen, and he had ignored me after that. Instead of using it for occasional events as I had asked, he was halfway to turning my once-tiny dive bar into a bar and grill.

I realized a month after we reopened there was no point in arguing. Whatever Oliver wanted was better for Kick Shot than trying to cling to my sad little existence. He hired a few guys for the back and a small serving staff to run food out or help the bartenders when it got too busy. We had a small but fully functional menu as well. I didn't deal with ordering the food.

I only had to show up and smile, so that's what I was doing.

"Hello, Ms. Leon!" a young woman said with a smile. Leslie was an eighteen-year-old, trying to earn a little extra money after school and gain some work experience during her senior year before heading off to college. "How are you tonight?"

"I'm doing well," I replied, staying where I was, at the backdoor and in front of the stairs to the upper offices. "Do you know where Oliver is?"

"He hasn't come down from the offices tonight," she answered, pointing at the ceiling. "It's busy tonight, so..."

"Go," I said, refusing to drop my smile, but it was an effort. It was why I never hired anyone myself. Keeping a smile was hard, even when I was in a fantastic mood, as I was tonight. Leslie ran off and hit a bell. Halfway up the stairs, I heard people calling out orders and drinks.

I found Oliver in his office. We didn't share it anymore, not that we had for very long. The Kick Shot of old had been burned down the month after he had been sent from London to help me. That was over a year ago. I was only supposed to have him for a year, but I didn't think I could let him leave, and he knew it. That was why he walked all over me. I'd given an inch, and he'd taken the state of Texas.

"Hey, Oliver," I greeted, closing us in. "How are you tonight?"

The twenty-three-year-old with auburn hair and a crisp navy suit was a very British young man, very proper about his appearance and behavior. It was stereotypical of me to think that way, but I had yet to meet someone who didn't know Oliver Price was a Londoner or Englishman the moment they met him. They saw what he wanted them to see. What most people didn't see was the anxious young man. They didn't see his need to please, his need to prove himself, his need to be perfect because someone in his life had told him he would never be good enough.

"I'm good," he answered, not looking up from whatever he was working on. "We're low on a few things, and I'm trying to get this order done. If I can, I'm going to try to convince them to accept and ship it to us by Monday."

"It's Saturday evening, Oliver. Can you really convince someone to send something out in that sort of time frame?" I sat across from him, watching as he filled out the order.

"I can," he said, not showing even the slightest belief that he would fail. "But they have so much paperwork."

"They always do," I agreed. "So, is there anything you need from me tonight?"

That got him to look up. "No. You're the boss. You're supposed to answer that question, not ask it." He grew more anxious with every word. I had to calm him down.

"You know more about Kick Shot now than I do," I reminded him. "It's Saturday, so if you need me to sign anything that might have been missed yesterday, now is the time." We had rules now. Everything that needed an owner's signature happened on or by Friday. Saturday was my evening with Heath, and Oliver wasn't allowed to come by and bother me with anything.

"Ah..." He shook his head. "No, I don't have anything." He went back to the form he was filling out, then snapped his fingers. "Did you know Dirk is leaving your territory this weekend?"

"No, but I'll ask him about it. Thanks for the heads up." I sighed, leaning back in the chair to get comfortable. "He needs to start telling me when he makes these plans."

"I'm sure he would have gotten around to it," Oliver commented lightly. "But I had you here, so..."

*Yeah, lie to make him look good. We both know he wouldn't tell me until I ask.*

"Yup. Do you know what he's doing?" I allowed the lie to keep from showing Oliver I was getting fed up with Dirk. Over the last year, I was beginning to realize why Niko sent him to me. While he was capable and intelligent, he was also fiercely independent and rebellious. After everything that had happened, both of my humans were required to tell me when they left my territory, so I knew everything was okay. They had to tell me where they were going and why. Was it overbearing? Yes. Was it for their safety and my sanity? Yes.

All I wanted was to know he would be safe wherever he went. I would never stop him from going anywhere or doing anything, I just had to know. I did it for Oliver as well, but each provided their own challenges as humans under my umbrella of protection. Oliver wasn't tough. He didn't have close interaction with werecats and didn't know how dangerous the supernatural world really was. He needed the protection because he was the most vulnerable person in my newly forming inner circle of confidants. Dirk, on the other hand, knew all of that and was technically my adult nephew, raised by Niko as his son. He knew all of it, down to the small details I couldn't put into words. He knew how to get himself out of trouble and demanded I trust him to do that.

After seeing Kick Shot burned down, Niko's back

broken, and my human family getting kidnapped by werewolves, trusting someone with their own safety was hard.

"I think he's going fishing." Oliver frowned. "I don't understand why people find that fun."

"Fish tastes good," I answered, shrugging. "I'll ask him about it before Heath gets here. Again, thanks for the heads up."

"Have a fun evening," Oliver said, smiling at me as I stood from the cushioned leather chair. His smile was young and suggestive. He and Dirk knew about Heath and me. There wasn't really an option to keep a secret from them. Luckily, since I was their boss, they gave their loyalty to me and kept the secret of our relationship, with as much care as my secret identity as a supernatural. That didn't stop them from teasing, but only when no one was watching or listening.

I left Oliver in his office, glad to see him having a normal night. Heading back down the stairs, I found Dirk right where I figured, behind the bar pouring a beer for someone. Kick Shot was loud tonight, with over fifty people, and it would only get busier on a Saturday night.

"Dirk, I want to talk to you," I declared, walking behind the bar. It should have felt good, but with the rebuilding of the bar, something strange had happened. This spot was no longer *mine*, and I felt surprisingly out-of-place now. It helped me with the process of letting go of my old way of life. This wasn't *my* bar with someone new behind it. This was Dirk's place and whoever he helped hire to help him. It was made with him in mind, with things arranged the way he liked them for convenience.

"Like you do every Saturday before you take off," he said, sliding the drink to the man waiting for it. "What's on my boss' mind tonight?"

"I heard you might be going fishing this weekend," I explained, leaning on the counter behind the bar. "What spot are you hitting up?"

"Fucking Oliver," he muttered, looking up at the ceiling for a moment before looking down at me again. Dirk was tall, much taller than me. "I'm not going far. A one-night camping and fishing trip, that's all. I just want to enjoy some of this Texas wilderness, and I have a friend who knows it well. Nothing big, but it'll be a nice break, and the weather is good."

"Okay. Take a gun for protection. We don't have much dangerous wildlife, but you know how it is."

Dirk only nodded, and I let the conversation die as I felt movement through my territory. Heath was coming. I didn't feel like hovering over Dirk's safety when I knew my night was about to get much better. I didn't want anything to sour my good mood.

"He's on his way?" Dirk chuckled when I started. "You get a dreamy look on your face when he's on his way. I have no idea how you think you're going to hide this from your family if they ever visit."

"Our family," I reminded him, smirking as he gave an annoyed grunt. "Niko looks at you as a son. I don't know why you fight it so much."

"You didn't grow up with them," he fired back, keeping his eyes on his work as he made another drink.

"The education, the expectations, the strangeness. You have to admit, all of you are strange."

I opened my mouth, about to tell him I wasn't strange at all. Before I met my werewolves, that *might* have been true, but even then, I was an oddity in the werecat world, more withdrawn than most. Strangeness was part of my life the moment Shane and I had gone over the side of that cliff. The moment Hasan decided to Change me into a werecat. Not only did I become a werecat, but I was suddenly the youngest member of a powerful family that ruled over all the others. And I still found ways to be different from them, going further outside of the bounds of normal than any of my siblings.

And that was just me. Niko was born to a werewolf family. Mischa had a village of descendants that were essentially a cult. Davor was a certifiable genius. The list went on. There were seven living children of Hasan and one that was murdered long before I was born. The only passably normal one out of the entire lot was Liza, and I never had the pleasure to meet her.

"You're right. We're all a bit strange," I agreed.

"And you are by far the strangest," he said, looking over the customers around Kick Shot as he handed off the drink to a server to run to a table. "Falling for a werewolf. You know, you're lucky Niko raised me. He might be the only one who wouldn't care. I certainly don't. You do you."

We could get away with these conversations in Kick Shot even more than we used to. With it becoming more and more busy, people paid less attention to us. No longer did I walk in and greet everyone by name, nor did everyone look to me to set the tone for the night. I was a background figure in the place I had made. Dirk was the bartender, but no longer did people wonder why a new guy was in my spot. He was just one of six people who rotated through the week.

"I think I'm lucky you just don't care."

"No, I really don't." He sighed. "I never really...got it."

"If it helps, I don't get it either." I gave him a wry smile.

He chuckled again, nodding as he waved a hand, telling me to leave so he could focus on work.

"Dirk, text me when you're heading back, okay?" I said as I started backing away from him.

"Fine. I don't know why you're so worried, but fine."

"I'm serious, Dirk. After everything that's happened—"

"I know," he hissed. "But stop hovering so fucking much. I'm not Oliver. I was raised by Niko, and he did a damned good job of it."

I stared at him for a minute, wondering if the attitude that flared up would fade away again. I watched him work on it, finally throwing a washcloth onto the countertop.

"Sorry. I hate hovering. If it helps, I'll be with someone who knows what to do in case something happens."

"Okay." I let it go and headed for the back door. I had places to be. It wasn't until my hand was on the door his words really sank in.

*I need to figure out who he hangs out with. It can't be...*

"Wait! There were a couple of people looking for you

earlier tonight," he said quickly as if he had just remembered. "I told them you didn't come in much on Saturday nights, and it was better if they tried again on Tuesday."

I looked back at him, frowning. "Did you take a message?"

"They didn't want to leave one. They wanted to talk to you, not me," he said, shrugging. "It seemed weird at the time, but it got busy fast, so I didn't put much thought into it. They left when I told them you weren't available tonight."

"Thanks. If you see them again, let me know. I would stay and interrogate you about them now, but..." I smiled. "It's Saturday." I was in a hurry.

He nodded and smiled knowingly. "Go enjoy your night off, boss. I'll write down what I remember about them and leave it in your office for you."

"Thanks."

I walked out the back door right on time to see Heath's truck come around the back of the bar to the staff parking area. I leaned on the wall and crossed my arms, waiting for him to park. He jumped out of his truck, looking around cautiously. We were always careful. He didn't go into Kick Shot anymore, for any reason.

When his eyes found me, he gave me a crooked smile and started walking toward the trail to my home, passing the Private Property sign. I followed, jogging to meet him there. We didn't touch until we were out of sight. The moment we were certain no one was watching, he pulled me in for a fierce kiss that took my breath away.

When it was over, I was left stunned.

"Hopefully, that puts you in a good mood," he murmured, his lips brushing mine.

"I already was, but that certainly helps. What's wrong?" Holding onto him, fistfuls of his shirt in my hands, I kept him next to me.

"I need your help."

## 2

# CHAPTER TWO

*I need your help.*

Those words never boded well for me. Whenever someone needed my help, I ended up either killing someone or nearly dying, usually both. As a werecat, I was powerful, stronger than any werewolf I had ever come across, which meant lots of people wanted me to help with dangerous issues.

'I need your help' were four words that immediately sank my mood.

"I don't like that," I said, letting go and stepping back. "We've had a lot of peaceful months recently. Please tell me we aren't going to Europe or something. Our trip to Russia was enough excitement to last a decade."

"And that was after a trip to Washington State," he said, chuckling at my panic. "It's nothing like that."

"No one is trying to kill us? No one has found out about this? None of that?" I was honestly surprised.

"None of that," he promised, grabbing my hand as he stepped closer to me again. "Scarier."

"Oh, now I'm really worried," I muttered. "Not helping."

"I think Carey is about to...uh..."

I could smell his embarrassment even better than I could hear it in his words. Something with Carey wasn't scaring him, but it was out of his depth. Considering he was over two hundred and fifty years old, there wasn't much out of his depth. What could a thirteen-year-old girl do that would be something Heath couldn't take care of?

The answer came to me slower than I was okay with, but once I figured it out, I nearly burst out laughing.

"Oh!" I did laugh then. "Really? You need my help with *that*?" I leaned over, wild giggles distracting me from whatever he was trying to say. When they slowed down, I straightened up and leaned on him. "Heath..."

"Laugh it up. I've never dealt with it before." He was stiff and started walking to my home in the woods. I followed, snorting repeatedly as I tried to stop my laughter.

A werewolf born before the American Revolution was scared of his daughter starting her period.

When we walked up the steps to my front door, I was finally composed. I put my hand on the door to stop him from opening it.

"I'm sorry. I shouldn't have laughed."

"I knew you would. Not that much, but I knew I would get a snicker at least. I know it's surprising, but I've never had to deal with this before. Sons don't lend themselves to teaching this particular set of skills and information. Added to that, I come from a time when...

women didn't share this particular issue with the men in their lives."

"No human women in your pack ever thought to educate you? You've had lovers before. Carey's mother was human." I opened the door and held it for him but let him pour his own drink, seeing how he went for whiskey instead of beer. He poured a second and slid it to me.

"Adult women enjoyed a few nights with me, then went to live their own lives. They weren't committed relationships where we lived together and I was in their business twenty-four-seven," he reminded me. I drank my drink slowly as he threw his entire drink back. "Carey has been acting stranger every month, Jacky. You've seen it. She's telling us less and less about school, and when I asked about it, she told me she wanted to figure out her own problems. Problems. She's about to turn fourteen. She's not supposed to have *problems*. She's supposed to hang out with kids her age and have friends, hobbies, and all that."

"I know that," I said carefully as he poured a second helping of my whiskey for himself. "She's a teenager, and she's around intelligent, independent people. She has you for a father. Her classmates know what happened in Dallas, and they know who her family is. Of course she's not having a normal existence at school, Heath. That's... expected. That doesn't make it okay, but that's...Unless you change her name and send her to a boarding school, there's really nothing else you can do."

By the look on his face, I could see he was considering it.

"Heath..." I tried to put a warning in that.

He hired the best tutors, and Carey took extra classes. She was well ahead of her grade level. Her projects were literally child's play for her. Even if she didn't do extracurriculars, she would probably get into whatever college she wanted. She certainly didn't need to go to a boarding school to get ahead.

He sighed and put his drink down without swallowing all of it this time.

"Which gets us to tonight's problem," he said, looking down at his glass. "You know, a werewolf can smell these things, right? Very minor differences in a woman's scent throughout their cycle. As an Alpha, I trained myself to watch for them. That way, I could be careful with the human women in my pack." He gave the glass a sheepish smile, as if he was thinking about those times in his pack, definitely a happy memory. "I gave away a lot of chocolate."

"My sense of smell isn't nearly that strong. That was very sweet of you, though."

"I tried." He sighed again. "I caught it in Carey's scent yesterday. I'm not uncomfortable with periods, they're a fact of life, but I'm...I'm not used to being the one responsible for making sure a girl is ready..." He groaned, and I watched the stressed father run a hand through his hair. His grey-blue eyes were particularly stormy at that moment. "I don't know how to talk to her about it, or..." His face flushed a little, just a light pink. I had never, in the two and a half years of knowing this man, seen him blush like this. It was fascinating. "I don't know what to buy for her."

I snorted and had to put my drink down to consider that. A mental image filled my mind and sent me into a fit again—Heath and Landon, each with a deep frown, standing in the feminine products aisle, staring at a literal wall of products. There would be a debate on the merits of each product and the differences between a light or heavy day. It was an utterly horrendous moment I wished I hadn't thought of, but I saw the problem as I laughed hysterically.

Knowing them, they would buy everything, and Carey would drown in all of it, if the embarrassment of the situation didn't get her first.

"I can solve this," I declared, slapping my hand on the island counter in my kitchen. "It's very easy. Do we have a few days before it starts?"

"A week if my memory serves right." He stared at me as if I had grown a second head.

"Tomorrow, we'll go bowling, although it's not bowling weekend, and I'll take Carey after. She can crash here for the night, and we'll talk it out, then I'll take her to the store. I used to have a cycle, so I understand, although it's been over a decade." I tapped my temple. No werewolf or werecat had that sort of cycle. Our fertility was something of a mystery to everyone, but I had grown up human. I knew all about what Carey was going to have coming for her. "See what I did there? You don't need to have the talk anymore. After I drop her off at school on Monday, I'll drop off the stuff at your house. Then you'll know what to replace when the time comes!" I smiled. "Easy as that."

"You make it sound *too* easy," he said cautiously. "Are you sure I shouldn't...talk to her?"

"What you can do is keep everything supplied and listen to her when she tells you something feels wrong. This doesn't have to be a big event, Heath." I watched the tension leave him as he listened to what I had to say.

"We've...had the *talk*, obviously," he said, drumming his fingers on my counter. "So, I guess I can leave this one up to a woman to deal with..."

"You are such a control freak," I teased as I walked closer to him. "Heath, I can handle this, and we won't ever talk about your talk with Carey ever again. Do you know how hard it was for me to listen to a thirteen-year-old girl rant about her weird dad giving her the sex talk when I'm sleeping with him? 'What would my dad know about this, anyway? He hasn't been with anyone since my mom, and I'm thirteen! He's old. Things were different back then.'" My imitation of Carey was, in my opinion, spot on. Heath's full lips curled into a smile—an embarrassed, rueful smile—as his eyes filled with fatherly exasperation.

"Can we laugh about how she thinks thirteen years is a long time?" he whispered with a smile, leaning in to kiss my cheek. "Thank you, by the way, for making this easier for both her *and* me."

"You two are my most favorite people in the world," I replied, shrugging. "It's not a big deal, and it's not something you needed to worry about. You know I'll give either of you any help I can." I elbowed him playfully. "And thirteen years *is* a long time. We're not all ancient freaks who have seen the world change. I'm not even forty, so don't try to give me years I didn't earn yet."

"Fine, fine," he conceded. "Now, what was your plan for tonight before I decided to dump my parental duties on your head?"

"Honestly?" I looped my arm in his and started walking, dragging him into my living room. "I was sort of enjoying that conversation because I was really worried you were going to need me to fight someone, and honestly, I'm tired of fighting. Any other normal family stuff? Are you okay with my plan for bowling tomorrow?" I released him to sit on my couch. Putting down my drink, I grabbed my remote and turned on the TV, letting whatever was on play as background noise.

"Well, it's just going to be me, you, and Carey," he said, sitting beside me, his arm making its way over my shoulders as I leaned into him, getting comfortable. "Landon is going fishing."

I blinked a couple of times, then smiled. "I knew it," I said, reaching for my drink.

"Knew what?" Heath chuckled, his chest shaking under my head.

"Dirk is going fishing, too, and he said the friend he was going with knew how to handle things if they got dangerous. You know I don't like when Dirk or Oliver leave my territory." I sipped my drink. "But he never told me who the friend was, and I wasn't willing to ask. Dirk gets cranky when I get nosy."

"They talk all the time."

"I know, so I considered Landon was an option, but I also know Dirk has other friends. I think they're just a cover for him to live a normal sort of life. They don't know he's German or anything, but they're still his friends."

"I'm glad to see Landon making a friend." Heath took the remote and started surfing for something to watch like he always did. "Does it bother you that they're friends? I can put an end to it. It would piss both of them off, but Landon would understand if I approached it from a political angle. It's weird enough that we're hiding you and me. Landon becoming friends with Niko's adopted son adds another layer of complication."

"No, it's better than him running around with humans. I don't have to worry about his safety when he's hanging out with Landon or any secrets slipping," I said. "I just find it amusing he's trying to keep it from me as if I couldn't find out from someone else."

"It's a test," Heath declared, shifting around to get more comfortable under me as he hit play on a movie.

"A test?" I frowned at that. "What do you mean?"

"I raised three kids, and he sees you as an authority figure. He's testing your limits. He's wondering if you're just worried about him, or maybe you're too controlling for him. There's a fine line between worry and paranoia, or anything worse. Werewolves often do it with pretty much everyone. I got it from every member of my pack, every day." Heath ran a hand through my hair. "I find it more amusing that it's Dirk, who was raised by Niko…"

"And Niko was raised by werewolves," I finished, nodding against him.

"He's quickly becoming the only person my son likes

enough to have as a friend. Landon has always been withdrawn, as you might have noticed."

That made me snort in agreement. It took Landon over a year to have a full conversation with me, and I had seen him nearly every week.

"It takes him a long time to decide if he can trust someone. He never got comfortable in the Dallas pack, you know. People would rather talk to me than deal with Landon. He's purposefully made himself intimidating to protect himself, and that never really comes off. But today...he spent the entire day preparing for this fishing trip. And he's warmed to you. It took some time, but I think living outside the werewolf world has done good things for him."

"That's nice," I said softly. I felt petty pride that Landon had warmed up to me, but not his own pack. Last year, he had started talking to me like a normal person. Well, as normal as Landon got. He was still quiet much of the time, but when he wanted to be in a conversation, it wasn't short, simple responses. "I'm glad it's those two. There are worse people for Dirk to be hanging out with. At least with Landon, he can talk honestly about us. And I don't mean this." I waved a finger between us. This wasn't about our secret relationship. This was more. "I mean all supernaturals. Dirk grew up with them, and I can always feel this...undercurrent. He has opinions about our kinds he's not willing to say out loud. Maybe Landon will give him an outlet or a different impression of us."

"I've noticed that in my time with him as well," Heath agreed. "But I never smell anything from him that worries me." He moved an arm and started rubbing my back. "Let's leave it for the night. There's whiskey calling my name and a beautiful woman sprawled all over me."

I could go along with that. We drank our whiskey and watched the movie he picked out. Eventually, the whiskey was gone, and the movie was ignored as I kissed him in the glow of the screen. He growled as I positioned myself to straddle him. It was a sound that I craved.

This was our time—our time to be a normal couple, to talk about everything under the sun and the people around us. It was our time to be everything we wanted to be. No one was watching us. Here, on this night and in this space, we weren't two supernaturals going against centuries of hate and war. We were just two people, and nothing could stop us from doing whatever we wanted.

He wrapped his arms around my waist as I slid mine over his shoulders.

We always took full advantage of this time that was only ours.

An hour later, we made it to the bedroom.

3
---

## CHAPTER THREE

Heath was gone when I woke up. He always was, so it wasn't him specifically that upset me. It was the reason why. He always left right after the bar closed, never giving anyone cause to think he was staying the night with me.

It was the same bittersweet Sunday morning I had every week. It was always worth it, though.

I grabbed my phone to check the time, yawning as I tried to remember if we'd decided on a time for bowling. Luckily, I saw a text from him telling me bowling was at two, and it was only noon. I had time to wake up and get ready without rushing out the door. It was going to be an interesting enough Sunday without any effort. I didn't need it to be more difficult by not getting the time to take a nice, hot shower.

By one in the afternoon, I was nearly ready and decided to take the last bit of time I had to manage my family obligations. I opened my laptop on my kitchen's bar countertop and started clicking through my recent messages. One stood out, an update from Jabari from the night before. There were several replies to it as well, making me interested in whatever small family drama had played out while I was sleeping with a werewolf.

**Jabari:** Zuri is still MIA. She left for Tanzania back in August, and I haven't heard from her since January. I hate when she goes to run around with Mother without any of us.

I snorted, rolling my eyes at the obvious jealousy from Jabari. At least they knew the mysterious woman everyone called our mother and Hasan's mate. I reached for her name, knowing Hasan had told me once before—Subira. Enigmatic, wandering in Africa because she hates the modern world Subira.

**Mischa:** She normally comes back a lot faster. Didn't she have a small thing with one of the rogues in your area before she went off with Mom?

**Jabari:** Yeah, she had to force one of our rogues to settle down, but I don't know enough about that situation to tell you more. I wasn't involved. I stayed in South Africa.

**Hasan:** They're fine.

**Jabari:** How would you know? You never come to Africa anymore.

**Hasan:** I received a call from them two days ago. They might be out for a couple more months. They wouldn't tell me why they're staying out so long, but they're powerful women, and I'm certain Zuri needed a break from all of you.

I laughed softly, knowing that probably had Jabari fuming. He and Zuri were twins, and I could almost relate to that. Once, I had that unbreakable bond with my twin, but now it was very fragile. Even after several months, I still only got the occasional text giving me an update.

*It's better than nothing, I guess.*

I almost closed the message program Davor had made for the family when I saw another message I wanted to read. It was from Niko to me, so I assumed it had something to do with Dirk.

**Niko:** Hey, Jacky. I was hoping for an update on Dirk. He was only supposed to be there for a year, but he's been avoiding telling me when he will be back. I understand things happened, and they couldn't work for you for several months, but I do need a time frame. We're two months past when he was supposed to return.

I could hear his words in my head—a concerned father, worried about when his son was going to come home.

*I'll tell Dirk that Niko is hoping he'll go home. It's honestly his decision, not mine. Well...I could fire him, but I don't want to. He's good at his job.*

With that on my mind, I closed the messaging app and shut the laptop. I grabbed my keys and wallet from the counter, leaving in the hope of beating Heath and Carey to the bowling alley.

I jogged to my car, then raced to the bowling alley, testing out the new things Heath got me for the little Nissan Versa hatchback. A Christmas gift, he had claimed. I'd finally let him take my car for the day, and he had it tuned up with new tires and everything, but that was the normal stuff. He also claimed there was magic on my car now, something I couldn't tell on my own until I sniffed hard and was looking for it. There was something I had heard called a Look Away charm, a fae spell to stop humans from looking too closely at something. Apparently, it was standard for most supernaturals to have a supplier for simple tricks like this, but I had never engaged with the larger supernatural world. My one run-in with a fae left me with magic I wasn't supposed to have. My run-ins with vampires were hit and miss, but always violent in some way.

While Heath—and my life—was forcing me to learn and acknowledge the larger world more than I ever wanted to, that didn't mean I wanted to engage with it regularly. I was hunting for an elusive balance between the two extremes. I needed to know everything but stay disengaged. I had already caused too much trouble for my own good.

So, I let the werewolf get my car tricked out with magic but didn't go with him to do it.

Beating the Everson family to the bowling alley, I grabbed our lane, rented shoes, and ordered a large pepperoni pizza by the time they walked in.

"Everything is on the way. Just get your shoes!" I called from across the bowling alley. Heath smiled and waved, but his greeting wasn't what bothered me. It was fairly normal.

Carey blushed, looking down at her feet when someone laughed in the arcade section of the bowling alley. Frowning, I turned to see who it was, seeing some kids around her age.

*Oh, we're already at that stage. Catty girls. Fantastic.*

I nestled into a seat and watched Carey as she got her shoes and came to sit at our lane.

"You know them?" I asked softly, not pointing or looking at the young teens.

"They go to my school," she mumbled. "It's fine. They're all assholes."

"Language, Carey," Heath said, but there was no anger behind it.

"Sure. Let's just bowl." She got up before Heath and I could say anything else.

The entire bowling thing was tense. The kids didn't cause any problems for Carey, so I didn't see if it was really bullying or just some laughter at my accidental, embarrassingly loud behavior. I knew what the problem was. Carey was hanging out with her dad and some lady. She didn't have any friends her age and was the odd one out. It killed me a little. I had been right when I explained to Heath that it was unavoidable, but it didn't make it easy to deal with.

"Did you get enough to eat?" Heath asked Carey.

I hissed, and he looked up. Glaring at him, I shook my head.

*Don't fucking hover, Heath. You'll make her seem like a kid when she's not one. The other kids will notice.*

The irony of my thoughts wasn't lost on me.

*No wonder Dirk hates when people hover.*

We made it outside without another incident.

"Well, maybe we can do something else in the future," I said, looking back at the bowling alley as we made it to our vehicles. Heath had parked right beside me. "You didn't seem to have much fun today."

I didn't need to direct that statement.

"Yeah," Carey sighed, still looking down.

"Have either of you ever gone paintballing or played laser tag?" I looked between them. Heath nodded.

"The Dallas pack used to keep a place open for everyone to play on weekends."

"Really? There's probably somewhere nearby. We can try one of those next time. Carey?" I watched her carefully.

"Yeah, that would be cool." She sounded so disinterested, as though I was some old lady, trying to relate to a teenage girl. Today was supposed to go smoothly, and it was an absolute failure.

"I'm going to assume you don't want to hang out today," I said, leaning on Heath's truck. "I asked your dad last night if you wanted to, then I would take you to school tomorrow, but..."

She looked up finally, her eyes gaining some of their normal brightness.

"Really?"

"Yeah," her dad said with a small chuckle. "You've been strange, so I'm dumping you on Jacky because I can't deal anymore."

"Let's go!" Carey was already running to the passenger side of my car. I smirked at Heath and shrugged.

Sometimes, teenagers were mysteries. Sometimes, they weren't.

"I have a couple changes of clothes for her at my place," I reminded him when he opened his mouth. "We'll be fine."

"Her schoolwork," he said, opening the door to his truck.

"Wait, you brought my backpack?" Carey looked over my car with a deep frown of her own.

"Of course. Jacky and I planned this, so I prepared." He grabbed the backpack and held it out for me. I threw it into my backseat and waved at him.

"Drive safe," I ordered before getting into my car. Carey jumped in next to me and quickly put on her seatbelt. The moment we were out of the parking lot, I dove into my interrogation.

"What's up with you?"

"Nothing."

"Look, I'm not your parental figure and never tell your dad shit. I even let you curse. I don't care, but you were in a terrible mood while we were bowling. I think I deserve to know why you were sour for the entire surprise get-together your dad and I tried to pull off for you."

"What if I don't want to tell you?" she fired back. "Are you going to force me?"

"No," I conceded. "Because there's..." I sighed, knowing she was about to hate me. "There's a reason you're with me today that might be a little more important."

"What?"

"I'm taking you shopping and not the good kind."

"I don't like that. I don't like this type of surprise," she said, huffing. "Let's just go to your place and play some video games or something."

"This is important," I said sadly. I drove silently, and she groaned as I pulled into the local Walmart. We'd been here before, and most were unimportant visits, but today wasn't. I sniffed the air, but Carey didn't smell any different than she normally did. She was cranky with everyone, but recently, that was becoming more common.

"Tell me we're just getting groceries," she said, glaring at the store.

"Nope. I think we quickly need to deal with something, then we can never bring it up again if you don't want to." I stared at the store as well, not cutting the engine off yet. "Your dad is at a loss, and I'm assuming your brother is, too. You know, you have to talk about things if you want to resolve them. Brooding in silence doesn't help anyone and will probably only hurt you in the end."

"Sure. Why are we at Walmart?" She was short with me, but I didn't get onto her for it. There was only one thing I ever wanted from my strange aunt-like relationship with Carey, and that was her trust. If I got snappy back with her too much, I would lose that trust.

"To deal with a problem neither of your werewolf family members has to deal with."

"Because they're werewolves?"

"Because they're men," I said, sighing. "And also werewolves. Werecats don't deal with it either...but I used to. I'm all you have to help you before it happens, so..." I looked at her, watching her work through it. "Carey, we're here to prepare you for your first—"

"I hate you," she declared. "Yeah. I hate you, I hate Dad. I can't believe we're doing this. This is so embarrassing. Wow." She undid her seatbelt then jumped out of my car, slamming the door.

I turned off the car and got out more slowly, then went to her side as she glared at the ground.

"Carey, seriously. This is important, and I hate it too. Most women hate it, but it's...unavoidable."

"Could just make me into a werewolf or something," she said, glaring at me.

I hissed, looking around the parking lot before replying.

"Really? You want the life we live? The danger of people trying to kill us and fighting all the time? Just last year, I had to fight against my own kind, then save my human family when they were kidnapped by Russian werewolves." I shook my head. She didn't know what she was asking for.

She opened and closed her mouth, and I watched her fight an obvious pain eating at her, but since she didn't want to talk about it, I didn't pry—not yet—but obviously, this conversation was coming up on us faster than I wanted.

"Let's go get this done. I promise once it's over, everything will be a little easier," I said softly, gently touching her back. She leaned in, her way of saying it was cool if I put my arm on her shoulder. I held her to my side as we walked in.

"Why do we have to do this today?" she asked softly as we drew close to the aisle we needed.

"Not to weird you out, but we're pretty sure it's close," I said quietly, looking over the options. The branding had changed in the over ten years since I needed to be here, but the products were the same. "As a parent, it's

31

obviously expected that your dad talks to you about all of this."

"But he's never done it before," she finished, nodding. "Yeah. I mean, thanks for bringing me. You're way better than Dad or *Landon*." We both laughed softly at that idea, and I was immensely glad she saw reason. When she stopped, I waited for whatever was next. "Lots of girls in my class already have theirs, and I knew mine was coming soon. I couldn't avoid it forever, right?"

"Sadly, no," I said softly.

"I wish I was born a werewolf, like Dad," she mumbled, grabbing a box off the shelf.

*There it is. That's what it is.*

"You know, it's always been weird being the human in the family. Like super weird. Dad had to make all sorts of rules, so Richard and Landon didn't invade my privacy all the time. If I was a werewolf, I could be more like them, and the rules wouldn't matter so much. Instead...I don't really fit anywhere. Not with my dad and Landon. Not with the kids at school, who are all human with normal human parents. Did you know they keep asking Dad to be in the PTA? He turns them down because he thinks it's a trick. A trick! Why is it a trick? Why can't he try to be normal, too?"

"They're looking for him to mess up in public to justify their behavior," I explained, grabbing another box. "This was my favorite brand."

"You mean like lose his temper with them?"

"He's an easy target for those sorts of tricks, yeah." A sad fact of life. "He explained it to me before. He would be an easy one to sue if anything went wrong. And natural human instinct tells them not to trust him or me or any of our kinds. They need to create a reason to feel that way instead of just accepting the fact of it. He has to be on his best behavior all the time, and that's harder when his kids are involved. What do you think would happen if some boy was bullying you, and he found the kid's parents? What if they didn't care? Do you think he would tolerate that?"

"No," she said in a small voice.

"I'm sorry you don't live a normal life," I whispered, looking down at her. She threw a box into our basket.

"It's fine. It's just getting *harder*. I don't even have others like me anymore. The pack had other kids growing up with werewolf parents. We all hung out at school when we had the chance. People left us alone because the werewolf kids hung out with us, too. If I was a werewolf, people would at least be too scared to laugh at me or tease me."

"School sucks for everyone," I said, hoping it was any sort of consolation prize.

We finished up in the aisle quickly. On the car ride to Kick Shot, I gave her all the advice I could, knowing I had finally softened her enough to listen. As we walked to my home, she seemed even lighter.

"Sorry for the attitude," she finally said as we walked through my front door. "I was fine until those idiots laughed. I was so embarrassed and don't even know why."

I had a few guesses, but I kept them to myself. She probably knew exactly why but didn't want to admit it.

"Carey, my best advice is this. Do better than them. Be

smarter. Ace tests and kick ass. They're trying to bring you down to prove they're better than you. Don't let them. Be pretty, be tough, be whatever you want to be. Don't let them dictate the terms of your life. It's your life, not theirs."

She nodded, and the smile she finally gave me was everything I always wanted from her—happy, fierce, and ready to take on the world.

"You're right," she agreed.

"Yeah, and just think…they don't have a bunch of cool ancients willing to help them ace their history exams and research papers." I shrugged. "Or an ancient warlord teaching them to use the bow. It's their loss."

"Yeah, it is," Carey said, that smile continuing. Then she looked at the bags, narrowing her eyes on them. "Are you really sure it's coming soon?"

"Yeah, and I'm one of your emergency contacts to pull you out of school. If you need it, just call me."

"You're the best."

"I know." I didn't really know, but I always appreciated the sentiment.

## CHAPTER FOUR

I dropped Carey off at school on Monday, watching her go inside as I thought about what she had said the day before. She was being teased, and there wasn't much any of us could do about it. I could only hope she took my advice to heart and was strong. The alternatives weren't that great, and I had explained those to her as well.

Boarding school was a bad idea to her, while homeschooling had made her a little excited, which meant I'd lightly drop the idea on Heath. If he had time for it or the money to afford it, a solid private education was possibly a perfect solution for her.

Or she would lose all possibilities of having human friends, and we'd further entrench her into the supernatural world we didn't want her to be a part of. It could go either way.

When I arrived at the Everson household, Landon was pulling up in his truck. I waited for him to go into the driveway first to claim his spot, then pulled in behind him.

"How was the fishing trip?" I asked loudly, as he grabbed a large pack from the back of his truck.

"Fine. Caught a couple of fish for dinner and breakfast. Nothing special," he answered, eyeing me as I walked closer. "What are you doing here this early?"

I held up the Walmart bag in my hands. "Fixing a problem for you and your father."

He snorted in derision as if there was no way I could ever fix something for them. I kept the bag where he could see it, and he finally gave in to look inside. His eyes went wide as understanding dawned.

"Ah..." It was probably the best thing he could have said.

"Mm-hm." I smiled sweetly. "In return for handling this, I'm going to extort you now." His narrowed-eyed stare was intense, but I held firm. I was getting very good at playing the werewolves into my favor.

"Why me?" he demanded. "Extort *him*. He's the one you're sleeping with."

"Because you hang out with my brother's adopted son, and I'm concerned about him."

Landon sighed as defeat hit him. "That's right. Dirk was pretty annoyed you found out about the trip before he could leave. He's fine. I'm not going to betray his trust beyond that."

"If there was anything concerning—"

"There's not," Landon growled softly. "But...*if* there was, I would certainly tell someone." Landon threw the large bag over his shoulder as if it weighed nothing.

"He just wants to live his own life, Jacky. That's all. Let him."

"All I ask is he tells me when he's leaving my territory. How hard is that?"

"That's for you and him to work out." He shrugged. "Get the cooler. It's empty."

I helped him, chuckling as he started sorting through everything with an exasperated look on his face.

"You okay?" I finally asked, watching him dump everything.

"I used to go fishing with Richard, and he was always here to help me put this shit away," he answered. "Just annoyed."

"You could have forced Dirk to help you."

He only shook his head, then waved me away. Landon wasn't trying to be bossy. He just didn't always have the patience or energy to remember words. Heading inside their home from the garage, I put the bag on the kitchen counter for them to handle later. I wandered the house until I found Heath's office and saw him glaring at his computer screen. I could tell the moment he caught my scent, and a very wolfy grin came over his face.

"How was your night with Carey?" he asked as if I was going to tell him it was terrible, and he could laugh at me.

"It had a rocky start, but we figured it out. What you need is on the kitchen counter. I'm heading home."

He growled softly, but I was already moving out of his office, closing the door in his face. He caught me before I made it to the front door, pinned me to the wall, and leaned in for a kiss.

I could have gotten away, but there was something

thrilling about how Heath worked. He put very little effort into being anything but a werewolf, while I worked so hard to pretend I was human.

"Take it somewhere else," Landon growled from the next room.

"Move out," Heath growled back. "My house. My rules."

Landon's grumbled response was lost to me. I raised an eyebrow at Heath.

"We haven't lived together for this long in decades. We've remembered why he and Richard got their own homes," he explained, leaning back in to put his forehead on mine.

"Is he going to move out?"

"He's looking around at houses."

"How are you and Carey going to do without him?"

He shrugged. "He'll probably be over here all the time, but it's the principle of the matter. He's an adult man, and I think we're all recovered from the Dallas coup and relocating. Time for him to reclaim his own space." He slid a hand down my back and brushed over my ass. "Now, why are you running away? We don't get much time during the week, and I promise, there's no one watching my house. We could steal a few hours."

I went through what I had to do for the day. The only reason I wanted to get home was to get some sleep before I dealt with bar work in the evening. Kick Shot was closed on Mondays, but it was a good day for Oliver and me to break down what would happen during the week.

"Sleep," I finally answered. "Something you won't let me have if I stay here."

"You're right." He chuckled and released me. "I wouldn't. Drive safe."

We kissed one more time, and I headed out.

When I made it back to Kick Shot, I noticed someone parked in the driveway who hadn't been there when I left. It wasn't uncommon for people to stop their cars in my parking lot to check maps, but I had them towed if they stayed too long. It was such a rare occurrence, I could remember every time it was needed.

I went to the car, frowning, seeing no one was inside. I took a picture of the license plate for future reference. The windows were dark, but I could see it was kept clean, and there was nothing out of place to me. It belonged to humans or was used by humans because there was no scent of magic or any sort of supernatural on it.

*It's too normal.*

I didn't like that I couldn't see anyone around. I sniffed, catching the scent of two people, and started to follow, wondering where these two people had gone after dumping their car in my parking lot. I didn't like where I was going as I headed around the bar toward the trail to my house. The Private Property sign was still standing as I walked past it. I followed the scent into the trees off my trail, wary what these humans were doing. I didn't have a gun on me, something I wished for now. While I didn't particularly need one, it was useful when I needed to keep up appearances as a human.

I didn't move quickly, keeping my eyes open for anything. Nothing seemed out of place except their scents. I never caught them. They kept moving, leading around in a semi-circle back to the bar. When I made it back to my parking lot, the car was gone.

*At least I got the plate. I'll give it to Davor and see what he finds out.*

The entire event left me bewildered and paranoid. I went into Kick Shot, knowing I wouldn't be able to sleep now. I locked my office door, an unnecessary security feature but a comforting one. I emailed Davor the license plate with an explanation from my office computer, which was a keyboard and mouse on the desk and the monitor attached to the wall to my left, out of the way. The tower was carefully hidden away in the bookcase built around the monitor, so no one could do something crazy like ripping the hard drive out. It was somewhat paranoid but also very nice and high-end. Heath and I had spared no expense making this office, with his years of advice about security involved in its planning.

It didn't take long for Davor to get back to me, only five minutes, which told me the man was bored with whatever else he was doing.

**Davor:** Probably some idiots considering buying the land from you. We've dealt with it before.

**Jacky:** Can you look into it anyway?

**Davor:** Obviously. It's you, so the probability it's something dangerous is more likely. Even then, with how many dangerous incidents you've had over the last two and a half years, the likelihood of another is very slim.

**Jacky:** Let's play like the odds aren't in my favor, okay?

**Davor:** Are they ever?

I cracked a small smile. Davor was an asshole, with little capacity for normal emotion, in my opinion. A genius of ridiculous levels, he spent his days coding, building new systems, and managing the electronic security for most of the family. Not me, though. He let me use what he developed, but he didn't offer his free time to help me. I either had to ask and make a good case or go without. I was pretty good at going without since I wasn't willing to get into stupid fights or involve Hasan. It helped that I went without for several years for my own reasons. It was good training for Davor's continuous coldness. The good thing was, I had learned something important about him. He liked numbers. When he was talking numbers, he was in a good mood.

Not twenty minutes later, my phone rang, and I answered without looking.

"Jacqueline, Davor said you had trespassers on your property." Hasan's immediate concern was touching but made me want to roll my eyes. I was hit with the sudden realization Dirk was right.

Hovering was shitty.

"It's fine. It's going to be fine. It was two humans and a car. I sent everything about the car to Davor. He didn't need to tell you about it."

"He didn't. I'm sitting next to him," Hasan said. "Davor can't help but mumble to himself as he types."

*Shit. I forgot Davor was spending time with Hasan right now. It's the anniversary of Liza's death, isn't it? They warned me like a month ago, and I completely lost track of the date.*

"Tell him he can work on it later. I don't want to impose on your time with him," I said, rubbing my temples. "I wasn't thinking when I sent it over."

"He can do it now," Hasan said with a chiding tone.

"It's your safety, something I'm very much invested in, and I know if we don't do it now, you'll find some way to get into trouble before we can stop it. Like *last time*."

I winced. "Yeah."

Last time. The time when I flew across the country and got involved in a situation I had no business being in, without telling any of them until it was too late to get out of it—that time. The time my twin sister murdered a man for a self-righteous reason, and I vowed to get her out of trouble for a similar self-righteous reason. The time my human family was kidnapped, and I convinced my family we needed to fight the werewolves instead of making a trade.

*That* time.

"What are you doing right now, other than trying to find intruders on your property?" he asked.

I considered what to tell him. My life was fairly stable now.

"Well, I'm not normally up this time of day. I took Carey to school this morning because I let her stay at my place last night. I was going to head back to sleep, but..." I let him fill that in for a moment. "Now I'm going to try to get ahead of work before Oliver arrives."

"Stay safe." There was no missing the order in those words. "Davor will get back to you, probably this time tomorrow."

"Thanks." I hung up first, then leaned over and put my head on my desk. I didn't like things out of the ordinary. I considered texting Heath about what happened but decided against it for now. There was no reason to worry him so early.

I didn't want to come off as paranoid either. Deep in my bones, I felt a creeping sensation of something bad coming. Maybe I had finally gotten into enough trouble to have developed a survival instinct.

*What can I do? Dirk left me a write-up...*

I searched my desk and found it on top of some reports I'd had the two young men working as my managers write. They were personnel reports, write-ups on their feelings about the rest of our staff. I had no intention of bringing any more humans into my secret. I didn't want a large staff, but it was good to be prepared, to know my employees, so I could work with them if anything came up.

I looked at them for a moment, wondering if something bad came what I would do with them—even more people relying on me, now for work to pay their bills and support their families.

*Well, first, I have to know if there is anything wrong.*

I started reading the handwritten information from Dirk, trying to put my troubles at ease. Two people, one man and one woman, each wearing casual clothing. Dirk's description of their fashion choices was spot on. He was observant, but I had a feeling that was something Niko taught him. He memorized details with apparent ease and had told me about them so casually as if he barely even thought about the two humans looking for me. It was good, certainly better than I could do. I was still working on that, trying to take in details, part of the natural safety precautions of being immortal. Hasan told me a decade ago, memorizing the little details was important—a mole, the density of someone's freckles, or a small pockmark—anything and everything. As an immortal, you could never really know when someone was going to pop up into your life again or what their motive was.

I was terrible at it. I knew faces but couldn't remember all those details. Dirk, while frustrating for me, once again was proving himself too useful to ever get rid of.

*Shit, and Niko needs a timeline for when he's getting his adopted son back. I'll ask Dirk about that today after I tell them about the visitors on my property.*

I waited in my office for hours until I heard the familiar sound of footsteps coming up the back staircase. They were quiet, and a yawn made me smirk. I heard Oliver unlock his office, then come to unlock mine. He opened it, looking bright and fresh, his eyes clear with shock as he saw me. Dirk was behind him, with dark stains under his eyes. It was clear who didn't get enough sleep.

"Why..." Oliver looked down at the doorknob, then back at me, obviously confused by me locking myself in the office.

"Earlier today, two humans decided to go on a walk through my woods," I explained, leaning back in my chair. "I didn't see them because I didn't want to take too much of a risk. I tracked their walk, which went precariously close to my home, then led me back to my parking lot, where I had found their car. I didn't recognize the scents but sent Davor a picture of their license plate to run."

They both watched me in a still silence as they

thought over what I told them. Dirk gently nudged Oliver farther into the office, closed the door, and relocked it.

"Is there anything we can do?" he asked, looking at me.

"Keep your eyes open like you have been. Davor thinks it might have been some real estate people. It's a... decent idea, but it could have been anything. I didn't find anything hidden on the little walk they took other than their footprints."

"Niko...once had a couple of teenagers trespass his property because everyone knew someone strange lived there. Most people avoided it completely, so it got to be a bit of a legend," Dirk said thoughtfully as he sat down across from me. Oliver fell into his seat silently, looking between us.

"You think I might have had a couple of dumb idiots, thinking they could get a peek at my house? Have a laugh?"

"Or a make-out session?" Dirk shrugged. "Could you tell how old they were?"

"Adults. Teens normally have messy cars," I said, sighing. "But...there's always been questions from the people who come to Kick Shot whether or not I'm human. I could see someone finally deciding to look a little closer..." Which didn't bode well for me.

"This is why Niko doesn't go to his businesses regularly," Dirk pointed out. "You might need to cut down on visits to Kick Shot and let people forget about you for a little while."

"But..." Oliver frowned. "Everyone knows about

werewolves. Why not let them think you're like Alpha Everson? A wolf outside the pack."

"Because it's..." I didn't continue, knowing Oliver was right. "Are you saying I should stop fighting the rumors?"

"Yeah. The more you fight them, the more people will want the truth if they think you have a secret. They know you're...off." Oliver looked at Dirk for confirmation.

"He has a point," Dirk agreed.

"Then it's settled," I said decidedly. "I can do that. If anyone asks either of you if I'm a werewolf, don't deny it. Just say I'm a private individual who enjoys owning a bar, and I hope to run Kick Shot for a very long time."

"That's a good line," Oliver said appreciatively. "If they ask about anything else, we'll categorically deny it. You're not a witch or fae, which would be the next two most likely questions. Humans don't really know about the rest of the supernaturals."

"Shit, I barely know about the rest of the supernatural species," I commented with a snort. Heath was trying to teach me, though. While my ignorance worked when I lived alone, it didn't anymore. Four sparse years of education from Hasan was slipping away, thanks to disuse and my personal experience with a handful of species, but there was so much to know. Dozens of types of supernaturals lived around the world. The big five were always mentioned in conversation, thanks to their positions on the Tribunal, but it was the smaller groups that were the most interesting. Like the newly discovered cambions. An entire supernatural species had been discovered and joined the Tribunal. Heath mentioned it over dinner one Saturday evening, laughing when he realized I had no idea it had happened, even though Hasan was one of the people who knew the most about them and worked closely with their leader.

*Well, Hasan did say he likes to keep his work separate from his family...very separate.*

"Sometimes, I wonder how you made it this long," Dirk teased.

"Thanks," I replied dryly, narrowing my eyes at him. "We're all on the same page, right? Let them believe I'm a werewolf and hope interest dies down?"

They both nodded, then Dirk got up to leave. Oliver and I dove into the start-of-the-week papers, and I tried to ignore the nagging feeling.

*Something is coming.*

## 5

# CHAPTER FIVE

The days continued to turn. An uneventful work week turned into a normal Saturday night off and a lazy Sunday.

"Looking forward to the full moon tomorrow night?" Heath asked as we walked down the trail the night before.

"Ambivalent to it."

We had talked about a lot but not the trespassers on my property. I told him everything else, though, like the decision I came to with Oliver and Dirk. He'd gotten a laugh out of the idea that people were so willing to believe I was a werewolf.

Now I was reading a book and waiting for the moment I knew I needed to head outside. Like all the moon cursed, I had a sixth sense for it. The curse activated on nights of the fullest moon, right on schedule, and only once the sun went down.

The book was good, part of a long series I couldn't put down now, a long-running mystery series, something to lose myself in when television started to bore me. I liked to read, even though I rarely found time. Hasan had sent me the Spanish editions for Christmas when he had learned through the grapevine I was studying the language. While I was by no means a conversational speaker of the language yet, I was beginning to make enough progress to read, with some assistance. I looked up words I didn't understand on my phone more frequently than I cared to admit, but it helped.

I put the book down and looked out the large windows of my home, seeing how the red glow of sunset was taking over the world. Standing slowly, I felt the pull of magic, a whisper asking me to head outside, to wait. I followed it, slowly stripping as I made my way, dropping my clothes wherever. By the time I was on my front porch, I had nothing left on, and the sun was nearly gone. I closed my eyes to breathe in the fresh night air. There was nothing unusual on the breeze, so I let that lull me into enjoying the night to come, letting go of the paranoia I'd felt for the last week.

There was no one out there.

When the sun was gone, I didn't fight the shift. I never did. When I was a young werecat, Hasan had taught me to go with the Change, flow with it, akin to going down a river. Like getting swept under a strong current, going with it was safer than trying to swim against it. I had embraced that lesson and learned to swim with the current, taking myself through the Change faster than most werecats my age. I ignored the pain and moved through it as my body rearranged itself into a new form—just under thirty seconds. It was as fast as I could go, and

I was damn proud of it. Most of my family took just over a minute. Werewolves took upwards of fifteen minutes. I was the youngest person in the family, and I matched Hasan's speed through the Change, and it was through sheer force of will.

I shook, feeling the familiar, heavy weight of my werecat body, a saber-toothed feline reminiscent of something from the end of the ice age. I weighed more than an adult male lion and was considered small, thanks to my age. Jabari and Hasan both weighed over nine hundred pounds, practically double my size. Mischa and Zuri were the closest to my size, but both of my werecat sisters were thousands of years old and had finished filling out, unlike me.

I jumped off my porch and headed into the woods. The first thing I had to do was hunt, take a kill, and appease the feral side of my nature that came out to play during the full moon. Thanks to an out-of-control population, finding whitetail deer was easy, and no one noticed something was taking kills year-round. I caught the scent of several that had roamed through my woods over the last few nights and picked a buck over any of the does.

Once my mind was made up, my body entered hunting mode. I lived in the backseat of my own brain, letting the instincts take over and the cat be what it was meant to be—a hunter. It prowled through the trees until it finally caught sight of its prey. I felt my muscles tense as it lowered itself into a crouch, then I felt the twitch of muscles ready to release and take down its quarry.

It was easy to think of the cat as something *other* in

moments like that, but I knew it wasn't the case. I used to believe the cat was something different from me. I would feel the needs and feelings of the cat and think I had to fight against it, but it was really just a different way of thinking inside my own mind, a different set of skills to draw on, and a different way of seeing the world. It was still *me*. I had to let go of human thought to truly embrace what I was.

It made life easier.

The kill was fast, and the meal was hearty. It felt good, and once those instincts felt as though they had their fill, my more human mind took control once again.

*I have hours to waste now. I think that's the worst part about this. Once a month, I have to stay up all night and can't even get anything productive done.*

It was close to midnight when a howl caught my attention. Heath and Landon often ran out of my territory on full moons to hunt on their own, but I felt them reenter my territory earlier than usual tonight. It wasn't a real cause for concern. They came back when they took their own kill together and would spend the rest of the night running along the trails near their home.

Heath did exactly what I thought he would, but Landon took a different route, making me curious. I got up and started trotting, not in any particular hurry. I had the clear advantage. When they were inside my territory, I knew where they were at all times. The territory magic was the one thing werecats had over werewolves, while they had pack magic, the ability to communicate in their wolf forms. I had both, but I was the exception—a very strange exception. The ability to use pack magic had been granted to me by a strange fae who ran a motel and gas station with his human wife and the sons he had with her. I never saw him again after that and hadn't gone looking.

I didn't get too close to Landon, but it was the direction he was headed that made me too curious for my own good.

*He shouldn't be headed this way. He knows better.*

I stopped nearly a hundred yards away, staying downwind of him. I watched as Dirk left the home he shared with Oliver and went outside. It was obvious Dirk could see Landon and knew who it was. It was also clear Landon's visit wasn't a surprise. I couldn't hear what was said, but Landon lowered himself to the ground.

Then his tail wagged.

*Ah. No problems here, then. Just him bothering a friend.*

I took a step back as Dirk's laughter rang out. He went inside, and I chuffed in feline laughter at the clear yellow tennis ball in his hand when he came back out.

"I told you if you came and bothered me on a full moon, I was going to treat you like a stray dog," Dirk said loudly before he threw the ball. Landon ran after it as Dirk laughed.

I stepped back again, turning my head in Heath's direction. He had to hear about this. I took off in a full run, racing through the trees, carefully crossing roads until I made it to the edge of Heath's property. He was hanging out in the large field that was his backyard, probably near the stable where a little pony lived for Carey. The horse was comfortable with the werewolves now, but it was still skittish around me.

"Heath!" I called out. "You won't believe what I saw!"

"Yeah, I can only imagine," he replied, a clear chuckle in his words. "Landon said he was going to go mess with Dirk for a laugh tonight."

"Dirk is making him play fetch."

Heath's clear laughter made me want to smile as he appeared in front of me. He was a big wolf, nearly shoulder to shoulder with me, although I still had him on weight, probably a hundred pounds.

"I wish I could see it, but I can't sneak as well as you," he said, coming to sit beside me. "Did they know you were there?"

"No, I stayed downwind and gave them some distance. I just wanted to see what Landon was doing going near them on a full moon."

"We hunted. He's in control," Heath said, bumping me.

"I figured."

We sat together in the dark, looking over his property as if we were waiting for something. We weren't. We didn't often spend time during a full moon because when we met, we weren't sure if our instinctual sides could get along, especially at the beginning of a full moon. The need to hunt, to kill something and eat it was a pressing one, and we were never sure if we would turn on each other.

"Zuri is still on vacation. Jabari is getting annoyed," I said, offering up a small piece of my family's dramas since I knew his so well.

"When were you going to tell me about the people who wandered around your property?" he asked suddenly, ignoring what I said.

"Let me guess...Dirk told Landon, and Landon told you."

"No, I could smell them on the trail when I visited yesterday, but you didn't acknowledge it, so I held off. If Dirk tells Landon anything, it certainly doesn't make it back to me," he retorted. "The scents were faint, but they weren't there the week before."

I huffed. "Last Monday, I found their car when I got back from dropping Carey off at school. I followed their scents, but they made it back to their car before I could get eyes on them. I played it safe since I didn't know if they were armed. The plates on their car were a dead end. Nothing's happened since."

"You aren't worried?"

"Of course I'm worried, but I didn't want to make a big deal of it. If something else had come up in the last week, I would have mentioned it, but nothing did. I'm going to wait to see if anything else comes up. Some of my family are convinced it's just some idiots looking over the property, thinking they might want to make me an offer. Dirk, Oliver, and I also talked. I mentioned that last night."

"You didn't tell me why it came up, though," he reminded me.

"And now, you know." I bumped him with my shoulder. "You don't really have a leg to stand on here, Heath. You're the werewolf who never really explained to me how werewolves grow stronger as they grow more dominant, but who didn't want to admit he was more of an Alpha than the Russian. You could have taken that pack last year."

He growled softly. "Fine. You got me. It's not something I'm comfortable with, you know. I never expected it to happen." He laid down in the grass. "I've never wanted to be anything more than what was needed. I became an Alpha, fought for it because I needed the position to protect my sons. If I was in charge, no one would try to hurt Landon, who was becoming a vicious fighter to protect himself. The only reason I've defied them and stayed here is for Carey...and you. It didn't start with you, but it became you."

"You knew you would lose all your support and friends from Dallas the moment you decided to retire." I still hated that. I disagreed with the idea Heath had to keep his distance from a pack that used to be his family. "You needed something to help you protect your daughter, Heath, and I was the clear choice. They can't blame you for that."

"They don't, not in so many words. Besides, I'm glad I don't have any connection to the Dallas pack right now. I'm still...trying to figure out what to do with the information I have on them." He sighed. "I've decided to keep it in my safe until I need it. I don't like blackmail, but I'm not better than it. I've lived too long to ignore the option, but I won't use it until it's the only thing I have."

"You're a good man, Heath. And I promise, if anything comes up that might pose a danger to you, Carey, or Landon, I'll be the first to tell you. I just don't want to create trouble where there might be none. I'm tired of the trouble we've had over the past couple of years. I'm certainly not trying to look for or create it where there might not be any."

His mental laugh echoed in my head.

"I'm going to head home," I declared, stretching.

"Can I come?"

"Don't you have to get Carey to school after sunrise?"

"Nope. She's taking the day off," he replied. "Ah..."

I looked toward his house, then back at him, understanding, thanks to our previous conversations.

"Well, you should stick close by then. She might need something. Have you two talked about it yet?"

"Not yet," he admitted. "It's a conversation I've never had, so I'm...waiting for her. If she needs me, I'll be there for her."

I chuckled mentally. "You're a good father, Heath Everson. Don't forget that."

He nodded as he stood. We went our separate ways, Heath heading toward his house and me heading toward mine. I passed Landon on the way home, seeing him cross a road to get back home as well.

When I made it home, I jumped onto my porch and looked over my woods.

That feeling I couldn't shake came back, as though someone was watching me, which made no sense. There was no one in the trees.

*I'm just paranoid. Heath got me thinking about it, and that's it.*

# 6

## CHAPTER SIX

Tuesday came, as it liked to do every week. Normally. I wasn't anxious to go in during the slowest days, but I was antsy to keep my eyes on everything going on. I couldn't shake that feeling.

I left my home and looked at the trees, wondering if someone was there now. It was unlikely, especially since Kick Shot was open. If anyone was trying to go around the building to the woods in the back, someone would let me know the moment it happened.

As I looked at my woods, I remembered the people who had come onto my property. They had been human and therefore out of the sight of my territory magic. If I hadn't caught their car in my parking lot, I wouldn't have known they were even there until I caught their scents, and by then, I would have had nothing on them. The license plate hadn't been helpful, but it had been something. I knew something to look out for, a type of car at least.

I started walking, taking extra care to catch any

possible scent. The full moon was two nights ago, which made it even more unlikely someone was around.

When I reached Kick Shot, I walked in through the back and plastered a smile on my face. I waved silently at my employees as I made my way into the front. Tuesday was a small crowd, mostly my old regulars. They didn't come by on the busy nights as much anymore, but Kick Shot was still a quiet place for them to drink and hang out on the weekdays. Joey and his friend John were laughing over a game of pool. A server blew past me and placed two beers down on a table near them. John checked her out and I had to hold back a growl. He didn't say anything, and he didn't touch her, so I let it go and focused on Dirk behind the bar.

"How was the full moon?" I asked nonchalantly.

"The same as always," he answered, clearly not finding anything odd with my question. I always asked how the full moon went for him and Oliver.

I nodded silently, then sat down, looking over the bar again. I heard a glass placed on the bar top and turned to see a glass of water next to me.

"Thanks," I said, sipping it.

"No problem. Tuesdays are boring."

"Aren't they?" I sighed. "I should get upstairs and talk to Oliver. We didn't have our weekly meeting yesterday."

"He understands," Dirk said, chuckling. We didn't need to say why the meeting was skipped. I needed sleep and relaxation after a full moon. Now that I wasn't the lone bartender and owner, I skipped work the night after a full moon. Monday evening's weekly meeting was no exception.

"Still," I said, sighing. "I'll be back down here once I know everything is good for him."

"Do you want to help behind the bar tonight?" He actually gave me a smile. "You can. You just can't take the tips. You don't need 'em."

"Ha ha. I'll think about it." I hit the countertop and got up, taking the water with me. As I walked up the stairs, my phone vibrated. I checked it before walking into Oliver's office.

**Heath:** Care to come over for dinner with the family tonight?

**Jacky:** I'll think about it. I was considering sticking around Kick Shot. Let me check on a few things and get back to you.

I put my phone away and gave Oliver's door two knocks.

"Come in," he called. I walked in but didn't say anything as I walked around his desk and looked at his screen. Oliver was too professional and awkward to be doing anything at work he shouldn't be.

"Working on the schedule? Do you need any help?"

"No, no," he said, leaning back in his chair. "I finished it yesterday, but a couple people have asked for certain days off and some switches, so I'm updating it to account for those."

I nodded and went to my seat. "So, how was yesterday without me? Anything I need to look at?"

"Kick Shot won't fall apart because you missed one weekly meeting. I swear on it," he said, smiling at me around his computer monitor.

"How was your weekend, otherwise?"

"Uneventful. You know me. I'm not Dirk. I don't... know anyone here and don't really think I want to." He wrinkled his nose, then shook his head. "I'm finally getting a car, I think. Tired of Dirk needing to drive me around. He's really nice about it, and I help with petrol, of course, but everyone in America needs a car. I'm still not used to it. I used to bike or use public transit in London to get anywhere I needed to be."

"Yeah, living in the country does make it hard to get around without a car," I agreed. "If you want help looking, I'm more than willing to take you. Hell, I'll cosign a loan with you if you need it. You're responsible enough."

"Ah, I was just going to buy something used for cash," he replied, dismissing me with a wave of his hand. "I don't need something brand new and big like my roommate. Something like your little hatchback is perfect for me, really."

"Are you sure?" I didn't want him in something that was just going to break down in a year or give him problems.

"I might take you up on the offer to go car shopping with me, but that's it," he said, smiling. "Okay? Does that make you happy?"

"Perfectly," I said, smiling back. "I mean, you're not getting a used car just so you can dump it easily when you leave, right?"

"Leave?" Frowning, Oliver's youthful face got wrinkles he shouldn't have for at least two more decades. "I don't plan on leaving. It's my first car. If I wreck it, it won't be expensive to deal with."

I laughed and remembered there was a conversation I had avoided for over a week. I never did ask Dirk about when he wanted to go home to Niko.

"What's wrong?" Oliver was still watching me.

"You don't plan on leaving?" I asked softly. "At all?"

"Why would I?" He shook his head. "Why go back to living in London, where I would have to either work with my family or find a job outside your family? I like working here. I'm confident in what I can do for Kick Shot, and you trust me with it. It's more than London could ever give me."

"You've definitely become a lot more mellow in the last year," I said, trying for a smile again.

"Have I?" He smiled, a blush creeping up. "I was frantic when I came to Texas, wasn't I?"

I put two fingers close together and laughed as his blush deepened.

"You're a great manager, Oliver. I asked about you leaving because I need to talk to Dirk about something. Maybe you can give me some insight because you live with him." I put my hands together and sighed. "Do you think he wants to go back to Germany?"

"He hasn't said anything to me about that," Oliver replied, shrugging.

"Not at all? Don't worry about it," I said quickly, trying to stop the conversation before it went too far.

Oliver gave me a confused look as I stood.

"Are you sure?" he asked, watching me back away.

"Yeah, yeah," I said. "It's not anything you can help with, I promise. Text me when you want to go car shopping."

He nodded, then went back to work. I left the office, frowning.

*Do I have to send Dirk back? Does he want to go? Is Niko going to push this?*

I didn't have any answers, so I headed back downstairs. I couldn't pull Dirk away from the bar at that moment, so I took a seat where I could see the entire space. He hovered close, tsking after a moment.

"What?" I asked him, huffing.

"You didn't bring the glass back down. I'm going to have to send someone up to get it later." He put another water next to me, shaking his head. "Lazy."

"Wow, you're going to call me lazy? You do remember I ran this place by myself for several years, right?"

He shrugged at my retort.

"You are so mean to me," I muttered, shaking my head.

"And you hover," he replied. "But you know, we make the best with what we have."

I glared at him but couldn't bring myself to get truly angry, probably because the comment was actually kind of funny.

"We're never going to get along, are we?" I asked. The question seemed to startle him and forced him to put down the glass in his hand.

"I thought we were?" he said with obvious confusion.

I opened and closed my mouth, now startled myself. "This is how you talk to people you like?"

"This is how I talk to everyone," he corrected. "You hover, and I don't like it, but that doesn't mean I don't like you. I love working here. Texas is nice. It's giving me the chance to practice all the things Niko taught me, like talking like an American. That's fun. I'll be able to use it one day, unlike French. I don't care for French."

"How many languages do you speak fluently?" I asked curiously. More than curious—intrigued. Dirk was an enigma with a complicated upbringing, wrapped in the attitude of a cranky mid-twenty-year-old man.

"Four," he answered quickly. "I'm also passable in two others. German, my first language, English and French, tying for second. I also speak Welsh fluently, and I'm passable in Arabic and Zulu."

"That's a wide range of languages for someone your age. Let me guess, Arabic and Zulu are thanks to—"

"Niko wanted me to make a good impression," he said, cutting me off with an annoyed expression. "And I speak all of them as if I'm a native except for the last two. I'm more of a tourist with those, definitely not native, but..."

"Passable," I said, nodding. "That's really interesting. Why didn't you go to college? You're obviously a lot smarter than I am, and I got into medical school."

"You had to have learned languages," he said, staring at me as if I was pulling his leg.

"I went through the courses and survived them," I replied with a chuckle. "But they never stuck. Over the years, I've lost them. I'm teaching myself Spanish now. And don't avoid the question. Why didn't you go to college?"

"You're not going to let this go, are you?" He poured two beers and put them on the bar. One of the servers came by and picked them up while we sat in silence.

"I can if you want me to," I said softly. We stared at each other until he sighed.

"When I was at the age to go, I was tired of trying to be perfect for him," Dirk answered softly. "I got a job and just wanted to get out and be my own person. Never looked back. He's never really forgiven me for it. He might not admit it, but he had a plan for me. He wanted... a *son*."

*Ah, shit. Niko, you've loaded this man up with so many expectations, you chased him away.*

"Thanks for sharing that," I said, swallowing. "Look, if you want to be a bartender for the rest of your life, I'm not going to stop you. I was just curious. No judgment from me. Be whatever you want, just come to work on time."

He nodded, giving me the strangest look. "Thank you."

"No problem. I get it. I wanted to be a bartender for the rest of *my* life, too." I smirked and finally got a chuckle out of him again.

"That's a very long time to be a bartender."

"Isn't it?"

*Well, it's not the 'go back to Germany conversation' we need to have, but it's something.*

Not long after Dirk and I entered in companionable silence, an interesting pair walked into the bar. Their navy blue suits stuck out. I knew that color, but the reason for seeing them here at Kick Shot eluded me. There was no reason for them to be here.

I stood slowly as the pair looked around. Some

people glanced their way, but most of the bar's patrons continued on with what they were doing.

Then they looked at me as I stood for their inspection, not trying to rush them. I met the dark brown eyes of a stern man matching Dirk's description. He reached down and revealed his sidearm as he pulled out his badge and flashed it.

"Jacky Leon, I'm Special Agent Collins with the Bureau of Supernatural Affairs. This is my partner, Special Agent Miller."

You could hear a pin drop in the bar. In the corner of my eye, I saw how tense Dirk was, unable to stop staring at these agents.

Every country had a department that handled supernaturals in some way or another. In the United States, a new department had been created, the BSA. A quiet organization, they really only dealt with the werewolves and the small occurrences of fae or witches being outed.

"Is there something I can do for you?" I asked, trying to be respectful. My last and only run-in with this organization hadn't gone well.

"We need to speak to you, preferably privately," Special Agent Miller said, looking around the room again.

"Oh, is the big bad BSA coming after our werewolf?" Joey laughed across the room. "I always knew you were one. Not sure why you denied it." A few people laughed.

"Yeah, you even hang out with that werewolf from Dallas. It's fine, though. You know we don't care," John added, laughing with his buddy.

I wanted, for a split second, to kill those idiots, a vicious instinct rooted in self-preservation. At that exact moment, my eyes probably flashed gold, but some things were truly uncontrollable. The rush of the feeling came so fast, I was hopeless to stop it from presenting itself for just a single second.

"You can talk to me in my office upstairs. Please follow me," I said softly, trying to reclaim my calm. "Dirk, do you need anything?"

"No, boss, I'm good," he said, visibly relaxing. "I've got things down here."

I patted the bar and started walking, letting the agents decide if they wanted to follow me. My gut told me this was bad. My instincts screamed for me to stop this meeting, but I had no reason to. There were rules against guns in Kick Shot and on the property, but that was because I served alcohol. I didn't need some idiot getting drunk and deciding to shoot someone. I couldn't throw out two government agents for having their required sidearms, no matter how much I wanted to.

The walk was quiet, and since I was leading, I could barely catch their scents. I didn't know yet how they were feeling through that needed sense. I didn't know what they were thinking because they offered no other indicator. Up the backstairs, the only sound I could register was my own heartbeat, pounding like a drum leading up to some event. I knocked on Oliver's office, then ducked my head in without waiting for a response.

"I have a meeting. Dirk will explain," I told my manager, then quickly shut the door before the agents drew close enough to look inside. I didn't even give myself time to make sure Oliver registered what I had said. I just had to trust he had listened at that moment.

When we made it to my office, I held the door open for them to enter with one hand while gesturing at the seats in front of my desk.

"Have a seat," I said softly, then closed the door as they sat down. I walked around my desk and sat down, putting my hands on the desk, and looked between them. Special Agent Collins had dark eyes that reminded me of Zuri and Jabari. Their eyes were also that dark brown, so close to black, especially when they were in a mood. For Jabari, that was common. Zuri's eyes tended to lighten up more than they darkened.

*That's it. He has Jabari's eyes. He's calculating, a warrior looking over an opponent. That's why I'm getting this vibe.*

Special Agent Miller was physically tense but didn't feel as threatening. His brown hair was boyish in cut and style, and he seemed fifteen or twenty years younger than his leading partner. It was a startling contrast to Special Agent Collins' crisp, military fade.

"What can I do for you, gentlemen?" I asked simply. I could smell them now, closed in my office. Their scents couldn't escape, and the air wasn't on. Everything they felt would expose them and give me an idea how to handle this.

"That is a somewhat complicated question, Miss Leon," Collins said, leaning back in his seat. "First, I need to explain some things. We're Special Agents of the BSA, not the lower ranking agents you've met before. We handle...particular circumstances."

I didn't say anything when he paused. I wanted him to

keep talking because the more he had to talk, the less I needed to. I wanted to reduce the chance of giving away something about myself. It was the best I could hope for in this situation. I had done it before with the BSA's visit about Carey last summer and was confident I could do it again.

While the pause continued, I came to the decision this had to be about Heath and Carey. I didn't know if they were trying to take her away or get Heath in trouble for something, but I was confident this was about my Everson family. I had to be careful if I wanted to fully protect them. Heath followed me to the other side of the world for my family. Dealing with these BSA visits was the least I could do for him and Carey.

Finally, the special agents realized I wasn't going to say anything.

"We handle first contact," Miller finally snapped, annoyance thick in his scent, probably impatient with my refusal to speak.

The words snapped like a whip and sent me into panic mode.

## CHAPTER SEVEN

*First contact.*
*They know about me and would never dare show up here unless they had proof.*

It shattered my plan into a million pieces. I lost the air in my lungs and my train of thought. A strange lightheaded feeling hit me, and I felt strangely bold for a moment.

*There's no way. They didn't catch me being supernatural. This...this can't be happening.*

"First contact?" I asked, leaning forward and daring to laugh. "What? Am I a fucking alien? What are you talking about?"

They looked between each other, and Collins was the one who reached into his pocket, pulling out a simple, harmless USB stick—it should have been harmless, but I knew what sort of damaging information could be kept on those little fucking things.

"Reactions like yours are common," he said, putting it

down gently on the desk, moving slowly for me. He was smart enough to be cautious.

*Or he knows enough to be cautious.*

"I bet," I said, letting the disbelief drip from my tongue like acid.

"Now, first contact isn't as bad as it sounds. We at the BSA don't out people for their status as supernatural. Normally, we open a dialogue to work with the new supernatural. We just become...handlers, in a sense, until the negotiations are done. We just want to make sure human laws are being followed, and if you are edging around the laws, they're for reasons we can allow. Financials are often something we turn a blind eye to unless there's evidence of insider trading. Normally, supernaturals keep their money clean, though, even if it's under fake names. Once we're done, we switch with someone experienced to work with you in the long term."

*Yes, we keep our money clean. We hire the best to do that. Hasan told me never to worry about that sort of thing.*

"I'm still wondering how you can possibly think I'm a supernatural," I said, blinking, pretending to ignore what he was trying to explain. "Is this some way of pulling my leg for getting pissed at an agent you sent to Heath last year? He's a friend. I'm protective of him, he's a wonderful father, and she was a hateful bitch. She wanted there to be something wrong with me because it was pretty obvious she didn't like how I was so trusting of the werewolf family. What was that woman's name..."

"Agent Robinson, who was promptly reassigned from interacting with supernaturals and has been reprimanded for her behavior," Collins said, crossing his arms. "Why don't you just...take a look?" He slowly pushed the USB closer to me.

I finally grabbed it and plugged it into the USB slot at the back of my keyboard. While they watched, I turned on the monitor from my desk, punched in my password, and clicked to the new folder waiting on my desktop.

It popped up and destroyed my life.

I didn't need to click the images. I could see the night vision images with clarity just from the surveillance. High quality, trail cam surveillance of me jogging past on a broken-in trail I used as a werecat. I could see the detail of my stripes in the strange green vision of the world. I could see my long fangs, just over four inches of bone ready to kill. A later picture showed matted fur, right after my kill.

"Looks like I have a prehistoric beast in the area. Thanks for the—"

"Click the video," Collins said, no longer entertaining my denials. He wasn't annoyed like his partner; he wasn't angry. He was talking to me like he would talk to a child who didn't want to admit she stole cookies from the kitchen. If anything, he was too patient.

The video was the last file and filled the forty-two-inch screen. The sun was going down, and I could see my house through the trees. My heart pounding, I watched as I walked onto my front porch completely naked. My face wasn't blurred, but someone had been nice enough to blur my private areas.

I felt sick to my stomach.

*How kind of them. How so fucking kind of them.*

"When we opened the investigation on you, we were

of the same mind as the gentleman downstairs. We believed you were a werewolf who lived off the radar. We tried to talk to you about it just over a week ago, but we couldn't get your bartender to find you for us. It's obvious he protects you. So, we decided we needed hard evidence and completed our official investigation by installing surveillance on your property. With the evidence, we were going to give you and Heath Everson a firm reminder that werewolves who operated businesses in the United States had to disclose that information. It's the law. It's one thing to take a background role in hopes people ignore it, but you flatly denied it."

"Because I'm not a werewolf," I whispered, unable to tear my eyes off the screen. It was a horror show of my own making. As the sun went down, the camera flipped into night vision, but even that couldn't obscure what it was filming. There was no reason to deny it anymore—they knew I wasn't a werewolf.

I Changed, right there on my front porch, caught by a camera that had to be farther away than it appeared. It was zoomed way too close on me, catching the detail of my bones and muscle moving under my skin, my fur growing out, and the deadly long fangs extending from my own, very human canines.

When it was done, I darted off-screen, far more agile than I should be as a nearly five-hundred-pound prehistoric cat.

"You are most definitely not a werewolf. We've never seen anything like you before," Collins said softly.

I wasn't paralyzed. In fact, I had never felt a more pressing need to get up and move around. I put my hands on the desk, trying to think. I wanted to pace. I pushed myself to a stand and saw how the agents reached for their sidearms.

"Miss Leon—"

"I just need to stand," I whispered. I finished my movement and took a step back from my desk, turning to look out the window behind it that looked over my beautiful trees.

The beautiful trees that were obviously no longer safe for me.

Nowhere was safe for me anymore.

Not even my own territory.

I wanted to vomit. Something insidious crept through me, a feeling I had little experience with. I crushed it, needing to think. I didn't have time to indulge it.

"What are you planning?" I asked, refusing to look at them.

"We're not...planning anything," Collins said, clearly choosing his words with care. "We're here to open a dialogue with you and your kind. You're the first thing we've ever seen like you, and we're not in the business of outing the supernaturals we find. We know there are thousands out there, but there are many we can't prove. The United States of America holds the position that we need to understand all the creatures that live within our borders. We need to be able to work with you. Since you're the first of your kind ever found, you find yourself in the unique position of being someone who can help us."

"How?" I asked, not bothering to elaborate.

*This was never supposed to happen.*

"Well, you can tell us how your kind works—"

"No," I hissed softly. "How did you figure out I'm not human?"

"You want to know about our investigation of you?" Miller huffed. "We don't—"

"It started a couple years ago, Miss Leon," Collins said quickly. I didn't turn around, but it was clear he was shutting Miller down before the younger one could say something stupid. "The coup in Dallas."

My blood ran cold. My hands were shaking, so I folded my arms and tucked my hands near my armpits to steady them. Looking into my woods, I tried to find solace in them that was continuing to escape me.

"The coup," I said as the memories came back to me —Carey's amazing run to get me to protect her, her being taken, me stupidly and bravely going into the city to get her back to protect her again because I couldn't bring myself to admit failure. She had been such a young girl. I couldn't fail her. "I remember the coup."

"We had never heard of you before, but during the coup, there were whispers about a woman who helped Heath Everson defeat the uprising and save his children. We were all sad to hear Richard had been lost, but at least Heath got his two youngest back. We heard about a woman people didn't really want to talk about to us, not in any fashion, official or unofficial."

I wanted to laugh, but the feeling was bitter. I hadn't known they had given Richard a tragic death. He'd been the greatest betrayal of the night.

They were sad to hear he died?

I had killed him to protect his sister.

"It's illegal to out another supernatural," I explained as if the words were coming out on autopilot. "If they had told you about me, they would have forfeited their lives."

"We're the United States of America. We could have protected them."

"You keep believing that," I said, hearing and regretting the deadpan way I spoke those words. It turned the words into a dangerous threat. I didn't say them with a laugh but with the utmost confidence. The United States could never protect someone from the Tribunal. They would be crushed.

"We're not here to exchange threats," Miller said, definitely playing the more aggressive of the partners.

"If the coup didn't give me away, what did?" I asked, ignoring his little outburst. I turned back to them but stayed where I was. I was concerned about the sidearms. If I took a step toward them, they could put me on the ground if they didn't feel safe.

"We heard several disturbing things, but mostly, we could track you through Heath Everson. He only recently stepped down from power, and while we didn't have him watched, we heard his name come up enough to keep record of everything. Heath helped save a werewolf in Seattle from a trip gone wrong. Reports were, they were kayaking, and the other three drowned. And there was this woman with him who made everyone a little on edge and annoyed he was with her. Then there was the Russian pack incident last summer," he said, tilting his head to the side as he waited for me to recognize that.

"I helped him save the wolf," I confirmed because they already knew that. "And I know all about Russia."

"Oh, Russia is the one we can definitely pin on you," he said, leaning over. I had a feeling Collins was pleased with himself, even though his scent betrayed nothing but pure confidence in what he was presenting. "You helped bring down a pack run by a despot who abused so many. When new werewolves are brought into the country, we interview every one of them. It's a deal we made with the North American Werewolf Council. Now, they're all coached well before they ever talk to us. While we were managing all the new werewolves, someone slipped and mentioned Heath...and Jacky in our company. We made the connection with you from your incident with our agents last year."

"Why are we telling her this?" Miller demanded.

"Because she's an interesting case," Collins replied, not looking at his partner. I stared down the older partner. To him, I was the most interesting thing in the world. He was genuinely enjoying unraveling this mystery to prove to me I wasn't as smart as I thought I was, or that he was smarter than a new supernatural who had hidden for so long. "Aren't you? When we got your name, we noticed some interesting...coincidences around you. We were able to trace back to your human identity because we knew what you looked like after learning your name. You don't talk to your human family any longer, hiding from them probably since you became what you are. While you were in Russia, they were on vacation."

"That's right," I confirmed. "I heard they had a lovely time."

"Your twin changed jobs at the same time."

"Not everything has to be connected," I said, warning in my tone. "I keep away from them because they were never a very good family. I keep away from them because I like living my own life. Now, I need to know what you want. Are you going to blackmail me? Are you here to get me to expose others? Let's fucking hear it." I couldn't hold back the snappy, snarling rage at the end. The fear ate at me. I didn't have training for this situation. This was never something Hasan and I had talked about. I was responsible for exposing werecats to the humans.

This was all my fault. Me and all my good intentions over the last two and half years led to this. Special Agent Collins had been kind enough to give me the entire detailed play-by-play of how they found out about me. Now, I had to pick up the pieces and figure it the fuck out.

*My family is going to blame this on Heath. I know they are. They're going to tell me I was too close to the werewolves.*

*And they're fucking right.*

"We truly just want to talk to you," Collins said, leaning forward again. I inhaled deeply, knowing my eyes went gold as I did. There was no anger on their scents, but for a quick second, there was fear. "We're trying to open a door for both our kinds. You don't have to live in the dark."

"I don't break any laws. If you just want to talk, then I think we're done here," I said stiffly. "I have nothing to say."

"Fine." Special Agent Collins got up first, gesturing for his partner to follow him. He didn't seem angry, as if he was expecting this turn. "We'll come back in a couple of days. Don't go anywhere, please. Maybe when you've had some time to think, you can start to see how this might be a good thing. Miss Leon, you're a supernatural who lives in secret. Imagine how your life could change if that wasn't the case."

I walked around my desk, keeping my hands curled under my arms, keeping them from being the threat. I opened my office door and waited. Eventually, the BSA agents relented and left.

"Two days," Special Agent Collins said softly as he passed me. I watched them walk down the hallway and saw Oliver coming up the stairs, his face a shade paler than I was used to. He glanced at the agents, then down the hall to me. The agents looked him over as well as he tried to press himself up against a wall to let them pass. Neither of us moved until the agents' steps on the stairs ended.

Oliver spared no time after that, walking down the hall to me.

"Jacky—"

"Shut it down," I ordered as he got to me.

"What?" he stumbled to a stop.

"They know. Shut it all down," I repeated. "I need to call my family."

I closed the office door in his face and locked it, my hands still shaking.

*I need to call my family, but what the fuck am I supposed to say?*

# 8

## CHAPTER EIGHT

I didn't make it a step, freezing in place as the panic gripped my heart and threatened to stop it. Oliver knocked and jiggled the door handle.

"Jacky, what's going on? What do you mean by 'they know?'" Oliver kept trying, but I made no effort to unlock the door.

I took three steps back, bumping into the chairs.

I could still smell them—the agents. I could still smell them in my office.

"Jacky?" Dirk called, a loud series of thumps on the door. "Jacky, we need to know what's going on."

I stumbled, trying to get around the chairs and my desk. I looked up at the monitor and saw where it was paused, staring at my house in night vision. I couldn't forget what I saw play out.

They didn't just have pictures of a werecat. They had me Changing. They had both me and confirmation of a new supernatural species. This wasn't the case of some cryptid, where people on the internet debunked the images as some sort of prank.

This was real.

I fell into my chair, barely hearing Oliver and Dirk, both in full panic mode now, trying to get inside.

I reached out to the mouse and went back to the beginning of the video, watching it all play out. I rewatched my Change over and over again, letting it sink in.

My phone started going off, but I ignored it as I pulled my knees up and began to rock, trying to contain my pure terror.

I had exposed the werecats. There was no going back from this. There was no hiding from this. Even if I disappeared for a few decades, they would know me the moment I came out of hiding. They would look for others.

Years and years of secrecy. Years of Hasan saying he wanted to carefully plan the outing of the werecats if it needed to happen.

And I had ruined all of it.

"Jacky, please," Dirk said, more desperate than frantic. His deep voice broke through. "We're here to help you. We need to know how."

*Need.*

I needed to keep protecting them. Dirk and Oliver were human and too close to my family to get out of this unscathed if I didn't do this right. I didn't want them to become targets of the BSA to get information.

And I needed to protect my family. I couldn't let the BSA drag me into the public eye and out my siblings or my father. Hasan was on the Tribunal. If they got too close to him and discovered that, I would be single-handedly responsible for outing the shadow government of the supernaturals. My life would be forfeit, and so would many others.

I needed a plan.

I stood and took a deep breath, then walked steadily back to the door and unlocked it, opening it slowly to reveal the scared faces of my two humans.

"I'm sorry. I needed a moment to collect myself," I said, looking between them. "Come in, and I'll explain."

"Should we close the bar down?" Oliver asked as he walked into the office first and sat down where Miller had sat.

"No. No, leave it open for the night. Actually, we're not closing down at all. We're going to continue like nothing happened."

"What happened?" Dirk asked, his desperation gone. He walked in behind Oliver and took the door from me. He was solid, my nephew. I had to remember Niko trained him from a young age. He was ready for these moments.

I went back to sit at my desk as he closed the door and locked it. I didn't answer his question, just pointed at the monitor, rewound a minute in the footage, and hit play. I didn't watch the scene play out on screen again, opting to watch their reactions.

"I know how to find those cameras," Dirk whispered. "And before anything else is said, let me check the room for bugs."

"They never left those chairs," I said softly. "And..." I

pointed to the USB. "They gave me that."

He nodded and began his search around the chairs. I pulled out the USB without bothering to copy the files. I knew the tricks employed here. If there was any sort of malware on the USB, it would hopefully stay contained. I would need Davor to look through my system remotely and through the USB to clear it. Only then would I feel safe copying the files onto my PC to send my family.

"Clear, but let's take that out of the room," he said, pointing at the USB.

"Go ahead."

He grabbed it and left the office in a blur, coming back only a moment later.

"We're secure to talk now. So, they caught you on camera changing."

"I didn't see any trail cameras. I don't know how they did it," I admitted. "I followed those two people through my woods, and they were definitely the ones who set up the surveillance, but I didn't see it."

"Walk me on the trail they took, and I might find it. We can do it tomorrow at dawn. Don't go home tonight. Do everything here in this office, then crash at our house or something." Dirk was more solid than me, and I took some comfort in that.

"I take it Niko was prepared for these kinds of situations?" I asked softly.

"Not this one specifically. We were bugged and spied on by a lot of people, mostly werewolves and other werecats, the occasional vampire. Most people in Europe choose to deal with Niko over Davor, thinking he might be less prickly, which he is, and would equate that to him being an easy target, especially since he had me. Niko taught me all of this to protect myself and him. If you need a room cleared of surveillance, I can handle it for you."

"Thank you," I said softly. "Now to the important parts of this conversation. As you saw, they know I'm a werecat, but they don't know what a werecat is. I'm the first they've caught on camera. They want me to...make a deal with them, I think. I give them information about our kind, and they let me live openly as a supernatural, like the werewolves. Well, maybe not exactly like the werewolves, but similar enough."

"That puts other werecats at risk," Oliver pointed out. "Doesn't it?"

"Yeah," Dirk confirmed.

"They're already at risk," I whispered, looking down at my hands. "They've picked me apart. They know my tricks, the tricks Hasan taught me and uses to protect us from human eyes. They went through my finances and know my human name. They know Gwen changed careers. They know my family went on vacation last year. At least *that* story is holding up." I growled as I looked up at my two employees, my humans who knew and helped me in the task of being supernatural. They, at the end of the day, were my cover. "By knowing all of those things, they can watch for others using them. They can try to find gaps in the protection of other werecats. This is...I don't know how I'm going to tell my family. I only have forty-eight hours until the BSA comes back and expects me to make a decision. I don't know what's going to happen if I don't play their game. I don't know what they have up their sleeve." I stopped and spun my chair around, looking out the window behind my desk. "But I know how they figured me out, and that's...that's what is going to get me killed in the end."

"Boss?" I could hear Dirk's frown.

"They heard about me in passing during the coup in Dallas. They knew I helped Heath save a werewolf in Washington. They...finally got my name in Russia, and I had already run into them at that point. My connection to the werewolves exposed me and my entire kind." I leaned over and put my head in my hands. "I'm going to need to take the consequences for that."

"They don't even know you and Heath are..." Dirk cursed.

"Are they going to make us leave?" Oliver asked in a small voice. "I like it here. I like working with you."

"I don't know," I whispered. "I don't know if they'll let Heath and his family stay. I don't...If they have footage of that, they have footage of Heath coming and going from my place. They probably don't even know they're sitting on a bomb."

"Oh, fuck." Dirk's chair clattered as he stood. I heard him pacing.

"The footage doesn't seem clear enough to show what happens in my house. My windows are purposefully tinted for that, but it doesn't look good...walk into my house with a werewolf on a Saturday and him sneaking out early in the morning, hours later."

"No, that doesn't look good at all," Oliver agreed. "Would anyone hurt him for that? Or you? Or would they just make you break up?"

"Worst-case scenario, Hasan is forced to pick between me and his position over the werecats. If he picks them, and he should, I would be forfeit. Heath would have the same problem. Werewolves all over the world would be up in arms. They would expect him, as a traitor, to be put down. Then there are the would-be accusations of seduction, in which case, each side would try to place the blame on the other. A great way for that to play out would be if a werewolf claimed I was trying to spy for the werecats or vice versa, Heath spying for the werewolves. This can go wrong in all sorts of ways."

"And you did it anyway," Dirk pointed out. He was so frustrated, the smell of his aggravation thick in the air.

"Yeah, I did," I agreed, nodding as I turned back to them. "Old rivalries and wars shouldn't have the power to stop me from spending my time the way I want to. Old prejudices shouldn't be my or Heath's problem. So, I did it anyway."

He paused in his pacing and looked at me, then nodded slowly. "You're right."

"We're going to deal with this, one problem at a time," I declared. "There're cameras in my woods. Dirk, do you know what sort of tech they might have used?"

"I can find them. You take me where those humans went, and I'll find and get rid of the cameras. The photos and video help. They give me the angles and positioning. I just need someone to lead me to where they are." He was confident, and I trusted it.

"Thank you. Oliver, you're going to be working Kick Shot alone. I'm going to keep Dirk with me for a while. Get someone to cover his shifts until further notice."

"Okay," Oliver said, nodding. "I'll keep up appearances here. No one will know anything is wrong if I can help it."

"Why?" Dirk asked.

"You know our family," I reminded him. "And you're obviously good at this. I want you near any of the meetings going forward to look out for bugs and shit like you have here. You have an eye for detail. I don't. I know you don't want to use all the things Niko taught you and understand you want to make your own path, but I need you right now."

"All right," he said, nodding once again. "I can do this. I've got your back."

"Now, you need to call your family," Oliver whispered.

I winced. "Yeah, I know."

"They might have really good advice," Oliver pressed, suddenly perking up. "They could know how to fix this."

"That's what she's afraid of," Dirk muttered.

"Oliver, get back down to Kick Shot and make sure everything is running smoothly," I said softly. There was something I needed to clear up before I made this call. It was going to get brought up. "I need to talk to Dirk about something."

"Okay..." He stood slowly, looked at Dirk, who shrugged, then walked out.

"What do you need, boss?"

"Niko wants to know when you're going home," I explained, meeting his stare. "He expected you back at the end of the year. You weren't supposed to be here. He understands everything that happened, and that the year didn't turn out as planned, but he wants a timeline."

"We're going to deal with this right now?" Dirk sat back down, looking away from me. "Really? There's something else going on—"

"If he feels you're in danger, he might tell me to put you on a plane without us discussing it first. So, do you want to go back—"

"If I wanted to go back, I already would have," he said softly. "I want to stay here and help you. I want to work at Kick Shot. We just had this conversation downstairs. He has all sorts of expectations of me I don't want. I want to make my own life, and I know you're more willing to let me do that than he is. He tries, but..."

"I get it," I said softly. "I never got the impression from Niko that he had a plan for you. He's always seemed to have...the best of intentions when it comes to you. Now it makes total sense." I chuckled darkly. "Parents."

"Yup."

"So, you want to stay for as long as you want to stay. No real timeline, huh?"

"No timeline," he confirmed.

I nodded slowly, then went to my keyboard and mouse, then started the process of reaching out to all of my family members, letting them know there was an emergency in my territory.

It didn't take long for a video call to start, only a couple minutes of dreadful silence. I answered, letting it engage the webcam at the top of the monitor, then pointed where it could see me and my entire office, including Dirk, where he was seated.

It was time for me to face the music.

## CHAPTER NINE

Hasan was the first face I saw with that familiar concern. Guilt ate at me at that moment, watching him take in my appearance on the screen and register that Dirk was there as well. Jabari and Mischa were there next, then Hisao, Niko, and Davor. Davor being last surprised me. He had dark bags under his eyes as if he wasn't sleeping properly, and I recognized the space around him. He was still in Hasan's territory and at our patriarch's estate. Zuri's absence made sense. There was no real way to get ahold of her, though I had sent her the same emergency message as I did everyone else.

"What's the emergency?" Hasan asked, obviously trying to keep any sort of emotion out of the words. He wanted to approach this calmly, but the undercurrents of worry and annoyance were clear, even though he didn't want them to be.

"Davor, can you perform a sweep on my system for malware?" I asked, ignoring the question.

"Why is Dirk there?" Niko asked. "Dirk, is something wrong? Were you hurt?"

"Do I look hurt?" Dirk asked, scoffing. "Jacky will get to it."

"I'm trying to reason out why you're here since you don't want to be involved with the family, but you're here for an emergency call. Growing up, you never wanted to be on calls with me, and bartenders don't get the privilege of these calls, either."

"He's not my bartender anymore. He's..." I looked at Dirk.

"Head of security?" he offered, shrugging.

"Sure," I mumbled. "Davor?"

"I'm on it," he growled softly. "Anything I'm looking for specifically?"

"Not...not really. I was given a USB to plug into my computer and want to make sure it didn't leave anything it wasn't supposed to."

"Okay..." Davor's confused expression persisted as I saw my mouse pointer moving around my screen. He had complete remote control over my computer. "I'm not finding anything. Tell me if anything starts acting weird, and I'll come back into it."

"Can you please tell us why you needed us?" Mischa huffed. "This is an emergency, right?"

I felt sick. "Dirk, go get the USB and let's plug it in for Davor to clear."

Everyone waited in silence, the look of confusion spreading. Dirk came back in quickly and plugged it into the USB slot in my keyboard I had used.

I watched Davor pale.

"What the fuck am I looking at right now?" he asked softly.

"The emergency, but I want you to clear it of any sort of malware—"

"There's nothing. You can copy those files and send them to everyone," he growled softly. "Fuck."

"Davor? Jacky?" Hasan was sitting up at attention, leaning forward. "I don't like secrets, and neither of you has ever been the type to beat around the bush, as the humans say."

Davor did it for me. I watched the files copy on my screen, then dropped into an email that was sent out to everyone in the family.

"Take a look," I whispered. "Davor, can I eject the USB? We haven't broken it open for bugs and—"

"Destroy it," Davor snarled.

I nodded to Dirk, who ripped it out of the slot and left the room again.

"Oh no," Mischa gasped.

"While you look at the email Davor just sent out, I'll explain," I said, clapping my hands together. "Today, two special agents from the BSA came to Kick Shot to talk to me. They specialize in what they call 'first contact.'"

"They have *pictures*," Hisao growled.

"And a *video*," Jabari snarled. "The pictures we could avoid, but they have her Changing!" He started a long string of what I guessed were profanities, but I didn't know or understand the language. He picked up and threw his mouse, then stormed off the video feed.

"Jacqueline, how did this happen?" Hasan asked, not reacting in any overt way compared to my siblings.

I opened and closed my mouth. Not even a year ago, I sat on a call with Hasan, Davor, and Zuri. After Davor left, Zuri had tried to talk sense into me. She tried to warn me staying secret probably meant I had to distance myself from the werewolves. I hadn't taken her advice. Instead, I went to Russia and got into a whole different league of trouble.

Now, a world power knew about werecats, not just from fuzzy photos. They had a name and face because I played too closely with the werewolves.

Just like Zuri had tried to warn me about.

She probably didn't see this coming, but she knew the risks I was taking before any of my siblings and tried to head it off before it became too much of an issue.

"Jacqueline," Hasan repeated. Jabari fell back into his seat, glaring at his camera.

I swallowed. "They first heard of a woman helping Alpha Everson in Dallas..." I started, repeating what had been told to me, all the way to the BSA check-in for Carey and my conflict with one of the agents, which the family had already known about. All the way to Russia, where hundreds of werewolves had seen werecats help free a human family taken hostage, with Heath Everson standing tall against their new Alpha trying to take over.

"I don't know who slipped my name to them," I finally said, refusing to look up at my camera or at my monitor. "They didn't tell me. Someone slipped something about Jacky and Heath in their presence or something..." I spread my hands and chuckled darkly. "They put it together on their own. Heath's new friend in Jacksonville, the woman who watches his daughter and helps out with her growing up."

"And again, it comes back to the werewolves," Mischa said with a soft growl. "Always with the werewolves."

"We need to know who gave Jacky's name to the BSA," Hasan said softly. "Someone, look into that. I need to know if it was accidental, as though they were being watched and didn't know, or if they purposefully exposed her. Hisao, be ready. If someone purposely exposed Jacky, you're going to get a call. I'm going to need you ready to get on a plane."

"Yes, sir," Hisao whispered.

Chills went down my spine. I hadn't even considered that. Being purposefully exposed was so against the Law, it was considered the bedrock of supernatural society. We could kill each other all we wanted, but we didn't get the human authorities and government involved. We did everything we could to keep them out of it.

"We need Zuri back," Niko said. "She would know exactly what to say to get Jacky out of this problem."

"There's no getting out of this problem," Davor snarled. "They have her on video, Niko. They know about werecats now and not just some measly fucking rumors we can avoid and slip past. We're either going to have to make Jacky disappear or leave her out to hang. I vote the latter. It doesn't change the fact they know us now. We're step one into going public to humans. I know we've toyed with the idea, but this? This is out of our hands, and it's because she couldn't fucking stay out of trouble. Jacky has to stick her nose into everything and go ten steps too far every time she's given the opportunity. Now it's come back to not only bite her in the ass but everyone here."

That stabbed me through the damn heart, and I didn't even like Davor.

"Zuri would know how to make this work for us," Niko snapped, lowering his head as if he didn't feel like dealing with Davor's aggressive meanness, either. "She would spin this and say we're accelerating our plans for something, or we could use this to help us in the future. We're a family, and we work together to fix these problems."

"What, like werewolves?" Davor snarled. "Like they work together? Is that what you mean, Niko? Like how Jacky works together with the werewolves, which is what got her found out? Or maybe like the werewolves who worked together to kill Liza. IS THAT WHAT YOU MEAN?" He was roaring at the end, making things shake in my office. I quickly silenced the call, hoping no one outside the office heard the outburst.

The deafening silence that followed was almost worse than the screaming. Davor went pale and pulled away from his computer. I looked for Hasan and realized he was gone, so silently disappearing from his spot that none of us had noticed.

A moment later, his large hand reached out and grabbed Davor by the back of his shirt, yanking him off the screen. I didn't turn the sound back on. I didn't want to, seeing the expressions of my other siblings. Dirk walked back in at that moment and sat down slowly. I glanced at him, wondering what he decided to do with the USB. He must have read my mind.

"I put it through the industrial garbage disposal. It's in a thousand pieces now."

"Thank you," I said softly. "We're muted, and they're silenced. Davor just said something he shouldn't have to Niko."

"Was it about Liza and werewolves?" Dirk asked, leaning onto the other side of my desk.

"Yeah," I confirmed.

"It happens. Niko gets on to me about not being closer to the...family,"—he waved a hand at the monitor as he said it—"but he's always been an outsider. I noticed it when I was a kid. He thinks like a werewolf when you compare him to everyone else in the family."

"This might be surprising, but you know all of them better than I do," I said, leaning toward him. "They didn't want a sister. They were still getting over Liza. Hasan met me and Changed me as an adult. I wasn't, in any way, raised with the family the way all of them were."

"I remember hearing about it," Dirk admitted. "Niko didn't know how to approach the situation. He admitted to me, he pretty much shut down when he met you."

I huffed. "Yeah, he didn't talk to me for years, not that most of them did, but his silence was always one of the more noticeable ones."

Someone was waving on the screen, so I turned on the sound again and unmuted my side.

"Yes?" I asked softly. "I'm in a public place and didn't want anyone to hear any of that."

"Davor won't be back," Hasan said softly. "Not until he can control himself."

"Okay." I looked at Niko. "Are you okay?"

"I'm fine," he said softly, looking down at something and never looking back up. "He's grieving still. He'll always grieve. She was the love of his life."

*That doesn't excuse him being a mean asshole, but if that helps everyone in the family sleep at night...*

"Niko is right, we need Zuri, Father," Jabari said, quickly getting the family back on course.

"Well, Zuri is unavailable," Hasan retorted. "And unless you want to upset her and your mother, you will help us here instead of chasing her down."

"She would be a better public face for the werecats," Jabari countered.

*Better than me, sure, but...I think I'm better suited.*

The idea came to me quickly. I didn't have to put anyone at risk, not even Zuri. I didn't want to. This was my fuck up. My actions brought this on everyone here. I needed to protect them, and I had an idea how.

"Look, I'm not even...close to Zuri, but I can get through this with everyone's help," I said. "There's no reason to expose anyone else in this family. Hasan is a member of the Tribunal. Jabari, you and Zuri are in charge of the largest werecat population in the world. There are not many of us here in the Americas, but I'm American and modern. Yeah, Zuri is the politician, the one who used to be a queen, but...I'm one of them. The BSA...they might be able to relate to me the best. I was born and raised *here*. If this goes public, I'm the one who doesn't seem like an ancient powerhouse no one can understand or relate to, but someone people can...know. I'm a business owner and an American who just so happens to be...not human. Right?"

I second-guessed there at the end, looking between the faces of my family.

"That's what I was thinking," Hasan agreed softly. "I'm sorry we have to put you in this position, but I don't see a way around it."

"They can pull up my school records and see I was a normal kid...a normal human *American* kid. They can't do that with any of you."

"This will go worldwide," Mischa countered.

"Then we pick who works the best in each area, even if it's someone not in the family. We hire someone to be the face."

"And lose power?" Hisao asked, raising an eyebrow.

I bit my lip and looked at Hasan.

"Not lose power, solidify it by giving people power we can take away," he said, nodding slowly. "After what happened last year, maybe it's time we show werecats we can trust those who are the most loyal to us."

"Zuri is going to hate this," Jabari snapped. "She's worked damn hard to keep us in power, Father, and part of that is refusing to bend...on anything."

"Zuri will understand the need, and there's a chance she will be back before this goes international. Until then, we need to address the problem in front of us. The United States of America knows werecats are real, and they know Jacky is one. What do they want?" Hasan was cool and calculating. At the end of the day, he was the one in charge.

"They were a little vague about that. They want to know more about our kind, for sure, but the purpose is... elusive. They did try to sway me with the idea I could live openly as a supernatural, never have to move around again."

"When do you see them again?"

"They're giving me forty-eight hours to think about things. They asked me not to run."

"Press them for more about their side of the bargain. Ask them to keep werecats out of the public eye. If they have to, they can just call us moon cursed, and I'll talk to Callahan and Corissa to see if we can hide in the shadow of the werewolves. Hopefully, we haven't upset them too badly after last summer." He rubbed his jaw. "I knew Changing you would be something, but Jacqueline, I was really hoping we were beyond this very troublesome part of your life."

"I think we're only getting started," I whispered, "but I was really hoping we were past it too." *I'm in a romantic relationship with a werewolf, so it was bound to come back eventually, but I was really hoping I had more time before something came for me. I certainly wasn't expecting this.*

I knew I was walking a very fine line. My dealings with werewolves were the reason I was caught, but I had no intention of losing Heath in this process unless lives depended on it and only if lives depended on it.

*Maybe not even then.*

"I'm going to go," I said finally. "I need...some time to really let this sink in, and there are still cameras on my property. I'll let you all know how the next meeting goes."

"Jacqueline...if you make this worse, I'm bringing you home," Hasan warned softly. "Other than that, just stay alive."

He hung up, and I quickly followed, knowing his

warning wasn't a joke or a game. I had been in too much trouble, and the stakes were always so damn high. Now I was playing a role that should go to my sister. Zuri was perfect for this. She knew how to talk to people and play the field. I was a child, playing in my older sister's shoes, although I had some experience. I was obviously pretty good at talking to werewolves and navigating those issues, or so I wanted to believe. I used to be pretty popular among humans, as Gwen tried to remind me repeatedly.

"I'm going to print those pictures to use as reference to find the cameras," Dirk said after a few moments of silence. "Tomorrow. It'll be too hard to find them in the dark."

"Yeah..." I agreed. "I'm going to sleep in here."

"Are you sure, boss?"

"Positive. You can do whatever you want, but dawn tomorrow, we're going in and clearing out those cameras. Make sure you get some sleep."

I covered my face with my shaking hands as he walked out. I felt sick.

My family hadn't even asked how I was doing. I held back the tears as I sat there, trying to keep the crushing wave of emotions from destroying me. I wasn't ready for them yet—not yet.

## 10

# CHAPTER TEN

I did exactly as I told Dirk I would, sleeping in my office. Oliver checked on me before he left, but I told him I would lock up. I locked up all the doors, then to my office, continuing to hide from the world and my own trees.

At dawn, I went downstairs, holding a folder, and saw Dirk driving up. He drove around and parked at the back. I walked back there, watching him jump out in fresh clothes, something I didn't share. I didn't change, not wanting to walk home to do it. I didn't trust my forest anymore, and that was the first thing I had to fix.

"Are you ready?" I asked as he stepped closer. Holding out the folder, he took it without a word, flipping it open to see what I was giving him.

"I'm ready," he agreed. "And you can call on me any time to come out and sweep the area if you want me to."

"That would be...very nice," I said, sighing. "I'm going to need to give you a raise."

"Yeah." He nodded. "Yeah, you are," he said with that

casual "fucking deal with it" tone. It made me crack a smile. We both started laughing, the first time I had honestly laughed since the day before.

"Let's go," I ordered, wiping my eyes. I led him into the trees and took the trail. I couldn't forget following the scents of the trespassers. I should have approached them while I had the chance. I'd known it was fucking fishy and played it too safe. Now I was paying for it.

Dirk stopped before I did, tsking.

"Here." He held up a photo and moved around in a circle. "Yeah, it's somewhere here. Did they ever go too far off the trail?"

"I..." I couldn't remember.

Shrugging at my inability to give a response, he put the folder down and kept the one photo in his hands, then walked deeper into the brush and cursed.

"Got it," he called out. "It's still on. Hey, motherfuckers, found you." He waved in front of something. "Nice little high-tech piece of equipment. Don't try billing us for this."

"Does it have audio?" I asked, watching him reach into a bush.

"No, but I bet someone can read lips, and they'll figure out what I said." He pulled out something I had never seen before. The camera thing was no bigger than a watch face or a quarter and only half an inch deep. "They crammed everything in here. Watch battery, tiny camera, like for a cell phone, and the ability to send information somewhere. It's not supposed to work for longer than a couple weeks, I bet, then someone comes in and picks it up to dispose of."

"Have you ever seen anything like it before?"

"No, but humans and supernaturals are always trying to push the boundaries of surveillance tech. I've found things just as interesting."

"So, do we just destroy it? Or..." I had no experience in this.

"Send it to Davor, normally," he said, flipping it over in his hand. "That's what Niko usually did, even when they weren't talking."

I frowned. "They often don't talk?"

Dirk put the little camera in his pocket and sighed.

"For about three months every year. The month before the anniversary, the month of the anniversary, and the month after the anniversary."

"And he goes to Hasan's to hide during the anniversary month."

"Yeah, he's an asshole, but he's one of the family, *right*?" Dirk's sarcasm didn't go unnoticed, but I didn't call him out. "He's never really been mean to me, but you... Yeah, he fucking hates you."

"I don't need the reminder. Seems you got lucky, though. Niko's adopted son and my employee, and he's not an asshole. That's a damn miracle."

"Human *and* young. He's known me since I was a kid," Dirk reminded me. "But...he's one of the reasons I would never be a werecat. Well, they're all why I don't want to be a werecat."

We kept walking as I thought about his words. It was clear Dirk wasn't interested in being a werecat. I didn't know my family had a part in shaping that opinion. Now that he said it, it made all too much sense.

"Yeah, if I had met the entire family before it happened, I wouldn't have been interested, either," I agreed.

"I mean...who wants to live like that? Alone." Dirk slowly shook his head, walking next to me as we kept on the trail. "No...I want to forge my own path, and I don't want to be alone like that. You're different. You haven't been ancient for long, but they all have issues with change. Funny, because they do it once a month, you know? And they're all alone and honestly *like* it."

"We have the entire family," I countered—a large family in werecat terms.

"Yeah?" Dirk laughed. "And the *one* member of the family who has a lover, a real mate? Hasan, the oldest of all of you, sees her maybe once a decade if that. Niko has seen her a handful of times his entire life, and he loves her like a mother. Can you honestly say that's a way to live? Can you imagine living like that with Heath? I know that's already a complicated situation, but go with the example, please."

"I...I can't," I agreed, relenting. "And I've never met her."

"Yeah. Until you showed back up in their lives a few years ago, they didn't talk nearly this often. You've breathed some life into them, but really, they all fuck off to their own corners of the world and do their own things. Look at Zuri. She's been gone for months, and there's no getting her back until she's ready. One day, I bet you'll have the same urge. You'll get up, decide to go for a run, and that urge won't stop. You'll come back in a few years, but by then, everything will be different.

That's distinctly a werecat thing. It's just so damn lonely to me."

"Did Niko ever do that to you?" I asked softly, looking up at him.

He was right. I had already done it, just differently. I had fallen prey to the need to be alone, disappearing from the lives of my family the best I could for over six years. It had felt right, and I had been mildly content with the loneliness. If it wasn't for Heath and his family crash landing into my life and my territory, I would have easily gone back to that life.

"No, which is why I think Niko is too much of a wolf. I..." Dirk stopped as if he realized he was about to say too much. "Let's get back to work."

"Okay," I said softly, letting him end the conversation. Dirk saw too much. I already knew that, but he was wise to be so prickly.

We found three more cameras and the large, live video feed to my house. All in all, there had been five little pieces of tech scattered in my woods. Every time we found another one, a sick feeling rolled through me, and I succeeded in crushing it. I had to fix this, and to fix it, I had to hold it together. I had to.

"Why am I worried there's more?" I asked softly, focusing on something other than that nasty feeling.

"There might be, but we're at the end. I can do another walkthrough, though. I caught two they didn't even need." Dirk seemed unconcerned. "I think I got them all, but we'll find out, won't we?"

"Don't say it like that. You'll have me too paranoid to go home."

"You want my recommendation?" He eyed me. "Get a driveway. Make some official paths and use those exclusively for a while. Really wear them in. Make this place more official and put a fence around some of it. Barbed wire is all you need. If you make it even remotely harder for them to sneak in, they'll be less likely to try."

"Does Niko use a fence?"

"Everyone uses a fence," he said, shaking his head at my reluctance. "I don't know how you've survived this long. I really don't."

"By not knowing anyone. I didn't even tell people I was Changed by Hasan for over a decade. He didn't introduce me to anyone outside the family those first few years, then I pretended as if I didn't know anything once I was out."

"You *don't* know anything," he said with a huff.

"And here I thought we were getting closer."

"Yeah, well, someone has to keep you on your toes," he said, finally smiling. "If I'm going to be your head of security, I have lots of experience living with Niko, and he taught me everything about staying safe in our world. You're all paranoid in your own ways. Look, those are just suggestions off the top of my head. I can reach out to Karl, Niko's current head of security. I grew up with him hovering when Niko wasn't around. He'll be able to give me more advice. I bet Heath and Landon have some things they could add, too. But...you don't do well with change. We all saw that play out when Kick Shot was being rebuilt. So..."

I closed my eyes. He was right. At the mention of Heath and Landon being involved in this, I realized I never texted Heath back, never said if I could make it to dinner, which I had completely forgotten about. I didn't even have my phone on me anymore. I left it in my office.

"What you're saying is I should take your advice and try to just deal with it because it's better for me in the end."

I normally hated having too much—too much security, too much change—but for a clear moment, one I didn't voice, I wanted them to put up fifty-foot walls around my house if they had to. Anything they needed to do, I would deal with.

"Yeah," he said softly. "I...get it. No one wants someone else running their life, but when lives are on the line, I get up, and I fucking do something about it."

"We're a sad pair," I said, chuckling. "Yeah. Yeah, whatever you come up with, I'll try. I can't keep getting caught off guard like this."

"I'll call Landon and—"

"I haven't told them yet," I said quickly. "Let me talk to Heath first. I'll drive over in a couple of hours, and you can tag along to talk about new security."

"I mean, the bar's security is great. Heath's company did a great job with that, and I know you have control of it. I've never been to your house..."

"Hasan recommended someone to do it," I explained. "Look, let's get inside and just chill out while I contact Heath."

He waved for me to lead the way. I chuckled. Sometimes, his behavior was so at odds. He was definitely rebelling against the life Niko had wanted for him, but oddly, he was very good at it.

*He wants to do it his way, and his opinions on werecats are...well-informed.*

He sat down on a stool behind the bar as I went to grab my phone. Heath hadn't reached out, and I wrote it off as him assuming I got busy. It happened, and he wasn't exactly a pushy or overbearing sort of man who needed to know every little thing all the time. It was one of the reasons I appreciated him so much. We lived our lives and found a way to do that together sometimes, but we didn't take each other's lives over, something my fiancé, Shane, and I had done. We had become each other's world to the point where nothing else and no one else mattered. It had been romantic but overwhelming to consider now that I wasn't a human, and my brain didn't work the same way. Heath just wanted a place in my life and wanted to give me a place in his.

When I got back downstairs, Dirk was sipping a drink.

"A bit early for that, maybe?" I said lightly as I sat across from him.

"We're dealing with a world-changing event, and now I have a job that fucking terrifies me, but no one else can do it, so I'm going to do a little breakfast drinking," he countered. "Just the one to take the edge off."

"You're a little young for that, aren't you?"

He gave me a flat stare. "You were getting married, then became a werecat at my age. One early morning drink on the first day of a new job I'm technically unqualified for, is not something you get to get on to me for."

"Touché," I said softly, looking at my phone. My hand

froze, and I looked back up at him. "You knew about Shane?"

"Who doesn't," he muttered before taking a long swallow of whatever he had made himself.

I shook my head, realizing my life was family gossip. How I didn't already know that was beyond me. I probably knew, but it never sank in. Dirk was having a strange effect on me, making things clearer for me than they had been my entire damn time as a werecat.

I hit call for Heath, knowing he was probably eating breakfast or getting out of the shower. It rang three times before he picked up.

"Jacky, good morning," he said in a voice I could only describe as confused and a little husky. The huskiness reminded me of evenings when I knew he was the happiest to see me.

"You're on speaker. Can you and Landon come over to Kick Shot, or we can head over to you? Dirk and I need to talk to you."

"Is this an emergency?" he asked, the huskiness gone.

"Yeah. It's why I didn't get back to you last night." I took a deep breath. "You'll be doing the werecats of the world a very big favor if you help me with this."

"I don't like the sound of that. Come over. You sound like you haven't slept. Maybe a change of pace, a new space, may help clear your head."

"Yeah...I've been at the bar all night," I said. "We'll be right over."

"Change your clothes," he ordered softly.

"How did you know?"

"I know you," he said simply. "Drive safe."

"Will do," I promised. I looked up at Dirk. "I'll go change."

"I'll be waiting. Want to take my truck? It's nice and new, not a disaster like your Nissan."

"Sure." This helpful Dirk was very strange.

*Maybe it's because I won't force him to go home...or he pities me. Also, how did he throw an insult into that offer?*

## CHAPTER ELEVEN

We were at Heath's home in less than thirty minutes. He met us at the front door, opening it before I could knock. He gestured for us to quickly come in. Landon was nearby, waiting at the bottom of the stairs. I ignored him and stared at Heath as the Alpha closed the door.

"What's going on?"

"The BSA visited me yesterday, and it had nothing to do with you and Carey. They've been watching me. They know I'm a supernatural."

It was Landon who started whistling, low and persistent, probably in shock. Heath growled in his direction, and I turned to see the younger werewolf lift his hands.

"Sorry. Just not what I was expecting to hear this morning. Why are you here?" His final question was for Dirk.

"I'm her new...head of security," Dirk answered,

clearly unsure of the terminology, or maybe because he was talking to Landon. Landon's eyes went wide.

"Do you have training in that?"

"He's the best I got," I said, cutting in as Heath reached out and grabbed one of my hands. "He was raised by my brother, so he knows a few things. He was able to get the fucking cameras out of my trees."

"Okay, let's go to my office. Now." Heath started walking, and when I didn't move, he nearly pulled me to take a step, which was unlike him. "All of us. Let's go. Jacky, you'll explain everything when we get in there."

Once we were all in his office, he closed the door and sat down, running a hand through his perfect hair, messing it up in a way I was all too familiar with.

"How?" he asked. "Are you okay? I wouldn't be."

"I'm fine. Let me explain..." I explained every aching detail and watched as Heath grew more and more guilty. He slumped back in his chair when I got to the end.

"It was us," he said plainly.

"It was us," I agreed. "I...overstepped the bounds, doing what I have been, and now I'm paying for it." I pulled out my phone and flipped it around in my hand. "I wouldn't change it, any of it, I just wish it didn't play out like this. Heath, Hasan threatened to take me home if I screwed this up anymore, and...these photos are from the last full moon." I held out my phone. I had put the pictures and video on it for future reference the night before. "Which means they probably caught you coming and going, too."

"Oh no," he whispered, taking my phone. I watched

him scroll, and when he stopped scrolling, I knew he was on the video. "So, you talked to your family already? You made a game plan with them? Because I can't...guide you through this. I'm a werewolf, and sticking my nose about you going public or working with the US government is... way out of line. There's no way either of us could justify it. I helped the werewolves go public, and I could maybe tell you about those meetings, but beyond that..." He seemed a little lost. I knew Heath Everson liked having a plan. Plans were good. He could control plans, but this time, he had to be on the sidelines. For both our sakes, he had to stay out of this one.

"Yeah, we've already talked, and it went as well as you can expect, but I need something from you," I said softly, sitting down across from him. "Dirk and I need to shore up my security problems. I was hoping you and Landon could help him with that."

"Good work on getting the cameras," Heath said, looking over me. "I can help contain your property, fencing, and maybe a few of your own cameras hooked up to your office at the bar or in your home. Jacky...I could turn your house into a fortress in under a month if that's what you need."

"I'll pay you," I said quickly, swallowing. "Or you can just give Dirk some names and—"

"Are you sure you want that?" Heath shook his head. "Jacky, you love living in nature and seeing your trees. I'm talking about putting up a wall and a gate."

"Whatever you have to do," I said, suddenly frantic when he put my phone down on the desk between us. I looked down to see it paused on a scene from my house and remembered that sick feeling again, making my stomach twist. "Whatever I have to do. I'm about to be the United States and werecat liaison or something. Heath, this is big now. This isn't me going off and getting into a fight. They're coming to me. They know my name! They put up cameras pointed at my house! They have *video of me*!" I began to shake as tears filled my eyes. "PUT UP FUCKING WALLS!"

For the first time since I saw the video, the sense of being violated hit me fully, like a battering ram on my emotions and my self-control. I had been holding on, trying to address the problem, making my emotions wait, but nothing could burn out the feeling I had the moment I saw myself on camera. I remembered how they blurred my body, but they had seen *me*. I was accustomed to nudity in front of the people I *chose* to be nude around and for practicality among werecats. That was something I accepted.

These were strangers who recorded me, saved it, watched it, and learned my darkest secret, then had the audacity to think blurring my tits meant anything. Somewhere out there, someone was probably still replaying the unaltered version, not seeing a damn thing wrong with it. Someone who didn't know how much they had fucking hurt me—or maybe they did and just didn't care. They saw my scars and the sick way my bones shifted under my skin.

They saw my truth, and they were going to have it forever. My privacy had been ripped away from me, and there was nothing that could get it back.

I crumpled and sobbed, my shoulders shaking as it washed over me, and I felt the need to throw up.

Two strong arms wrapped around me and pulled me off the chair into a lap. Curled on the floor, I sobbed into Heath's shirt until it felt as though there was nothing left.

"I've got you," he whispered into my hair. "I'm here."

"She...she seemed fine..." Dirk was trying to say.

"Let's give them a minute," Landon said gently. I heard the door open, boots leave, then the door close once again.

"Let it out," Heath said, ignoring the conversation.

I took a ragged breath. "I...I need to get to work. I need—"

"You need to come to terms with what's happened," he said strongly, holding me in place.

I pushed away from him and off his lap, reminding both of us who was the stronger species. I fell back on my ass, hitting my tailbone on his hardwood floor when I couldn't find my feet.

"Come to terms with this?" I clutched the front of my shirt, hissing the words. "How can I ever come to terms with the fact I was filmed naked on my own porch? On my private property? And I exposed my entire fucking species!"

"I don't know," he said gently. "I don't know how, but you need to feel what you're feeling, Jacky. I'm sorry, but you need to work through it. If you keep burying it, you're only going to hurt yourself or someone else."

"I want to hurt them!" I roared, going feral as the human words turned into an animalistic sound. My body was triggering the Change. My jaw cracked and shifted as I tried to close it.

"If you don't calm down, there's a chance you'll do something you can't come back from," he said quickly. "Jacky, listen to me. When moon cursed lose control like you are right now, they don't always come back from that Change. *Please.*"

I saw the tears in his eyes, the horror and desperation on his face as I snarled in his direction and finally heard what he was saying.

"Think of Carey," he pleaded. "Please don't lose it now."

I took a deep breath and held on. The rage and violated feeling inside of me was upsetting that primal part of me, that instinctual beast that was a corner of my brain.

He was right. If I let the Change take me right now, it could very well be my last.

Inhaling deeply again as my body shook violently, I fell forward and cried out, but I kept my human shape. He touched me gently and slowly hauled me back onto his lap.

"Please don't scare me like that again," he murmured, holding onto me. "I know what they did to you. I saw it. It's wrong, and they didn't just violate you. They violated your entire species. They violated everything you try to protect. They don't understand. They'll never understand."

I slowly stopped shaking.

"They've done it to werewolves," he continued,

rubbing my back. "As much as I want them to stop, I can't make them. They try to see us as citizens, but they barely see us as humans. They don't care that you were raised like any of their daughters were, and I'm sorry they don't care. I'm so sorry."

"I'll make them understand," I said hoarsely. "Watch me."

He didn't say anything in return. When I moved to get up this time, I was steadier. He got to his feet only seconds later.

"If you make this a fight with them, it could jeopardize other werecats," he said softly, a warning coming from his good nature of wanting to see everything turn out okay.

"I won't make it about the werecats," I said softly. "I'll bring it up after everything else is figured out. They can't...they can't do that to people." I pointed at my phone. "They...they have copies somewhere, Heath. Someone is probably showing someone else right now, talking about this new freak they found."

He hugged me again and rocked gently. This was what I had wanted after my family yelled at me and each other. This was what I wanted from them, just for a moment. I was sure they didn't mean to hurt me. They were in panic mode, too, trying to figure out what to do with this new revelation.

I didn't need to ask Heath.

Heath offered it without words.

I clung to him, knowing how I fell for him, why he was such a vital piece of my life, that I was willing to risk everything to be with him. He didn't need me to ask. He only needed to be in the same space as me.

"How are you so good at this?" I asked, leaning into his chest farther, putting my weight into it, practically letting him hold me up.

"The truth or the poetry?"

"Both?" I frowned into his shirt, wondering what he meant.

"The poetry is, I love you, and my favorite place to be is with you. I'll give you anything you need, whenever you need it. The truth is, I'm an Alpha werewolf, and this is my job, to know the needs of the people who are in my life and make sure they're taken care of. Giving that to you, even though you're my lover and not my pack, is something that comes as naturally to me as breathing."

"There are bad Alphas," I reminded him, pulling back.

"There are," he agreed. "They do the same thing, though. They just do it in their own awful ways."

"Ah."

The off-topic conversation took my mind off the video, off the photos, off the problem, but I knew I'd have to get back to all of those things soon.

"I see them again tomorrow," I whispered, going back to the conversation. "They gave me forty-eight hours to figure out what to say to them after I decided to throw them out."

"Better you throw them out the first meeting than attack them," he said, nodding. I felt his cheek rubbing my hair.

"I didn't want to attack them at that moment. I don't

know what I wanted. To turn back time?" The hug ended naturally this time. Heath took a step back, putting his hands in his pockets as he stared at me with those stormy grey-blue eyes. "Do you really think I was about to..."

"I've seen enough werewolves do it, I know the signs, but...I know werecats do it much less frequently than we do. I don't really know, but it was too close to something I had seen before," he said as if he was admitting something painful.

"What would you have done?"

"Put a silver bullet between your eyes," he whispered, reaching out to push my hair out of my face. He meant every word, and there was no guilt. He wasn't blocking his scent from me to make it even clearer. He would do it. There wasn't another option. I'd be a danger not just to him but to Landon, Dirk, and Carey as well.

"Good." That was the correct decision. It might have seemed harsh to anyone else, but the Last Change meant becoming a monster. It was the reason movie werewolves existed and why so many people truly feared them. All rationale was gone. The ability and need to kill anything and anyone that might threaten the moon cursed was all that was left. When a moon cursed was pushed to that point, everything was a threat.

He dropped his hand and sighed. "Tomorrow—"

"Landon! I'm ready to go! Isn't Dad taking me to school today? He promised he would."

That voice was like an electric shock on my system. I wiped my eyes, wanting to see her, but I wasn't sure how I looked. I had just had a breakdown.

"She can't see me like this, can she?" I asked, looking at the door.

"You look like you're tired," he said diplomatically. "You can always see her, but she'll know you've been crying." In the background, Landon was consoling his sister about their dad not being available.

"Okay..." I took a deep breath. "I'm going to go see her, then we'll talk more."

He followed, silent, patient, and always at my back. She was standing at the end of the hall near the front door as Landon pulled on some shoes.

"Dirk, why are you here?" Carey asked innocently.

"Ah, uh..." He looked around and caught sight of me before anyone else. "Jacky and I had to stop by for something important. There she is." He pointed at me.

"Hey, Carey," I greeted with a smile, even though it felt shaky and weak at best. "Heading back to school, huh?"

"I went yesterday, too," she said, coming up to me for a one-armed hug. When she stepped back, her calculating mind worked on what was going on as she looked me over. "Why did you need Dad?"

"Werecat things," I said, shrugging. "Sorry, but it's above your pay grade."

"Oh. Well...since we didn't hang out on Monday, do you want to do something today? Or tomorrow?"

"I might need to hold on for a week. This is big, but you'll be the first to know when I have time," I promised.

*Will I still be allowed, or will the BSA think I'm too supernatural for her?*

Another thing I would have to clarify at the second meeting.

*I wish those guys hadn't been so vague.*

"Okay, cool. I got to head to school. Feel better, okay?"

"I will," I answered, giving her a thumbs up.

She didn't move, her grey-blue eyes, exact matches to her father's, studying me.

"Have a good day." She still didn't move as if she was daring me to say I would have any other kind of day.

"You, too." I didn't think Carey had ever seen me like this. I didn't normally present myself to the public, then break down into tears.

"Carey, come on. I don't want you to be late for school," Landon said. "Let's get out of their way."

"Where's my hug?" Heath demanded, finally stepping around me. Carey stuck her tongue out at him and walked out the front door, making me laugh.

"No love from that child," Heath muttered. Landon shrugged, and Heath glared at him next. "No love from any of you."

Landon walked out, giving everyone a silent wave. Dirk was the last of the "kids" in the house, awkwardly standing in the entryway near the living room.

"She just walked downstairs, ate a pop tart, and acted like everything was totally normal," he said, looking at me and Heath as though he didn't honestly know what to do.

"I've finally discovered a Dirk weakness," I declared. "Children!"

"Not funny," he grumbled. "Not many of them in our family."

"There really isn't," I agreed. Then I sobered. "Sorry about..." I pointed aimlessly over my shoulder.

"You don't need to apologize," he mumbled. "Are...are you feeling better?"

"Yeah. Yeah, I am. Let's get to work. I don't need walls, but..."

"We can do something that matches the area," Heath said patiently. "Let's talk. Let's try to fix this."

## 12

# CHAPTER TWELVE

I stood in my office, watching out the window as Heath, Dirk, and several men I didn't know, talked about the little trail that went to my house. Heath was moving a pointed finger along the edge of the parking lot, right at the tree line, saying something.

"We can...along here...barbed wire. Country...gate..."

I could only really hear bits and pieces when his voice went a little louder, and the wind outside died down. It wasn't a blustery day, but there was just enough to mess with my acute sense of hearing. I knew what he was telling them, though. They were the fastest plans we had ever thrown together since we met. Kick Shot had been a slower rebuild, getting the details perfect because it was a place of business.

This was a needed security blanket, so I could feel safe in my own house. The physical look of the design didn't matter, only the practicality.

There would be a new barbed wire fence woven through my trees as a clear line people couldn't cross.

Cameras and microphones would be tucked around the woods, carefully wired to a power source in my house. I would lose the trail and get a real driveway, with a country-style gate, something you would see on a farm. It suited the area more than a high-level mansion gate, and I didn't want to stand out too much. I would park my car at home for its security, so I could see it. Motion detectors would tell me when someone was walking or driving down the driveway toward me. The gate would open automatically for people with a certain type of receiver. It was all very fancy, high-tech stuff. Heath had said it was this or magic, and since I was a werecat and so sensitive to magic in my territory, he figured I would like tech better.

He wasn't completely wrong. I would have preferred never having either.

*We don't always get what we want, and I have to address what I need.*

I was losing a lot of what I loved about my little corner of the world, but I was a werecat. I could adapt to physical changes in my world.

What I couldn't deal with was the violation of my territory and feeling unsafe in it. It wasn't just that I was a woman recorded on tape. This had tapped into something primal, a fear of any of my species. The territory we claimed was our kingdom, the place where we were the dominant power. When someone drew close to the center, our home, the place we laid our solitary heads, the more likely we were to kill those people.

I had fought that instinct, playing safe when I knew people were walking around my woods. I was paying for it now, with the ever-present sick feeling I couldn't go home because it wasn't safe and the idea I would never feel so comfortable again. I knew I had done it to myself.

That was why I let those men change something so vital to me.

I could tolerate the driveway, the barbed wire fencing, and the technology that ruined my pristine forest, but I couldn't tolerate the feeling that felt like a slow rot.

I couldn't watch anymore, turning to check the time on my monitor, its blue glow cold comfort. At least my computer was clean. They weren't going to get me through it.

"One hour," I whispered. "I have one hour." With a shaky inhale, I knew the second meeting was going to be just as hard as the first. Looking down at myself, I was proud for just a moment. I had made it home for a simple shower, with Heath, Landon, and Dirk all hovering in my house—a silent guard. They weren't just there to protect my privacy, but to make sure I didn't lose control like I did in Heath's house.

Once the shower was over, I put on a crisp suit and hunkered down in my office. Landon went to be with Carey while Heath and Dirk worked with the guys Heath had called the day before, once we were settled on what I wanted for security.

I sat down and sighed, but even as I tried to relax, I was ever vigilant. I could hear them still talking, then trucks revved, and some drove away. The back door opened and closed, then footsteps on the back staircase. I could hear their conversation as they headed to my office.

"Do you know what my kind calls your...dad?" Heath asked, unsure about Niko's title for Dirk.

"The Traitor, right? I had heard some use it against him." Dirk shrugged.

"Yeah. He's interesting, though. One of my favorites from Jacky's family."

"He's not bad." Dirk was about as evasive as he always was when Niko was brought up.

I let my mind trail off, considering Niko for a moment. The Traitor was Niko's unofficial title in the same way people called Zuri the Politician and Hisao the Assassin. He was the Traitor, not because he betrayed his werecat family, though. He'd been born to werewolves, and his family didn't want to get involved in the War raging at the time. They had been slaughtered. Hasan rescued Niko, finished raising him, and Niko decided to join the werecats instead. He'd "betrayed" the species he had been born to. He was a traitor to many werewolves old enough to remember, and others used the name just because they had heard it before.

It was an interesting story, but I knew the quiet man who had lived through it. Dirk said it right—Niko was pretty much always an outsider. I had a rocky start coming into the family, but from everything I knew, Niko's was worse, thanks to the circumstances of the time.

As they walked into my office, I looked up and smiled at the two men.

*At least I have the support here. My family will catch up. They always do.*

"They'll begin work tomorrow," Heath declared. "I was up all night, drawing out the designs, and they got the final measurements needed through today. The driveway and gate will come first. The barbed wire fence will have to be done without a design plan because we don't want to cut down any trees. They'll have to go in and see what they can do. I'm calling the techs from my company tomorrow to talk about how we're going to wire in cameras and mics. It's do-able, but it'll be hard."

"How much is this going to cost me?" I asked, leaning onto my desk.

"I think you might want to ask Hasan to cover it," Heath said carefully. "At least the technical portion. The driveway and fencing are pretty cheap, all things considered."

"Seriously, Heath. How much?" I asked again. I couldn't ask Hasan for help right now. Well, I could, but I didn't want to. I brought this on my family, and I would eat the costs. I would do everything I could to keep them from getting more involved than they already were.

"The driveway and fence will be close to $50,000. The technical side will probably run close to a million out of pocket. They're going to be breaking out some high-end, possibly prototype stuff for you, especially when you tell them what was used to watch you."

"Those are already in the mail to my brother, so I hope you aren't thinking about giving them what the BSA developed," I said, sighing.

"No, no. And those weren't developed by the BSA. They were developed by the CIA. Werewolves, however, already told both organizations if we get our hands on it, it's ours. They should be careful with their equipment. Finders keepers." He gave me a wolfy smile, all teeth and definitely not nice. "I've broken down a number of their pieces with my own hands after finding them in my offices and in my backyards when I was an Alpha. They know better."

"Didn't it bother you to be spied on?" Dirk was hovering by the door, so I pointed at a chair. "Sit down. You probably need to hear all of this."

He fell into a chair as Heath casually strolled around the desk and leaned over me.

"It bothered me," he confirmed, kissing my cheek. "But I was already outed. I was more upset when Carey was young. I threatened the agents I knew in Dallas that if I found another camera in my backyard where she played, I would break their legs, so they couldn't run on the next full moon. I would let my pack show them werewolves could, in fact, eat people, and some of them learned to enjoy the act. My daughter was off-limits to the spying. All the children were, no matter the species. If they wanted to see any of them, they had channels to do that. I would have killed them if there was video similar to yours for *any* young werewolf."

"Would you have really eaten them?" I asked softly, looking up slowly. Heath never, even at his most fearsome, struck me as a man-eating type.

"I do what I have to," he answered enigmatically, pulling away. He fixed his button-down, making sure it was properly tucked in. Gone were the casual jeans and tight-fitting shirts. Today, he was in the business slacks that reminded me of the day I met him. This was business Heath or more aptly, Alpha Heath. He'd dropped this image over the two-plus years he'd been in my territory, but today it was back.

"I should go before they get here," he declared. "They'll be early to throw you off your game. They're going to come in hard and fast with demands and questions, trying to put you off-balance. Hold your ground and make your needs and demands clear. If you press your side, they'll be forced to listen. They'll railroad you into a bad deal if they can. The BSA isn't out to hurt supernaturals, but to better understand us and how we can be useful to the United States. They want to know how we can be used and controlled. Don't give them an inch. Their goals are important enough, they'll listen once they realize you're not going to back down."

"Thank you," I whispered. "Dirk, go with him. Heath, can you keep..." I waved a hand at Dirk. I was already a bit frazzled by my upcoming meeting. Heath's purposefully focused advice only made me more worried. We had already talked about how he couldn't, under any circumstances, get involved.

"By the time everything is done, he'll be ready to manage it. Promise." Heath smiled and thumped Dirk's shoulder. "Let's go and give her some time to breathe before this happens."

"Boss?" Dirk watched me. "Do you want me to go? I can stay and get whatever you need during the meeting. It'll be fine."

"Kick Shot is closed for the night. I have a plan, one I can do on my own. Go with Heath. I'll text or call to check in once it's done."

"You might need back up," he retorted.

"You seem awfully helpful for a nephew who doesn't want to be too involved in the family," I said with a smile. "Go be helpful by learning more from Heath."

He looked between me and Heath, then got up. They both waved before Heath closed me back in my office. I sat in the quiet and listened as their trucks pulled away, tracking Heath as he drove toward his home. After a moment, I stood up.

I had a plan, and I needed to be in the right position for it.

I went down to the main floor, going behind the bar without pausing. There were a couple of cars in the driveway, but I had the Closed sign lit up, and there was a small sign posted out front saying I needed the space for a private event on short notice. There would be a sale on Friday for those that were unhappy about it. That had been Oliver's idea when I told him I wanted to keep Kick Shot closed for the night.

I rearranged bottles, placing everything I used the most where it had once been. I wanted to be comfortable but hadn't wanted Dirk to see me doing this to his precious set up.

*Not that he's ever going to get back to it.*

Once I was done, I turned and grabbed a glass, making myself a drink to calm my nerves and give me something to sip on, but not the type of drink I was worried about losing my wits. I fully intended on loosening up the agents, though, and having a drink myself could make them more comfortable to indulge.

*They wanted to come for me, a bartender. I'll show them what a bartender can do.*

## CHAPTER THIRTEEN

I watched as they drove up and parked near the door. Special Agent Miller was more confused and curious about the Closed sign than Special Agent Collins.

They didn't come up to the door immediately. While they parked close, it was still ten feet from the front door. They hovered at the back of their SUV, looking at the bar. Collins went to investigate my little sign while Miller stood with a deep frown.

"Why did she close? In training, they say supernaturals try to keep the appearance of normal as much as possible. Closing a bar mid-week without warning doesn't seem normal."

"She knew we were coming this time and probably wanted to have a more private meeting," Collins replied. "That's what the sign says. She needed the bar for a private event."

"Why do they all own bars and restaurants? Have you noticed that? A bunch of werewolves invested in this kind of stuff. A couple of the fae we've found have as well, and the witches have their own types of...places of business."

"I think it's a community thing. A restaurant is part of the fabric of a town and lets them feel included when they aren't." Collins shrugged. "It's also a forever growing and changing industry. People like to eat out, and people like to drink. Money."

"Didn't you work with Heath Everson, the werewolf who lives nearby? He had a couple of restaurants in Dallas, didn't he?"

"In Dallas, yeah. That's why we were picked for this. I wish you could have met him. Maybe we can do a drive-by of his place and see if he wants to talk."

I raised an eyebrow. Maybe I could get more information from Heath. If Special Agent Collins was from the BSA offices in Dallas, Heath would probably know more than he realized. Collins might even be one of the people who tried to spy on Carey and knew how wrong a bad decision could go when playing with supernaturals.

"He knows about her, right? If we took him in, maybe he could break and give us everything we want to know,"

"He definitely knows. They've been hanging out for a couple of years and are both supernaturals, but I wouldn't count on Heath breaking. He's an Alpha, one of the biggest in the United States, and after the Russian incident last year, rumors say he's probably one of the top ten or fifteen Alphas in the world. He'll die before he breaks...or he'll kill us," Collins said with a huff. "Besides, we *don't* do things like that. I know you come from the

CIA, and it's different over there, but we don't interrogate like that in the BSA."

I watched out the window, glad they were dark enough to hide me from their sight. I didn't have any lights on because *I* didn't need them, especially not when I was on edge. My eyes were probably bright gold and full feline. The humans would, though, and even better, they didn't know how good my hearing was when the world was otherwise silent. To me, they sounded like they were whispering, but it was easy to listen in on them when there was no music playing, and the wind had slowed down at the perfect moment. Collins lit a cigarette as he checked his watch.

"Still got fifteen minutes. We'll see if she comes out to us or if we need to knock."

"Do you think she'll still be hostile?"

"I don't think she was hostile when we saw her on Tuesday. I think we scared her. When it comes to supernaturals, you'll know when they're hostile. They'll make it painfully clear."

*Do we? Maybe you have a sense of self-confidence you don't deserve.*

It was easier to focus, knowing they were out there, enjoying a cigarette before they had to come in for a meeting. It was easier to ignore the sick feeling in the pit of my stomach, knowing I had to be ready for anything. They had scared me, he was right about that. At the time I threw them out of my office, I hadn't been thinking about killing them. I had just been sick and wanted it to end. I had wanted to hide and needed to call for help.

*Today will be different. It has to be.*

Collins dropped the cigarette and stomped on it, leaving the butt in my parking lot. That pissed me off. I had ashtrays and smoker's poles to hide those dirty little things. They came to the door, and Miller knocked while Collins looked over his shoulder as if he was checking their six to make sure no one else was there.

I went to the door at a slow pace, not rushing. When I opened it, I nailed Collins with my gold stare.

"Go get your cigarette butt and put it in a smoker's pole," I ordered, knowing I shouldn't have let it piss me off, but this place was *mine*, and he was going to respect it. He seemed confused when he turned back to me. Miller's eyebrows went up as I pointed between them. "You dropped it on the ground and left it there. Go pick it up." I didn't budge.

Collins looked back again at the spot he dropped his cigarette, then back at me. He must have realized I was serious and I'd been watching them. He walked back toward their SUV, picked it up, and shoved it into the top of a smoker's pole close to the front door.

"Sorry, it's habit. I'll be more careful in the future," he said, entering that polite front I had experienced from him two nights ago. This time, there was a strain to his words.

He didn't like that I had been watching them.

"Come inside." I opened the door more, stepping out of the way for them to enter.

They came in slowly, looking around the dark bar, I knew they could barely see. I walked to my place behind the bar and flipped on the display lights, giving the room a nice warm glow that didn't reach into the dark corners. It was low light, but it was enough.

"We're going to stay down here tonight," I said simply, sipping my drink as they looked at each other. "Want anything to drink? I used to be the only bartender here, so I know my way around the alcohol, and our liquor license is perfectly legit."

"We don't drink on duty," Collins said, sitting down first. "But thank you for the offer." Miller followed his lead and noticeably left an empty seat between them.

"Just want everyone to be comfortable."

"Jacky, maybe we should—"

"Jacqueline," I snapped softly, cutting off whatever platitude or comment Miller was going to say. "You can call me Jacqueline or Miss Leon, but Jacky is not a name that'll leave your mouth tonight," I said, a low growl in my words at the end. "You two blindsided me the last time you were here. I bet that makes you feel powerful, having all the cards and all the power. When I have to sit and talk to people I don't like, they do me the respect of calling me Jacqueline or Miss Leon. I don't like either of you. Those are your options."

*I'm Jacqueline, daughter of Hasan, motherfuckers, and you're going to learn I play hardball when I have to.*

I had them terribly off-balance. Miller cast a glance at Collins, who watched me with narrowed eyes. There was no feigned politeness in his expression now.

"Miss Leon," Collins decided, nodding. "We won't try to be too familiar. Have you thought about what we talked to you about on Tuesday?"

"Yeah, I've thought about it. If you want me to tell you

anything about my species, you're going to make me some promises. They'll be in writing, signed, and sent to whoever can make these things official, and I'll follow up to make sure the BSA doesn't try to screw me before the end of this."

"There is no *end* of this." Collins leaned forward. "Hopefully, this is the beginning of a new alliance between your species or those who live here in the United States, and the BSA, representing the United States. An alliance that will bring your kind out of the dark to become average citizens of our country and will help us further understand the underground world of the supernaturals who live beside us."

"And if my kind doesn't want to be citizens of the United States?"

"We're not talking about anything different than the werewolves, Miss Leon. No draft sign-ups, no militarization of your kind. Only that you go public and abide by the laws."

"We have different needs than the werewolves, Special Agent Collins. First, you'll never know who the others are of my kind unless it's needed. You got lucky, or maybe very unlucky, you found me and not any of the others."

"What can we call your kind?" he asked carefully.

"Werecats, one of two moon cursed species. Werewolves are like...our cousins, but don't let that lull you into a false sense of security. We're very different."

"Werecats...That's why you shifted on a full moon like werewolves. It's the same type of curse, meaning it presents the same dangers. You won't give us names or identities for other werecats? That won't work for us, knowing you're the cousins to werewolves, who can accidentally turn someone with a single bite, and that bite could just as easily kill someone," he said, watching me as I sipped on my drink. "We need to be able to track these sorts of issues."

"It's called *Changing* someone," I pointed out. "Which I'm sure you already knew, even if you don't understand the importance."

*And they never will unless the vampires decide to come out and tell them that Turning is something they do. We Change humans into a new type of beast, vampires Turn them evil. Or so the saying goes.*

"The reasons you're worried are something we can talk about after you promise to give something to me."

"What else do you want?" Miller asked, more frustrated with me than Collins.

"We don't want to be public. We want to remain a private species. We don't want the world knowing the word werecat, much less seeing pictures of us. Let us hide behind the werewolves, blend in with them." I wish I'd heard back from Hasan before this meeting. He said he would talk to Corissa and Callahan. I hadn't. I sent him more than one message throughout the day, but he never got back to me.

Miller chuckled. "You're ballsy, but why are you the one doing the bargaining? Isn't there someone in charge we can talk to?"

"When it comes to werecats in the United States, I *am* the one in charge," I answered honestly, staring him down. "Like I said, you were both lucky and unlucky to find me first. You found someone who can bargain with you, the only person in the country allowed to, but it also means you'll only ever know my face. I'm not giving you any of my kind."

"Really?" Miller leaned forward. "*You?* You're thirty-eight, which is young compared to the leaders of the werewolves. Heath Everson is over two hundred and seventy years old, and you expect us to believe you lead the werecats in the United States?"

I shrugged. "Believe it or not, I'm all you have and all you'll get," I promised.

"We need something to take back to our superiors that will show you're serious," Collins said, sighing. "What else do you want?"

"Like werewolves, we're exempt from your military drafts if they ever come back, and protected from forced research. You'll respect our internal laws, and we'll respect yours. The general things. I still don't really understand what you want from me."

"It's what I've been saying," Collins said, his jaw tensing. "We're just trying to open dialogue between our species and integrate you into the United States as citizens, just like we did with the werewolves. You pose more of a threat when you're allowed to remain secret."

"Would you like to know the difference between werewolves and werecats?" I said, leaning in. "They wanted to be part of your world. Werecats don't. You'll need to do better, because if you can't convince me what you want is worth my time, I'll disappear, and you'll never find another one of our kind." I smiled. "Guess who holds all the cards now?"

Oh, that last comment was completely unnecessary, and everyone at the bar knew it. Special Agent Collins stood up and fixed his blazer.

"Please don't disappear before I can get back to you," he said. "I'll take what you've said to my superiors. If you don't mind, we'd also like to verify your position among your kind through the werewolves we know."

"Do that," I purred.

Collins tapped Miller on the shoulder, and he got up and followed his older partner out of the bar.

I took a deep breath and sagged once their SUV left my parking lot. I couldn't take a long break. I pulled my phone from my pocket and called Heath.

"Jacky?" he asked quickly. "Is something wrong? Is it already over?"

"They just left. I need you to tell every werewolf you know that the BSA only knows about me. They don't know who Hasan is or anyone else, just me. They're going to verify my position as the werecat in charge of the United States. They don't know that extends to Canada or South America. They can let my region slip, but if they mention Hasan's name, they're outing him."

"Okay, I'll spread the word," Heath promised. "This is going to cause a stir."

"I know," I whispered. "Thanks for watching out for me. Will this get you in trouble?"

"No. This is a higher priority than the push-back-and-forth bullshit between our kinds. This is secrecy, which is respected by all. That's the official stance of the North American Werewolf Council and the Tribunal. You don't need to worry about me getting in trouble for this." He paused. "Are you going to call your family? I just want to make sure I don't interrupt anything if...I wanted to come over later and check on you."

"Yeah, I need to call them next," I confirmed. "I'll let you know when it's safe to come over. You can send Dirk my way if he's still with you."

"I'll trust you to do that. He's right next to me. I'll send him back."

We mumbled goodbyes and hung up, practically at the same time. After that, I texted Oliver to come to Kick Shot as I locked the front door and headed up the backstairs. I was going to need more help than just my newly picked head of security.

*I wonder if Oliver is going to be okay with a pay raise and a new position.*

## 14

# CHAPTER FOURTEEN

I was in my office when Oliver and Dirk walked in together.

"I picked him up on the way over," Dirk said, pointing at the young man. "I'll sweep downstairs for anything the good agents left behind once you're done with me."

*Good. He's on top of everything. On to the important question.*

"Oliver, will you be my personal assistant?" I asked without any sort of preamble. I watched him stumble and reach for the back of a chair.

"What?"

"My personal assistant. I need someone who knows contracts, can take notes, and is able to manage my schedule. This is going to get crazier, I can already feel it. I need someone, and I trust you. Do you have training in it?"

"Um...yeah?" Oliver sat down slowly. "Is there no one else you can call?"

"You'll still be doing everything with Kick Shot, for

the most part, but when I'm needed as...whatever I am now, I need someone who can help...track everything." I clicked through to my calendar on my computer, which showed up empty. "Look. There's nothing there."

"Ha ha..." Oliver whined.

"There's no one else I can call unless I want to ask a sibling to send me someone else, but I think I got lucky with the two of you. If I told them I was in the market for a personal assistant, they would suddenly have a great person to spy on my every movement. This person would learn about Heath, for example." I clasped my hands together. "I told the BSA I'm in charge of all the werecats in their country, so..."

"Oh, fuck," Dirk said, sitting down now beside Oliver. "Did you have to?"

"They wanted to write me off, thinking I wasn't in charge, probably hoping I would give up someone like Hasan or Zuri for them to talk to. They were fishing. They didn't realize I wasn't the bait. I'm the fish. They left in a hurry when they realized I wasn't going to give them any information until I had some simple assurances from them. Oliver—"

"I'll do it," he said quickly. "It's...it's just a lot really fast. Um...I'm going to need to use the business credit card to set some things up and get everything I need. I played as my parents' personal assistant while learning the restaurant business. It's a common thing to do in the family, to be an assistant for someone you want to be. I don't want to be a werecat, but if you need me to juggle things, I can do that."

"Feel free to hire another manager for Kick Shot you

can delegate to. Dirk is learning on his toes how to be a head of security." With that settled, I started asking the family to join me for another call to update them on tonight's meeting with the BSA.

"Yeah...should I get to work?"

"Yeah," I said, staring at my monitor. Before Oliver made it out of my office, I turned to him. "Hey." He looked over his shoulder. "Thanks. We're all in a bit of a trial-by-fire moment. Thanks for agreeing to step up and help me out. I really appreciate it."

He nodded, a blush taking over his pale, freckled face before he thought to duck and get out of my office before I asked for something else from him.

"You really know how to blindside the people in your life," Dirk pointed out.

"Says the guy who knows how to sweep for surveillance and never mentioned it," I retorted. "Look, I'm trying to..." I ran a hand over my hair as the call from Jabari began. I clicked answer before finishing what I was saying to Dirk, ignoring my eldest brother's annoyed and stern face. "I'm trying to manage this, not just to protect myself but everyone here and in the family. That means if you're here, work with me, and you know about werecats, it's all fucking hands on deck." I looked back at the monitor, not smiling as Jabari sat there alone. None of my other siblings bothered to join the call yet.

"Hello, Jabari."

"How did it go?" he asked sternly, keeping it professional, waiting for a report from a good little soldier of the family.

"I railroaded them into leaving without anything but

our name and our desire for privacy," I answered. "Well... there's a little more than that. They know we're werecats. They know we're cousins of a sense to werewolves and about the full moon problems that entails. They had that from the video. Two plus two equals four, right? I just gave them something to call me, really. They know what I want—protections for our kind, privacy for most of our population, me being the exception. They know I am in charge of werecats in the United States. They didn't believe that last part."

"They need to," he said stiffly. "Do you have a plan for that?"

"Yeah. I sent them to the werewolves. They were already planning to talk to them. They know I've had a lot of interaction with the werewolves. I sent Heath a message, passing along what needs to be the public story. Hopefully, everyone listens and gets the message in time that the BSA only knows about me. Not you, Hasan, Zuri...or anyone else."

"Good, that works. Father spoke to Callahan and Corissa. You impressed Corissa last year, and she heard his plea. It's going to cost him some political power, but they're willing to let us hide under the guise of being werewolves in a sense to the public. It's tricky, but since you're the only public werecat, I'm certain you can pull it off. You have Heath to help." That last sentence felt like a condemnation.

*After working so fucking hard to be a part of this family, I'm back in the fucking doghouse.*

"Is anyone going to join the call?" I asked softly.

"Father might," he answered. He seemed uncomfortable with something.

I waited a moment for more. It probably took me a whole two minutes to realize Jabari wasn't going to continue.

*Father might?*

I took a deep breath and nodded. "Okay. Is there anything else you want to talk about with me?"

He leaned forward and lowered his chin onto his hands, propped up on his elbows, studying me as though I was something he needed to fix.

"When is this going to stop?" he asked softly.

"Dirk, can you step out?" I asked softly, turning away from Jabari's intense stare. Dirk was gone without needing any sort of push, casting me a sympathetic glance, a look that told me he would be right outside the door. Once he disappeared from view, I heard no footsteps. He was really going to stick right there in case I needed him.

*Niko, you raised a damn good young man.*

I looked back at my monitor and sighed.

"I tried," I whispered. "I tried, Jabari. I'm doing my best right now and don't need to be treated like a criminal. I haven't disagreed with a single thing you or anyone else has said since this started, so please don't ask me when this is going to stop. I *tried*. I kept my head down for months. I got my business running again and focused on that. I'll remind you that my business was burned down because your old enemies thought I would be the easy target, the example they could make. And what was it I did that started all this? I protected a little girl. Then I helped *you* in Washington. Russia is the only time I ever did anything that truly went against what this family was about. The only time!" I snapped. "So, don't you fucking ask me when this is going to end. Don't you dare play this up like I'm the fucking problem child when all I'm trying to do is make everyone proud of me! To keep them safe!" I was out of my chair.

"All I've ever tried to do is what I had to, so I could fucking sleep at night! And yeah, it started because I broke the Law and did everything in my power to save a *child*." I shook my head and exhaled. "I can't believe this." I started to laugh as someone else joined the call. I didn't look up to see who it was, sinking back into my chair and laughing until I cried. Then another person joined the call...and another.

"Are you okay?" Mischa asked softly, visibly upset. "Do you need someone to talk to? I knew this was going to go wrong. I fucking told all of you."

"Give her a moment. I would never intentionally hurt Jacky. I didn't mean for it to go this way. I told all of you she would be handling this," Jabari growled. "And I don't need to hear the 'I told you so,' Mischa. You know who needs to hear that."

*And there's the protective brother, back again. That's the curse and magic of this family—too many big personalities.*

It was eight strong personalities, always going against each other, always snapping at each other, but also willing to kill for each other. I was one of them. I knew that. I hated Davor, but if he had been the one taken by Lani's friends, I would have been with them, trying to get him back.

Now, he saw me break, and Jabari knew to back off once that happened.

"I'm fine," I declared once I could breathe again. I looked up to see everyone on the call except Hasan. "Jabari, you give the update."

They all looked at each other, and Niko was the one who spoke up.

"We were listening in," he said softly. "*Davor* hid us from your view."

*Oh. Oh, so they all heard that outburst.*

I was so distracted by that thought, by the embarrassment, I didn't take much time to consider Niko's tone.

"I told you this wouldn't shake Jacky enough to change her," Jabari said, a small smile forming, but I didn't know who he was talking to. "You wanted to see how she was taking this, but I told you, nothing rattles Jacky enough to stop her from getting the job done. You need to have a little more faith in her."

"That was a fucking test?" I asked, raising my eyebrows, furious at the implication. I glared at Jabari. "When I see you again, I'm going to gut you, old man. Do you hear me? I'm going to cut you open and spread your entrails all over the fucking room. That was cruel. I'm not here for family mind games. I have a bit of shit on my plate if you haven't fucking noticed!" I was screaming again.

Jabari lowered his head. "I'm sorry," he mumbled. "*Some* of us were worried you were going to crumble under this sort of pressure, and I didn't know another way to show you were still going strong. I wasn't one of them, and I didn't mean to push too hard."

Jabari just kept his head down, refusing to look up at me or anyone else. He wasn't the only one. Davor was looking away as well, and he had been the one to hide everyone.

How this happened was suddenly clear, or at least the source was. 'Some of us' was probably only *one* of them. Mischa, Jabari, and Hisao? They all knew I could handle situations under pressure. Niko was quiet, and he wasn't mean. He trusted me, or so it seemed on most days. Zuri wasn't in contact with anyone.

It could only be Davor.

*Did you get what you want, Davor? Have you embarrassed me enough to be happy yet? I can forgive all of them for being strong personalities because I'm the same way, but you are a monster, cruel piece of shit who can't get over himself. I'm fucking done with you.*

I glared at the camera, hoping Davor realized I knew it was him.

Thank the gods for Mischa, though, because the silence was unbearable. She finally spoke up, looking upset.

"I'm not one of them. I know you can handle this. We've spent the last few days supporting you by handling some of the public relations issues. We reached out to all the werecats in your region to tell them you were exposed but handling the situation as quietly as possible. They've all wished you well and good luck. Some wanted to extend their encouragement behind your idea to keep them secret and you becoming the public face for werecats with the humans in America. You stepping up meant a great deal to them."

"I'm sorry I didn't reach out to them, but..." I shook my head. I didn't talk to the werecats in my region often, but Everett proved they could and would call me when they needed me. Sometimes, I checked in with them, but I wasn't friends with any of them, especially after Lani's betrayal.

"We started the moment the last call ended. It was Jabari who recovered the fastest and realized you would be too busy handling things in your territory to really do anything outside of it. Niko was the one who suggested we reach out in your stead. We've known all the werecats in your region longer than you have, so we have a relationship with them."

"Thank you," I said softly, rubbing my face. "I'm tired, so—"

It was that moment Hasan decided to get on, looking the tiniest bit flustered. He was still sitting down when his camera came on.

"What do I need to know?" he asked. Before anyone could answer, he growled softly, and his face grew hard. "Something upset several of you. I can see it on your faces. I am tired of these little dramas. We have better things to do than fight with each other. You were all better behaved during the war. This is not the time to start crumbling internally and falling prey to infighting. Whoever needs to make an apology had better do it quickly, preferably when I'm not here. Am I clear, *children*?"

Three of Hasan's children were thousands of years

old, but at that moment, we were all younger than him, which was all that mattered.

*If we're going to fight like children, he's going to treat us like children.*

In near-perfect unison, all six of us said the same thing.

"Yes, Father."

"Now, tell me what I've missed," he ordered.

Everyone else filled him in on the important details, and when they were done, he nodded, looking down at a notepad on his desk.

"I just spoke to the Tribunal as a whole. We need to convene if a species was outed, especially when it's one of our own. While they were surprised this was happening out of my control, they weren't particularly surprised it was happening in general. Every year, humans learn our tricks and grow better at identifying them."

"I told her Callahan and Corissa are on our side," Jabari said quickly.

"Yes, and that's important. I spoke to the fae king and queen about how they handle these sorts of situations. Oisin, the fae king, says their policy is to leave people out in the cold. They know they're not secret, but if they let a fae or two die every so often, it's not their problem if a fae wasn't smart enough to fool humans. They expect 'better' of their kind. We can't do that, obviously. I wouldn't do that to the worst of the werecats. The vampires obviously had no advice, but the witches were an interesting talk."

"It's different for them. They are human, so many governments turn a blind eye, as long as the witches don't involve themselves in something they shouldn't, like human politics or wars. An ironic twist, considering humans used to burn anyone they thought was a witch. Some countries still do, but they're growing rarer by the year and are places no supernatural wants to live. Chasing away supernaturals is bad policy, thanks to the economic boom of the werewolves and their long-term enterprises. That's why many nations allow them to stay, even if it's covered in thinly veiled disgust." Jabari talking about long-term economics wasn't something I'd expected out of today's conversation.

"I do believe they are trying to reconcile the evils they have to deal with," Hisao said softly. "They have bigger beasts to hunt, and witches could be their allies one day in the future, sharing that humanity with them. We've been watching this unfold for decades."

"I wouldn't put it past human governments to try to conscript witches into their service," Hasan agreed. "But that's not the point, and I believe we're a long way from that becoming an issue. The witches had some advice. Johann thinks we continue to push for privacy from the public eye because it works for them. Witches, when their covens and schools are found, though it's rare, protect the privacy of lower members and students. That is for any country that isn't hostile to witches without recourse, where the rules of secrecy are stricter. There's only been a handful of cases, but that knowledge of how witches in the United States deal might help you bargain with them."

"This is all well and good, but what do we do if the people Jacky's dealing with don't cooperate with her demands for privacy and maintaining our secrecy?" Davor asked, his voice rougher than I had ever heard it.

"We adjust as the need arises," Hasan said simply. "I'm trying to reach Zuri and Subira again, just to talk this out with them. They're off doing whatever it is they do."

Strangely, Hasan didn't seem okay with that. I knew he loved his mate, and Zuri was the daughter the rest of us wanted to be, the most helpful and balanced of the entire family. Something was making him uncomfortable with the long-term visit Zuri was having with the mother I had never met.

"When was the last time you saw Mother?" Mischa asked, smirking. "Or are you jealous of Zuri, too? Father—"

"She visited me after Niko and I arrived home from the hospital during his recovery," Hasan answered a little stiffly. I could see Niko's face turning pink.

"Oh!" Mischa started laughing. "Niko, was it your first time being there while they brought the fucking house down?"

I sputtered, not needing to hear that. No wonder Hasan and Niko never mentioned her visits.

*That's awkward as hell.*

No child, adult or not, wanted to hear their parents, supernatural or otherwise, having sex through the walls.

Hasan recovered quickly. "Jacky, just continue with what you're working on. Keep your head down, don't draw attention to yourself. If I can, I'll get Zuri in contact with you, even if we can't make it a family call."

"I thought you said we couldn't go looking for them." Jabari narrowed his eyes.

"I was hoping Zuri would check in again and see something happening. I don't like dragging her away from her time with Subira." Hasan, at that moment, was more of a father than a ruler. He was trying to honor the needs of one of his daughters and regretted having to put his foot down, had avoided it even.

"Father, I'll do my best if she's unavailable. I promise." I felt like a kid, hoping for her father's attention, love, and pride.

He sighed. "You always do your best, which is what scares me sometimes. You don't know how to do something halfway, and subtlety, my lovely daughter, is lost on you more often than not. It's okay, though. I'm behind you, ready to help every step of the way. We're going to see you and the werecats through this." Hasan and I stared at each other, unable to break eye contact. His next words surprised me. "She told me you were going to be a bigger change than I was expecting for this family, and that I underestimated how different you would be from your siblings."

"Zuri?" I looked up again, frowning.

He shook his head, then disconnected. Everyone was silent for a moment, then quickly said goodbyes, hanging up as well.

Dirk walked back in, and I looked over my shoulder at him.

"Subira," he answered. "Comments like that are always Subira."

## CHAPTER FIFTEEN

I tried to get back to normal. The next day, Kick Shot opened, and I sat in my office, watching Heath and Dirk once again talk things out with different contractors. The next day was the same.

And the next.

And the next.

By day six, I wanted to scream. No word. My life, and potentially the lives of werecats everywhere, was stuck in some sort of strange limbo. I didn't even get to see Carey. We decided to tell her about the BSA finding out about me because it was safer if we didn't see each other. She had deserved the explanation, but it left me in not only limbo but a boring, lonely hell.

I sat at my desk, listening to the music below and the contractors wielding their chainsaws. For a driveway and a gate to go in, some trees had to be taken down. It wasn't enough to distract me from the stuck feeling.

I had Special Agent Collins' card, but I didn't call. If I made the first move, I was giving them power in the negotiations for no reason. They would know I was worried and scared and would use that against me. Every time I had the urge to pick up that card and call, I envisioned Zuri—ancient, patient, and deadly. She knew how to handle these situations. She was key in gathering allies during the War about eight hundred years ago and key in keeping me from politically destroying the family every time I walked out of my territory.

So, I put the card away again and watched as people cut down my trees, waiting for any word or warning of what was coming next. Someone walking up the back steps made me turn away from the window. As the person drew closer, I heard someone else jogging up the back and down the hall, seemingly trying to catch up.

Landon opened my office door without knocking. The door didn't open the entire way, hitting a small pile of dirty laundry I was now keeping in my office.

"Do you ever go home and sleep?" He made it clear through the long, slow look he gave me, I didn't look good. Then his eyes moved over my desk, seeing the takeout boxes. I hadn't cleaned up the office yet. Since I had no meetings or calls in nearly a week, I had no outsiders to show I was doing okay.

"I'm fine sleeping right there," I answered, pointing to my chair. "Until this is done."

He didn't look amused.

"Is there something—"

Dirk ran into the back of Landon as he tried to stop. I felt something bubble up, and the laugh that erupted from me was loud and obnoxious as Dirk and Landon tried to shove each other away and find their own place to stand.

"Tell him I don't need some fucking weird training exercise in the woods," Dirk said, turning his heated stare on me.

"He does. He needs to learn proper self-defense techniques, how to use a gun properly. He needs wilderness survival training. I've been thinking about this for days. As my father's second, protection of the pack was one of my highest priorities." Landon closed the door and locked it. "While you refuse to see my father as your Alpha...it's time for everyone to settle in with the fact you're his mate. I won't see your vulnerability become a vulnerability for my father. Which means your safety is important to me."

I sat down slowly and gestured for them to take seats. Dirk glared at Landon, Landon glared at me. I wasn't sure why I was getting glared at. I hadn't said anything yet.

"I'm not your father's mate because a mate is someone you've permanently bonded with, like a marriage in our kind," I said softly, leaning in. "Which is not what Heath and I have. The idea he and I could even be on that path can never leave this room. As for the rest...I can physically protect myself. You know that."

"I'm older than you, so I know what's at stake," Landon snapped. "I'm more than a hundred years older, in fact. If you don't want Dirk to be a good head of security for *you*, then think about the fact that Carey comes over here. Think about how you and my father keep making enemies, and she's going to be the one caught in the middle. Why not have Dirk trained to at least take care of her safety if it ever comes to it?"

I opened and closed my mouth, having to kick myself for treating Landon like I did Dirk for a moment.

"You're right," I conceded. "So, what do you want Dirk to do?"

"I'm going to take him with me for a few days while things continue to be worked on here. It will be basic lessons and to set him up with the equipment he actually needs. I was thinking about a trip to the Market, and I'm going to contact my supplier of silver bullets. He needs a sidearm, at least."

"Jacky, this is crazy. I know how to shoot a gun. I mean, come on. I lived with Niko most of my life. Do you really think he didn't teach me all of this?"

I took a long, slow inhale, ignoring Dirk as his rant about Landon continued. For two and a half years, Landon never worried about his sister's safety with me and never worried about my safety at all. Even after the coup in Dallas, the events in Washington, the werecats that abducted me, or even Russia...none of it ever made him question the safety of my territory for his sister.

The long, slow inhale told me a story Landon probably didn't want Dirk to know. He wasn't scared for Carey. He knew I would die for her. He knew his father would die for her. *He* would die for her. He wasn't scared for me or Heath. He had seen both of us handle problems effectively.

He was scared for Dirk.

I thought about a wolf playing fetch under a full moon.

"Do whatever you want with him," I declared, shrugging. When Dirk sputtered, I gave him a side-eyed look. "Even if Niko taught you all of that growing up, when was the last time you employed it? Go freshen up your lessons and get a new perspective on how to do those things. I've been spending the last several months sharpening my knowledge of the supernatural world because I had forgotten a lot Hasan taught me, and I was woefully ignorant of other parts. You can do this."

"So, you know what I meant by the Market?" Landon asked.

"The fae black market, or the Market, is a pocket dimension where supernaturals from around the world can gather to barter. It's okay for anyone to go except the fae, who are banned by their own rulers," I answered. "Never been but sounds kind of neat...and crowded." That made me wrinkle my nose. "Yeah, Heath explained it to me. I know a lot more now. I just don't need to interact with it all."

"I don't need this," Dirk said again, shaking his head.

I smiled a little as Landon stood.

"Come on, we have a trip to plan. Your boss said so."

As Dirk stood, I paid more attention to my nose. Dirk, always trying to rebel even a little, glared at me, then at Landon, then stormed out of the room. I took a slow, deep inhale and caught the anger in Dirk's scent...and the lust in Landon's. He *liked* Dirk being cranky and angry.

When I looked up, Landon was looking down at me.

"He doesn't need to know," Landon said softly.

"Okay. I wasn't going to say anything."

He seemed satisfied and walked out after Dirk.

I slowly lifted a hand and put it over my mouth, leaning back in my chair to consider what to make of *that*. Landon had unceremoniously told me he was gay last summer. On most days, it never crossed my mind.

*I don't know how Dirk feels about it. Does Dirk know? Is this my business to worry about? Am I worrying for nothing? Dirk's not bad. Neither is Landon. They'll figure it out. They're both grown-ass men. Landon said it himself. He's over a hundred years older than me and has all that experience to back it up.*

*It will be fine.*

*Right?*

Frowning, I stood and went to my window, seeing Heath talking to Landon while pointing at Dirk. Once Landon and Dirk left, using Dirk's truck, my werewolf looked up at my window before getting back to work. The contractors needed him constantly to push through these security renovations. Once they gave him a chance to slip away, he did. I listened to him walk up the stairs and down the hall. He came into the office, then I heard the soft click of the door locking.

When I turned toward him, he captured my mouth with a groan. The kiss was deep and passionate, even a little needy. If neediness could be attractive, Heath had mastered it. He knew just how to apply the right type of emotional pressure to be sweet but not creepy or controlling. He pulled away at just the right moment and wrapped an arm around my waist.

"Thank God for your dark windows," he murmured. "Landon said you approved his little idea. He told me about it last night and had thought Dirk would be interested. When Dirk shut him down, I couldn't back him up because Dirk isn't one of my werewolves. Why did you say okay?"

"Because Landon isn't doing it for me, as your lover, or for his sister, who he knows will be kept safe. He's doing it for Dirk...and I appreciate that," I answered, sitting on the edge of my desk. "Did you know...Landon is attracted to Dirk?"

"I had my suspicions," Heath confirmed. "For a few months now, maybe since Landon met him. Landon can't do what I can, but he finds his own ways to keep his secrets, and I've never pried into his romantic life. Or Richard's, for that matter. Landon's a grown man. Richard was the same." He stepped close again and put his hands on either side of me on the desk. "And I don't gossip about them, either."

"I wasn't trying to gossip! I'm wo..." I thought better of what I was going to say. "It's not my business."

"No, it's not," he agreed, leaning in to put his forehead on mine. "But if you were about to admit you were worried about how this might play out, don't think you're alone. Landon has never been in a steady relationship... ever, Jacky. In the hundred and fifty years as an adult, he's never had...a boyfriend."

"I can imagine why," I countered.

"The only reason I found out my son was gay was he couldn't hide it when he was young," Heath explained softly. "Not because I caught him with someone, either. I could smell it when he lost his train of thought and stared at someone he liked. The reason he was so attached to Richard was Richard spent the better part of four *decades* keeping Landon *alive*. Richard supported his little brother without question. Werewolves wanted to kill my son for accidentally offending them because he found them attractive. I...I wasn't the best father back then. I supported him, but I..." He looked guilty, lowering his head. The first soft hint of shame filled the air.

"It's a long, complicated story, Jacky, and I'm not the man I was a hundred or a hundred and fifty years ago. I woke up and changed my way of thinking. I'm worried because this is the first time in probably twenty years Landon has shown an interest in someone, and he's never been in a world that might actually accept him for who he is. I'm glad we're moving in that direction, but werewolves...werewolves aren't humans. Landon might finally find acceptance for his sexuality in the modern world, but he might never find it among his own species. Add in a vulnerable human boyfriend, lover, or a husband is now an option...I'm worried, too. But I'm going to let him work through it and just watch his back."

"Were you a victim of your time?" I asked in a small voice, reaching up to touch the five-o'clock shadow he was sporting. Landon was still with his father, which told me they worked it out, but it was important to my relationship with Heath to know just how bad he might have been over a hundred years ago. I didn't want to wake up one day and realize I liked a man who was still holding onto any cultural rules I wanted no part of.

"I wasn't so bad as to be a danger to my own son. I never hit him or berated him. I loved him too much for that," Heath answered. "I just thought 'I can fix this.' I thought I was a good father, looking out for him. I also kept him from being hurt, like Richard, but I was more withdrawn, looking for a solution rather than just letting him be who he is."

"Oh." That was a revelation. It wasn't the best, but it could have been worse. I still wanted more of an explanation.

"For those first few decades, I introduced him to women." Heath was still looking down in shame, the scent of it thick in the air. "I tried to get him to at least try to pass as straight, but every time I saw it go wrong...I knew I hurt him by trying, and I didn't know how to fix it. I always thought 'maybe the next one will accept him,' and he just tolerated it without question. He could have left, but he never did. One day, I was talking to a young werewolf woman and asked about introducing her to Landon, as I had tried before. She was my last attempt. I had known she was a forward thinker, but I figured that would just help her accept my son as her husband, and there would be nothing wrong with it. She said something interesting."

"What was that?"

"My son wasn't wrong. The world was." He smiled as he looked back up. "And the world changes all the time. Since that conversation, knowing she was right, I have backed my son in every case. I didn't just protect him and refuse to speak about the manner. I started to put energy into it. Any pack I've ever been the Alpha for since has respected him, or wolves have been asked to leave. I banished people who tried to hurt him. He and I have never really had a conversation about it, but when he became my second in command, which was about...

seventy-five years ago, he said he didn't know a better Alpha to serve. I'll never forget that moment." He sighed heavily, betraying his age and life experience. At that moment, he was definitely a man who had lived well over two hundred years. "You probably think I'm a terrible man now. I know the modern times would look at how I treated Landon and hate me—"

I put a hand over his mouth.

"I think you did what was best for the time, and when you learned there was something even better to do, you did it instead," I said softly. "I can't judge the life experience of two men a hundred years before I knew them, and you obviously don't act that way today. Landon is still by your side, and Carey has a wonderful father. I'm sorry I brought this up. This was a heavier conversation than I think both of us wanted to have today."

"You're the first person I've ever had outside the family who I could be truly honest with. You know, raising Landon, watching him become the man he is...it's one of the reasons I make sure I evolve with the times. I don't think getting stuck in the past, set in my ways, would have kept my son with me."

"I...I only brought it up to keep my mind off..." I waved my hand around, frustrated with my own situation, but dropped it after a second. "I am so... honored to be the person you tell these things to. We'll both watch out for them. Okay?"

"With you helping me, how could anything go wrong?" He finally laughed, brightening in front of my eyes.

"Very funny," I said, pushing him away slowly. He

tried to stay where he was but failed, laughing harder. When he sobered, he was still smiling.

"Look, if you want to gossip about them to get your mind off things, that's fine. Let's just keep it to a minimum, though."

"Okay." I remembered I had never asked him about something from the last meeting. "Do you know a Special Agent Collins?"

"He's a *Special Agent* now, huh?" Heath groaned. "Yeah, I know him. He's one of the two that have been coming by?"

"Yeah, him and Special Agent Miller," I confirmed. "I heard them talk about you for a minute outside before the last meeting. I've been so wrapped up, I keep forgetting to mention it. Was he one of the agents you threatened when they were spying on you and Carey?"

"Yeah, he was one of them," Heath said, stepping back. He put his hands in his pockets and looked toward my window, with a faraway expression. "Agent Collins was a rookie when I first met him before Carey was born. He respected me the entire time I worked near him and was often one of the first BSA agents to arrive on the scene when there was a mix up between any humans and my pack. He was never out to get me in trouble, but he wanted to do his job to the fullest, which made us butt heads. He was the one who didn't think it was a big deal to keep surveillance on me. He has a lot of integrity, so he didn't consider how videos of my daughter could be used against me. I made him learn. It was the last time I spoke to him. They took him off the Dallas pack for his safety, not because his superiors think he did anything wrong.

No." Heath shook his head slowly. "They didn't want me to kill him because he did it so well."

"Should I be worried?"

"Unless he's drastically changed, he's by the book and respectful. He's stubborn, though—"

My speakers started to ring, and I turned quickly to see a call coming through on my monitor. Heath took it as his cue to leave without goodbye, which wasn't unusual. That was just how we handled this situation.

I picked up and saw my sister.

"Zuri!"

## 16

# CHAPTER SIXTEEN

I had never been more relieved to see her face, but it was off. She looked tired, in a modest home, a little too close to the camera. All of it was wrong. She wasn't dressed in expensive clothes, just a simple, somewhat plain dress from what I could see, and her hair wasn't immaculate.

I always thought if I went on a vacation, I would want a week in Zuri's life—treated like a queen, people fanning me, and handling everything, so I never had to get up and clean. It seemed her vacations were the exact opposite.

"Hello, little sister," Zuri greeted, giving me a kind smile. "I'm sorry it took so long for me to find out what was happening and reach out. I've read everything and caught up on the situation. Before we get into any of that, please tell me...are you okay?" The concern touched me, and I swallowed back emotion.

"I'm...I'm going to be fine," I said, giving her a half-truth.

"Don't try to play that game with me," she warned. "I've heard about all of it, from the family's initial reaction, to Davor's...abhorrent behavior. I know all of you can handle this situation without me, but I'm...Jacky, who has been taking care of *you*?"

*Heath.*

I couldn't tell her that. Her concern for me—immediate, not an afterthought—touched me. I refused to stress her out on her vacation, though.

"This is just a stressful—"

"Do not try to justify the way this makes you feel by saying it's stressful," she growled. "And don't you dare play nice for Davor's sake. He's not playing nice for yours. Don't you worry about that, though. I'm going to make sure he's taken care of. Father obviously doesn't have him well enough in control."

"I wasn't going to try to justify what Davor did," I fired back. "He's a mean asshole. He's been mean to Niko. He's been mean to me. I don't know why everyone puts up with him. I'm just not...my feelings don't matter in this. We have a problem to fix, and it's my fault...again. I'm an adult who can admit I made decisions that led to this, and now I have to focus on finding a solution."

"Jacky..." Zuri shook her head. "My lovely sister with a big heart...I saw the video."

That cracked through my defense. "I'm fine," I whispered—I was until that moment.

"You look exhausted, and your office looks like you've been living in it. I see the pile of dirty laundry and the takeout containers. I'm not a fool. You've been sleeping in your office. A werecat staying away from the center of her territory is a werecat who is not doing *fine*. That is more important to me than anything you have or haven't done. We can talk business after I make sure you are okay."

*Shit, I didn't have the chance to clean up.*

"I berated my idiot twin in an email when I saw Niko's email about Davor. Jabari was only trying to do what I do…he just has no finesse. If he could do it well, he would have known Davor's little idea was terrible and that you aren't okay at all." Zuri's jaw was tight. "If he was good at it, he would have known Davor's intention to make sure you were 'up to the task' would be more detrimental than helpful."

"I told you if you called her, you had to remain calm," someone said out of view. There were a million ways I could describe the voice—low and husky, definitely a woman, patient but stern. My heart pounded as I realized who it had to be.

Zuri was with Subira, the mother I had never met. I didn't really see her as my mother, but she was definitely special to the family, and seeing her was obviously rare. Now, for the first time since I had become a werecat, I heard her voice. My palms went clammy, and I rubbed them together, wondering if she could see me when I couldn't see her.

"You're right, you did," Zuri said. She took a long deep breath, closing her eyes as she held it, then slowly released. She did it three more times before she looked at me again. "I wish I could fly out to you, Jacky, I do."

"Any advice would be appreciated," I countered. "What's going on? You've been MIA for months."

"We'll talk about that later. First, we need to talk

about you. How are you feeling?"

I remembered the sick feeling when it had all started—the violation of my privacy, the exposed feeling, my blurred body.

"I really am doing better, but when I think about it...I feel violated," I admitted. "I'm not sleeping in my house, and I'm getting new security installed. Dirk is really stepping up for me, talking to..." I trailed off, letting Zuri fill in the blanks.

"You can say his name," Zuri said softly. "Heath is a good werewolf, and he's been a wonderful friend of this family."

"*This* family?" My eyebrows went up. He was certainly my friend, more than that, but I didn't remember any point where it was suddenly decided he was everyone's friend. He and Jabari didn't get along at all, Davor hated him from a distance, and Niko was interested, but I knew they didn't talk. Heath had no chance to build a friendship with everyone in the family.

"By being a friend to you, he is a friend to this family. I don't want to make the distinction anymore. My... perspective may have changed recently, and I'm not going to give you a hard time for letting him help you."

It felt sudden, but I had no idea what Zuri was going through to prompt this sudden acceptance.

"Okay...yeah, I went to Heath. After I called the family, the next day Dirk and I cleared the cameras off my property, then I went to Heath to talk about new security Dirk and I could manage and find names of contractors to install it...and I broke down. Right there in his office. I fell apart."

Someone whistled off-screen, and Zuri sent a glare in that direction.

"Is someone else there? Besides...Subira?" I asked, frowning deeply.

"Yes," she answered but offered nothing else. "And said person is supposed to be out for a time, so I could speak to you alone." She continued to glare in that direction until something happened that made her content again. "Gone now. Continue."

"I am so lost right now." What the fuck was Zuri into? Was it a friend? Another werecat? A human?

"Jacky, I really can't—"

"You can; you're just too scared to," Subira said from wherever she was hanging out off-screen. "She's your sister, not one of your brothers. It's really those boys you're hiding from. Let her know. If you open up to her, she will be more willing to open up to you. I know I don't need to explain this."

"Okay, but at the end," Zuri said, running a hand over her face. "Jacky, let's just stay on topic right now."

"Sure. What would you do in my position?"

"Exactly what you are doing. Keep playing hardball with them. Remind them you are going to live for an eternity, and you can always bargain with the next generation. The thoughts and ideas of men change rapidly, the world moves swiftly. You can bide your time to get what you want. They can't. I don't have a problem with you telling them all about us. Because we're so closely related to werewolves, they know our weaknesses. They don't yet know our strengths, but if they want to, they need to give you *everything*." She reached out, and from the look of it, she was touching the screen.

"I don't want you to keep looking like this, darling. Please take care of yourself. That worries me more than the humans, do you understand? You have it hard in our family as the youngest. You've forged a different path than what we're used to, but I am curious to see where this path leads. I came out here because I'm tired. I thought it was because of the drama you had caused, but in reality, I was just tired of the life we live. I don't want to see you become one of us—one of Hasan's powerful and reclusive children with no hope of normal lives. I want you to keep fighting for what you want in life. I just want to see you live through it and be happy."

I blinked several times, tears filling my eyes. "What's gotten into you, Zuri? You used to demand that I be every bit the queen you believed I was."

"You're a werecat and the ruler of your territory. You were always a queen to me. I should have said it more often. Seeing you like this...hurts me." She blinked as well, and I caught the glisten of her tears. She took a deep breath. "Oh, I'm so damn emotional these days."

"You can tell me what's going on. I told you about my breakdown."

She nodded and leaned back from the computer. Something seemed off as she turned in the swivel chair, but when she stood up, the situation became very clear.

It was a beachball-sized problem.

"Oh my god, you're pregnant," I gasped. "Oh my god." I leaned back, then rushed forward, getting closer to the screen. "Oh my god! Zuri! What?" I threw my hands over my mouth, trying to remember coherent thought, but Zuri backed away, showing me the entire story, posing with her hands wrapped around her belly.

"I met a man at the beginning of my vacation, and my...preventative measures failed. In an unlikely turn of events, I discovered I was pregnant shortly after this man decided he needed to head home...in the Sahara Desert." She smiled, but it looked tired. "You can't, under any circumstances, tell our father or any of our siblings about this. They will come out here and find me. They will force me to live with Hasan until the baby is born. I want to give birth with Mother attending me and let this child be born in the wilds where I believe it will belong, where I feel most at home." She slowly ran her right hand over her baby bump.

"The...the other person..." I pointed, but I didn't really understand why.

"The father," Zuri answered softly. "His name is Kushim. He's an Immortal. He was passing through my territory, looking for a rogue who had stolen something from him. We connected as I helped him and decided to have...a bit of fun, thanks to that connection."

"Let me get this straight. You met an Immortal, had sex with him once, and got pregnant, defying all the odds since it's really rare for werecats to get pregnant."

"Oh, it wasn't a one-night stand," Zuri admitted, smiling. "More like a two-month stand. We got out of bed to eat, and we talked." Her smile turned dreamy. "About pirates and bandits through the ages. It was so...perfect." She sighed happily, and I saw her cheeks darken with a blush.

"See, this is how you ended up pregnant," Subira said, walking on-screen and pointing a finger at her daughter.

I lost all the air in my lungs. She was so short, probably five-foot-two, and had long, beautifully braided hair like Zuri, though Zuri towered over her, closer to five-foot-nine. The face, though—Zuri had inherited her beauty from this woman. Subira laughed, and it was at Zuri's expense, who laughed along. This was the bond between a close mother and daughter.

I finally saw more than just a painting of this woman, and the painting didn't do her justice.

"Immortals are immune to magic and nullify it in other things when they touch it," Subira continued. "You were so enamored with your bandit, you didn't consider while you made love to this man, his touch would stop the spells protecting you from pregnancy. That, my lovely daughter, is why I told you to not fall for love!" She was still laughing as Zuri waved her off.

"You love Father!" Zuri reminded her, grinning.

"I do," Subira said, her smile also turning peaceful as if thinking of Hasan was her favorite thing to do. "He's a fool, that man, and you'll learn your bandit is as well. Love tends to do that to men."

*Oh, they're still both madly in love with each other. It's not just Hasan.*

*Will Heath become a fool? I have to watch out for it now.*

Subira finally turned on me, her smile not fading, only changing. It became indulgent.

"And you," she whispered, coming closer to the camera. "I expected we would meet under different circumstances. I have been told Hasan calls you

Jacqueline, but...if I may, I would like to call you Jacky like the others do."

"Jacky is fine. Why haven't we met yet?" I dared to ask.

"Imagine being Changed by a man like Hasan, introduced to all of our children, then told you're one of them now. It's easier to finish easing someone into the family slowly. If you had stayed with Hasan for the decade he needed to teach you, I would have visited, but..." She trailed off, considering me. It felt as though I was being disassembled and my every part checked for defects. "You had to reckon with some uncomfortable truths, and I decided I wouldn't involve myself and rush you or pressure you in any way. I have heard of your adventures, though." She raised an eyebrow at me, amused as heat flooded my cheeks. "And what adventures they have been. We'll talk about them one day." She stepped back again and lifted her hands. "I can't stay. I've been making a potion for Zuri to help with her discomforts. I need to check on it."

Then she was gone, leaving me and Zuri staring at each other.

"That's really not how she wanted to meet you," Zuri said as she came back toward the camera and sat down in her swivel chair. "At least the initial introduction is over."

"She's..."

"She's our mother," Zuri said with a wise nod. "She's special."

"I think I caught that," I whispered. "A potion? Is she..." I leaned in close. "Is she half-witch?"

"There's a reason she had to leave the second Tribunal seat empty," Zuri said softly. It clicked for me as

Zuri said it—half-breeds couldn't hold ruling positions. Subira, a witch making potions, couldn't also rule the werecats on the Tribunal. It was a conflict of interest, people would say. "And...a reason *I've* had to leave it open."

Spells. Potions. Runes of power, symbols that have magic no matter who uses them.

"Are you—"

Zuri put a finger over her mouth, and I stopped, not daring to go further. This was a secret. Mother wasn't, not really, but Zuri was.

"Everyone in the family knows Mother is a witch. Normally, she tells you, but you hadn't met her yet," Zuri said softly. "She was born one and Changed into a werecat later. The story is more complicated than I'm letting on, but there are some things she needs to tell you. Jabari is cranky right now because I'm blocking his connection with me."

I just stood there, giving my sister a wide-eyed, confused stare. She chuckled softly.

"Jabari and I were born twins of a magic user. We have a connection. We can feel each other over vast distances, though at a certain point, it grows weak. Mother, for my pregnancy, has helped me block that connection, so he can't track me down. It's something we've never told anyone, except Mother."

"Why are you telling me?" I asked, laughing in shock. "What? I'm...the last person in this family you should give your secrets to right now."

"Because I know one of yours," she said softly.

## CHAPTER SEVENTEEN

I stopped laughing and stared in wide-eyed horror at nothing, unable to look up at her on my monitor.

I only had one secret.

"You didn't treat your own injuries last year," she continued. "You went to see Heath. When you left his home, you were running. Look at how Heath treats you, little sister. His love and devotion are clear."

I took a long, ragged breath.

*How does she know that?*

"Who are you going to tell?" I asked softly.

"No one," she said simply. "Not a soul. Not even my twin."

"Why?" I looked up at her again, stunned yet still fearful.

"Because I'm having a child with an Immortal. Really, Jacky...I'm not going to tell anyone. The heart is the heart. That has been made very clear to me recently." She turned and smiled. Lifting a hand, she beckoned for someone to join her without needing to say a word.

The man who walked onto the screen had a swagger that couldn't be denied. He was covered in scars, but not ugly because of it. Once, he would have been a heart-stopping, good-looking man. Now, he was definitely a man who had seen more battles than I could comprehend.

"This is Kushim," she introduced. "The bandit who very effectively stole my heart."

"My queen, I do believe you gave it to me," he murmured, leaning down to kiss her. It was so tender. When he looked at the camera, he waved. "I've heard about you, Jacky Leon, through the grapevine, not just from your sister. An old friend of mine runs the Mygi thing."

Zuri practically rolled her eyes. "Hospital. He runs Mygi Hospital. Most people call him Director Johannsson."

"Yeah, he and I met," I said, clicking my tongue on my teeth. They hadn't been pleasant phone calls.

"If you and Heath decide to go public, you have two allies in us," she said with her signature smile. That smile said, 'I rule this world, and I get what I want.' "Or if you two decide to end it without ever going public or decide you don't have a future together, I'll be here with a child for you to cuddle and play with to ease the bruised heart. But I won't out your relationship. This..." She pointed at Kushim, then patted her baby bump. "This has changed me."

"You could have outed me beforehand," I pointed out. "Why didn't you?"

"I wanted more evidence and decided I was just going

to avoid the situation entirely. I didn't want to unleash drama on the family after what had happened to you with Lani and the other rogues, but I did give you a warning last year. I meant it. You *needed* to distance yourself from Heath. When you didn't and everything with your human family had settled, I decided I wanted to go on vacation. Give you more time and a break from the pressure and give myself time to think. I was tired. Sadly, now there's so much other stuff happening."

"Yeah," I agreed with a huff. "Um…since you know about Heath and me…the BSA might have evidence of it, too." It felt wonderful to get that off my chest. It was even better to know I had a friend in the family who would protect us. Finally, I wasn't keeping a dark secret. My sister knew, and she didn't just want to keep the secret for me, she decided to trust me with her own.

Except, that feeling ended with Zuri's response. I didn't exactly give her good news.

She straightened her back and frowned. "Explain."

"They didn't send me a video of anything about it, but I know the day they had to have put their surveillance in. Heath and I were meeting every Saturday night at my house, a pattern we had already established because he would come to Kick Shot for a drink every Saturday. It's how we got so close, I guess. The full moon was on Sunday night. The timeline means they would have recorded Heath coming and leaving my house."

"You need to ask for that footage," Zuri said, more worried than she had been. "They don't know how bad it is, right? Have you said anything to them about our kinds being enemies?"

"No, and I don't think any werewolves have mentioned it, either," I confirmed.

"Don't. Don't ever mention it. The moment they know, they'll know they have something to use to blackmail you. That's bad. This is bad. This is worse than I assumed. From what I've been told, everything was smoothed over for the werecats about you being found out by a human government, but...I don't think we could smooth over you being with a werewolf yet. Not at the same time. That's something we need to do in a controlled release, and only once the family knows." She took a deep breath. "I'll continue to think about this. Don't fret. You can trust me to do everything in my power to protect you."

"Don't put yourself at risk for me again," I pleaded. I remembered the rebar in her chest. It could have killed her. It *should* have killed her.

"Unless our own family tries to kill me, I won't be at risk of anything," she reminded me.

"And me?" I asked honestly. It had been one of my biggest concerns. I could never truthfully guess one way or the other if my own family would turn on me for being with Heath.

"I wouldn't let them even if they tried," she said, full of a conviction that made me love her. "And really, there's only..." She counted on her fingers, probably weighing and measuring each of our siblings and parents. "Davor, Jabari, and Mischa would be the problems. Niko would die for you, die to protect this life you're building. He's wanted peace between the races since I met him. Hisao would find the killing in war needless, and he might be angry with you but silently. He doesn't raise his hand against family...under any circumstance. I mean, if you tried to kill him, he would fight back, but he would then leave you for one of us to deal with. It's a rule he has, something Mother taught him when he was young. Mother and Father...Mother isn't an issue at all."

"You told her, didn't you? I mean, she probably heard us."

"I didn't need to tell her," Zuri said with a flat stare. "I was telling her about your adventures, and she asked when you fell in love with the wolf and how no one else has realized it."

"I hadn't even met her!" I was incredibly uncomfortable with that.

"She's like that," Zuri said, just as unamused as I was. "Father...Father keeps his own counsel on you and Heath. He loves you and wants you happy and safe like the rest of us. Heath isn't safe for you, but Father also hasn't forced you to kick those werewolves out. He's protective of you when the rest of us become too, well...us. You didn't have the easiest start in the family, and he blames himself."

"Maybe if he stood up to Davor—"

"He knows Davor is his fault. He's trying. He is. If he can't get Davor in line and I can't, I'm going to ask Mother."

"Why is Davor his fault?"

"What kind of example does it set when a man who lost his daughter decides to abandon all of his responsibilities and hide for a century? Sure, Father was grieving, but it was selfish grieving. None of us spoke to him much for those years until he Changed you. Davor, having been in love with Liza, got to see that as an example and thinks he can behave however he wants because he's grieving. It's been over a century. This family has dealt with loss before, and we've never tolerated someone to behave as Davor has for this long. I blame Father for disappearing and allowing Davor to spin out of control. Davor never listens to us unless it was an area of our expertise, but he listens to Father without question. Father needs to pull the trigger on our brother. He needs to go in and take his territory if Davor can't finally clean himself up, especially when we're dealing with something this big." Zuri was huffing and furious again. I remembered the threat Zuri was mentioning and the shock it had sent through the family to hear it.

Kushim knelt next to her and rubbed her thigh. Definitely, a man trying to calm down his pregnant lover. It was affectionate and sweet.

*They fell in love quickly.*

"You promised your mother," he reminded her.

She took several deep breaths. "I did, I know. I should go lie down."

"Maybe," he said, smiling a little, twisting the scars on his face.

I felt like the third wheel.

Nodding, she stood slowly, Kushim standing with her. He was *tall*, Hasan or Jabari tall.

"Jacky, email me when you hear back from the humans about another meeting. Keep me updated. I won't get on family calls, and I can't come to you because of this,"—she gestured to the baby bump—"but I'm here for anything I can do."

"Do you think I can do this?" I wanted her reassurance.

Zuri tilted her head to her side, frowning. "Of course, I do. I know you're willing to do whatever is necessary. I saw it with my own two eyes, the dedication you have. I was there when you fought and executed Lani for her betrayal. And while my twin is an idiot, he believes it, too. As do Mischa and Hisao, who saw you go across the world to rescue your human family. And Niko, who saw you overcome one barrier he never could and become friends with the werewolves, the people of his first family. We're a rough family and are unaccustomed to being proven wrong or being forced to accept change, but you have our support in this. If they have all forgotten to say it, I'm sorry."

"I just wanted to hear it from you. You would be so much better at this than me."

"Would I?" She shrugged. "I'm an ancient, withdrawn from humanity, and I come off that way. I think the instincts of our family...no, *your* instincts for this are good. Maybe what humanity needs to see is someone like them...someone like you. Someone modern who best understands the world they live in and ours." She smirked. "I couldn't have picked a worse time to get pregnant, though. Sitting in on those meetings would have been a good course of action for me. We could have worked together, maybe."

"Not that we picked this," Kushim said, coughing softly. "Or that I mind the situation. You're fucking gorgeous as a pregnant woman." He reached out and touched the bump gently, smiling. "And I did this."

"Don't get it into your head, we're going to do this again," she said, looking down at his hands.

"Why not? The making was certainly one of the best things I've done," he countered, pulling her closer.

"Don't make me kill you again," she said, both warning and joking. She didn't elaborate as Kushim started to laugh. She reached out, and the moment her fingers touched the keyboard, the video call disconnected.

I was left staring at a black square.

*Don't make me kill you* again? *What?*

"Well, that was something," I declared, promising myself I would unpack every detail I could about that conversation the moment my head was clear enough to try—witches, an Immortal, and a *baby*.

I couldn't honestly decide what was most surprising, but I was happy for Zuri. Leaning on my desk, I thought about her story about her first son and how that had turned out. She deserved a bit of happiness, and she looked happy. Kushim wasn't the sort of man I ever thought she would be with, but there was a wonderful duality to them. My mind had a million trains of thought, all trying to go at the same time, so focusing on the cute new relationship my oldest sister found herself seemed the easiest.

*Queen and bandit. That's cute. Will the baby be a little royal like Zuri or a dangerous little criminal like him?*

*I'm going to be an aunt. I wonder how Hasan is as a grandfather.*

*Zuri is a witch, and Hasan doesn't know. That's pretty crazy. I can't believe she told me.*

*She knows about me and Heath. I need to tell him.*

That last thought made me feel more urgent than necessary. She didn't plan to out me, but letting Heath know about this massive revelation was important. I grabbed a light leather jacket and walked out of my office. Oliver poked his head out of his office as I passed.

"I'm heading out, running some errands, and I need to talk to Heath. Dirk isn't around, so you're on your own."

"I'll lock your office for you," he said.

"Text me if you need anything from the store or anything else," I said, looking back at him before going down the stairs. I saw his wave and knew he heard me, feeling confident he could manage the bar on his own. Slipping out the back, I got in my car, then texted Heath, telling him there was something important I needed to tell him.

*I don't need to go there, but I need to get out of this bar. I can't keep living like this, only going home for a ten-minute shower and sleeping in my office. When was the last time I left to buy groceries or anything else? I have to somehow reclaim that feeling of security.*

I had to wait for nearly five minutes to get out of my own parking lot, thanks to a rush of people driving by. It happened. Sometimes, there were no cars on the highway where I had built Kick Shot, and sometimes, there were too many. I looked at the time. It was six, and it all made sense. People were still trying to get home from a long day of work and responsibilities.

As I waited, two trucks pulled up behind me. One honked for me to hurry up, so I stuck my hand out the window and flipped him the bird, getting him to honk louder.

"Wait a fucking minute, asshole," I yelled out the window. "I own this fucking parking lot!"

The honking stopped.

It was another minute before there was a gap to get out of Kick Shot's parking lot. The honking truck hit the gas, too, causing the tires to squeal as the truck stayed on my bumper.

## CHAPTER EIGHTEEN

I lost the asshole in town. As I passed through, my phone started to ring.

"Hey." The way he said it, deep, calm, and pleased, sent shivers down my spine.

"Hi," I replied. "I'm on my way over. I needed to get out of the bar. That call was Zuri. There's some stuff I need to tell you in person."

"Carey and I are about to have dinner. I'll make sure to set a third spot at the table for you. We're going to be talking about her upcoming birthday, too. That's just around the corner. She's already got a horse. How do I top that?"

"I...I don't know," I admitted. "But you'll figure it out."

He chuckled. "I'll let you drive. See you soon."

"Definitely," I promised. I dropped the phone back into its cupholder. Heath didn't like me talking and driving because I didn't have a fancy dashboard that picked up my calls.

*Oliver isn't the only person who needs a ride. I need to update.*

I was minding my own business, driving the speed limit thanks to the traffic, and finally hit an open stretch of road when a new truck decided to get right behind me and stick to my back end like he was glued there. The road clear, but this guy—I assumed a man was driving—hovered right behind me.

"Pass, asshole. What the fuck is wrong with everyone driving today?" I checked my rearview mirror. The windows were too dark for me to see anything, but I hit the gas, trying to pick up a little speed. Five over would have to please this guy.

He matched me and stayed there. I rolled my eyes before focusing on the road. Trying to ignore the truck, I thought about how I was going to tell Heath about the call with Zuri. That was the least pleasant part of this small diversion. Heath's cooking was better than any takeout I could get, and an evening with Carey would be good for me, too. I hadn't seen her since I had broken down at their home, mostly because I just wanted to hide in my office and didn't want her to see the sorry state I was in.

I heard the glass shatter and felt glass sting my face, cutting open my cheeks. I closed my eyes for a moment. Something stung my shoulder, and the suddenness made me jerk the wheel without thinking. My ears were ringing as I straightened myself out.

*What?*

It was then my mind registered the gunshots tearing up my backseat and dashboard, then the sound of silenced gunshots, hidden under the roar of the wind through my broken windows.

I looked up at my rearview mirror to see the truck wasn't there anymore, forcing me to look back if I wanted to see who was shooting at me. I took the risk, trying to turn to look over my shoulder without sending myself off the road. The same truck was there, and there was someone hanging out the passenger side window, holding a gun I couldn't identify. He was reloading already, which gave me a moment's break.

I focused on the road again, slamming the gas pedal to the floor. I slid down, trying to keep a view of the road and stay safe at the same time. The fact I had only been hit once was a blessing. Shooting out of a moving vehicle was harder than the movies and video games made it seem.

I heard one of my tires pop and started losing control, then a bullet clipped my right hand, barely missing my head. I dropped the hand into my lap, hissing as adrenaline kept me focused on driving.

The truck decided to ram me, and my little Nissan Versa couldn't take it. I went off the road, bumping into the ditch on the side. The stop slammed my head on the steering wheel, causing the damn car to honk. I groaned as I sat up and grabbed my phone.

*I need to call Heath.*

This was car accident number three for me. Luckily, it was the least severe. As the truck stopped on the side of the road, I unclicked my seatbelt and crawled to the passenger's side. I got out of the car as the two guys got out of the truck and started firing blindly into my car.

There was no one around. I was out of Jacksonville, on the stretch of highway between my town and Tyler. Heath was only five minutes away, but there wasn't anything with good enough hearing to catch the silenced gunfire.

"Die, you fucking freak!" one of them screamed.

*Freak? Who are these guys?*

"We don't want your kind here!" he continued.

"I don't know what you're talking about!" I yelled back. "I own a fucking bar!"

"We know what you are!" More gunfire.

*That's why you're not getting close, huh? You're going to stay up there and eventually hit me.*

*Two options—fight or run as a human. Can't Change. Don't have time to strip, and my clothes will get in the way if I don't.*

The answer was clear. I didn't know who these two were, but it was broad daylight and on a main road. They were bold for trying to kill me right now, but I wasn't bold enough to kill them. The BSA was already onto me. Killing humans, no matter why, wasn't something I could do right now.

I waited for a moment of silence, then took off into the trees, running faster than I believed I had ever done before. I heard them firing and saw bark explode on the trees, but I didn't look back, didn't have the luxury of looking back. I ran until they stopped shooting. I ran until I knew they couldn't catch me. I just ran. Luckily, I knew the terrain. This was my territory. I knew every game trail, every path people had worn down with their dirt bikes and four-wheelers. I angled and headed in the direction of Heath's home.

My legs were on fire when I decided to slow down to a jog. I looked back, seeing only trees, and finally stopped.

"What the fuck?" I asked, then winced as the throbbing pain in my shoulder made itself known. I reached up with my free hand and gingerly tried to find where I had been hit.

*Just a graze. Oh, that could have been so much worse. They knew I wasn't human and were trying to kill me.*

It didn't take a rocket scientist to figure out what that meant. The BSA either just tried to have me killed or had a leak in their organization. There were fringe organizations that killed supernaturals, but they rarely made the news. Most supernaturals were hard to kill. They would rant and rave about the dangers of werewolves, witches, or fae, but no one took them seriously. There were lots of people who didn't like supernaturals, but most of those people preferred to ignore the new reality that supernaturals existed.

I never gave the fringe killers any thought and had never heard of a case where they actually succeeded. Living in secret meant they were never going to be a threat to me.

*But I'm not living in secret anymore. The BSA caught me.*

I focused on everything around me as I tried to call Heath.

"Heath?" I said when I heard him pick up. All I got was a crackling noise on the other side. "Heath! Someone ran me off the road. They were shooting at me. I'm out in the woods near your place, and I'm walking. I would love a ride, though." I knew he had off-road vehicles for simple work around his property. A ride on a four-wheeler would have been nice.

The call disconnected.

"Fuck!" I snapped, shoving the phone into my pocket. Useless.

*Walking it is.*

It took twenty minutes. A five-minute drive was a lot longer on foot through the hilly terrain of East Texas. I had to cross two back streets, hoping none of the humans who lived there saw me. I found his property line and was so exhausted by the time I staggered into his backyard. At first glance, I didn't see anyone, but I knew my service was better near his place. As I walked to his back door, I pulled my phone out and sent Oliver a quick text to stay safe, and I would explain more when I had the chance. Then I sent a message to Hasan, asking for the family to get back together, telling him I was attacked and would be home soon. Texting with one hand was a pain in the ass, but I was trying to ignore the terrible throbbing pain coming from my bleeding right hand. I certainly didn't want to look at it.

I heard screaming in the background, someone saying my name, but I didn't look up, glaring at my phone, waiting for my texts to be read.

By the time I made it to Heath's backdoor, he was there, opening it with a terrified expression. I shoved my phone back into my pocket, looked between them, then entered the house in silence. Carey was pale, but she wasn't screaming anymore. Neither of the Eversons said anything as I went to their kitchen and grabbed the ice pack I knew they kept in their freezer with my left hand. Heath grabbed the first aid kit and met me at the table.

"Want to tell me what happened?" he asked, his voice tight. "Carey, find some towels, so we can clean up Jacky."

"Okay, Dad." She ran out of the dining room.

"I was run off the road," I said simply. "Well, I was also shot at, a lot, but the off the road part is the reason I'm walking through your backdoor looking like I got into a fight."

"I'm going to assume nothing is too bad if you're here like this," he said, the tense note in his words refusing to give way.

"A graze on my shoulder, the bump forming on my forehead, glass scratches from the windshields being blown out." I lifted my right hand, which was a disaster. "This. I'll need a hospital. The bullet hit and broke bones. It wasn't a hard enough crash to deploy airbags, though. I don't know if the bullet was silver. I didn't have time to really register the pain. Once I had the chance to run, I did."

Carey came back with an armful of washcloths, went to the sink, wetting one, then gave it to me.

"Thank you," I said, trying to give her a smile. I winced as I wiped my face. "They called me a freak and said they didn't want my kind around this part."

Heath paused as he looked over my shoulder. "Extremists?"

"The BSA must have a leak," I said softly. "I'm going to handle that. I need a ride home, though. My Nissan is out of commission. Ironically, I was considering finally buying a new car."

He didn't look amused. "I'll get you back to the bar. You're handling this well."

"I'm not handling it at all," I said softly. "I'm pretending as if it's a normal day, and eventually, that's not going to work. We both know that, so I would prefer to continue ignoring what this means for me and just get on with what needs to be done about it."

He nodded.

"Carey, you're coming with us. If we have an extremist group going after Jacky, there's a chance they don't like werewolves, either."

"Why me and not you, though?" I hadn't thought about that yet, but Heath brought up a good point. "You're out. They know you're a werewolf. They would have only just found out I'm a werecat."

"You're alone and vulnerable. That's how wolves stay safe from these people. Witches, too. There's strength in numbers. Attack one of us and get the pack or the coven. Do they know you lived?"

"They didn't follow me into the woods, they were smarter than that, but yeah, they know I lived. If they really want me dead, they'll try again." I winced again as Heath cleaned off my injured shoulder. "Silver?"

"Yes," he whispered. "You're in for another scar."

"Fuck." I huffed. "Probably a lucky guess, yeah? Werewolves, werecats, both change at the full moon, both weak to silver."

"I don't like that they have silver in general. I'll need to tell the NAWC you've run into humans using silver and trying to murder a moon cursed. This is a problem." He stood and sighed. "There's not much I can do more for you other than clean it up. You got lucky, Jacky. You got really lucky. You do need a hospital for that hand, for X-rays and setting. That needs to happen before you do anything else."

"I know. I got lucky they had bad aim. They damn near took my head off—" My phone started ringing. I tried to pull it out, but Heath got it when he saw me fighting to get it. He answered, then held it to my ear.

"Are you okay?" Hasan demanded.

"I'm fine. I need a small hospital visit for one of my hands that was hit, and bones were broken. A few scratches and a couple of new scars—"

"Who did this?" Hasan snarled. "I'm going to start packing—"

*Oh, no. No, no. No, he's going to stay right where he fucking is.*

"Humans. They shot at me, ran me off the road, then shot at me some more. Look, I know you want to descend on my territory with everyone under the sun, but I really think that's only going to make this worse. Somehow, these humans learned what I am, learned I'm supernatural—"

"Yes, I do want to descend on your territory. Do you honestly think we won't come and defend you—"

"Hasan, listen to me. There's a human government involved. If you get involved, if any of our family gets involved, we'd expose how powerful we are, how old we are. We're older than the werewolves. They'll put that together." He didn't reply, but I heard a soft, unending growl. "On top of that, you are a member of the Tribunal. Do you really think the Tribunal is going to be okay with more of the members being in the public eye? Callahan and Corissa from the werewolves already are. Let me handle the BSA. They leaked me to someone, or they hired someone to kill me. I can deal with this. I won't have all our plans at keeping the werecats out of the public eye ruined. I won't have it. I won't put everyone in the family at risk. I have backup. They made it abundantly clear that they know I hang out with Heath. I have other allies. There's no reason to give them information they obviously don't deserve."

I heard his exhale of defeat as he saw my reason.

"Get to the hospital," he ordered. "Send an email report of the full attack. We won't come yet, but if you find yourself backed into a corner, get out of there."

"Yeah, you don't need to tell me twice."

"And tell Alpha Everson thank you for continuing to be an ally to the family."

"I can hear you," Heath said. "She was on her way to my place when it happened. She came walking up to my backdoor. I'll get her to a hospital, then back to her bar."

"Good. One of you, keep me posted. I need to tell your siblings what happened."

"Bye." I hung up and looked up at Heath. "Let's get into the car and get moving."

## 19

# CHAPTER NINETEEN

After we loaded into Heath's truck, Carey in between us, I thought about how that call ended.

"He's going to ask why I was coming over."

"You were dropping off something Carey left at your house," he said quickly. Simple white lie no one ever had to verify. "That way, you weren't staying over and hanging out with me or her. Just dropping something off, then getting a move on. They won't think anything of it."

"Why are you lying?" Carey frowned at us. "Werecats can smell lies, and she was just coming over for dinner. Will I have to lie, too? Lying is wrong."

The scent of Heath's regret was strong. I knew he didn't like lying to his daughter, and he just set a bad example of creating a lie for me to tell my family.

"We're not asking you to lie," I said softly. "Only that I will."

"Yeah, but why?" Carey crossed her arms. "Both of you tell me lying is bad. Why is it you get shot at but need to lie about coming to have dinner with us? We're your friends."

"We'll talk about it later," Heath said softly.

"Werecats and werewolves don't like each other. People don't like that your dad and I are friends, and they would prefer we stop being friends, Carey. You know that. I've explained it before."

"But you've had dinner with us before, and they know about those, don't they? I mean, Dad goes to Kick Shot and hangs out with you every weekend."

I didn't understand why Carey was attached to this. Her confusion was obvious, but one would think me bleeding in their dining room would allow a small white lie.

"Carey, this is complicated," Heath tried to say.

"You're using me to lie. I don't want to be used for a lie that doesn't make any sense. I thought people didn't lie about who they were friends with if those friends were important to them."

"You and your dad *are* important to me," I said softly. "Heath, she has to know. It's actually part of the reason I came over. Zuri figured us out."

"Figured what out? I can help keep this big secret if someone tells me what it is." When neither of us gave a reply, Carey slumped between us. "Really? I don't like this. I don't like knowing Jacky has to lie about coming over to dinner with us. Do you always do that?"

"Yes," I answered softly. "I never tell them about Heath and me hanging out away from Kick Shot, where he's technically my customer."

"Why?"

"Because we don't want them to find out Jacky and I are dating," Heath answered, keeping his eyes on the road.

Carey's eyes slowly widened. I waited as she absorbed the information.

"When did that start?" she asked, looking between us. "Tell me, when did this start?"

"Officially? My birthday last year, but we were already considering it after the werecats attacked me," I explained. "Carey, it's not smart for your dad and me to be together. People will think it a betrayal. They won't understand, so we have to keep it a secret. Your dad doesn't come to Kick Shot on Saturdays. He comes to my house and watches movies. It's...the one time we can be normal."

"So, you've been lying to me..." She was hurt. I could see how hurt she was, then she turned on her dad. "You've been using me to get to Jacky!"

"No," he growled.

"Like I should believe that. You've been lying to me for a year!"

I winced as a headache started.

"Please, stop yelling. He didn't use you, Carey. We didn't tell you because...we weren't ready."

"I bet Landon knew," she countered.

"He's an adult and a werewolf. We couldn't keep it from him," I reminded her.

She crossed her arms, huffed, and fell back, ignoring both of us.

"I just got shot at, Carey, so please forgive me if I don't have the proper sympathy for this attitude right now. He didn't use you to get to me. In fact, you accidentally brought us together, and that's just the way it is. We were planning to tell you, but the time was never right. It's not a good time right now to be talking about this."

"You've been using me as an excuse to hide it. That's the only reason you hang out with me, isn't it?" she softly whispered, refusing to look at me. The words cut me.

"No, and the fact that you would think that is more painful than anything those assholes did to me," I said in the same low whisper. "Where would you get that idea?"

She shrugged.

I looked over her at Heath, who wasn't happy with how this turned out, either.

"About Zuri," I said, deciding Carey would need time to stew. "She figured us out last year. She knew I went to you to fix me up after Lani's execution. She said she could see how you felt about me, but she's not going to tell anyone. She's, uh, decided she's going to back us up if and when we go public."

"What brought that on?" he asked, frowning. "She's not pro-werewolf."

"She's pro make her sister happy," I said, trying to smile, remembering how sweet my oldest sister had been on the video call. I couldn't tell him the full reason—the baby and the new lover—not until I had her approval, which probably wouldn't be until the baby was born. "You haven't given her a good reason to dislike you enough to try to put an end to it."

"That's good," he said, giving me a tired smile. "Now, let's focus on your amazing ability to get shot at."

Snorting, I rolled my eyes and looked away from him.

My hand throbbed painfully. Before we got in the truck, Heath made me wrap it in a towel. When we pulled up to the hospital, he and Carey stayed near me as the hand was looked at in the ER.

"It's a federal law to call the BSA when a supernatural comes into a human hospital," Heath whispered to me as we waited for the X-rays to come back. Sitting with Carey in a patient room, it was the first chance we had to speak to each other since we entered the building. "I forgot. The hospital I took wolves to in Dallas treated us special because we find it an invasion of our privacy. Seattle is the same way. Most human doctors don't agree with the rule."

"Are you saying they're going to call some BSA hotline because you came in with me?"

"Yes." Heath sighed. "Sorry."

"Well, that complicates things even more, considering I think the BSA or someone in it tried to have me killed," I growled, kicking the rolling doctor's chair across the room and into the cabinets. "Heath, a warning would have been nice."

"Would it have changed anything? You needed to come to the hospital, and the BSA already knows about you. I bet they're watching your credit card accounts. They would have seen the charge and known you were alive."

"Damn it."

He was right, but I still wanted to be mad. He let me fume, placing himself between me and Carey as if nothing was wrong. We didn't say anything more, which gave me a precious moment to calm down enough to survive the doctor when he walked in.

"It needs surgery and pins," the doctor said as he put x-rays up where we could see them.

"No metal," I said quickly. "You're going to have to figure out how to set it without all that."

"Ma'am, my best medical advice is pins—"

"I turn into a creature every full moon. I don't want metal coming out of my paws while the bones try to heal the right way. If you get it in the right way, I can Change, and the bones will begin to fuse in the right ways. If that goes wrong, I can suffer them being rebroken and trying again, but I can't do metal."

Heath stepped up closer. "Sir, we do it all the time in Dallas when a werewolf breaks a bone. There are no security cameras in here, so Jacky will be able to shift back and forth without anyone knowing it's happening. You'll be able to take more x-rays once she's back in human form to verify how it went, but the metal really can't happen."

The doctor looked at Heath, then back to me.

"You own Kick Shot, yeah? My buddies and I go there sometimes. I didn't think you were a werewolf," he said, tilting his head as if he couldn't wait to go tell everyone about this new and exciting piece of gossip.

"Doctor-patient confidentiality means none of your buddies will know, right?" I asked, glaring at him. "I hate threatening people, but if it gets out, I'll make sure you never work a day in your life."

"Of course, of course." The doctor nodded quickly, going pale.

"Don't tell any of the nurses, either," Heath ordered. "This is need to know, and they don't. You'll pull out the smallest fragments of bone, push them into alignment, then leave. Say you're letting the painkillers kick in."

"Yes, sir."

He sat down and put my hand on a rolling tray in front of him. He didn't seem comfortable, but the bleeding had slowed enough for him to work. I growled and whined as he pulled out chunks of my bone. He kept checking the X-ray, then went back to work. Once the broken bone chips were out, he gently pushed the remaining bits of my hand in the right directions, which nearly made me scream. Heath shoved the towel, once on my hand, into my mouth to bite into.

"You've got this. It hurts worse because it's silver. Do you feel any left in there?"

I shook my head. If there had been any silver left in the injuries, I would *know*. Luckily, both had been grazes.

When the doctor was done, he rolled away.

"That's all I can do," he said, pulling off his gloves. "I'll step out to give you time. Stick your head out to let me know when you're done." He left us there, and I started stripping, trying to do it with one hand. Heath came closer and helped, but when I looked at him, my face heated.

He was helping me strip in front of his daughter. Even on a normal day, this would have been strange. Today wasn't a normal day. From Landon and Dirk, then Zuri, then guns, Carey learning about us, and now this, the day was so far from normal. I wasn't sure if I could ever go back to normal. Normal seemed like a faraway hope.

I glanced at Carey to see her staring into her lap, tastefully not staring. I would bet money on Heath teaching her that at a young age. Just because it was practical for werewolves to take their clothes off didn't mean they wanted to be stared at. I was grateful Heath was a thoughtful father and Alpha, and had taught his daughter that.

Once everything was off, I backed up and pushed into the Change, whining as my wounds hurt. Everything hurt, like always, but my hand was a mess as it turned into a paw. It didn't just need to reform, it had to regrow bone and figure it out. It took me longer to Change, thanks to my hand and the lack of a dangerous imminent threat, something that usually forced me to Change as fast as possible.

There was a knock on the door as I finished.

"Who is it?" Heath called out, glaring at the door, then put his body in the way in case someone tried to open it.

"Special Agent Collins and Special Agent Miller of the BSA," Collins answered.

Heath glanced back at me.

*"Let those motherfuckers in to see what they're dealing with,"* I said using my personal form of pack magic. I moved to get out of sight, so Heath could safely open the door.

I laid down as the door opened and watched them walk in, looking around at the typical adult height of looking. It was Miller who looked down first.

I snarled as I stood.

"Holy shit!" He reached for his gun, but Heath grabbed his wrist, stopping him.

"She's Changed to heal," he said quickly. "She's just giving you a scare."

"She? That's Jacky," Collins said softly, blinking several times as I leaned closer to him and sniffed. Carey giggled softly.

"They're scared of you, Jacky."

*"Good. This is their fault."*

She laughed harder, and damn, it felt good. She had stewed in silence since she shut me out in the truck.

"What happened? We got a call you showed up with a woman and your daughter," Special Agent Collins asked, trying to look away from me to meet Heath's stare. It proved difficult. I was a very dangerous animal, taking up most of the room with my nearly five-hundred-pound, mostly muscle frame. "Why does she need to heal?"

"That's for her to tell you," Heath replied, shrugging. "I'm not getting involved with Jacky and the BSA."

"Please, you're involved with her—"

Heath grabbed Miller faster than anyone could stop him.

"My personal relationships aren't for gossip. Neither are hers," Heath warned. "You don't know a damn thing. Anything you think you might know should be forgotten and never mentioned again. Okay?"

"We won't bring it up again," Collins said, trying to get between Miller and Heath as my lover snarled at the human agent. It was hard to do because Heath had the man by his shirt with both hands. "Please understand the only people who have seen the entire footage from Jacky's property are in the room," he said softly. "We only passed along the proof that Miss Leon is supernatural."

"And wouldn't my relationship with her be evidence of that?" Heath asked, his glare still on the agent he was holding, even though his words were for Collins. I didn't move, not wanting to upset an already delicate situation. No one liked a giant saber-toothed cat walking up to them in enclosed spaces...except Carey. She trusted me in this form almost more than she did when I was in my human one.

"No. You've always had...relationships that weren't our business. Being romantic with the woman who helps you with your daughter is something we expected. There's no reason to verify it, and it doesn't change anything." Collins was trying his best, but he didn't know what Heath and I would have to deal with if they leaked it. That had to change, but I didn't want to give away everything, only the most basic of facts.

*"Tell them if anyone finds out, they're putting our lives at risk."*

Heath repeated my words in his own way, which caused eyebrows to raise. They had no idea things were hostile between werewolves and werecats. They had no reason to, something I had assumed from the beginning.

"Now, please step out, so Jacky can reenter her human form," Heath ordered.

"We'll be right outside."

"Meet us at Kick Shot," Heath corrected, growling softly as he let go of Miller with a shove into a wall. The audible thump of the human's back hitting the stone bricks made Miller wince. That had probably hurt enough to leave a bruise.

"Fine." Collins cast one last glance at me before leading his partner out.

With them gone, I flexed my paw, testing my claws. Everything looked normal. There was pain, definitely, but it was dulled in this form. I initiated the Change, quickly getting back to a form that worked better in a human hospital. I flexed and twisted my hand, not enjoying the scar.

"It works," I declared. "Something feels a little off, but I bet an X-ray will show it's just the place where it healed."

"Be gentle with it, anyway," Heath said in a whispered command as he reached for my extended, healed hand. He took it gingerly and inspected it. "Everything feels right to me. Let me get the doctor for another X-ray. The bones will still be broken, but they should be well on their way to healing the right way. You've got some scabbing, but he should be able to brace it."

"Then we can get out of here," I said.

## 20

## CHAPTER TWENTY

"This is where I drop you off," Heath said as he parked at the back of my bar. "I'll find your car and have it towed, hopefully before a cop finds it."

"Thank you. I'll need to replace it." I ran my newly healed hand over my face. "You'll see. It's bad."

"Want me to take it straight to the junkyard or bring it here?"

"Junkyard. I won't be able to get an insurance claim on it, I bet. I don't think there's coverage for assassination attempts."

"No, they don't have anything specific for that. I've asked." His sympathetic smile was almost enough to make me laugh, but the smile faded, and we were both left looking at the reality of the situation. Someone had tried to kill me. "Are you going to be okay?"

"Once I yell at these two, I should be," I promised. I was talking over a silent Carey, who was between us, trying to be unseen. I looked down at her and bumped her gently with my shoulder. "Are you going to be okay?"

"Yeah. I'm not the one who nearly died today," she mumbled. "You need to be more careful."

I didn't like hearing that from someone about to turn fourteen, but it was the same thing I was hearing from every adult I knew. From five thousand to fourteen, the advice was the same.

"I'm trying. Look, if you want to talk about your dad and me, we'll tell you everything once we have a chance—"

"Whatever," she said, shaking her head, looking down at her hands in her lap. "I don't care."

Looking up at Heath, we both knew she had lied, but neither of us was in the right headspace to call her out. I didn't have the time, and he was at a loss how. We'd have to talk much later about this situation.

There were too many people to handle—the BSA, my family, Heath, Carey, Dirk, and Zuri. I couldn't handle them all at once, and sadly, Carey was the odd one out this time. I couldn't handle any of them if I was dead.

"You should care," I finally said. "Now, I need to get inside. You two get home safe. Text me when you do, please."

"Will do," Heath swore.

I got out of the truck and waited for them to leave before heading inside, where I found Miller and Collins sitting at the bar, looking wildly out of place.

"With me," I ordered them from the back. They got up, leaving my human bartender confused. It wasn't Dirk, so he didn't know what was going on, and I intended for it to stay that way. I led the agents upstairs into my office.

"Miss Leon, please allow us—"

"Someone in your office leaked my identity and my supernatural status," I began, cutting off whatever Special Agent Collins wanted to say. "Let me be clear. This won't be tolerated, and I won't be offering any sort of information to either of you beyond this point. You'll fix this. You'll catch the leak, and you'll verify it's no longer a concern before you get to ask me for anything. Is that clear?" I waited, glaring at them from behind my desk. They were both stunned by my accusations.

"How did you come to *that* conclusion?" Miller demanded, the younger one the first to get angry, of course. "We would never put someone's life at risk by leaking their identity without a plan in place. We certainly wouldn't give it to murderers."

"Someone in your office exposed my identity to radicals or extremists who tried to kill me. They opened fire on me in my car, ran me off the road, then tried to mow me down with a rain of gunfire. I'm lucky to be alive. They made the amazing comment they didn't want my kind around. They wanted me dead. Luckily, they didn't want to chase me down when I made a run for the woods. That might have saved my life and theirs because if they had chased me down, I would have Changed and killed them. Who knows if I would have been hit by another of the fucking silver bullets they were using!" I snarled, slamming my hands on my desk. "You have a leak. There's no fucking way they learned about me otherwise. Fix this."

"We don't have a leak," Collins snapped back. "We've been in talks with our superiors for the last week, trying to get you what you wanted. We verified your position here in the United States with Alphas all over the country to make sure we could bargain with you instead of someone else. Damn it, in a couple of days, we were going to call you and finalize what we could. You're going to throw all of that—"

"Yes," I hissed. "Someone is trying to kill me or get me killed, and there's not a good explanation for it right now except you two or someone you work with. Until that threat is over, I can't bargain with either of you. Sorry, but I won't be in the weakened position of *trying to stay alive* when making important decisions for my kind. These things have a priority list and *not dying* tends to be at the top."

*Most of the time.*

"We'll fix this," Collins said as he walked back and grabbed the doorknob. "We'll fix this. We'll figure out who is actually trying to kill you. Maybe then, you'll believe us. The BSA didn't do this."

"Sure it didn't," I growled, letting sarcasm drip like acid. "But when you find the leak in your organization, make sure you let them know one thing."

"What would that be?" Miller crossed his arms, his offended glare making me scoff.

"That you aren't dealing with werewolves. You're dealing with their bigger, meaner cousin. If you think I'm big, I know a couple of werecats who hit nine hundred pounds, and they're furious about this."

Both men paled.

"We'll fix this," Collins promised again, his voice losing some of its power.

"Do that," I snapped, then watched them storm out of the office.

Once they were gone, I lost the power that had been keeping me going. I didn't do well with the alone thing. Sinking into my chair, I hit a name on my contacts, starting a video call with anyone in the family willing to pick up. Since the two humans never got the chance to sit down, I didn't concern myself with the possibility of listening devices.

Niko joined the call, so I canceled the others before they picked up. I was just looking for someone to talk to, not a full family meeting.

"Hasan told everyone what happened," he said, looking at me with a worried expression. "Is there something you need? Do you not want the family?"

"I just want someone to talk to," I admitted. "About anything."

"Ah." He had sympathy for me. "How's the hand?"

I lifted it and moved my fingers, showing off the brace and wincing in the process. "Not good as new, but it works. Thank goodness I'm not an artist. It'll heal just as expected."

"It'll change your penmanship," he said as though he was offering some known advice. It was odd he decided to talk about the broken bones and not the BSA agents or the humans that attacked me. "I've broken each of my hands in the last eight hundred years. It's probably the most annoying area of the body to break."

"Does that include your back?" I asked, tilting my head to the side as I tried to understand his priorities.

"Uh...no," he stated, chuckling. "No, that one was worse, but I had the hospital. Hands are more annoying to me than arms and legs. I need my hands, and they heal wrong so easily." He lifted his left hand to show me something I'd never noticed. The knuckles seemed out of place. As he showed me, Hasan got on the call but remained silent. "Broke this one about twenty years after I was Changed. So long ago, it wasn't well known how to set bones right. There's no fixing it now, and it took me a decade of practicing my penmanship to get back to where I was."

"Ouch." I didn't like the look of that. "I should tell you about the BSA agents and what happened. I should also give someone a report about the attack on me."

Niko chuckled sadly. "Take a moment and breathe, sister. Gossip about the sad family dramas for a moment, or just tell me how you feel and ignore the bigger problem. I was trying to give you a break since you said you just wanted to talk. You seem tired, and your office is disgusting."

*Fuck, I still haven't cleaned it up.*

"He's right," Hasan added. "Take a moment to just breathe, Jacqueline."

"I actually called right after I threw the agents out, and it is important. I told them there wasn't going to be any negotiating until I figured out who leaked my identity. But...taking a break is nice," I agreed. "I was nearly killed today," I whispered, letting it sink in and grew vulnerable. "Again. In my own fucking territory." I covered my face and leaned over. "What am I doing wrong? Why can't I have a normal life again?"

"Because you want to do what's right for everyone,

and we live in a world that doesn't openly reward that behavior. In fact, many punish it," Hasan said gently. "Are you okay?"

I blinked back tears as the pressure left my shoulders for a moment, hearing those words.

"No," I answered honestly but couldn't tell them all the reasons why. "How can I be okay?" I looked up at the monitor.

"If I had the answer, I'd give it to you. You know you can talk to any of us privately if you need to let go of any frustrations. You also know I would be there in a second if it was the right decision, something you fought." He shifted in his seat and leaned back, getting more comfortable. He was right. "As for the problems you are facing, this family is facing…you made the right decision with the agents."

"That's good. I could always call them back. They're obviously staying in the area to keep close to me. I wish I knew where—"

"I'll have Davor look into it. Their names?" Hasan grabbed a notepad and pen.

"Special Agent Collins and Miller. No first names. I never asked."

"We'll find them," Niko promised.

"I'm going to jump off, then," I decided. "That's all I have, so…"

"Stay for a moment, please," Hasan said quietly. "Good night, Niko."

"Clean that office," Niko said, giving me a sympathetic look.

Hasan didn't speak again until Niko disconnected. I

looked at him, knowing I was a mess. My clothes were torn and dirty, and I probably had dark bags under my eyes from lack of sleep. He obviously wanted to say something.

"I don't want to lose another daughter," the old male whispered. "Please tell us when you need us. We're supporting you in every way we can, but we're not there to keep you alive."

"If I have anything to say about it, you won't. I'm not in the mood to die, but I am in the mood to take a long nap." I sighed, knowing my sad attempt at humor failed. "You're upset with me, aren't you?"

He didn't answer for a long time, studying me. Hasan was good at choosing his words carefully.

"I was," he admitted. "When I learned what happened, as you explained it, I was upset. Right now… I'm beyond that. Upset is a natural response but also reactionary and not productive. I would have been upset with any of your siblings if they had done anything you have done, and it led here. But I sat back and thought about it. We live in different times. Once, supernaturals lived openly because humans couldn't stand up to us. Then they were able to fight back, and we retreated. Maybe it is time for us to find peace through all species, human and supernatural. I let myself and my children be led to war against the werewolves on multiple occasions, even though I've fought for a truce most of my life. Humans are the next largest threat to our kind, and this could be a good first step, even if it came without me controlling it."

"So, instead of being upset, you found a way for this

to be useful." That sure did a lot to make me feel better—not.

"It's easy to be upset the moment something happens. It's a failing I will probably display in the future, but it's not the correct response. I thought I should stop being upset with you for being you," he said softly. "This is you. You save people and fight for what you believe in. And like all my children, I need an adjustment period to come to terms with who you are." His wry smile was one I had seen before.

"You should ask Zuri and Jabari about their youth. Against my wishes and the wishes of their mother, they ruled a continent. Or you should ask Mischa about when she went rogue and how angry I was. Or when I learned Hisao was acting alone and training new assassins in the process, something I had expressly told him not to do because I didn't want him training someone who could one day return to kill *him*. It ended up being his calling. You are just the most recent in a long line of children doing things I wished they wouldn't." He rubbed his jaw. "These are what humans would call growing pains, and our family goes through this with every new family member. In the end, if you live through these things and you're happy, I will survive, and so will your siblings. Besides, you've proven to have solid judgment."

"I feel terrible, you know. I never wanted to expose werecats. That wasn't something I dreamed I would ever do."

"Would you go back and do anything differently?"

"No," I said quickly, the answer easy.

I yawned, exhaustion catching up with me from the emotional and physical toll of the day.

"And that, my dear daughter, is why I stopped being upset." He took a sip of a drink. "Now, you should rest. You've had a long day."

I clicked the disconnect and sighed, leaning back in my chair. A nap sounded good. The bar was still open below me, people around and having a good time.

I yawned, then I was out.

## CHAPTER TWENTY-ONE

I woke up, gasping, looking around my dark office wildly for some sort of danger. A moment later, I realized there was nothing there, then groaned as I leaned over my desk again. I'd woken up with a headache, my head throbbing in pain.

*I should have drunk some water. Stupid.*

I checked the time and groaned. It was three in the morning. I was still tired, and the bar had been closed for three hours.

*What woke me up? The dehydration headache?*

I got up slowly and stretched, yawning again as I tried to make a plan of action. Stress and dehydration were problems one and two. The fact I was so tired was problem number three.

*Nothing I can do about the stress. Water, ibuprofen, then back to sleep, I guess.*

I headed downstairs, another yawn punctuating the situation. I was at the bottom of the staircase when warning bells went off in my head, and paranoia hit.

*What woke me up? I had woken up in a panic. Why?*

The bar was dark and quiet. I sniffed the air and frowned. Kick Shot was one of the worst places for my nose—too many scents of alcohol, food, cleaner, and the patrons who had been there during the evening before.

I walked slowly into the kitchen, hoping to get the glass of water I wanted, then lock myself back in my office. I found a clean glass and turned on the tap. The running water was loud, making my head pound harder.

Something creaked and made me turn slightly, angling myself to hear the noise better if it happened again. My hearing was so sensitive in the quiet night, I could hear the water in the pipes and the night breeze hitting the trees. One of the first things I had to learn as a werecat was how to tune out the background noise and find the important sounds. It wasn't something I worried about anymore, naturally focusing on noises out of place. Normally, a building creak wasn't something I worried about—if I did, I would never sleep again—but Kick Shot was a new building now. The creaks of an old home simply didn't happen in my bar.

Another creak, so soft it would have been drowned out by any other noise. A human wouldn't hear it, and usually, I wouldn't either.

I looked at my glass, then turned off the water, turning slowly toward the open kitchen door to the rest of the bar. Softly putting the glass on the metal table in the center of the room, I moved toward the open door. I grabbed a knife as I walked, listening to the soft shing of metal as it was pulled from the knife block.

When I entered the bar, I was able to see perfectly

well. There was no one there. I turned on the lights, letting my eyes adjust to that light. Even though I could see in the dark, having the lights on made me feel safer.

*I'm just on edge.*

There was no one in the bar, no one outside the bar, no cars suspiciously parked out front. I was completely alone.

Going back into the kitchen, I grabbed my water, turning the lights off as I headed back upstairs. I wasn't tired anymore. I was wide awake, my heart pounding as I tried to shake the feeling I was in danger, but I wasn't, not at that exact moment. I went into my office and locked the door, frustrated my feeling of security didn't come back.

*This is werecat paranoia. This is what we are. I just need...*

I put the glass down before I threw it in anger. I would have felt safe in my own home, but I couldn't anymore.

*I've dealt with attacks at home before. Why is this such a problem? Why does this one freak me out more than the attack last year by the rogues? Is it because rogues are a normal problem and humans aren't? I don't fucking know!*

My hands were shaking as I sat down.

*I need to get over this. I can't live paranoid and afraid of who might be watching. They know what I am now, so it's not like it can get much worse.*

I drank my water as soon as my hands stopped shaking enough to hold the glass. I drank every drop and knew I needed more, but the idea of walking out of my office again *terrified* me.

Wanting to feel safe, I stripped and Changed, entering my werecat form. I was powerful, and the new building was built to accommodate my size, so I could fight back if anyone tried to come for me. I didn't get back to sleep, though. Lying down, my eyes refused to close. I stared at the door all night, waiting for the sunlight to enter my window again. I listened to every creak, every odd noise, things I normally blocked out, but I was too hyper aware to sleep.

It was a long few hours, but when the sun came up, I stood, Changed back into my human form, then put my clothes back on, even the brace for my hand, though another Change had helped it heal even further. Better safe than sorry. I knew I needed a shower and a change of clothes, so I walked back home, enjoying the sunrise.

*I can't live like this. I won't live like this.*

When I walked into my bathroom, I caught myself in the mirror and realized I looked haunted.

*This was the face everyone had to see yesterday? Wow.*

I was a mess, even if I didn't look injured anymore. Changing sped up the healing process, so there was only minor bruising left, but Changing didn't fix my clothing, the exhaustion, or pretty much any of the mental issues causing my eyes to remain gold.

*A shower will fix some of this.*

Showering washed off the dried blood and dirt I should have dealt with the night before. It was enough to help me feel more awake as I put on clean clothes.

As I went back downstairs, I realized this was the first time I had been in my house alone since I broke down at Heath's home. I wasn't nearly close to that now, but I was still edgy. It was something to take pride in, though. The initial shock was gone, and Heath had supported me for over a week, but I was back in my house without anyone watching my back.

*Still paranoid as hell, but an improvement for sure. I'll take what I can get.*

I took a moment to make coffee, knowing I was going to need the boost to make it through the day. Looking out my large windows at my trees as I sipped the first piping hot taste of much-needed caffeine, I took solace that I wouldn't actually lose this view. Sure, I was going to get a driveway, but Heath was making sure it was out of sight of my big windows. I was getting a fence, but it was going to be barbed wire in the surrounding forest, not a large wall around my house.

In reality, very little was going to change. He and Dirk had looked out for me when it came to the security changes. I would get a new security hub in my house as well, but that was happening last, once they figured out how to wire everything or if it needed to run off wifi. I preferred a hardline because wifi could be hijacked.

*It's not so bad. I'll survive.*

The thought made me feel better, something I desperately needed. Just being in my favorite place, watching my trees, made me feel better. I knew no one was watching me, and if anyone attacked me here, I was fully able to do with them what I pleased.

*Maybe tonight, I'll come home.*

I finished my coffee and put the mug in the sink, then spent an hour wiping my kitchen down and dusting around the house, keeping my space nice. Even though I was trying to do better, there was still a moment, as I stood alone on the stairs, the worry came back. Was someone watching me? Dirk didn't sweep the woods for people, and I hadn't been out there in over a week. The contractors had been working on the upgrades, but not me.

*No. Finish cleaning, then go into the woods. Or just don't. What are they going to see? Me drinking coffee and cleaning the house.*

I vacuumed and mopped the different floors next, reorganized my movie and book collection, then found the book I never finished on the coffee table. Picking it up slowly, I stared at the cover. This was the last normal thing I had done—reading a book on a lazy Sunday before a full moon.

Keeping the book with me, I walked out of my home, leaving it spotless. I was still in a cleaning mood, the drive to get back to normal, even though the paranoia followed my every step. I went back to Kick Shot and cleaned my office, took out the trash, then grabbed the laundry. I was going to have to walk back to my house, and that was exactly what I did. I even put it in the washing machine and started the load.

*Someone tried to kill me yesterday. If I let them take my normal life away from me, they win. No different from the rogues. I kept living my normal life then, even with the paranoia. No different at all.*

It was different. I knew it was. I could feel the werecats, knew they were there, knew what they were doing the moment they tried to enter my territory. This time, I was up against humans—weaker, fragile, mortal, but they could hide. I had no idea where they were inside my territory or when they would strike again. The werecats couldn't sneak up on me, but the humans had already proven not once, but twice, they could. First, the BSA, then the fanatics trying to kill me.

By the time I got back to the bar, I'd made the decision to walk around to the front. I wasn't sure where the urge came from, but remembering the startled way I woke up and the paranoia still haunting my every step, I wanted to look around.

Nothing seemed unusual until I caught the scent of spray paint as I rounded the corner to see the front of the building. I started walking faster and saw the message spray-painted on the door.

DIE FREAK.

I didn't scream or freak out. I calmly took my phone out of my pocket and took a picture, sending it to Heath, Dirk, and Landon first, then to my entire family in a separate message.

This was what must have woken me. I could feel it. I had slept through whoever did it, but the headache might have distracted me from hearing them drive off. Even if I had heard them, I would have thought they were just driving down the highway that early in the morning.

They were smart, putting it on the door, not a window where I would have seen it coming downstairs.

My phone buzzed repeatedly in my hand.

**Heath:** I'm on my way over.

**Landon:** Bringing Dirk back. We'll clean this up and check for fingerprints.

**Jabari:** They're blustering because they know you survived yesterday. Common tactic to keep you scared. Don't fall for it.

I put my phone away and went inside, sitting at the bar with the front door open to see the message. The only reason I wasn't scared was something didn't make sense.

If they wanted me afraid, they should have sent this message before they tried to kill me. This was just overkill. The puzzle pieces didn't fit, but I couldn't do anything about it.

I waited until Heath parked in front of the bar. He looked at the message as he came in.

"Odd that they wrote this after they destroyed your car and tried to kill you. Their motives are already pretty obvious," he mentioned softly, leaning down to get an even better look at it.

"I was just thinking the same thing," I said, sipping on water I served myself. I didn't need the headache coming back. "But you know, idiots."

"Idiots is the simplest solution."

"Jabari said it's bluster because they know I survived yesterday."

"Also a firm possibility," Heath agreed. When he looked up at me, he smiled, showing the same lack of concern I was feeling. "You look good, healthy even. Been a while since I've seen that."

"I took a shower and cleaned my house," I said, chuckling. "Decided living in my office wasn't doing my mental health any favors."

"I was going to give you another week. I considered saying something yesterday, but then you were attacked, and it didn't seem like the right time." He came closer and grabbed my knee. We were alone, and I enjoyed when his hand went from my knee to my thigh slowly, testing the waters. We never fooled around in the bar, but he seemed excited to see me looking more like normal.

"I'm glad you reconsidered being an Alpha," I teased.

"Never an Alpha." he reminded me softly, then pulled his hand away and put both in his pockets. It was the easiest way for us to keep our hands off each other in a public space. "Are you waiting on Landon and Dirk?"

"Yeah," I confirmed, taking another sip of my water. "I know you don't want to give me advice about my situation with the BSA, especially not specifics about negotiating with them, but I threw them out yesterday. I think they're the leak. You agree about that, right?"

He frowned, looking away, working through the situation in his head. Then he shrugged.

"It's a strong possibility. There are other options, but..." He shook his head. "I don't see how the pieces fit for those. You've made enemies among the werewolves, you know."

"Obviously," I said, chuckling. "That's not a surprise."

"But no werewolf I know would give your information to human fanatics to kill you. If someone in the supernatural world wanted you dead that badly, they would hire a professional. Hisao isn't the only assassin in the world, and you aren't an ancient with thousands of years of experience. It wouldn't be hard for someone to take you out. The only thing you have going for you is your territorial magic, which would give away an assassin before they made it here. They would have to try to catch you outside your territory, which means even more planning. The most logical solution is the BSA has a leak, and now extremists have your information."

"So, I shouldn't bargain with them until they fix this leak."

"I don't know," he said honestly. "My situation with them was much different than yours. I don't know how willing they are to play hardball because you shut down negotiations."

"My family thinks I did the right thing." I put my water down and leaned on my hands. "And I think I did the right thing, but I'm not sure. I threw them out because I was angry, but was it really the best decision?"

Heath sat next to me, leaning on his hands as well, matching my pose.

"Only time will tell. Now, my favorite bartender, care to get me a drink?"

Laughing, I got up, but the only reason I did it was he called me his favorite bartender. It was as though we were back to those initial strange Saturday nights, with me behind the bar and him trying to know the woman his daughter trusted so easily. Two people, practically strangers, trying to understand each other and build a newfound friendship, even though the world didn't want us to.

As I poured him a soda, I thought about the pieces at play—me and my family. I was the defender now. I knew I would be physically safe if I called them here, but then the entire ruling family of the werecats would be exposed to the BSA, something no one was comfortable with. I had Heath, Dirk, and Landon as my help here, along with Oliver to an extent, but I wanted to keep him out of danger. I also had the BSA agents.

When I put Heath's drink in front of him, he said something that took my mind off the BSA agents.

"Carey yelled at me last night," he said softly. "About us."

I sighed heavily. "How mad is she?"

"She just yelled. Said it was wrong for us to keep something like this from her for so long. I don't think that's all that hurt her, though. There's something deeply wrong, and I can't force her to tell me. I took it last night, then fired back with the fact that you and I are adults. We don't answer to a thirteen-year-old girl."

That made me wince. Not exactly the softest way for a father to deescalate a fight, even if he was right. We didn't answer to a thirteen-year-old girl, and her fourteenth birthday wasn't going to change the fact she didn't get to control our relationship.

"I...don't know what I would have said, either," I admitted. "She's so mad. I get she should have known sooner, but it puts her in the position to lie for us, and she was never supposed to have to."

"Yeah, we really screwed this one up," he agreed. "Danger at home tends to bring these things into the open. The fact only Zuri and Carey know, through all of this, is astounding."

"The BSA knows," I reminded him. That was dangerous enough.

He nodded, going quiet. Neither of us was in the right headspace to also deal with Carey. It was the anger of a teenage girl or the rage of two species and people trying to kill me.

*I hate putting her on the back burner. I hate it so much.*

"Let's take her out today. Get her out of class and take her somewhere," I said, crossing my arms with a nod. "Once this is cleaned up, we can slip away and bowl when there's no one around or go paintballing...anything. Well, maybe the movies since I have this." I lifted my brace.

"I like that idea. She's been feeling left out, and I don't know how to get through this bumpy patch. I really don't." Heath finished his soda.

"We'll get through it together," I promised. "There hasn't yet been a situation you and I haven't been able to get through, and most of them were a lot more dangerous than a human teenager."

His laugh was like music and the perfect balm to my soul after the rough week and a half I had lived through.

## CHAPTER TWENTY-TWO

Landon and Dirk showed up like bats out of hell, screaming into the parking lot and jumping from the truck as if they were ready for war. Heath and I greeted them with simple waves, forcing them to slow down.

"I figured we would be dealing with more...hysterics," Landon said, his nostrils flaring as he looked at me, then the door.

"Yesterday, someone tried to kill me, so..." I shrugged innocently, realizing I had never told Dirk or Landon what had happened.

Heath chuckled as both of them paled. Obviously, Heath hadn't reached out to his son, either.

"You were away, and I knew you two were safe. There was no reason to bother you," Heath said, still chuckling. "As you can see, she's fine. Carey and I are fine. This is just a new development in the new situation. Go about your business. Jacky and I are going to take Carey out for a bit of fun today because she's furious with us."

"I need more explanation than that," Landon growled.

I chuckled this time and explained how the attack went down. Dirk's eyes went wider, but Landon nodded wisely.

"You handled that right. Good job."

"I'm so glad I have your approval," I said, smiling. "You can tell Dirk all about how I did the right thing as a lesson. We're going to go. Get the fingerprints, then scrub that off before the opening shift gets here."

"We got it," Dirk promised. "Just, uh, don't get killed. Are you sure this is safe if you were attacked yesterday?"

"My father wouldn't go anywhere with Carey if he didn't think it was safe," Landon said stiffly. "He's not a fool, right?" He looked at his father.

"I think they were tracking Jacky, but if they fuck with me or Carey, they've got every werewolf in the United States after them. I think we're the best shield she has right now."

"And not dying? That is number one on the priorities list," I told him, patting Dirk's arm. "I talked to Niko last night. Nothing important, nothing about you. He didn't even ask, but I bet he wanted to. Just felt like I should tell you."

"I'll give him a call to tell him I'm okay," Dirk replied, sighing. "He's probably expecting it."

"Probably."

"We'll keep in touch," Heath promised. "Stick together?"

"We will," Landon agreed, already heading for my door with a bag in his hands.

Heath and I got into his truck together.

"I need to buy a new car," I pointed out. "Can we get that done before we pick up Carey? Shouldn't take too long."

He started to laugh and didn't stop until we were nearly at Carey's school. He was still chuckling softly as he parked.

"The joke must have gone over my head," I muttered.

That made him laugh harder, but he didn't get out of the truck yet. When the laughter finally subsided, he turned to me with a grin I could only describe as absolutely devious.

"You need to buy a new car, and you think it won't take too long?" he asked. "With me there with you? I might not try to be your Alpha, but let's be honest about something." He leaned over the center seat of his truck, inching closer. "If I go with you to buy a new vehicle of any kind, I'm going to do my damnedest to make sure you get the safest, most advanced thing I can find on the lot. Then I'm going to drive it and your happy ass to my guy in Dallas to have a roll cage added and a bit of his fae magic. I won't be able to help myself, Jacky."

"So...I'm buying a new car without you." *Decision made, then.* "Good to know."

"If you value your sanity, absolutely go without me." He smiled. "But please try to get something safe."

"I'll consider it." I had no intention of telling him what sort of car I was going to get. I was going to buy it without his Alpha ways influencing my decision.

He huffed, rolled his eyes, then got out of the truck. I waited for him. Carey would have only been at school a couple of hours, maybe not even that, so it was a pretty strange morning. When they walked out, Carey was frowning at the truck, but she didn't see me yet. As they got closer, I saw her expression change to downright brewing anger. I knew the look. Her father got it when he was pissed off. She threw her bag into the back as Heath opened the door and held it for her.

"What are *you* doing here? I want to go back to class." She didn't get in, glaring at her father and me. The question was for me, but the demand to go back into the school was definitely for Heath. He didn't say anything, a stone wall to her anger.

"We're taking you out for the day," I said. "Just the three of us, to talk this out. I don't want to put you on the back burner, Carey. I want to make sure you know we didn't mean to hurt you. Things happened, and hurting you was an accident. Give us a chance to talk to you. Plus, you get to skip school."

She got in the truck and sat in the middle, pulling on her seat belt in silence. Heath got in last, and we left the school with the cranky teenager.

"Someone tried to kill me yesterday—" I reminded her.

"And you're fine," she fired back. This was the dramatic antics of a betrayed young teenager. Her priorities were all messed up, but I didn't hold it against her. I continued with what I was saying.

"Which makes it all the more important I make sure you know you can still trust me with anything. That I trust you and respect you."

"Really?" she snapped. "Trust? You've been lying to

me!" She put her feet up on the dashboard. I knew that wasn't going to play out well. Heath didn't take his eyes off the road, just reached out without even glancing in her direction, grabbed one ankle, pulled the foot off the dash, and pushed it down back to where it was supposed to be. He didn't have to do the second; she put that one down on her own.

"Can we please be civil?" Heath asked desperately. "Be mad but be civil. I can take the anger, but that doesn't mean you get to act out and break the rules." At her huff, he growled, low and soft. "We're not trying to invalidate your feelings. We're trying to apologize."

Carey looked down. We spent the drive in complete silence. I was frustrated and hurt, but I knew she was justified to feel the way she did. Heath was right. We didn't want to invalidate her feelings. We wanted to apologize and get to the root of them. Heath said this was pretty extreme, and he was right. It was one thing to be upset, but this was fury, something neither of us expected. Even when we had talked about telling her, we hadn't expected this level of anger at us.

Heath drove us not to something active but to the movies.

"We can catch something early, and no one will have to talk to anyone. I'll get the tickets," he declared, parking. He got out, ignoring both of us, his frustration clearer than the sun. Carey grabbed my arm, a clear sign for me to stay where I was.

"We can do something else. I just wanted to spend some time with you before work and—"

"My entire life, there were women from the pack who

wanted to be my friend to get to my dad," she whispered. "They would help me with my homework and offer to babysit me. They would tell my brothers to go off and have fun, that they would watch me. They would be really nice to start, but then it always happened the same way. My dad wouldn't give them the time of day, wouldn't let them stay for dinner, told them no when they offered to join us on family trips, and there were a couple he threw out of the house. Finally, he asked me to tell him when any of the women were being *too* nice to me. He didn't want to see me used by them to get to him. I didn't think you would be one of them."

"Carey..." *Oh, shit.* "I'm not like that. I know you probably don't believe me, but what I have with your dad doesn't change what I have with you. It wasn't even supposed to happen this way. I didn't think your dad and I would get close, much less become friends."

She sighed, heavy and beyond her years. It was easy to forget Carey wasn't a normal thirteen-year-old about to turn fourteen. This was the daughter of a werewolf Alpha who had lived for a couple hundred years, who had complicated brothers and a family that needed her to help protect it. This was the girl who ran away from home to get away from the pack coup, found her way to my bar like her dad had planned, and knew what to say, even though she was tired and terrified. Even though she didn't know who I was.

"I don't think you are, either," she admitted softly. "I think my dad used me to get to you or something. I think..." She threw her hands up. "I don't even know who to be mad at. You both lied to me. You've been using me to be together. I want my dad happy, and I want you happy, but I'm mad. I'm mad because you didn't tell me. It reminds me of those women who never told me they were nice to me because they wanted to get my dad. Because he's the *Alpha*, he's important, because they thought he would buy them nice things and give them something special or whatever."

"We didn't use you. Feel free to be angry with us for lying to you, but neither of us intentionally used you to get to each other. We did a lot of traveling together. We nearly died a couple of times, and when everything got bad, he was the one person I knew could handle me leaning on him. But using you never crossed my mind or his."

"Really? I mean…I guess you did go to Russia together, and he helped save you from those bad werecats…and you helped him save me….and the vampires…" She trailed off and nodded. "Yeah, that makes sense."

"Maybe you should tell your dad all of this, too, so he understands."

"He's not easy to talk to, sometimes," she mumbled. "And like, I knew something had to be going on. He's seemed happier. And he goes to you for advice about me, which I don't like, but it's whatever. He's a guy, and I'm a girl. I hear other girls get embarrassed by their dads, too. Apparently, that's a normal thing. I was really happy you took me to the store and not him, and neither of you gave me 'the talk' about you know what." She shrugged. "Maybe I just don't like how you lied. Were you going to tell me before you got married, or was that going to be a surprise, too?"

"We were going to tell you...eventually," I said, unable to really answer. "I can tell you that your dad and I have never talked about marriage. Right now, we're just trying to find a way to be together without getting in trouble." I took off my seatbelt and sighed. "Ready to follow him? He probably has the tickets now."

"Yeah..." She undid her seatbelt next.

I opened the door and stepped out, stretching my arms over my head, feeling much better about everything.

I got out of the truck and felt the gunshot before I heard it. It sent me back into the door, and I purposefully threw myself back to fall into the truck. Carey started screaming as she grabbed my shirt. I knew I was bleeding, but I did my best to stay down and push her away.

"Pretend I'm dead," I fought to say through the pain. "Pretend I'm dead." I looked down, knowing the windows were too dark for anyone to see inside. They hit me in the side. I tried to breathe and thanked my lucky stars that nothing sounded like it was in my lungs. It hit my abdomen in the side, which hopefully meant my lung was safe.

Heath appeared at my feet, his face sheet white. In the background, tires squealing got his attention for a second.

"Gone?" I asked softly. There was so much I needed to say. "Don't tell my family. Get Carey home. Keep Dirk safe."

"They're gone. Let's get you to the hospital—"

"I can help," someone said, running up. I saw Collins come into view next to him. "I've been doing a stakeout on you but didn't notice anyone else watching you until it was too late." He was looking down at me, at the injury, but his words were clear and precise. He didn't let the injury shock him.

"That sounds incredibly suspicious, *Daniel*," Heath snarled.

"I got the license plate of the truck that just drove off, *Heath*," Collins snapped back. "And I can get her airlifted."

Heath looked at me, and I nodded.

"S-Silver," I groaned, clutching my side. The burn was beginning to set in. A bad gut shot was fatal upward to twenty minutes if the bleeding wasn't too bad. That meant the silver had time to settle into my bloodstream and cause problems.

"Shit." Heath pointed to the back of his truck. "There's a first aid kit in the back. Get it, Daniel. Jacky, we don't have time to send you to Mygi. I'm going to ask for them to take you to Dallas, okay? If you can make it, I want you at Dallas."

I tried to nod. Carey was crying over me.

*I've been here before. She's seen me die before. I can't...I can't do this to her again.*

"Keep your eyes on me, okay?" Heath asked.

I tried. I tried so hard. Collins was gone from my sight, and all I had to do was stare at Heath and his blue-grey eyes. That was all I had to do.

I failed.

## CHAPTER TWENTY-THREE

I woke up to beeping machines. I tried to sit up, but there were so many tubes, and my throat burned thanks to one. There were also straps on my wrists. I fought against them, trying to scream. The beeping grew faster, and people rushed into the room. They worked around me, and the world went black again.

The second time I woke up, the situation was similar.

"You know you need to dose her more often!" Heath's roar broke through everything. "Give her something that will actually put her out!"

The third time, there was no tube in my throat, and I was able to gasp for breath. I tried to sit up, and this time, there were no straps. I tried to look around, but the world was hazy.

What I did see was Heath, coming quickly to my bedside.

"Can't even keep you out for twenty-four hours," he said, sighing heavily. "They got the bullet out, and you got fucking lucky. It could have punctured a lung or torn up your liver. As it stands, it caused internal and external bleeding, but your organs made it out, unscathed, mostly. Your liver was nicked. They also treated you for silver poisoning. It should nullify the effects and let you Change, so you can speed up the healing."

"No broken bones that need to be set?" I asked.

"Nope," he answered, snappy with me.

"You seem mad," I commented as I moved slowly, letting my legs fall over the side of the bed. "I'm sorry Carey was there to see it."

"She told me you ordered her to...pretend like you died." He rushed to my side to help me up. "You Change, and I'll explain why I'm angry."

"Okay," I murmured. I undid the tie of the hospital gown and started pushing through the Change.

"I'm mad because once they got you into surgery, someone called the pack to tell them I had come by with a woman. They violated your doctor-patient confidentiality, and I had to square off with my old pack. That's not your fault. I told you I was bringing you here and should have expected the staff would rat me out. I didn't expect them to rat *you* out."

I was nearly a werecat by the time he was done talking. With nothing out of place, the Change was just fucking painful, but Heath was right about the silver.

I didn't spend long in my werecat form, going back to my human form as he continued to talk.

"Dirk, Landon, and Carey are at my house. Special Agent Collins was able to explain exactly what he was doing, and I'll vouch for him. He wasn't lying to me. He was following you to see if another attack would happen. He'd picked us up as we left Carey's school. He stopped across the street from the movie theater, just to keep an eye on us. It wasn't malicious or him trying to get your secrets. He was focused on making sure we wouldn't be attacked, and if we were, hopefully catching the men who did it."

"Well, he failed," I growled, my mouth still a little too inhuman to soften my words. I finished the Change and stretched before crumpling over in pain. "Stupid of me. Damn it. My insides hurt."

"Your liver wasn't directly hit, but it was nicked, remember?" Heath helped me sit down. "And there's the problem of having been shot. How can you forget about that?"

"Sorry, it's been a while," I snapped, but I wasn't angry at him. I was mad at me. As I sat back down on the edge of the bed, I knew I should take a week to properly heal, at least.

I didn't have a week. These guys wanted me dead.

"I don't care about the Dallas pack," I said, feeling overwhelming sadness hit me. "I told Carey to pretend I was dead, so the guys didn't come closer and try to take another shot. If I stopped moving and she kept screaming, they would leave. Collins showing up probably helped chase them off as well."

"Quick thinking." He sat next to me and took my hand. "But it terrified me. I was waiting in the theater. When I got out of the truck, I knew you two were going to talk, and I didn't want to interfere. She told me everything over the phone while I waited for you to get out of surgery. I saw you go down, then heard her scream, and I thought..." He brought my hand up to his lips and kissed it so gently. "I thought you were dead, and she had to watch you die."

"It's happened before," I whispered. "Last time, she screamed as I hit the pavement. Apparently, that time I flatlined and that fae and his wife brought me back. They were able to stop the bleeding, pull the silver out, and save my life."

"That fae..." He brushed my hair out of my face. "Have you ever gone looking for him to thank him?"

"I didn't look particularly hard, no," I answered. "Brin isn't the discussion, though."

"Brin?" Heath frowned. "Is that his name?"

I put a hand over his mouth. "Please, forget I said that. We have more important things to work on. I know I was shot, but we need to find these guys and put an end to their bullshit, so I can work with the BSA and resolve that situation. Hopefully, we'll figure out who the leak is." I dropped my hand. "Tell me what...Daniel said." I raised an eyebrow.

"Yeah, we used to be on a first-name basis, just to bug each other. I started it, and he fired back. He explained his partner, Miller, while he was tailing me, was working on finding out if there was any movement among the extremist groups the United States is tracking. I haven't heard back yet, but hopefully, they find something."

"Miller used to be CIA. They don't know I know that. I heard one of them mention it outside of Kick Shot."

"What do you think is your next move? At this point, I'll back you up, no matter what. I'm not fond of watching you get shot."

"I'm going to work with those two," I said, rubbing my hands together as I thought about it. "I'll tell them everything. They helped me. I still think one of their superiors is the leak. Hell, maybe it's Miller, but if I'm working with them, I can keep a close eye on them. I'll keep Dirk with me—"

"Landon and I aren't going to let you do this alone, so go ahead and put us in your plans, please." Heath's face was unmoving and unreadable, but his scent told me how angry and scared he had been. He would fight to help me now, and I knew I needed the backup.

"I wasn't going to leave you out," I promised. "They shot me in front of Carey. What if they had hit her?"

"I've already thought about that," he growled. "They need a reminder that supernaturals don't care what they think. They'll die if they hurt one of ours."

"Just what I was thinking. Let's get me out of this damn hospital and back to Jacksonville. I don't know how good I'm going to be in a fight, but maybe...maybe I can be the bait."

"Stupid but effective. I hate it, but I don't really see us finding them another way unless someone gets back to us on who these humans might be." He shook his head. "I can't believe I'm actually agreeing with this."

"Yeah, it happens sometimes. If we find another way, I'm more than willing to go for it, just as long as I get to talk to these people before anyone else. I want to know exactly who told them about me from their own lips. Can you help me make sure that happens?"

"I'll make sure, even if I have to tie those agents down for you to interrogate."

"Thank you."

He grabbed his bag from the recliner and dropped it on the bed.

"A change of clothes. Keep the bandaging on, please. You still have a hole in you that's trying to close."

"Yeah, I know," I said, smiling. Opening his bag, I found a comfortable pair of sweats and a t-shirt, nothing that could pinch or squeeze where I had been hit. "I can't believe those guys took a shot at me with a rifle."

"They can't be professionals," Heath said, sighing as he shook his head. "Thugs who may have never killed someone before or just idiots that own rifles. This is Texas. There are a lot of hunters."

"They had…" I frowned, trying to think of the best way to describe the guns they used when they ran me off the road. "Assault rifles. Like you see in movies."

"You need an education on that, don't you?" He chuckled. "Selective-fire rifles. If you don't know the type they had, that's fine. That doesn't really narrow down what we're looking for. Everyone and their grandmother own a needlessly powerful gun in this country."

"Yeah, but I didn't take you as someone who would find that a bad thing." I raised an eyebrow.

"I come from the era of muskets and cannons. We couldn't fire nearly 950 rounds in a minute. It took up to thirty seconds for us to reload our single shot. I find it excessive, that's all. It's not the people I don't like but the weapons themselves." He shrugged. "I don't like nuclear weapons, either. Or tanks. Modern war is not my scope of practice, and I find the ability to kill thousands of people so quickly to be…cheap, almost inhumane, but you'll never catch me saying that in front of anyone else. No human wants to hear a werewolf call them inhumane."

"Well, that's all really interesting to know. Can we get out of here? I'm beginning to really hate hospitals. Sad, because I used to really want to work in them, but… waking up with a tube down my throat isn't a pleasant experience. Intubation, not fun."

"No, I bet it's not," he agreed. He walked with me to the door, carrying the bag he brought. He held the door open for me and let me walk out first.

I could smell Ranger before I saw him, turning to nod in his direction.

"We'll get out of your hair now," I said, smiling pleasantly. "Have a nice day, Ranger."

"No explanation why you were shot and brought here?" He stood and crossed his arms.

"Ask your Alpha. I'm sure he's heard something about me recently that might shed light on this situation."

Ranger shifted uncomfortably. "That's why I'm here. He hasn't heard anything."

Heath stood behind me, and I could smell him but not his emotions. With another werewolf around, he had locked down his emotional scent.

"Really?" Heath asked, and I could hear that confused frown. "They never brought him into the loop?"

Ranger crossed his arms. "I can't say anything about that."

"Then we won't say anything about this," I said, shrugging. "Hospitals are fair game, just like airports. I don't know if it's me or Heath pissing off your pack, but it has to stop. I don't want to have to tell anyone important that the Dallas pack is giving me problems for passing through or using amenities I don't have in my region. We're going to leave now, Ranger. Tell your Alpha I'm tired of this conversation. This is the last time I'm going to have it without getting anyone else involved."

I started heading for a nurse's desk, hoping one of them could start my check-out process. Heath followed me and stayed quiet. I had my check-out papers thirty minutes later and was able to convince everyone I didn't need a wheelchair.

"Let's get back home," I said softly, sitting down in not-Heath's truck. "Landon gave you his truck?"

"Yeah. Mine went to the cleaners." He sighed. "I'm sorry about him."

"Do you know what's going on with the pack?"

"I know the...testimonies I've been keeping from last year, but I don't follow werewolf politics as much since Russia. I was pretty much shut out after that incident when they realized you leaned on me for information to help save your family. Saving a human family isn't something they punish people for, obviously, but they didn't like us getting involved. Though they were happy we shut down the Russian pack."

"So, a slap on the wrist punishment for helping me by cutting you out of their little ring of intel."

"Pretty much," he confirmed. "Now, let's get back to what we were doing. Finding the people who tried to kill you is more pressing than the minor dramas I deal with from others of my species."

"For now," I said, coughing innocently.

He chuckled and shook his head.

"Don't bring that sort of bad luck on us," he ordered, starting the truck. "We've got enough problems."

## CHAPTER TWENTY-FOUR

When we got back to Jacksonville, we stopped at the bar to check on Oliver. He ran out to the truck and looked me over.

"I'm fine. It was a relatively clean hit, not too much internal damage. I'll be sore for a week or so, but the more I Change, the faster it will heal. No bones, so that makes this a little easier." I patted his hand where he had placed it on my arm in the window.

"Okay. Okay. I know no one told your family. They haven't tried to get in touch, either. You might want to—"

"I didn't want them told and won't be telling them yet because they would show up. I have everyone I need to handle this and don't need to risk my family's identities getting into the hands of the BSA, and potentially whoever leaked my information to these assholes. I know it sounds crazy, but I'm not going to give them up just to feel better. I have two werewolves, Dirk, and two BSA agents...probably. I need to have a long talk with the agents. We can't stay."

"I have Kick Shot, and I'll fend off your family if they try to get in touch here," Oliver promised with a strong nod.

"Thank you. I just wanted to make sure you were safe, and so you could see me alive and kicking. I've been injured much worse." I grinned, trying to play it cool as if I had this all under control. I obviously didn't, but I had to try.

"Of course you have," he said, chuckling awkwardly. "Um...stay safe."

"I can't make that promise, but I promise to get these guys out of my territory, so we can get back to normal."

"I like that." He stepped away from the truck and waved. Heath took that as a sign we could go and gently hit the gas. I watched Oliver in the side mirror until I couldn't see him anymore.

"He's a good young man. Would make a terrible werewolf," Heath said with a small laugh.

"Do you judge everyone by if they would make a good werewolf?" I asked. I didn't do it as a werecat. For my kind, Changing someone was a special relationship, not one we did commonly, if ever, for many werecats.

"As an Alpha werewolf, I had to. Judge wrong and you would probably end up with a werewolf who couldn't handle it and hit the Last Change quickly or just die during the Change. Or wasn't the right fit for the pack. Or someone who, with sudden power, becomes a murderer and a maneater. We have to pay attention to these things."

"Have you ever met someone and knew right away they would make a great wolf?"

"Yes."

"Hasan said when he met me, he knew I would be a good werecat." I sank further in my seat, ignoring the throb of the hole in my side. "It's not normal for werecats to Change an adult stranger, though."

"I've Changed strangers. I was asked by other packs to handle a specific person because the Alpha was unsure of it doing it himself. I've asked other Alphas to do a number of people in whatever pack I'm leading as well. We're not attached to people we Change. They become part of the pack, not part of the family."

He drove us to his home. Dirk's truck was in the driveway first, with the BSA SUV next to him.

"I don't know if I'm ready for this," I said softly. I was the one who texted Special Agent Collins and told him to meet us. I was the one with the plan to bring these agents in, work with them, and help them understand what was really at stake.

I had to trust two total strangers, who might be the very people creating the threat on my life.

"There's not much of a choice unless you want to call your family," he reminded me as we parked behind Dirk. "And we know where that leads."

"Yeah." I undid my seatbelt and gingerly slid out of the truck to keep from disturbing my healing side too much. He jogged to get to the door before me, holding it open. Dirk was just on the other side.

"Don't. Die. Remember that?" His glare was one I had seen before—every time I pissed him off by hovering and trying to get in his business.

"I didn't, but thanks for worrying about me," I said with a smile. "Don't hover. I'm alive, and I'm here."

The chain he fired off of what I assumed were curses in German was impressive. He stormed away, and both BSA agents had to jump out of his way as he went into the kitchen. Pouring drinks for everyone, Landon looked up in time to stop Dirk from bumping into him and pointed to the drinks.

"Have one and calm down," he growled. "You're bothering our guests more than I am, and you're the human."

Behind me, watching the little scene unfold, Heath locked the front door.

"He's fine. This has been a stressful day," Collins said with a tight smile, then turned toward me, his eyes big. "So, you heal like werewolves."

"Yeah. I'm not one-hundred percent, but I'm functioning." I walked toward Landon and Dirk, letting Heath decide where he wanted to be. Landon pushed a drink slowly across the counter to me. Once it was in hand, I found a seat at their dining table. "Where's Carey?" I asked softly.

"It's nearly midnight..." Landon shifted on his feet. "I gave her some melatonin to help her sleep a couple hours ago. Once we knew you two were on your way back, she felt better."

"Damn it," Heath grumbled. "You know I don't like—"

"She asked. She knew she couldn't see Jacky until tomorrow, and she didn't want to toss and turn all night. It was half a gummy," Landon growled. "You weren't here, Father. I handled it."

"Thank you," Heath finally whispered, putting a hand on his son's shoulder. "Now, onto the important business."

"You asked us to be here," Special Agent Miller said, slowly walking to the dining room table. "I'm sorry for what happened this morning. The fact you're out of the hospital only twelve hours later…"

"Normally, if a moon cursed can Change, we heal faster. We just need to be awake. I'll be fine in a couple of weeks at the most."

"But we did the right thing by airlifting you out, right?" Miller sat down, not next to me, but close enough to show he wasn't scared. He was worried about my health, which put points in his favor.

"She would have bled out otherwise," Heath said. "With silver in us, we can't Change. Werecats have those same weaknesses as werewolves. We're the same curse."

"Just different forms," I confirmed, nodding slowly as Special Agent Collins sat down. Landon brought the other drinks to the table before finding his seat beside his father. Dirk was last, sitting between me and Miller. "Some other important quirks. We'll get to that. I need to ask you two to work with me right now. No reporting back to your superiors about what I tell you, no telling *anyone* what I tell you. We're both after the people trying to kill me. I don't know who told about me, but the information needs to stop moving. Have either of you told your superiors I was attacked?"

"Only the first time and that we intended to resolve this matter, so we can properly talk to you. We never intended to introduce a threat on your life," Collins explained. "But not about the second attack. Once that happened, we realized we needed to go dark and figure this out. The leak...might be the BSA."

*He's super upset about that.*

"Yeah, well...I'm going to tell you two some of what you want to know about werecats. In return, you will keep it to yourself, and we catch these guys. There's a lot at stake here. Not just my life, but everyone here. You...you put us in a difficult position the moment you showed up." I looked at Heath, hoping he would step in.

"We need your resources as much as you need our cooperation," Heath said, putting it into words better than I could. "Jacky is willing to begin giving you information about werecats, but in return, you have to acknowledge this isn't information for the BSA, yet. This information is to help you understand we need to be careful."

"And a somewhat thank you for saving my life," I added.

"We went dark. Whatever you tell us is between us," Special Agent Miller said, leaning to put his elbows on the table. "Right?" He glanced at Collins, who nodded.

"I think we're in extenuating circumstances. Where do we start? What do my partner and I need to know that could help us find these people?"

"Let's back it up. There're some things you need to know going forward that will help keep everyone here safe," I said softly. "You...have evidence there's some form of relationship between Heath and me. We need that deleted before we work with you further. Every trace of it has to go. If you can't do that, we can't work together."

"Why?" Collins crossed his arms, frowning deeply. "Don't misunderstand the question, please. I'm just trying to understand what we've stumbled upon. Obviously, it's a touchy subject."

Touchy was an understatement, but I wondered if he was being purposefully careful. Heath had attacked Miller in the hospital for not being tactful about the information.

"Werecats and werewolves are cousins, in a sense, but we're not allies or friends," Heath explained, sighing heavily. "In fact, for much of history, our two species have gone to war against each other, with the last leading to wide-reaching changes among supernaturals all over the world. There's still animosity between our kinds. Jacky and I are the exception, not the rule, of how our kinds work. In fact, there are many werecats and werewolves who would prefer Jacky and I never worked together again. They certainly don't know we're in any sort of personal relationship beyond occasional allies. We need to keep it that way. If we can't, you're putting the lives of everyone in this house at risk."

I thought about Zuri, who promised to have my back if our relationship got out. I thought about her new lover and the surprise of a baby on the way for her.

"Why..." Miller looked between Heath and me, seeming surprised. "Why have the relationship?"

"That's not your business," I said stiffly.

*Because I'll be damned if I let the world tell me what I feel is wrong.*

"Why not have it?" Landon snapped. "Their

relationship isn't the business of anyone but them, and they're asking you to respect that. Respect it."

Having been on the end of one of Landon's glares, I felt almost bad for the agents.

"We'll delete it," Collins said softly. "No reason for us to keep it." There was no lie in his scent, no deception that could be traced, but I could see from the look on his face, he was thinking about something. Miller's fear was clear. Landon was an intense man. "Why did you let us go to the werewolves to verify your identity?"

"Who else would you go to? They know who I am. Heath and I have been pulled into a lot of situations since we met, starting with me protecting his daughter during the coup."

"How does someone your age get to be in such a position of power?"

"That's complicated and will never be something we discuss." I leaned back in my seat. "What else? Should we go over the differences between werewolves and werecats?"

"If you're willing to. We don't need your information to help you find who is trying to kill you. We're grateful for the display of trust and thank you for telling us about the delicate situation of your relationship. We're willing to protect your privacy in that manner, but we don't need you to tell us too much. Seeing you get shot tells us a lot. Tells us we know a lot more than we thought we knew. We know werewolves are weak to silver, it's toxic in their bloodstream, and it's the same for you. We know you Change people with a bite, and the curse might kill someone in the process of them becoming a werewolf or a werecat. I presume it depends on the one who bites the individual. We knew you Changed during a full moon, so we already had some idea of there being a connection. Am I correct so far, thanks to that connection?" Collins wasn't making notes or looking at a reference. I could tell he had a fascination with supernaturals, but he didn't want to be one. He just enjoyed that there was something new and interesting at the same table as him. That must have been the thing that took him to the BSA for a job.

*He might be by the book, but he's interested.*

I nodded, then waved for him to continue.

"Then we can also assume, like Heath, you're living outside the community, but it's not normal?"

"No," I corrected. "Werecats live alone. That's the way we are."

"Ah." He frowned. "Isn't that dangerous? If you're enemies with werewolves, wouldn't you want numbers to match them?"

I shrugged. "That's for later." I gave them a look, daring them to test me on it.

## CHAPTER TWENTY-FIVE

"Then it's for later." Miller didn't make any attempt to disagree. Whatever bit of hostility he had for me when we met was gone.

*Maybe it's because I got shot, and it's probably their fault.*

"We can tolerate that." Collins was more eager to continue talking than his partner. "We just want there to be open communication going forward. If the BSA needs to know anything, we need to trust you to let us know." He nodded to Miller, who picked up the briefcase he had at his feet. "We want to update you before going further. Before this incident, I was planning to tell you we were willing to agree to your terms. You as our liaison with other werecats in the future, keeping your identity and theirs private unless there is a case when exposure is necessary."

"What about the Werewolf Disclosure Agreement?" Heath asked. "Werewolves are required to verify our identity to the public when we own a business. Jacky owns Kick Shot."

"That is werewolf-specific, and it's from the fact your packs would be considered parts of the economy with dozens of werewolf employees. Witches don't follow the disclosure agreement, either. It's not a hard sell to give werecats the same exception, as long as Jacky pays her taxes," Collins said as Miller opened the briefcase and took out a sheet of paper. "This is all tentative, mind you. We're not done negotiating, and this isn't finalized. This is a preliminary write up, but in light of the first attack on you, our superiors wanted to make sure you understood we're negotiating in good faith and want to make this work. Even if we don't get everything we want, having someone we can talk to from any supernatural species is better than not having anyone."

I took the paper offered to me—simple bullet points.

"That's going to piss off werewolves," I murmured, looking at Heath, who only nodded.

"That's something you worry about?" Miller put the briefcase back on the floor.

"It's something I have to worry about but not do anything about." I liked what I saw in the tentative agreement. It was simple. I would provide the BSA with information concerning the basics of werecats, something to help them expand their knowledge base. I would also let them know if there were any werecat-related incidents in the US. I would be accountable for any of the incidents if humans were killed. I would be expected to report conflicts that may endanger the United States or its citizens.

In return, werecats would get their privacy unless public disclosure was necessary and would be free of the

Disclosure Agreement. We would be given a seat at the table for all negotiations for future supernatural legislation, just like the NAWC. We'd be granted protections similar to the werewolves and witches in the cases when a human or human organization attacked us. There were even anti-discrimination laws about supernaturals.

And finally, the BSA would confirm the existence of werecats using my photos, but no videos with my identifying features. This was going to be a press conference on national television.

*Unavoidable, I guess. If they're making deals with a new species and pass laws, they need to admit the species exists. As long as they don't say my name or try to find other werecats, we'll have to make due.*

"What terms would force us into the open? Wrong way to phrase that...What would force me to tell people I'm a werecat?" I asked softly, not finding anything written about it. "And this is all contingent on whether the BSA is the leak or not."

"If the BSA is the leak, we'll adjust course, but I'm positive the BSA isn't the leak. We don't leak."

Special Agent Collins was so damn sure, I wanted to believe him, but damn, it was hard. It was a massive government organization. There was no way they didn't have someone in their ranks willing to out a supernatural to get her killed before a deal could be finalized. As long as the deal wasn't finalized, secrecy was the only protection for a supernatural.

"As for reasons to disclose the identity of a werecat?"

Miller shrugged. "Murder and conviction would release a werecat's name if that case landed in our hands."

"I would take care of it," I murmured.

"What if you commit the murder?"

"Someone would take care of it," I said softly. "But I see what you mean. If there's an incident, there's no reasonable way for the BSA to sweep it under the rug. Just means I'll have to work harder to keep you from needing to get involved."

"That's what the werewolves do," Special Agent Collins pointed out. "We let them because it's easier to work with than against supernaturals. We understand there are certain social and cultural guidelines supernaturals have upheld for centuries, and they prefer to continue to manage your criminals in your own ways."

"The United States isn't a perfect country, and there are politicians out there who want to change the laws around supernaturals, become more strict, but the BSA is resistant to anything that might disrupt the peace we've been able to forge with the non-humans of the United States." Miller's words sounded like a written statement just for moments like this. "And peace is the ultimate goal."

"No one wants a war with people who don't die very easily," Heath said with a dark chuckle. "Once the BSA realized just how many of us were hiding, even only werewolves, they decided it was easier to forge a path with peace than hate."

"Yes, sir," Collins agreed. "Less American lives would be lost, practically none. The murder rate of supernaturals on humans is miniscule."

*His tune will change if they ever realize vampires are real. Hopefully, none of them slip up in the next decade, so werecats can settle into this new reality.*

"I like this, but I'll need time to think it over when this is all said and done." I folded the paper into a small square and put it in my pocket. "We need to deal with the immediate threat on my life."

"All we wanted was for you to see what we were willing to do for you before moving any further," Collins said. "Let's move onto the incident from earlier today." He waited for Miller to get a folder from the briefcase again. "We ran the license plate on the truck. It's registered to a Sam Blake. He's not from around here, actually hails from Boston. Two men attacked you on the road. Can you give me a description of the vehicle? Maybe we can match it to this one."

"Black pickup." I closed my eyes, trying to remember. "Silver grill on the front. You know the thing, like Dirk's truck." I opened my eyes and gasped. "Dirk, you didn't try to kill me, did you?"

He glared at me.

"Jacky, don't mess with him," Heath smirked.

"Yeah, I don't remember anything except a black pickup. I'm not the best with cars or guns. I own a bar, so I can tell you every type of alcohol in stock, but I'm not...a truck girl. Or a gun person."

"Black is on the description. We'll go on the assumption it's the same truck, or there are two. Hopefully, it's the same truck. The last thing we need is to be dealing with more than two to four men. I would need to call in reinforcements. I'm lucky they haven't already forced me to do that, but then again, I haven't told them you were shot yet." Collins shook his head. "Miller and I aren't equipped to fight an army."

"They might find out soon enough," Heath commented. "Ranger tells his Alpha, his Alpha tells the NAWC, NAWC..." Heath looked at me.

*Hasan might find out before I have the chance to lessen the blow. Damn it. He would tell me if he's getting on a plane, won't he? I hope so.*

"Information moves fast in our world," I agreed. "But you don't need a BSA army. You have one right here. Two werewolves and a werecat can handle a lot. Heath and I have done dangerous things before.

"First, we need to figure out where these guys are staying. Then we strike, and I figure out just who they're getting their information from, who wants me dead."

"It's a simple plan. If we can't find them, we..." Heath growled. "We use Jacky as bait for another attack, hopefully keeping her from getting killed in the process."

"You could have let me say that, so it didn't make you want to gag," I whispered to him, knowing everyone at the table could hear me.

"It would sound even stupider coming from you than from me, so I decided to lessen the stupid factor of the idea," he retorted. "It probably surprises no one that I'm against the idea."

"I'm not too keen on it, either," I replied. "But we have to leave it on the table."

"Sure." He leaned closer to me. "We'll leave it on the table if you let me help you buy a new car beforehand and get a roll cage installed."

"You asked for this," Landon commented softly, looking across his father at me.

"We'll come back to it," I decided, and Heath chuckled softly. I turned back to the agents and drummed my fingers on the table. My side ached uncomfortably, and the pain was further in, that unreachable sort of pain I knew I couldn't rub and hope it would feel better. "Heath told me you were looking into movement from any of the major extremist groups around the country. Has anyone seemed suspect?"

"No, there hasn't been anything to lead us to believe any of the bigger organizations have attacked you. That made us think this might be a local militia, but with Sam Blake being from Boston, that doesn't seem to be the case, either. There's no stronghold there. Most militias that focus on supernatural 'threats' are in the Midwest." Collins kept his eyes on me, narrowing them. "If werewolves and werecats aren't allies or even close to it, do you think you might have some enemies among them? Maybe someone from the werewolves trying to kill you before you can make a deal with us? They know we're talking to you."

"I know they do, but if they wanted me dead, they probably wouldn't involve humans." *Oh, no, he's probably right.*

"Humans, no offense, are unreliable when it comes to killing supernaturals," Heath explained. "We're faster, more willing to kill to protect ourselves, and have very few weaknesses. A pack would much rather come into a werecat's territory with a large hunting group and kill the werecat before the werecat has a chance to call for help. It's happened before."

"Or they would get us to leave our territory," I added. "Something that baits us out."

"Territory?" This time, the curiosity came from Miller.

"Another time," I said quickly, a little pissed we had let that slip. Heath, to his benefit, smelled guilty. "I was shot today, so I'm going to head home and get some sleep. We can keep working on this tomorrow."

"Landon and I can keep watch if you need us. Kick Shot was burned down once before, and this group has vandalized it as well. Want to bet they'll consider it again?"

I nodded, liking the offer. "You can sleep in the bar if that's okay. I'm going to go *home*."

Heath stood and helped me to my feet. Landon was next. Dirk was the only one still seated with the agents, and that didn't last long.

"I'll give her a ride back to the bar," he said in a rush. "She's my boss."

"Okay," Heath agreed, chuckling. "We need to make sure we're ready for anything, so we'll meet you there. Kick Shot is still open, right?"

"Should be. That will keep me out of trouble for an hour or so as the last shift cleans up."

Dirk and I left after that, and once we were out of sight of the Everson family home, he cut off the music.

"We're not telling the family about this, are we?" he asked, squeezing his steering wheel as if it made him anxious or angry. His scent pointed to the former.

"No, not yet," I confirmed. "They'll show up and expose themselves, which ruins all the negotiating I've gotten done. Would I like them here? Yeah, if the BSA wasn't involved, but..." I shook my head. "Everything relies on me being in charge here, and with the family, I'm the bottom of the ladder, not the top."

"Yeah." Dirk nodded. "I'll keep up the story. How's the gunshot wound?"

"Healing." I lifted my oversized shirt and took a look at the bandage. There was some minor red showing through, a spot of bleeding. "It'll heal if I don't fuck with it too much. I got lucky, they only took one shot, and there were people around to help me."

"From what I heard, they only took one shot because they thought they killed you."

"Yeah, I did that on purpose," I said softly, still looking at the bandage. "I fell back and told Carey to scream. It was all I could think of. If they thought I was dead, she would be safe..." I closed my eyes. "I haven't had a chance to process it yet, so..."

We fell silent as he drove until we reached the parking lot of Kick Shot once again.

"You know I'm happier here in Texas than I have been anywhere else, right?" Dirk looked at me from across the dark truck.

"I think you've made a friend, and you're away from Niko," I said in return.

"Well, I lose both of those if you die, and you're my favorite person in the family. So please, whatever you decide to do to handle this, don't get killed. Oliver doesn't want to go back to London, either."

"I know. I know you two are counting on me." And so many others.

"Okay." He nodded. "And you can count on us, too. While you were down, Landon and I kept Carey with us and directed the contractors. They're moving fast. You should see all this done by the end of the month. Landon also has me set up." He lifted his hoodie and revealed a new sidearm. "No silver since we're dealing with humans right now, but he knows a guy he's going to hook me up with." He must have been satisfied I saw it and knew he was protected, because he cut the engine and jumped out of the truck. I opened my door but barely got a foot out before he was there, helping me to the ground. His truck wasn't small.

"If anyone comes at you while I'm around, I'm not afraid to shoot them," he said softly as we walked toward the trail to my home.

"Why?"

"You gave me space without making me fight for it, and it's let me grow the fuck up," he said, stopping at the new sign. "I'm going to check in on Oliver and my bartenders. Can you walk home?"

"Yup. I've got this," I promised. I left him there, walking the trail home alone. I didn't smell anything unusual. As soon as I got into my home, I locked the doors and checked the house, paranoia returning in full force now that I was alone.

Getting shot certainly hadn't helped me get over things and find normal again.

## CHAPTER TWENTY-SIX

Sitting at my computer, I wondered where to start. I opened my emails and decided giving the family a general update was as good a place as any. Keeping it short and sweet, I let them know the BSA and I spoke again, and I had a change of heart, wanting their assistance to find the leak and discover who attacked me, framing it as a way to prove their loyalty to clean negotiations. I scanned the tentative deal and attached it to the email, hoping for their opinions on it. It included exposing werecats to the public but not the identity of individual werecats. It would be similar to the fae, not the witches, but was better than what the werewolves had to deal with.

I hit send, then copy and pasted it into a separate email, but added extra, noting that Zuri needed to read this one, not the other. I included that I was attacked a second time, and one of the BSA agents had called in a helicopter for me. I was trusting her not to tell the family, to keep them out of danger, and made sure to add that to the email, making sure it was clear that I didn't want them to know I got shot.

After I hit send, I waited.

And waited.

I could have slept, but I knew one of them was going to be awake to see the email, eventually. I didn't think it would be Zuri, nearly an hour after I sent them out.

She didn't bother replying to the email. She called.

"You were shot?" she snapped the moment her face came on the screen. "Are you serious? You haven't told anyone in the family? How in the hell don't they know? Dirk—"

"Figured out I didn't have Heath send word and decided not to, either," I said, shrugging. "He's loyal to me, I guess."

Zuri shook her head slowly. "You know, when we talked just yesterday, when I specifically called you when I knew you would be up and hopefully in your office, I didn't expect you to get attacked. Not once, and absolutely not twice, in under twenty-four hours." She growled and leaned forward as though she was inspecting my image on the screen. "You don't look terrible, though. I take it neither of the attacks was too bad?"

"You probably know the details about the first one, broken hand, but that's...doing a lot better now. I've shifted a few times since it happened, and we made sure a doctor aligned the bones first. A graze on my shoulder, but the real loser was my car. The second...it was a cheap shot, Zuri. Wannabe sniper bullshit. Carey found out about Heath and me, so we decided to take her to the movies. I got out of the truck, and they hit before I closed the door. Luckily, I was smart enough to fall back into the truck, so they couldn't take another shot. Carey's screaming and the truck's tinted windows helped. They ran before they could verify if I was dead or alive."

"Definitely not professionals," she said softly. "I'm glad whoever shot you is stupid enough to fail twice, but it's also concerning."

"I'm convinced it's the BSA. They have a leak, and someone let slip that a lone supernatural is here. Finally, extremist humans have an 'easy' target. Gave them my name, and the game was on, you know?"

She nodded. "Makes them unpredictable, though. Professionals are impressed when someone survives, but others get frustrated. There's no honor among those who are just looking to kill for sport. They aren't looking at the skill and perfection needed for two great powers to go against each other. They only want death, and you have escaped it. If Hisao was trying to kill you—not that I believe that would ever happen—he would respect that you evaded him twice. He might even step back and consider his options and if the kill was worth it."

"Has anyone ever evaded Hisao twice?" I asked softly.

"No one has ever evaded Hisao once, from what I know," she answered, shrugging. "I'm glad to see you alive. The cheap shot, tell me about it."

I explained the injury, a gut hit that missed my organs by a slim margin.

"They moved too fast. If they had taken ten more seconds to line up a shot, they might have hit a lung."

"I know." I didn't deny that. "But you agree with me about our family, right? They can't come here."

"Well, we *could*, but it's not practical. It would take at least two hours for everyone to get in the air, if Mischa even could. I think Hisao is still commandeering their jet, so he would have to pick her up. I'm not coming at all, and you definitely don't want me in your territory right now. Plus, you do have back up. I know we all want to protect the family, but you have the ability to talk like the wolves. Very useful when you're with us, even more so when you're with the wolves. You can pack hunt if you have to. They're both capable." She touched the screen. "I'm just glad to see you alive. I won't tell Father yet—"

"He'll find out, eventually. One of the Dallas pack saw me in the hospital."

"Word travels fast," Zuri agreed, "but I think you have a few days, maybe even a week if you need it. Callahan won't stupidly give Father his condolences about his daughter getting shot. They aren't that close. When Liza died, the only reason Callahan offered his condolences was he had to since she had been killed by wolves. If you get assassinated by humans, he's going to pour himself a drink and have a toast."

"Would Corissa? She's the important one."

"She is. She's smart, but she's like Father. What is best for the wolves is not always the popular decision. It's not war or fighting, but peace and prosperity, something hotter heads disagree with. She's only the dominant in private, don't forget that. She won't jeopardize her mate's position by slapping him down in public where other wolves might see. The werewolves of her personal pack are completely loyal to her, and her objective is to keep them both on top, so they won't tell anyone. You shouldn't either. The fact she did it in front of Heath was surprising enough, but don't test her."

"It never crossed my mind," I replied, lifting my hands. "You never answered my question, though."

"She would...maybe have a private toast to the death of one of our family. Maybe. Depends on the family member. I don't know exactly where you stand with her right now. You embarrassed her husband, but you and Heath exposed a travesty of a pack to her, which he had been hiding. Now, she's able to clean it up. It could go either way. She would toast my death or Jabari's, without question. Not Niko....Actually, only Niko. She likes that he thinks like a wolf sometimes."

I nodded and decided it was time to get to the important part.

"Did you read the deal?"

"I did," she said, clicking around on her computer, probably pulling it up. "I don't like it, but I don't hate it. I don't think you'll get better. Specifically, I don't like that they're going to have a press conference about their discovery of our kind, which tells other governments we exist..." Zuri shook her head. "But I think it's the only way. We can't ask them for everything and give them nothing."

"Blaming them for the attempts on my life has been an easy way to get them to act in my favor. They don't want to ruin their reputation."

"Oh, that was a very smart play," Zuri agreed, smiling. "I couldn't have done it better myself. I'm about to have a baby, though, and now everyone is going to know werecats are something they need to watch for on the full moon. In reality, it doesn't change much, but this is it, the beginning of the slow leak of information about our kind to the world. Eventually, we won't have a choice but to be part of their modern, unforgiving world. I want my child to be safe."

"I know. How are you? With the baby and the man? I know we only talked yesterday, but...I'm still trying to wrap my head around it."

She laughed. "Yes, well, it's been fairly life-altering. Werecats, I have learned, are not immune to morning sickness. That was lesson one."

"Wait. You had a son before." I was sure I wasn't misremembering that.

"I did. He was adopted. This is my first blood child, not that it matters. When the time comes, this one will know about their older brother and what he did, all of it. This is the first time I've gotten pregnant. The dangers for women concerning childbirth are the same across most species, so I had decided never to have a blood child, one from my own womb. This was a surprise I decided to roll with. I have the resources, a mother with lots of experience with it, and a man willing to be a father to the baby. He was surprised as well, but as you could tell, he's definitely not unhappy."

"Yeah. Where are those two?"

"Running errands, getting supplies. The birth isn't for months yet, but you know, stocking up in case I pop early. Plus, Mother wants to know him better, hard to do when I'm always around, and he's focused on me and this." She ran a hand over her baby bump. "Plus, I couldn't call you until I got them out the door. I couldn't let Mother know you were hurt before I heard more about it. She would have gotten hold of Father immediately. She gets incredibly angry when one of her children is hurt."

"That's really weird because I've only met her once."

"You don't need to call her your mother, but I recommend accepting that she thinks of you as her child, even if she can be a bit absentee." Zuri looked around, seeming to check for them. "I'm glad you're not too badly hurt, though. Is there anything else you wanted to talk about?"

"Actually..." I remembered the odd timeline of the event, how the pieces didn't fit. "Did you see how they tagged my bar?"

"Yes, I saw the picture."

"What do you think about it? Something...felt off. The timing was wrong. Heath agreed with me, but...it slipped my mind after he and I got a laugh about how it was probably just these humans being idiots."

"I think you might be paranoid, which is a natural response to what's going on. I'm scared for you. I agree our family shouldn't go to your territory right now and wish this wasn't happening, but I don't think that means anything. They know you survived and were warning you. You're the one who foolishly decided to go to the movies with a werewolf and a human girl after that."

I winced.

"Yeah, I was holding that one back. Sorry." Zuri sighed. "I understand why you did it. They don't deserve to force you into hiding, and after seeing you on our last call, I'm also glad you made the decision to get out of the house and try to reclaim your territory for yourself. I'm conflicted. You haven't told me anything that would make me think it's not humans, Jacky, but...if it continues to bother you, look deeper. The only thing I can think of is a werewolf leaking your information instead of the BSA, and no werewolf is that stupid. We don't play those games."

"What if we do?" I asked quietly. "What if I finally pissed off the wrong person, and they decided it was worth the risk?"

"Then someone is going to die," Zuri answered. "Hopefully, it'll be them before it's you."

I didn't disagree.

## CHAPTER TWENTY-SEVEN

I couldn't shake it, even if it didn't make any sense. When I woke up the next morning, I was still thinking about the odd inconsistencies, the silver bullets, and that none of it made any fucking sense.

It was almost too easy to write this off as humans when I had enemies among the werewolves, but were any of them so stupid to hire humans and break secrecy Law to come after me? Especially since the BSA was hovering, and I had Heath at my back? Or even more pressing, the fact I was one of Hasan's children, helping him rule the werecats?

*Not that I do that job very well.*

From my understanding, my siblings had it harder, but they all had more experience. The werecats in the Americas were all fairly well behaved and came out this way to get out of the more populated areas of the "old world." I certainly didn't have to talk to anyone in my region more than once every few months, and most of those were courtesy calls to see how people were doing.

*I never got around to calling them myself when this started. Maybe that's what I'll do today?*

I had no idea what was on my list of things to do. I was still tired, recovering from being shot, but I didn't have the energy to Change *again*. Three times was enough for one forty-eight-hour period; four would be pushing it.

There were people trying to kill me, which took me back to the insistent feeling I had the moment I got out of bed and made my way down to make coffee. Something about all this was off, and I was on edge. I tried desperately not to show it, but I had nearly cracked in front of Dirk before I'd composed myself and been ready to talk to Zuri.

Now, I was alone, a mug in my hand, and no one around.

Sitting, I took a shaky breath. I didn't need to have another breakdown. People had tried to kill me before. Just because this was in my territory and the world was falling apart didn't mean I needed to break down again.

*I exposed my kind, I've made more enemies than I even know, and someone is trying to kill me in my own territory.*

*Again.*

I caught my reflection in the window—still looked barely thirty, as though I was youthful and vibrant, as I always would. No one could guess I was turning thirty-nine in only a few months.

*I'm going to be lucky if I make it to forty.*

It had nothing to do with Heath, though my feelings for him certainly complicated things. It was my decision to go to Dallas, my decision to put my middle finger up because I thought I had some sort of moral high ground. It was my decision to protect Gwen and go against the Russian pack instead of just taking the trade for my family because I felt as if I was too good for the easy solution.

I didn't regret those choices, but I knew, no matter which way I looked at it, I was paying the price for them now. The BSA had already made that clear.

Checking my phone as I poured another cup of coffee, I scrolled through my texts with the other. There wasn't much news. Heath had sent a text that he'd arrived at the bar, and Landon was going to run the property. He'd sent it around two in the morning. When I hadn't responded, he sent another, telling me to sleep well.

I smiled as I took a sip of my second round of coffee.

Was I going to feel the consequences of our relationship in some painful way? Yeah, probably.

Would I regret it?

Probably not.

I texted him back, saying thank you and good morning. He sent a picture back of him sitting in my office without me.

Well, if he's still around…

I put the mug down and hurried to get dressed, taking less than ten minutes to get presentable. I took my coffee with me. I was at Kick Shot in less than twenty minutes and found Heath standing in the doorway of my office.

"Good morning," I greeted. "I think I have a meeting."

"Do you?" he asked, giving me a hooded stare. "What's on—"

Landon stepped out of Oliver's office, fixing his shirt.

He looked between us, shook his head, then moved around me to get down the stairs. I heard the back door open and close, then his truck fired up. I met Heath's humored stare and started laughing.

"He's a prude," I commented lightly.

"He's not. When we moved back in together after Carey showed up, I made a promise to both him and Richard that I wouldn't,"—he gestured at me—"have a bunch of lovers in and out of the house. They made the promise in return. We just don't want to see it with each other."

"You had a bunch of women in and out of your house before?" I walked slowly down the hall, letting my fingers drag.

"I was a terrible man. Are you going to do something about it?" he asked as I took the final step. "Absolutely terrible."

"No, I really don't care," I admitted, shrugging. "I met one of those exes in Seattle. You know, funny enough, she thought I was into you. I'm still not sure what to think of that."

"Ah, yeah." Heath chuckled, then stopped. "You know...thinking about it, I see why so many women thought they could use Carey to get to me. I wasn't exactly hard to get before she was born."

"You were a single, attractive man, in an obviously lonely position. You had already lost two wives and had two adult sons. Why wouldn't you enjoy yourself? Doesn't sound like anyone was too hurt by it." I shrugged again. "And you aren't giving me any reason to think you're going back to that."

"I never made promises. I was always very clear about the sort of relationships they were, but...I'm glad to have found something a bit more committed."

"Me, too," I whispered, stepping around him to get into my office. "Do we have any plans today?"

"Daniel and his partner will be calling us around midday. It was a late night, and they still needed to run a check on who this Sam Blake is. They're hoping to know more for us by then. If not, they'll let us know we can hold off on another meeting."

"Heath..." I sat in my chair as he closed the door and sat across from me. "I've been really bugged by the inconsistencies."

"The door thing?"

"And the silver bullets. You said the humans didn't normally have silver bullets. Did you tell the NAWC about that?"

Heath shook his head. "Not until this is over. I know I should have informed them the moment I knew, but if they don't know you're under attack, I'm not going to give them reason to think you are. Besides, they don't know I know. You're the one being attacked."

"It doesn't make sense." I tilted my head to the side as I frowned, still uncomfortable with the strangeness, still wondering. "I mean...it's farfetched, but what if it is a werewolf?"

"Yes, you have upset people on the NAWC. Yes, one of them is Callahan, and he's got influence as the Tribunal werewolf, but he is still Tribunal. Do you think anyone could get away with it under his nose?"

"Look at Russia," I huffed. "He knew about that."

"That only hurt werewolves. As sad as that sounds, it only hurt werewolves, the people he rules. Letting someone or planning an obscure attack against you? That's an act of war that would destroy the Tribunal he helped create. Do you think he's that ballsy?"

"What if someone—"

"Jacky, I'm not going to tell you that you're wrong—you have an instinct and should trust it—but I was on that Council for years. I am genuinely uncomfortable with the idea they would pull off an assassination like this as a collective. I'm not saying it's impossible, but I... I can't see it, no matter how much I've fallen from grace. If it was them,"—he pointed to himself—"do you really think they would let me suffer another breath for defying them and staying here? For just being your ally? To them, I betrayed years of friendship by moving here and working with you, even if it was initially to protect my daughter when I didn't have a pack anymore. I wanted to retire, and they never understood that."

"No," I whispered. "You're right about that." I leaned over and put my head in my hands as I looked at him. "What if it's not the Council? What if it's just one werewolf?"

"Silver is expensive. It would need to be an Alpha, but I'm at a loss as to which Alpha would be your enemy and not mine."

"Unless it's not my enemy," I said, letting that idea dawn on me. "Unless it's a werewolf who is Hasan's enemy. Then I'm just an easy target."

"It's a possibility. We're not at war, but it may be a

sharp reminder to him, when one of his children steps out of line, they're willing to step in and correct it."

"Exactly." I dropped my hands. "And maybe they used the BSA coming by as a cover?"

"It works. Stage it as non-professionals. Would explain the odd little mistakes."

"They were cheesy...as if it was a standard dialogue. There's been nothing personal about the threats." I took a deep breath. "Are we overthinking this?"

"I don't know. It sounds plausible."

We stared at each other as the reality sank in.

There was a chance this wasn't humans committing random violence. There was a chance we were dealing with something that came back to the same issues we always faced—the delicate balance between two species who couldn't find common ground and with an explosive ability to hurt each other.

"Do we tell the BSA? It could be important." I stood and began to pace. "Who could it be? I'll take your word Callahan isn't an option. The Tribunal is too fragile, and if he attacks Hasan, Hasan will retaliate. With humans involved, the situation is too delicate."

"Could be anyone," Heath countered. "The last time —the *only* time—Hasan lost a child, that Alpha wasn't involved. I remember hearing the news of a young group of werewolves executed for it. I was around for that, and they kept a chokehold on that information. The identity of the pack and the Alpha was never made known, and anyone who was involved was sworn to secrecy, then the entire pack was split up. That's how serious we are about peace, Jacky."

"Liza was innocent," I whispered. "That's why. I've never heard someone say a bad word about her. I'm not her...I'll never be her. Someone could hate me a lot more than they could have hated her."

"It would be a crushing blow to Hasan's power if he lost a second child, though, especially since you're you. You've proven yourself to be an active player and a dangerous one." Heath stood and walked behind me, wrapping his arms around my waist. "That's the danger of fighting for what you believe in."

"Do you have enemies who may show up one day?"

"We met because some in my pack were angry with me," he reminded me. "And yes, I've made enemies, but I'm a werewolf, and my enemies are werewolves. Right now, I'm not a threat to them. If I become an Alpha of a large pack again or they find out about us? Yeah, I'll have problems." He held me tightly as my heart thumped in my ears. "But those are the risks we take."

"Some would call us idiots," I whispered. "You, over two hundred years old. Me, nearly forty. We both know the risks. It's not as if we're stupid teenagers who think love conquers all, or that things will be different for us."

"Who knows? Maybe things will be different. Zuri is on our side." He kissed my neck. "But let's get back on track. Someone wants you dead. Now we have options. It can be either human extremists, who have your information thanks to a leak within the BSA, or there's a slim possibility a werewolf is staging this to pin your death on the BSA and other humans to get away with killing you to get at Hasan."

"Do we tell Collins and Miller?" I asked, turning around in his arms.

"If we think there might be werewolves when we find these guys, yes. If we catch the humans, we can interrogate them, and if it turns out to be werewolves, we'll ask the BSA to kindly step aside. There's nothing they can do at that point that won't make the situation worse. The NAWC won't like seeing a werewolf arrested publicly for trying to kill you." He released me and sat down in my chair. "Did you look over the deal? Do you think you'll take it?"

"Probably," I admitted. "Zuri knows some are necessary evils, like pictures of our kind being released. They have to tell the American people something, right? When I was human, we wanted transparency. Funny being on the other side of things."

"Yeah, when the positions switch, it becomes harder to live up to those ideals. You understand the dangers better. What about the rest of your family?"

"I haven't heard from them yet, but they might be waiting on Zuri or Hasan to make the call. She made the call to me, but knowing them, there were discussions when I wasn't included. They'll come back to me when they have a consensus on the path forward. Luckily, I'm not making a decision today. Today, we need to find the guys trying to kill me. Did you or Landon run into anything last night?" I looked down at him, enjoying the way he stretched his legs out, unafraid to take up space in my office, to be there and make sure I knew it.

"It would have been the first thing I told you," he promised.

"I'm amazed you're not mad at me for getting shot in front of Carey. It was stupid and overconfident to think we could get away with a trip to the movies. My territory or not, it was stupid."

"You weren't the only one thinking it was safe. I didn't think they would hit you with me and Carey around. When they attacked you on the highway, you were alone. They tagged your bar. I didn't think they were bold enough to shoot you in broad daylight in town, with an Alpha werewolf and a human girl around. If they had hit Carey?" Heath growled. "They can't be foolish enough to think there wouldn't be retribution coming down on them hard. What they did was insane, Jacky, and they're going to pay for it."

"I know. So, what are you doing for the rest of the morning?"

"I need to get home, shower, and change. Then I'm meeting with the contractors all morning. They want to start getting your new security in the trees. I want to see how much space they can cover and make sure it's done right." He stood up and kissed me softly. "We'll spend the afternoon with Daniel and his partner. We're going to find these people. I don't care who sent the humans—they're going to pay for it."

## CHAPTER TWENTY-EIGHT

I met Landon, Dirk, and the BSA agents at Heath's home. Heath had given me a ride after he was done talking to the contractors. His home was better than the bar, which would open and have strangers going in and out. I walked in, threw my bag down, and stripped off my jacket. A light rain had started in the late morning, and now it was pouring down that spring rain that seemed to wash everything away and leave the flowers blooming. I spent most of the morning hours watching the rain while my family got back to me.

I was cleared to approve the deal with the BSA. The family would warn werecats everywhere there was going to be a breach, but no identities would be included, except maybe mine.

As I accepted coffee from Heath, I looked at my new head of security, just as unprepared for his job as I was for mine.

"Dirk, I know you want to stay and help, but can you

go back to Kick Shot and keep an eye on Oliver? He's vulnerable." I shook my wet hair, letting water fly, and making Heath chuckle as he stepped back from me. "I know you're taking this really seriously and want to be involved with every step, but I can't leave him without any protection."

"On it, boss," Dirk said, grabbing his coat. "Keep me updated?"

"I will," Landon said after I nodded. He looked at me as Dirk jogged out. "So you can focus on this, I'll text him."

"Thank you," I said, sitting down at the dining table. "So, what's our plan of attack?"

"Attack?" Collins sat down next to me this time. "We'll get to that. First, I have a full background on Sam Blake. He's not what we expected. I want to make sure neither of you has met him before."

"I don't like the sound of that." Nothing was as expected anymore.

"He's former military, a Marine," Miller explained, putting his briefcase on the table and unsnapping it. He held it open with one hand and grabbed a fat manilla folder with the other. "Discharged after five years and two deployments. He was picked up by a private security firm, but only stayed with them for a few years before shifting into…less honorable work." He dropped the envelope onto the middle of the table. "Do you recognize him?"

I opened the folder and looked at the picture carefully. I recognized the face, all right. I knew the cruel line of his mouth.

"Yeah...he's one of the guys who shot at me on the highway."

"I don't like that he's military," Heath muttered, leaning over to look from a different angle. "The U.S. Armed Services should behave better."

"He was squeaky clean while he was in. Once he was out, things started to fall apart," Collins commented as he reached out and flipped through the pages. "He was fired from the private security firm for failing in a protection detail. He injured himself while he was in, too. Tore his ACL at twenty-two, a hard injury to have before thirty. Surgery helped, but I bet it hurts on days like today. What concerns me is he's never been associated with any extremist movement. Where did he come from, and why now?"

I looked at Heath, who was too focused to notice me for a moment.

*I bet he's not an extremist at all.*

When he looked at me, our eyes met, and I knew the same thought was going through his head.

"I've never met him before," I declared, leaning back and letting them have the manila folder. "Do you think we can find him?"

The agents looked at each other.

"I don't think he was expecting to be seen or for you to survive...twice. I think when they shot at you at the theater, it was desperation. You were supposed to die on the highway, which explains the entire act and show. Shooting you on the open road, running your car off into the ditch, the continuous fire—one and done, make it big to send a message," Collins explained, sitting back down. "So, they put their motel room in Sam's name as well. And what's the message?"

"Or Sam is a fall guy, so no one else involved would get this pinned on them. We'll figure out what the message is when we get our hands on them," Heath pointed out. "And we can get our hands on them because they didn't see the job through."

"We can," Special Agent Miller confirmed. "We know where they're staying. *Now* we can plan an attack, then get on with our other business."

"What do we know about the motel?" I asked, putting my hands in my lap, trying to keep my demeanor calm. I didn't need to look bloodthirsty in front of the agents.

"It's in the middle of town, here." Collins pointed at a place I drove past frequently. "Sam Blake may be prior military, but he wasn't special forces. He was a grunt, and this kind of op wouldn't have been his thing. That would explain the piss-poor job they're doing."

"But why?" I asked, shaking my head when both agents and Heath opened their mouths. "I don't think anyone here knows the answer—"

"What if he's being paid?" Landon asked. "If he is, why not pay professionals?"

"Would professionals even take this job?" Heath asked, turning to his son. "Consider it. You're offered several million to take out…Jacky." I knew what he was about to say, but the agents were lost. Saying Hasan's name was a no-no. "Who would get revenge for that?"

Landon nodded, humming to himself, a deep,

thoughtful noise as he started pacing. "You have a point. There're repercussions for that."

"I know you rule North America as a werecat, but..." Collins leaned toward me. "I have a feeling I'm missing something here."

"You're missing a lot," I confirmed. "What I can say should be obvious. I have semi-control over this continent and South America. It's not all my personal territory, but I'm supposed to look out for the werecats here. Do you think the other continents don't have similar?" I tilted my head and smiled. "Or that I don't talk to them on a regular basis? Remember how I told you the situation about my position was complicated?"

"Ah, so we can't discuss that yet." Collins nodded. "But after this...would you care to open up about that part of things?"

"Depends. Are you okay with not hearing names?"

"Yes."

"Sure." I shrugged, then looked at Landon. "Any professional would have to be better than...you know." *Hisao.*

"There's no one in the world willing to play that game," Landon agreed, putting his hands on his hips. "But two punks, looking for an easy payment, probably not understanding what they're getting involved with? Do you know how many people are *that* desperate in this country and all over the world?"

"Too many," Heath agreed. "It's a theory. Thank you, Landon."

Landon only nodded. "Let me reach out to some of my contacts, the other seconds and inner circles. You know all the Alphas, but I know all the loose lips. I'll see if I can stir something up while y'all work out how we're going to catch these guys and where we're going to take them."

"Thank you. Hopefully, they haven't skipped town." Heath leaned over the map. "Can we get an APB statewide on the truck? Pull over, stop, and detain for those riding in it?"

"We can," Miller confirmed. "We'll tell them it's a federal case, and they are people of interest. Local sheriffs might get cranky, but the police departments should work with us." He pulled out his phone and walked off, making a call.

"Step one, catch them. Step two, find out how they learned about me and why they're trying to kill me. Step three, stop it from happening again. Great. Now, this motel…" I pointed at it and started telling them what I knew about it. I had stayed in it when I came to check out the area to move in and start Kick Shot. It wasn't an easy place to strike, thanks to being in town, but could be done at night. No one disagreed.

"So, we have until nightfall. Let's see if Landon can catch any rumors from the packs," Heath said softly, moving the map to look at it closely. "Do you mind staying here for the day? Where we can keep you safe?"

"I should say no on principle, but I'm not that bad. I'll stay. We're better in numbers, and it's not like I can get in my car and drive off. I still need to deal with that problem. Should have gotten a car the moment I knew I wasn't going to salvage the Versa."

"Yes, you should have…between the running

through the woods, two hospital visits, and getting sniped in a movie theater parking lot," Heath replied, his words so dry, I wondered if he needed a glass of water.

"Yeah..." I realized my error, putting too much on myself unreasonably. There was no way I was going to get a replacement in a day, much less during all of this. "I'll get it handled later. I'm just not used to having my car unavailable. Or, you know, being sniped in a movie theater parking lot."

We broke up, going into our own groups. Without Landon, a needed member of this strange little team, we couldn't really make plans. A werewolf second, with over a hundred years of experience, he could point out something valuable the rest of us missed. I made myself a drink and wandered into Heath's office for a quiet moment.

I didn't get to stay alone for long. Special Agent Collins followed me without his partner.

"I know you're cautious about telling me anything, but you and Heath seem like you have your own theories," he said as he sat down on the couch. "I was hoping you would share them."

I looked at him and shook my head. If I gave away my theory, I lost the upper hand, and I wanted the BSA to think I still believed they were the leak. The idea a werewolf was trying to kill me, using them as cover...that changed everything.

"Is there anything I can do right now to get your cooperation?" he asked.

"Finalize the negotiations," I replied calmly. "As they

stand, every bit of it, nothing added, no loopholes, no tricks. That's when I'll start giving you information."

He pulled out his phone and made a call.

"She likes the deal. Can we get a signature on it, so she can sign?"

"She's willing to sign, even though someone tried to kill her, and she thinks we leaked her identity? What changed her mind?" I didn't recognize the male voice with the light crackle being pushed through a phone. He was surprised by my decision.

"I think she's realized she's getting the best deal she can," he replied.

"I'll email it over. Boss already signed it when he gave his approval. We just need her. Once we have her signature, we can schedule a meeting to do the official show signing for the President."

"Do I need to be there for that?" I asked, raising an eyebrow. "Doesn't this need to go through Congress?"

Collins looked up and put the phone on speaker.

"You don't need to be there, and the President signs at the press conference. Congress is already waiting to vote. While you've been looking at it, we've already rounded up the votes we need to make this happen. Everyone is under a gag order for national security reasons until the BSA makes it public with the President's signing."

"He's our political and legal expert on these things," Collins explained.

"This wasn't a tentative deal, then. You wanted this handled quickly."

"The sooner we get a supernatural through the initial

negotiations, the quicker we can start working with them on other things. Supernaturals are a national security risk, a hole in our country. We'll do whatever is necessary, make whatever deal we have to, just to get someone to talk to us. The werewolves were easy because they had to talk to us, but they were tough negotiating the initial laws around themselves. The fae taught us a different lesson," the guy on the phone said. "They refuse to sit down with us at all, moving around our country without any sort of recourse or monitoring, and we know they are, but we can't catch any of them out to talk, especially not their leaders. We might not be able to get all the werecats out of you, but we have you. That's better than nothing. We'll take it."

"That's very pragmatic of you. Send it along." I crossed my arms and leaned on Heath's desk.

Collins ended the call. "We were never out to get you, Jacky. We're just thinking about how the future may play out. What if we had never made a deal with you, and a werecat killed someone?"

"I understand." I sighed. "Well, as long as it doesn't leave this room and that's moving, I'll talk to you. There's some information you need first to understand."

He perked up.

"Werecats have a different culture than werewolves. You probably see new werewolves every year, maybe ten or twenty a year, slowly growing but unstoppable. They commonly die pretty young, less than fifty years after they're Changed, so the large packs constantly need to replenish their ranks. It helps that there's a waiting list for people to become werewolves. Family of the pack first, employees of the pack second, and so on. This is information I was educated on ages ago...by my father."

His confusion was almost comical. Collins stood and crossed his arms.

"Your father is a human and has no ties to any supernatural organization, for or against."

"Werecats don't Change people the way werewolves do. We don't just pick random people to fill out our numbers. We're lonely creatures. We live alone, most of the time, and we have a different type of magic than the werewolves."

"So, you don't have pack magic...the ability to communicate in your animal form."

"Exactly," I agreed. "Instead, I have territory magic, which allows me to protect my space from invading supernaturals. This land is mine, even if it doesn't legally belong to me. To another werecat or any other supernatural, walking into my territory without my permission is a death wish. I'll fight tooth and claw to protect it." I sat down at Heath's desk, trying to get comfortable. It was the same chair I had in my office since I had let Heath pick out mine.

*"It'll be better for your back,"* he'd said.

"I see..." Collins sat across from me. "But how does this information factor into what we're dealing with?"

"Werecats don't just Change people. If I were to walk out there right now and Change someone into a werecat, by our culture, they would become my *child*. My responsibility to teach, protect, and help transition into our lifestyle. Anything they do after I let them branch out onto their own could come back to me, my failings. So, when I say I was taught by my father, I don't mean my human one. I mean my werecat father, the man who Changed me...and the ruler of the werecats. That's how I was put in charge here."

"Nepotism." Collins called it the way he saw it.

"I won't say you're wrong." I chuckled. "There have been a few werecats who have tried to kill me. They thought I was a failing of my father. His children rule all over the world, though. My siblings. So, when we were talking about the repercussions of killing me, we were talking about the ancients all over the world who see me as their wild little sister, who keeps getting into trouble. We're not a pack. We're a family, and we kill for family, even if we don't live together."

"And..." Collins took a long breath. "So, you were Changed by the ruler of all the werecats?"

"Yes. And no, you *don't* get to talk to him. You don't rule *all* the humans. There's a balance of power we need to maintain. He approved the deal, though. They all did."

Collins let out that long breath and sank in his chair. "How does one man rule an entire species?"

"Can't tell you that."

"Can you tell me anything else?"

"Well, if these guys were hired by werewolves, they might not be trying to kill me for being me, but to get back at my father. That's why I accepted the deal. I don't believe the BSA is the leak anymore. I think we're dealing with something a lot more problematic. A werewolf working to hurt werecats where it would sting the worst —killing another one of my father's children, which could potentially start another war. Don't worry, Heath and I have already brushed up against this issue a couple of times."

"Which part?" Collins demanded, a lot more stressed than I wanted him to be.

"The war part." I stood, walked around the desk, and out of the office.

## CHAPTER TWENTY-NINE

I was nearly in the dining room when Collins came running after me, broken out of his shock.

"I need more of an explanation than that," he snapped. "How often do the werecats and werewolves nearly go to war? What sort of tensions are we dealing with here? Do I need to call in a better negotiator? Someone who can talk this down?"

Heath was in the kitchen and dropped what he was holding. Landon caught it. Miller sputtered, spitting his drink out.

"Depends on who is involved," I answered, "and who finds out. Hotter tempers are an issue, and there are some. There's a lot of animosity between the two species of moon cursed. Heath and I are the exceptions, not the rule, remember?" I turned to him, stopping where I was as he barreled toward me. "The worst thing you can do is get more humans involved. If you expose the fact werewolves and werecats are enemies, you'll destroy the trust people have in both kinds once the werecats are revealed. Plus, it'll make the werewolves look like bullies."

"We do have the larger force," Heath agreed. "How did this come up? Why are we talking about war?"

"I was explaining to Collins the problem we have on our hands. I accepted the BSA deal," I explained. "My family was for it, so I decided to pull the trigger. My family's identities aren't revealed, though, so let's keep being careful."

"I'm lost," Miller declared. "Can anyone catch me up?"

"Jacky and Heath have a theory the humans were hired by werewolves to kill her," Collins explained quickly to his partner before glaring at me. "Because she's not just the ruler of werecats in the United States, she's considered the daughter of the ruler of all werecats. This is the kind of important information we need before we make deals with political powers!"

"Which is exactly why I didn't tell you," I fired back. "So you couldn't play hardball with me and try to get to my family. The deal is final. If it's changed before it comes to me to be signed, or if you call your people and tell them any of this, I'll make sure this goes wrong for everyone involved. Are we clear? I'll frame this as the BSA being incompetent, leading to extremists at my door, trying to kill me, and nearly killing a *human girl*. You can ask anyone in this room. I care for that human girl more than anyone here, and I'm willing to die for her. So, try me." I leaned toward him, shorter by a long shot, but still intimidating.

"She's got you in a corner," Heath said, exuding

patience and calm. "If that goes public, it doesn't matter what the truth is. There won't be a werewolf Alpha in the country willing to work with you. There won't be another supernatural species willing to broker deals. We can disappear if we need to...all of us."

"I can tell." Collins' jaw was clenched so tight, I wondered if his teeth were going to crack under the pressure. "Look, I just don't want this to potentially jeopardize human lives, okay? If there's a war—"

"There won't be," I cut him off, disregarding whatever worry he had.

"If there's a war, my people need to know who to talk to when it comes time to stop it before it hurts too many people. I need to tell my bosses exactly who you are." He pulled out his phone again. "I understand you don't like this—"

I grabbed his wrist and held it. He struggled, but I didn't budge. He looked up at me, his eyes going wide.

"Bigger, meaner cousin," I said with a small smile. "Werecats are stronger and faster than werewolves. A single werecat can take down ten of them before our injuries start to hurt. Entire packs go hunting when a werecat is the objective. They can't get into our territories, so they have to catch us outside of them. Don't you dare walk back on me now and break our deal, Special Agent Daniel Collins. You won't like my family when you've made us your enemy."

"For years, werewolves were so scared of her siblings, we called them by nicknames. We didn't want to say their names. Most werewolves still won't," Heath said from behind me.

"I would tell you there's some you need to worry about more than others, but they're all dangerous." I nearly laughed, thinking of my siblings as anything less than extremely worrying. "My identity wouldn't be disclosed to the media, which was a funny addition since obviously someone disclosed it somewhere. You made a deal. Honor it or destroy everything you've tried to build with the BSA. The problems between werecats and werewolves are fixed by better minds, ones who have fought for centuries, then sought peace when they had to reckon with the devastation war left. Anyone who tries for war now is put down with extreme prejudice. There won't be a war."

"But—"

"Just because I said we have to worry about it doesn't mean we're on the edge of one right now. It's always what our lives come back to, especially for Heath and me, two people going against the grain of the problems in our world. War is always on our minds. You're the one blowing this out of proportion. You'll be my handler, right?"

"Well, no, someone else—"

"Then get used to this and warn whoever comes next. Get used to the fact you might see things play out you can't do anything about. Humans won't die. We won't bomb half the country to kill each other. We're more sophisticated than that. You'll see random deaths all across the country. You'll see werewolf packs be destroyed from the inside, entire homes massacred but not a human among them. We'll wipe each other out before humans even know what's happening. You have to trust our rulers, people like me and Heath and the North American Werewolf Council, to work through these problems the right way. You didn't even know about them until I said anything, so don't pretend it's a pressing issue now."

"You're asking me to keep this to myself until the day I die."

"You and Miller." I glanced over my shoulder to see Landon holding a phone, Miller glaring at the werewolf.

"And what happens if we expose you and Heath?" Collins asked softly.

"You'll lose your werecat," I answered, squeezing his wrist just enough to add pain to the equation. "And none of my family will ever talk to you. You'll be lucky if there's a werecat who would even consider it a century from now. They might hate me, they might even be the ones to kill me, but they'll know you can't be trusted."

Collins dropped his phone, and I slowly released his wrist.

"I didn't expect things to be so...precarious," he admitted. "War is a touchy subject since that's what the BSA works so hard to prevent. When we initially started our policy of working with supernaturals, we realized how easily the werewolves had hidden from us and how easily they could have taken over our major cities without us having a chance."

"You're not the only one working every day to prevent a war," I growled. "But a war between werewolves and werecats isn't your business. You humans went centuries, forgetting we even existed, not knowing we were maneuvering right under your noses.

Don't act like we're suddenly a threat you need to deal with."

"You have a good point." He didn't reach for his phone. I leaned down and picked it up, checking for any recording being done, then broke it in half, meeting his stare.

"Just in case," I said softly.

"Please don't break mine," Miller pleaded.

"I won't because I'm going to point out something important," Landon said with a huff. "This is all just a theory, and it's a wild one at that. No self-respecting werewolf should hire amateur humans for a hit on a politically valuable target. If they did, they deserve what's coming to them."

"Landon…" Heath softly chastised. "I agree, but do we trust Miller not to run and tell his bosses everything? He's ex-CIA."

"If he's with the BSA now, he wasn't very good CIA," Landon said, snorting in humor. He didn't break the phone, but he did give me a chance to deescalate this.

"If you two are going to blow this out of proportion, you can both leave…without your phones. Expect us to frame this as if the BSA sold us out and abandoned us. If you want to stay, your bosses don't get to know any of this. If this turns out to be a werewolf, you'll follow the cover story we prepare, and my deal with your agency will remain the same as it was. There's a chance when we catch these guys, your job will be done, and you'll just have to be okay with that."

"Think about everything you can learn if you just follow along," Heath pointed out. "Instead of being reactionary to something that's a daily part of our lives, you can be the men who got the werecats to the table, instead of the ones who ruined the reputation of the BSA."

"We'll follow along," Collins agreed through clenched teeth. "You know I hate this, Heath."

"Yeah, Daniel, we all hate things, but we move on and work with it," Heath countered. "We don't get to decide how the world works. I don't, Jacky doesn't, you don't, and this is one situation where the status quo is very important."

"Then that will be our job," Miller agreed. "As your handlers during negotiations, Jacky, we'll maintain the status quo, so long as you don't keep us in the dark. If anything goes sideways, we do need something to tell our bosses afterward. Right, Daniel?"

Special Agent Daniel Collins, a by-the-book man, as Heath had said, was staring at me. I didn't really know what to tell him or what to say at this point. I had all the cards.

"I hate doing things like this," he said softly. "I think you hid too much during our negotiations, and I think this situation is much more out of control than it should be—"

"If you think this is out of control, I'm glad we didn't meet last summer." I looked at Heath, who shook his head, only his small smile giving away his amusement at my words.

"And I dislike being blackmailed or held hostage by a threat, but..."

*He fucking didn't.*

"That's too damn bad. Maybe if you didn't have a video of me on my private property, of my *naked body* during a full moon, I would have more sympathy. I don't," I snapped. "You violated my privacy and my rights as an American citizen, something I was *born* as. You exposed my kind to your government and jeopardized my position among the werecats, and there's still a chance this is the BSA's fault. Time for you to suck it up and deal because this is *my* territory. I deserve to feel safe here. I deserve my privacy here, and you took that away from me. A little blackmail? Consider what you have on me for a moment, then consider what I'm asking you for. I think it could be a lot worse."

"I was going to say that we can make this work," he snapped. "I'm obviously not the one with all the information here; you are. And..." He shook his head, lowering it and breaking eye contact. "You're right, our surveillance did catch you in a vulnerable position, one no person should be in. Miller and I are the ones who blurred you before sending it to anyone. No one else saw it, not even the two agents we had install the cameras."

I stepped back. "Really? There's not an unedited copy floating around?"

"No, I wasn't comfortable with it," he explained. "We've already deleted everything with both you and Heath."

I could smell no lie.

"Then can we go back to focusing on the problem at hand?" I crossed my arms. "If it's werewolves, you'll let Heath and me deal with this through the proper channels without getting your government involved? Let me promise you now, if there's anything I feel the U.S. can do for a situation, I'll let you know."

He nodded. "I can do that. I'll accept that promise."

"You can tell them about who I am later, just not yet. Not until that paper is signed. They don't get my father. They get me. That was my family's decision. Consider me the ambassador of the werecats, with all legal authority to make the deals necessary. Are we clear?"

"We're clear," he agreed. "I'm going to step out and have a smoke."

"You do that," I said, gesturing to the back door. He was gone in seconds.

"Daniel has a hot temper sometimes," Miller commented. "But he believes in people and in the work we do."

"Good to hear," I muttered, watching the back door. "Can we get to work now that Landon is here? Landon, did you learn anything?"

"Um..." Landon rubbed his hands together. "I don't keep in contact with them as much as I used to, but someone slipped."

"What about?" Heath asked, turning on his son slowly.

"Jacky, there are rumors about your...gifted ability," Landon said carefully. "It came up. One of them asked how I was doing, living near the werecat, and if I had any idea if the rumors were true. I asked what rumors. He told me some of the Russian werewolves were saying they could hear her here." He tapped his head. "People are starting to wonder, and it's getting around. No idea if any Alphas are paying it any mind because it sounds crazy.

The Russian werewolves were in a bad place when they got to the States, but some inner circles are whispering about it."

"You all gossip like old ladies," Heath accused as he sat down.

"I don't," Landon countered with a smile. "I just listen. Oh, Ranger is fourth in Dallas now. Tywin is still on the outs with everyone. Apparently, the Dallas pack can't keep up anymore. He's trying, and you taught him a lot, but he doesn't have your skill. Some think he stepped up too early."

"He was the only option I had," Heath muttered, shaking his head in disappointment. "Well, you were an option, but..."

Landon growled. "You will never see me be an Alpha. Not because of me, but because I hate the job. Being your second was a nightmare, and the only reason I suffered it was because I only had one other option. Being a rogue was worse." Landon grabbed his light jacket from the back of one of the dining room chairs. "I'm going to pick up Carey from school."

"Be safe," Heath ordered.

Landon didn't reply as he left.

"Once Carey gets back, we're going to get the plans ready for tonight. She can do her homework by herself in her room," Heath declared. Collins walked back in at that moment. "My son is picking up my daughter."

"I heard," he said as he tucked his pack of cigarettes into the inside pocket of his blazer.

## 30

# CHAPTER THIRTY

When Landon brought Carey home, she took one look at our group, waved, then took off to her room.

"Smart kid," Miller pointed out.

"Smarter than most adults," I added.

We got to work, planning our attack. Miller used a laptop to check if our target was still in the motel, and once that was verified, we knew what to do. It was decided everyone would go in human form to keep it from drawing too much attention. I would have a sidearm, but I was strong enough in human form to put up a considerable fight against a few humans. I didn't need to be a werecat. A silver bullet would kill me either way. The same went for Heath and Landon.

"This way, we can flash our badges to get us in. You'll be part of the 'team' instead of supernaturals. Even if someone gets a good look at any of you, it'll be late enough, we could say they're mistaken."

"I can shut down their security cameras just in case," Landon commented. "Or cut the power."

"Cameras. If you cut the power, it could create panic." Collins looked at the map and pointed to the main road. "We'll make this simple. Drive right up and hit the room while you cut the cameras and delete any footage that might catch us."

"It's an easy op," Heath said, nodding. "Landon and I have done similar with werewolves. Two humans aren't a problem. Even if there's more than two, Jacky and I are muscle. No one is going to beat us in a close-quarters fight unless they have time to get their weapons up."

"Then we need to hit fast, so they don't have a chance."

After that, we waited, going over the plan again. The agents revealed they had handcuffs on them, standard procedure, ready to make an arrest if it came to that. With that, we waited for dinner to be finished and for the sun to go down.

"Are you all going to do something dangerous tonight?" Carey asked as she ate, her curious and intelligent eyes looking around at us.

"Yes," Heath answered without missing a beat between bites of his casserole. That made both agents look up from their own meals.

"Well, be careful," she said, shrugging.

"You're okay with your father doing something dangerous?" Collins asked with a deep frown.

"My dad is a werewolf, so is my brother." Carey shrugged. "They'll be fine." Everyone with a useful nose could smell her worry, but she was a tough kid. She had seen her family betrayed from within, knew her father killed vampires, and rescued me from other werecats, then went to Russia. "No one beats my dad and Jacky unless they have lots of people or lots of guns."

Collins blinked several times. I enjoyed watching the exchange. It wasn't the most stable house for a young girl to grow up in, but Carey seemed well-adjusted.

"What if you get hurt?" he asked. Heath put his fork down at Collins's question and waited for his daughter's response.

"I won't. I mean, it's a possibility, but I know they'll do anything to stop that from happening. My dad is a werewolf Alpha. They do what's right, and they help people. People get hurt sometimes, but that doesn't mean he's a bad dad. I can break my neck on my horse, but that doesn't mean my horse is bad. That's called a risk." Carey finished her food and took her dishes to the sink. She stopped to kiss her dad, hug her brother, then me before she went upstairs. Before her door closed, we all got a chuckle.

"STAY SAFE!" she yelled across the house. "I'll lock the doors!"

"Thank you!" Heath called back.

The normalcy was a little strange, even to me, but Heath just smirked across the table at me. I knew Carey's feelings were more complex, but her willingness to put herself between us and outside judgment was touching, especially after the bombshell she had earlier in the week.

"The coup wasn't the first time she had a brush with

her dad and something dangerous," Heath said for the table, but it was pointed at me.

"You were a werewolf Alpha. How many challenges did you get after she was born?" I leaned back, putting my own fork down.

"None, but I had to handle other things. Landon had challenges, though."

Landon growled in a vicious but oddly pleased way, making the agents a little stiffer.

*Even Jabari gets weird vibes from Landon. Apparently, that's universal.*

"Let me get that." Heath reached out for my plate, and I slid it closer to him. I didn't want to eat too much. He took the plate and my fork, putting them in the sink with Carey's and his own. Landon went next, offering to take the plates for the agents, who handed them over silently. Landon ended up doing the dishes.

"I think I'm going to look for my own place tomorrow. Finally give that realtor a call," he said while the water ran over the plate he was holding, then tucked it into the dishwasher.

"Good. I need space." Heath picked up a book and sat down, flipping it open to read. I pulled out my phone and checked for anything from my family, Dirk, or Oliver. Kick Shot was doing well, with no incidents so far. That was better than nothing.

"Are we going to act this normal until the sun goes down?" Miller asked, making me look up at him.

"A hunt is a hunt, no matter the prey. No reason to be anxious," I said softly before looking back at my phone. "Right, Heath?"

"Yup." I heard a page turn.

"I'm thinking of something small, two bedrooms, maybe three. Lots of space to run on the full moon. Close by, so I can take Carey when you need it."

"You've lived with me for nearly fourteen years. I don't care what you get as long as you get out of my house," Heath said, chuckling. "Plus, I think Carey will like having space away from you."

"If I had the chance to get away from my sister at her age..." I trailed off. "I don't know. Maybe I would have liked it, maybe not."

"Gwen is your twin," Heath said, looking over his book at me. "A lot different than an adult sibling from a different time."

"Touché."

"This is surreal," Miller whispered to Collins.

"This is supernaturals," Collins replied, unsurprised by this part of the evening.

"If you don't let the bad parts of your life become overwhelming, you can strike a surprising balance," Heath explained, putting his book down. "You're new, Miller?"

"Yes."

"Well, I can't give you a normal look into pack life, but this is...pretty close. Normally, there are no werecats and a lot more wolves. We deal with a hunt at least once a month. Either the full moon or any sort of late-night get-together. Hunting humans or hunting a rogue werewolf trying to commit some crime in the pack's city? No different. I'm at home, I have the authority of the territory with me, and I have my right-hand man." He picked up his book and continued reading.

"Unless someone gets shot, we'll be fine," Landon said as he came to sit back down, a new sound, the dishwasher's gurgling rumble, added to the background.

Carey came downstairs four hours later, close to ten o'clock.

"I'm going to bed."

"Good night. Sweet dreams," Heath said, smiling at his daughter and putting the book down once again. "Remember—"

"I already promised to lock the doors. I'll lock my door, too. You make sure to lock the front when you leave, so I don't have to come down again." She went to the back, checked the lock, then moved on to windows she could reach. I knew this was Heath making sure his daughter remembered the vital survival skills he taught her since she was little. I thought it was a touch excessive, but I didn't help her.

She came back, hugged him with a yawn, and headed back upstairs.

"Now, we can go," he declared. Standing, his benign expression turned hard.

We silently went to his garage, where he unlocked his gun safe, something I still didn't have the combination to, not that I wanted or needed it. He brought out holsters and sidearms for the three of us.

"I got one for you a while ago, just in case," he admitted softly as I put it on.

"Mm-hm." I took the handgun from him and put it in the holster, after checking the safety and, thankfully, finding it on. I had no intention of taking it out and using it. In fact, I was planning on avoiding it. The less firepower used, the more likely we would take someone alive.

Once everyone was armed, we got into our separate vehicles and rolled out, Heath locking the front door using his phone.

"You have smart locks?" I asked. "I never noticed."

"I got them over winter and never thought it was worth mentioning. Your key still works on the back door. Now, I can check the locks when I'm not home. All the windows, too," he admitted.

"And I thought I was paranoid," I teased. "But really, that's a good idea. Do I have those installed at Kick Shot?"

"Yes, Oliver has control of them. I think Dirk does, too. You were so attached to just using your keys, none of us wanted to disturb that."

"I see." I chuckled, nodding. "It's just an app? I'll get the information and add the thing to my phone for security reasons."

"I could add it to your house, too," he murmured, leaning toward me as he drove with a smile.

"Is this how you win my heart now? New security features?"

"I like to think of it as mutually beneficial. You feel safer, and I know you're safer without being an Alpha installing things without your approval."

I leaned into him with a smile. It didn't last long. This wasn't a cute date, that was something Heath and I didn't get to do.

We were going to capture humans who were trying to kill me and figure out why.

"I guess it's time to get serious," I whispered, losing the fleeting joy. "What do you think we'll find?"

"I'm hoping we find the BSA is the leak, and they can work a lot harder to be careful with information of supernaturals," he said with a long sigh. "But I think we *both* know what we're going to find, even though it's not the most likely option."

"I wonder which of your old friends is trying to kill me."

"I'm wondering the same thing."

## CHAPTER THIRTY-ONE

We sped up to the motel, last in line. Landon went first, his truck barely parked before he was out and running to the main office. Miller jumped out of the large black SUV and followed him, pulling his badge out of his suit. All Miller and Landon had to do was cut the feed, which would only take seconds. Heath and I stopped behind the SUV, our seatbelts off the moment we were in the parking lot. I was able to get out of the truck, running toward Collins as he got out of the SUV.

We already knew the room number, knew it was on the second floor, but we didn't know exactly where it was in the building. We hadn't been able to get those building plans.

Heath was up the steps first. We triple-checked each door, making sure no one accidentally missed it. Miller and Landon came up the other side, running down the catwalk in front of the doors until Miller stopped and pointed. Even from the distance, I could hear loud music playing inside the room.

The others drew their weapons as Landon kicked open the door.

Everyone ran into the room, weapons up. I made it in last, the room feeling crowded. My nose was immediately hit by the stench of people who hadn't showered in days, stale beer, and a variety of fast food. My ears didn't like the music, not the choice but the volume. I used my foot to keep the door open, gun up to fire if it became necessary, as the guys rushed our targets.

I knew their faces. Shocked and paralyzed, I recognized their faces from the time they tried to kill me on the road.

"Hands up! Show us your hands!" Miller roared over the music. "Don't move and show us your hands! Keep them above your head!"

Landon grabbed one by his shirt and snarled, sniffing deeply.

"Stupid to be drinking," he growled.

Miller was right next to him, yanking one of the guy's hands behind his back.

I just stared as Heath and Collins tried to grab the other, who was screaming he didn't do anything. Then he saw me and lunged for something. Heath tackled him onto one of the small beds, holding the human down with ease.

"Didn't do anything?" Heath snarled in his face. "What were you about to do? Huh?"

Sam Blake was quiet now as Heath got off him and hauled him to his feet. Sam's glare was full of hate, but I didn't know why. Why did this human man, who I had never met, hate me enough to do this?

I was so focused on the fight, I hadn't been looking back out the door, covering everyone the proper way a soldier or agent would, so when I heard a gun cock behind me, I knew I was in a bad position.

This guy wasn't going to give me a speech about killing me. I dropped down and threw my head to the side, feeling the hot burn of the silver bullet on that delicate place where my neck and my shoulder met. It was a drop of lava, a searing pain like I had touched a stove—one of those heats that felt cold.

I lost the grip on my gun as I hit the floor and screamed, grabbing the spot where I had been hit. The bullet hadn't stopped when it hit its target. It had found another victim.

Special Agent Collins was down. He hadn't heard what I had and had no idea someone was going to shoot. I didn't know if he was alive or dead in that long span of eternity as I looked at him on the ground.

"MOVE!" Heath screamed.

Looking up, I saw the barrel of the gun. Without thinking, I grabbed it, pushing it away from my face, and heard it go off as I stared in the face of this new threat. I pulled down and brought the human to me, probably breaking something. He fell on top of me, yelling in either shock or pain. Yanking the gun from his hand, I pushed it away while he was trying to get his bearings. Taking a handful of his shirt to hold him in place, I nailed him with a right hook that sent him off me and onto the weird carpet flooring of the motel.

"You bitch!" he snapped.

I didn't give him a chance to say anything else,

lunging and holding him on the catwalk with my own brute strength, snarling in his face. He was reaching for something as I hit him again, breaking bones in his face. Something stabbed my leg, drawing forth a feline scream as I let my rage fuel me.

This motherfucker and his friends tried to kill me. I yanked out the silver dagger from my thigh and sent it into the man's shoulder, purposefully not fatal. He howled in pain now. When I reared back, ready to throw another punch, someone grabbed my wrist.

"We need him to talk," Heath said desperately. "You'll kill him, Jacky, and we need him to talk."

I yanked my hand away, but I pulled the punch, hitting the human just hard enough to knock his head on the concrete. He was still yelling as I got off him and used his shirt to haul him to his feet. I left the dagger in him as I spun him to hit a wall.

"Who do you work for?" I demanded. When he didn't answer as fast as I wanted, I grabbed the hilt of the small dagger and twisted, making him scream again.

"Jacky! Get him in a fucking truck!" Heath ordered. "We can't do this here!"

"How's Collins?" I asked, looking into the room. Collins was sitting up, looking dazed as Heath and Miller looked over his injury.

"He'll live. It looks like it went through, but he needs to go to a hospital. We're lucky it didn't hit Landon. Miller—"

"I'll call in the ambulance. You three get them out of here before the local cops arrive," Miller said. "We'll cover for you. Once they see our badges, they usually go about their business. Most local cops don't want anything to do with supernatural problems."

Heath nodded. I didn't stay after that, using the guy's shirt to yank him off the wall, practically dragged him down the stairs to Heath's truck. We only had two pickups and an SUV.

"I have the keys," Landon yelled, pushing his quarry toward the SUV. "Bring that one to me, and I'll tie him."

"Y-You're a c—"

This time, I didn't hit him, just shoved him into the side of the SUV without any sort of grace.

"Who do you work for?" I asked softly as Heath and Landon shoved in the two they had.

"F-Fuck you."

I shoved him at Heath, snarling.

"Take him and keep him from dying."

Heath looked at the dagger where I had stabbed the asshole as Landon rushed to tie the man's hands behind his back.

"He'll be fine. We'll take it out and patch it up at my place. Take my truck. Keys are still in the ignition."

Running to the truck as I heard the ambulances, I pulled out of the parking lot first, with the SUV then Landon's truck following. I didn't know who got that lonely duty with our new friends, but I hoped they were safe.

When we got back to Heath's home, I helped get the new captives inside before we sat them down at the dining table. Landon expertly tied them to the chairs while Heath went into the kitchen and grabbed his knife block. I found the first aid kit. As much as I hated the job, we didn't need anyone dying on us. They had questions to answer.

"Humans don't realize they're not powerful until they run up against a supernatural," Heath said as he slammed the knife block onto his dining table. "If you scream so loud you wake up my daughter, I promise you won't enjoy it."

"Daughter?" one said, looking around in fear.

"Yeah, the one someone shot Jacky in front of," Heath said with a snarling smile. "I'm Alpha Heath Everson. I used to rule the Dallas pack. It's nice to meet you young men. Behind you is my son Landon." Landon gave a vicious growl, making another of the humans jump. "And you all know the woman behind me with the first aid kit. That's Jacky Leon."

"You can't kill us. It's murder," said the one I stabbed, his breathing labored, and his shirt stained in blood, blood still spreading. The fact he wasn't unconscious yet was a testament to his will. "You owe us due process and—"

Heath pulled the dagger out of him, and the scream was ear-piercing.

"Father, you'll wake her up," Landon commented lightly, undisturbed by the noise.

"She's not in her room." Heath put the dagger on the table. "I asked her to sleep in the safe room tonight."

"Ah." Landon nodded slowly. "Good to know." Landon's smile was edging to somewhat insane.

*This is the edge people feel. That I feel.*

*He's willing and able to do violence and enjoy it.*

Heath took the first aid kit from me and patched up the shoulder.

"You three have been having a bit of fun in this town," he said, wiping the blood off his hands with a washcloth Landon handed to him when the patch job was done. "You've been trying to kill a dear friend of mine—" He started to gesture to me.

"You can't prove anything!" one of them yelled, struggling in his chair until he fell over. No one moved to pick him up, and the chairs were solid wood.

"You should let me continue," Heath said softly, looking down at the humans. "I'm Heath Everson, and in my world, your lives are already forfeit, but there's something you can do to fix this."

"We'll let you live if you explain why," I clarified. "Although we're not required to. One of you shot an agent of the Bureau of Supernatural Affairs, so you're not in the best position to bargain."

"We just...we..." One of them was more scared than the others. Two were silent, aside from the whimpers, but Sam Blake was about to crack. He was terrified.

"You just what?" Landon growled over his shoulder. "Thought you could kill an innocent woman because you don't like that she gets furry on a full moon? If that's the case, we have the responsibility to protect all supernaturals from humans like you."

Heath stopped his pacing in front of Sam and leaned down.

"And we're more than willing to end a threat," he said softly, calmer than his son.

"He promised," Sam whispered. "He promised. I don't hate supernaturals. He said I could be one—"

"Shut up, Sam! Once those agents get here, we'll get fifteen to twenty-five, then we're out. His lawyers will help us. Don't tell them shit!" The one I had stabbed was pissed at his buddy. I looked at him, crossing my arms.

"What's your name?" I asked, tilting my head to the side. I wanted to kill these guys. They were defenseless, so the feeling made me uncomfortable, but I wanted to gut them open and watch them die. The primal fear and anger I had been walking too close to for nearly two weeks were now dangerously close to the surface. I knew my eyes glowed gold as I glared at this human. Heath and Landon looked at me, and I could see the soft glow of their animal eyes as well, Heath's ice blue and Landon's a golden-brown, which seemed too bright for his face.

"None of your business," he muttered, trying to move his chair farther away from me.

"Let's do this differently then. We've given you three the chance to talk together. Time to talk alone." Heath nodded at Sam, and Landon moved to pick up the prisoner's chair, walking it out of the room. "You two behave while Jacky and I have a chat."

Heath and I followed Landon. I had never done anything like this, but the father-son pair seemed as if they had years of experience with these kinds of *talks*.

Landon put Sam in Heath's office, then left to watch the two left in the dining room.

When I entered the office, I heard the click as Heath locked us in with this would-be assassin.

## 32

# CHAPTER THIRTY-TWO

"Sam, if you tell us what we need to know, this doesn't have to be bad," Heath said softly as he leaned onto his desk. I walked around him and sat behind the desk. I couldn't trust myself not to kill someone, and I hit harder than the werewolves.

The idea of torture scared me, genuinely made me uncomfortable, and I wasn't sure I wanted part of it once it started. I had been acting in a fit of rage when I stabbed the human and twisted the knife.

Now my head was clear, and I just wanted to get to the real source of my problems. I wanted to know who started this, and I wanted to fix *that*. If these three were wayward souls, hired to do this, they weren't actual threats. They were just desperate for money or whatever they were offered.

Sam took a deep, shaky breath as he looked up at Heath, then at me.

"I don't want to die," he said, swallowing. "It was never supposed to go like this. We were told it would be easy, and it was for the good of..." Sam frowned at Heath. "You're a werewolf, right?"

"Yes," Heath answered, crossing his arms.

"The guy who hired us said it was for the good of all werewolves. He said if someone went against this, they were going against the pack, and..." Sam looked down. "The job was to kill this one chick because she was going to bring more problems for the werewolves, then he would turn us."

I could smell Heath's shock. Quid pro quo Changing was frowned upon. Every person needed to be carefully judged for their suitability for the Change. Each species had its own way of doing that, but quid pro quo wasn't considered acceptable in lieu of normal testing methods.

"Turn? Did he say turn?" I asked softly.

"Um...yeah?" Sam didn't understand my question, but that was okay. I raised an eyebrow as Heath looked over his shoulder at me. Sam didn't think he was lying, but there was a chance he misremembered, based on what word he wanted to use.

"It's just an interesting choice of words," I explained for Sam. "Werewolves and werecats *Change* people. It's a common misconception."

"Well, in reality, we just infect them with the same curse that causes us to turn into beasts on the full moon." Heath shrugged. "But turning isn't the normal word packs use. Let's stay on topic, though. Someone told you Jacky was a threat to the pack, and if you killed her, you would join the pack."

"Yes," Sam answered, nodding vigorously.

"Your knee is getting worse?" I asked, and this time,

Sam went pale, and I saw a bit of his anger and could smell it on the air like faint rot.

"I did everything for it, and it gives out on me. The pack is like the military, and I...I need that community. I have nowhere else to go. My knee won't let me go back to the military, and private security firms..." He shook his head.

"They're not the service." Heath was sympathetic to the plight of this veteran. "You seem like a good man, Sam, so I'm going to ask you to look at her." He pointed at me. "She was born and raised in this country. She leads a quiet group of people, all trying to live their lives, enjoy their freedoms, and work hard not to hurt people. In fact, unless someone forces their hand, she's part of a very peaceful family who preach peace and unity. The only pack that would be threatened by her is one that doesn't believe in those ideals, and that pack misled you."

Sam narrowed his eyes on me, studying me. "How can I believe that?"

"Someone asked you to commit a murder," I said, countering his question of our trust with some logic of my own. "Murder, Sam. When the pack faces a threat, the pack fights together. It's the werewolves' greatest strength and the way they win against things like me. Yet, for some reason, whoever told you to do this didn't send you with the pack. They sent three humans to kill a supernatural with silver bullets and no real plan. Does that make any sense to you?"

"He..." Sam looked between us. "Oh my God."

"He used you," Heath whispered kindly. "Preying on your need for community and healing for your knee. He didn't think any of you would live through this. He expected you to kill her, then to die for it." Heath reached out and touched Sam's shoulder, kneeling in front of the man. I now saw Heath had never planned on torturing anyone. He found the weakest link and did what he was good at. He was their Alpha for a moment, offering them wisdom and comfort, guiding them to where he wanted them to be.

"Why don't you tell us the entire story?"

"I got a part-time job as a parking garage security guard. Alpha Price and the Boston pack used it for a lot of things. We got talking a couple years ago, and eventually, he gave me a job in the pack, and I put in a package to get...Changed. I was never picked, but, uh, a week ago, he said he knew something I could do to get to the top of the list. He would Change me the moment it was done. He had them, too." Sam jerked his head toward the door. "She was going to destroy the werewolves, and if we killed her before she had the chance, we would be werewolves, too. That's it. I agreed to put everything in my name, so the other guys could be covered. Thought I was doing something...something good for the pack. I don't know how all this supernatural stuff works."

"Have you been having second thoughts?" Heath asked softly.

"Yeah, of course," Sam said quickly, the truth apparent through his scent and the pained expression on his face. "I was getting drunk when you showed up because I was getting cold feet, you know. We tried twice, and she's...right there." He nodded at me. "And like...she was hanging out with that little girl and you, and she's got the bar. I just didn't understand. David and Jacob said she must be good at keeping it secret, but..." Sam shook his head. "I was planning on leaving in the morning and telling Alpha Price I couldn't do it. We tried twice, and she was still alive, but sometimes missions fail."

"Most supernaturals are notoriously hard to kill. Don't feel bad about it." I honestly felt for this guy, something I didn't want to do. He'd shot at me and run me off the road. He or one of his buddies took a cheap shot at me, which was now aching painfully, thanks to the rush of activity. My neck burned, something I hadn't even looked at yet.

And Sam gave me the name I needed, so he wasn't too bad of a guy.

*Alpha Price.*

"We're done," Heath decided. "We're going to take you back out to the dining room. Landon will get you some water and keep you away from the others—"

"They won't talk to you, but I can tell you everything," Sam said quickly. Heath waved for him to continue. "David was the one with me when we opened fire on your car." He directed it at me. "I drove, and he shot at you. He told me to ram your car, so I did. He was the one who tried to kill you at the movie theater. I mostly drove us around and put stuff in my name. Now that I look back, I was the fall guy, wasn't I?"

"Probably," Heath agreed. "Someone got your license plate, which led us to your name. Then we saw the credit card charges for the motel. They were using you to keep all the evidence in your name. It could have been any two people off the street in that truck with you."

"Jacob's laptop will get him. He's a POG."

"What's a pog?" I frowned this time.

"Person other than grunt," Heath answered, chuckling softly. "Supply and tech guys, people who don't see combat very often, if ever. Grunts call them POGs. It's an insult."

"Ah..." I nodded. "What was Jacob doing on his laptop?"

"Tracking your phone."

I growled softly, and Heath lifted a hand.

"Let's get Sam more comfortable somewhere else, then we'll handle the others."

I stayed in the office as Heath and Landon switched who we had. Instead of going to David, the primary attacker, we took aim at Jacob, the POG, as Sam had called him.

Jacob didn't want to be in front of me. His hateful glare was one of those dangerous looks that told me I had made an enemy for life for the terrible offense of not dying.

"We don't need you to tell us who did this or why. I just want to know how you got my phone number."

"Fuck you," he snapped. "You fucking stabbed me, and now you're violating my rights as an American citizen."

I lifted my hands in defeat, looking at Heath to handle this one.

"Why don't you head home?" Heath asked softly. "You still have my keys, and now you have a name. Take it to your family and see what they say. I don't know Alpha Price that well, so I can't even begin to understand his motivation. I'll decide what to do with these three without you. I'll probably hand them over to someone we can trust to keep them alive until we can use their testimony."

"Of course. Call me tomorrow. Get in touch with Miller, too. See if Collins is okay." I didn't touch Heath or kiss him in front of this human, who would most definitely tell someone.

"It's on the to-do list," Heath promised. There was a heat in his eyes that made my toes curl, so I waved for him to come closer to me as if we needed to get away from Jacob to say something.

He followed me out of the office, and the moment no one was watching, I threw my arms around him, holding him tightly. He pushed me against the hallway wall and kissed me like our lives depended on it.

"I needed that," I said softly, leaning my forehead against his.

"You and me both," he said, chuckling as he lowered his lips to mine again.

If I had all night, I would have stayed. In a heartbeat, I would have stayed there with him, letting him be my rock, my friend, and my lover. I would have watched a movie with him on his couch and pretended like none of this was happening.

I didn't have all night.

I kissed him one more time before forcing myself to walk away and was able to get out the front door before I stopped to look at him through the window.

## 33

# CHAPTER THIRTY-THREE

It wasn't hard for me to contact my family even though it was well past midnight my time when I reached out. I was exhausted, but I wasn't done. Just because the threat was over from the humans that Alpha Price hired didn't mean this was completely over. I had a new target, and this one was an Alpha werewolf who tried to execute a member of the werecat ruling family.

"Do you have news?" Hasan asked before any of my siblings could get a word in. Many of them were still trying to find their seats, confused why they were getting called in the middle of the night. I hadn't sent an email or message, just called and let it ring until people answered. I cut the connection to Zuri, knowing she wouldn't show up. She would get a brief from someone, and I was in a bit of a rush. So much had happened in less than forty-eight hours, and I had to get everyone caught up.

"I accepted the deal with the BSA. They know I'm part of the werecat ruling family, but they don't know who any of you are. We caught the humans trying to kill me and discovered they were hired to play-pretend for a werewolf Alpha here in the United States who wants me dead." I rambled the information before anyone could interrupt. I took a breath and kept going. "Heath and Landon have the humans. One of the BSA agents was shot and is at the hospital as far as I know. The alpha is Alpha Price, here in Boston—"

Hasan's low snarl and the furious look in his eyes were supposed to tell me something.

"Do we know the name?" I asked softly, looking around at the surprised and somewhat horrified faces of my family.

"We were sworn to silence," Jabari answered. "But yes, we know the name."

Sworn to silence. Werewolf Alpha.

It hit me like a battering ram, a realization that shook me and forced me to sit down.

"Is this the Alpha who was involved with Liza's death? Who executed the wolves who did it, so...so he was let go? Is it?"

"Because he took the appropriate action, we were sworn to secrecy," Hisao said softly. "And promised not to take action against him, including encouraging others to be his enemies. We can't tell other werecats who was the Alpha of the werewolves who killed Liza."

They were doing so in as many words.

"Okay, this is all very pressing to deal with, but..." Mischa was glaring at me. "Jacky, you are *bleeding*!"

I looked down at my shoulder and groaned. "It's not

bleeding anymore. I'll have to peel my jacket off it, but it's—"

"You should go deal with it," Niko said kindly. "Were you hit during the capture of the humans?"

"Yeah, there was a third we didn't know about. He was able to get behind me. I mostly dodged his shot. I was grazed, and it hit someone else. I'll add it to the long list of times I've been shot or nearly shot." I didn't have that many scars, I didn't think, but there was definitely a pattern forming.

While they watched, I pulled off my shirt to show them it wasn't bleeding anymore. I had a first aid kit in the office. The little red boxes were everywhere now—three at Kick Shot in my office, Oliver's office, and the kitchen downstairs. There was one in my home, had been one in my car, and Heath kept them stashed in dozens of places as well. I was certain Landon would stash even more around his home once he got his own place. I knew Oliver and Dirk had one at their home.

Sitting in my bra and jeans, I let them watch me as I cleaned the wound, unperturbed by their presence. I slapped a bandage on it and taped it down, then put my shirt back on, bloody but my only option.

"Better?" I asked, looking up. "Look, there's a case that maybe Liza wasn't a one-off accident. He's tried to kill me now, and I have humans telling the truth about who hired them. He offered to Change them in return for my death, but let's be real, if they weren't killed by any of you, he would have done it himself."

My family just stared at me as if they weren't allowed

to say the obvious, so I continued, understanding they weren't just gagged because they promised. This was *magic*. Everything they had told me about Liza's death was *all* they could tell me.

*In the name of keeping the peace, they had to deal with letting Liza die and never getting to investigate the Alpha, who just moved to another pack with the protection of other werewolves. This is the sacrifice of my family. No wonder Davor is pissed. He never got justice. None of them did.*

*And they know it.*

"Just like he did with the werewolves when they killed Liza. This time, he tried to frame humans because if werewolves had attacked me, there would be no recourse for him, not again. We would have put it together." I pointed at them. "You could have told me you were magically gagged."

Hasan opened and closed his mouth, trying to say something. His face contorted, and he growled.

"We never saw a reason to. Do you really think it's something we *like*? We thought the situation was put to rest, Jacky. Liza's death has always been hard for this family. If we believed otherwise, we would have said something, put you on the investigation, or found some way to tell you more. But with the vow of secrecy, technically a geas, we've told you the story everyone knows. We believed it was true and *agreed* to it. A group of young werewolves thought they were doing something good by killing Liza. By the time we got there, our hearts broken, the Alpha involved had already executed the traitors of his pack who had acted on their own. Callahan and I both verified the Alpha hadn't lied about his lack of involvement, and we agreed to protect the Alpha's identity. Everyone who knew of the incident was put under a large spell by Alvina, a geas to protect his identity. Everyone who didn't know was free to learn the public story." Hasan rubbed his face. "Now, you're bringing evidence that we were all fooled, and this Alpha has acted *again*."

"Alpha Price," I said, repeating his name just for the hell of it since no one else could. "I know you can't confirm if it's really him, but I think we can get him for trying to kill me. I just need a meeting to be set up. I need to talk to the NAWC anyway about the deal the United States of America and the werecats have come to. I need to make sure they're clear the rules that apply to them and to us are different and for good reason."

"I can make that happen," Hasan said softly. "But why? Why do this? To you or to Liza?"

"I...don't know, but I have some theories. I'm sure you all can put it together, but I'll say them if you can't. I've made enemies here in the States among the werewolves, possibly around the world after my visit to Russia and getting involved in that pack's internal business. There's a chance he just thinks I should die for it. It's not unreasonable for him to think if he pinned it on humans and the BSA, he would be crippling our family in the United States for years to come. Even a century after Liza died, this family is obviously still not over it. Hasan gave up his Tribunal power for a hundred years and only came out of grieving for me. Imagine what losing a second young daughter would be like? Before me, Liza was the most vulnerable, and now I'm the most vulnerable out of us, especially with the exposure I brought on our people. He might just hate us, Hasan. He might hate everything we stand for, hate werecats. That could be it. He might even be the wolf who gave up my name to the BSA to kick this off, to make a situation where my death seemed likely."

"We never did find out which wolf gave up your name," Hisao commented. "It seems as though it really was accidental, an overheard conversation. There was no malicious plot we could find in that aspect, but this Alpha seems very adept at covering his tracks."

"If it's not him, and my exposure is really just all my fault, I'm willing to accept that. I'm glad the BSA isn't as terrible as I thought, knowing they have some procedures I don't agree with. Hopefully, I can have a strong working relationship with them going forward. But let's go back to the part where someone tried to kill me."

"It would cripple us," Jabari said softly, leaning over. "We couldn't do it again and let the people walk away without proper investigation. We would..."

"Executions," Hisao whispered. "I'd kill every single one of them."

"Then we're off to the races for war," Mischa said softly, opening her hands as if I should have known to expect this.

"I figured." I wasn't surprised. Hasan believed family was the most important thing and had pushed that into most of his children, which spiraled into more complicated things. An attack on this family was an attack on all werecats, a direct assault on the leaders of the werecats.

"I can set up a meeting," Hasan said, the fury in his eyes a bit scary. "I'll set up a meeting with Alvina, Callahan, Corissa, and the Alphas from the council."

"Alvina? The Fae Queen on the Tribunal?"

"Yes. She's the one who swore us all to secrecy, including the werewolves from *that* Alpha's pack. With her, we can lift it for a long discussion."

"Do you think we can get Alpha Price for this?" I asked, crossing my arms. "I have witnesses who will testify, whether they want to or not, or I'm willing to let Alvina rummage in my head for my secrets if that's needed to verify the truth of my words." I knew the fae could do that and some witches as well. They would go into memories and witness what I had seen and heard.

"She might want to," Hasan warned. "Are you prepared for that?"

"I'll have to be if it gets justice for this family," I said, leaning back in my chair. I knew what I was risking and could only hope Alvina would protect secrets she had no business having. She was the fae queen, though, so I couldn't really know how it would turn out.

My family deserved justice. Alpha Price couldn't get away with this again. Hasan and my siblings had fought for peace. They had allowed the werewolves to internally handle Liza's murderers, a token of peace to not further escalate the issue. They were living what they preached, and I had to protect that, just like I had to protect them from exposure to the humans.

"Set up the meeting," I said softly. "Oh, and the

humans, they actually attacked me a second time. They shot me in a parking lot. Special Agent Collins was able to get me flown to Dallas for treatment. I was treated and discharged the same day. It wasn't a good shot. I got lucky. These humans aren't professionals. Figured I should mention that before someone else does since a Dallas werewolf saw me."

Three of my family members put their heads in their hands. Jabari and Hasan were glaring. I knew everyone was on edge.

"I'm fine," I whispered, lifting the shirt to reveal the new fun hole that would scar within the month. "It's been a busy couple of days, and I didn't want everyone flying out to me."

"I give up," Hasan declared. "I'll set up the meeting. You can decide with Heath Everson and the BSA what you want to do about your human attackers. We'll support the decision, no matter what you decide. When does the BSA go public with the existence of our kind?"

"I don't know. We haven't finalized that part. I don't think it'll take longer than a few weeks?"

"Fine. I'm headed off to contact Callahan and Alvina to set up your meeting."

He disconnected, but once he was gone, none of my siblings left. In fact, they were all waiting for something else.

"Thank you," Davor whispered. "I always knew something was wrong with how she died." At that moment, I realized he hadn't said anything. Cutting, mean, awful Davor had been silent for the entire conversation. He wasn't the only one, but he was the most notable.

One by one, each of my siblings relaxed.

"We'll get justice for her," I promised him, then disconnected the video call.

## 34

# CHAPTER THIRTY-FOUR

It happened quickly. Heath agreed to hand over all three of my would-be assassins to an Alpha on the NAWC, picking his old friend Geoffrey Lewis, the Alpha of Seattle's werewolves. It had been a strange shuffle through Dallas, with that pack helping, but within twelve hours, the three humans had a new home in Seattle. Eighteen hours after I hung up on my family, I was talking to Alpha Lewis before our meeting, now that he had eyes on the three humans who had tried to kill me —repeatedly.

"Can I know why I'm holding these guys?" Alpha Lewis asked over the phone. "They're not happy, but they're not talking, either. They're the humans who have been trying to kill you, right?"

"Yes, and you'll find out soon," I promised over the speakerphone in my office at Kick Shot. "You may have received a summons to the meeting starting in...an hour. I can say it's a lot better for them to be with werewolves and werecats than for them to go to the BSA. You're lucky

I convinced my first contact special agents of that. One of them was shot when we were getting those humans into our custody, and they really wanted custody."

"The gymnastics you must have done," Alpha Lewis said with a chuckle. "Fine. I look forward to the mysteries being unraveled at the meeting. I'm glad to offer my holding cells to the people who rooted out the vampire corruption that was ravaging the mountains of my home."

"Again, thank you. Just keep them alive until we get through the meeting. Their fates will probably be decided there."

"Not hard to do. I put my personal guard on them. No one will go near them."

"You haven't told anyone about them, right?"

"Only Callahan, who was expecting it. Did you pass along word to him? He didn't seem surprised."

"Yeah, through proper channels," I confirmed. I told Hasan the plan for the humans guilty of attempted murder, and he had made sure everyone was up to speed.

Alpha Lewis was a good choice. He liked both Heath and me from the Seattle incident, even though it had been somewhat destabilizing for him. We'd rescued one of his wolves and killed the vampires who murdered the others. It had been a bad situation for my family as well because those vampires had killed two loved and respected werecats who'd had a peaceful arrangement with the werewolves in that region of the States.

"Should I be worried about this meeting?"

"I don't know if I can answer that," I admitted. "Look, I'll see you soon, and all will be clear. Thank you again for taking them off my hands. I don't have a mini prison at my disposal."

"Heath used to, then he decided to run off and try this whole being a single father thing." Geoffrey chuckled as he hung up.

I stretched and yawned. I wasn't low on sleep, but there was a lot happening. The last eighteen hours weren't only used to set this meeting up and deal with the humans, but also to work on the final details of the werecat and human relationship. Collins was fine, in a sling for a few months, and Miller was no worse for wear. They were going to release the information about werecats on Carey's birthday. I had agreed to the date because it wasn't going to interfere with the business at hand. Getting them to relinquish the humans to supernaturals had been difficult, but the BSA had agreed when they realized the PR nightmare it would be, and no matter what the BSA wanted, a supernatural was going to handle the humans because of their crimes.

Through it all, I was only focused on one thing, only one thread of this complicated knot that truly worried me —Alpha Price of the Boston werewolf pack, once the Alpha of Paris.

I had asked Heath for more information, nothing to do with Liza, and he had given me everything he could. The Alpha was stiff and quiet, known to only speak the truth. In the werewolf's six hundred years, he had never lied. It was such a big deal that Heath was confused how Price thought he was going to get away with this. I had no theories about that, either. Would he accept his punishment now that he'd lost, or would he fight back?

*The only way I'll get that answer is by going to the meeting.*

I dressed in a simple outfit, nothing fancy, not a suit or a skirt, just nice jeans, a t-shirt without a band logo on it, and a leather jacket without patches or holes. Most of my clothing was suited for working behind the bar, not in the office, and I was dragging my feet updating my look. I topped it off with simple black boots with a flat heel and no scuff marks. I wanted to be stable on my feet, just in case. I fixed my hair, letting it lie on my shoulders instead of throwing it up into a ponytail.

Lastly, I texted Hasan that I was ready to go, however he intended to get me to this meeting.

I was in my kitchen when I sent the text. A moment later, I heard a creak and turned to see my laundry room door open to reveal a beautiful woman, who looked like she walked out of a Tolkien novel and put on a classy, black business suit.

I knew her face and her name, but I had never seen her so closely.

Queen Alvina was drop-dead gorgeous, and her incredibly long, pointed ears seemed pronounced this close. She was only three steps away.

"Your...your Maj—"

"The children of Hasan may call me Alvina," she said quickly. "We've met before." Her eyes practically twinkled. "That was a very exciting time."

"Yeah." It had been at my trial.

"I helped with your human family's memories as well," she said softly. "Hasan asked me to open a door for you here. Sadly, favors aren't allowed between members of the Tribunal." Those twinkling eyes turned a little mischievous.

I didn't move, uncomfortable with the interaction.

"You've met at least one fae before," she decided, nodding. "Hasan knows too much about us and would have taught you to be careful, even if it's just following old human legends about us because they might turn out to be true. Very smart of you. I'm just teasing, though. I'm quite interested in seeing how this plays out today. Come inside." She stepped out of the doorway and held the door for me to rush inside, following me with a single step, and closing the door. I was in the Tribunal's pocket dimension, but I didn't recognize the space. She walked down the hall, and I knew I needed to follow her. She breezed into a room where Hasan and Callahan were waiting.

"She's well met, Hasan," Alvina declared. "If a bit *stiff*." She made a small gesture, laughing melodically.

"You can be frightening to people with little experience with fae," Hasan countered. I walked across the room to him, forcing me to pass Callahan, who looked up at me and nodded respectfully.

"Good to see you again, Jacky Leon," he greeted.

"Is it?" I mumbled as I made it to Hasan.

The werewolf laughed. "No, not at all. Hasan can't tell me the entirety of your little theory, but with Alvina here, I have a feeling I know what this is about." He tipped back his entire drink and placed his glass roughly on the center table. "We put this to rest a hundred years ago, but of course, the most inexperienced and wild of Hasan's children would think she's solved some great conspiracy that we need to handle right now. Why am I not surprised?"

I didn't say anything, knowing I should have kept my mouth shut. Hasan growled softly, but it was Alvina who cracked the verbal whip.

"You asked us to leave Corissa out of this meeting. Don't make me ask her to stop by to keep you on your leash, dog."

"Don't talk to me about Corissa. You can't keep your own brother in line. Either of them," Callahan snapped in return. "Oisin was helping hide an entire species from us, something we let slide to keep the peace, and Brion disappeared completely. Brion, a *founding member* of the Tribunal. The first and only to *leave*. Don't you dare come at me when the kings of the fae have been repeated problems for the Tribunal."

Alvina inhaled sharply. "For that, I can't wait to help Jacky expose whatever awful thing one of your werewolves did." She smiled sharply. "Knowing her and Hasan, I have a feeling I won't have to try to make it look bad. It just will."

I found a seat, not on any of the luxurious couches around the room, but at a small table on the side of the room, behind Hasan. I didn't want to be in the middle of a spat between two ancient beings. Hasan, however, looked eternally bored.

"One day, we'll give my daughter a good impression of this Tribunal," he muttered, looking away from both of them.

"Ah, yes. Hasan acting like he's better than all of us." Callahan snorted derisively.

"I *am* better than you," Hasan returned, not growling, snarling, or anything other than utterly bored. He wasn't acting the way I was used to. He was purposefully antagonistic. "Proven that time and time again for the world to see. And if you attack my daughter's abilities or intelligence again, I'll prove it again."

"I'll remind you that you were losing the war and had to accept some bad deals as punishment," Callahan growled.

"The war was eight hundred years ago," Alvina said with a groan. "When are both of you going to stop bringing it up?"

"Are they coming?" Hasan asked. "Your little council?"

"At least all of my closest advisors and Alphas *earned* their positions." Callahan looked around Hasan at me. "They weren't given the position for their loyalty. They had to *earn* that once they were powerful enough to lead their own packs."

My face heated.

Alvina turned to me and frowned. "My apologies. You must not have a good impression of the Tribunal. When situations have nothing to do with us, we're normally much friendlier. When we're directly involved, tempers get heated."

"There's no problem," I said carefully, knowing who I was talking to and in front of. If there was a problem, I would be offended by Alvina and Callahan.

"You can admit it," Hasan said, looking over his shoulder at me. "Alvina isn't allowed to play fae games here."

"Nope, I'm fine." I clasped my hands in my lap and waited.

It was a boring wait as everyone grew silent and stayed in their proverbial corners. It was nearly twenty minutes before the Alphas began to arrive.

I recognized only a few. Lewis, because I had met him, Harrison, from his voice and confused look at me as he greeted the Tribunal members present. Price, because Heath had given me a picture of them together at an event for Alphas over a decade before. There were eight of them in total, all exuding power. These were the eight most powerful Alpha werewolves in the United States.

*Heath used to be one of them.*

It was a chilling thought. Heath was more dominant and powerful than most of the men in the room. He should have been standing on the other side of the room, wearing a deep navy blue or black suit just like the werewolves near Callahan, giving me a distrustful look like many of the Alphas were. He wasn't, though.

He was living in my territory.

And he was mine.

"Today, I've asked you all to be here because of the recent exposure of the werecats to the United States Government. Hasan and Jacky are taking no offense to any of you about this situation, but they bring forth other charges," Callahan said, taking on the most professional behavior I had ever seen from him. "A group of humans made attempts on Jacky's life. From her testimony, these humans weren't extremists, working from a leak from the BSA, but rather using that as a cover to kill her under the orders of a werewolf in this room."

The growls from the entire group, including Geoffrey Lewis, actually scared me. I could beat a group of low-ranking wolves, but if these eight ever decided to hunt me down, I was fucking done for.

"That's insane," Alpha Lewis snapped, glaring at me. "Why would any of us do that? Jacky, come on."

"You have the humans in your custody. You can turn around and interrogate them yourself and smell there was no lie," I said softly. "Why do you think we gave them to a wolf pack?"

The truth of my statement dawned on Alpha Lewis, who nodded slowly.

"I do have them in my custody now," he agreed. "I see. You picked an ally you knew, who you could trust not to turn around and kill them, to help cover it up if it is true."

"Exactly."

He nodded respectfully, knowing he had been used, but he couldn't do anything without smearing his own honor.

"Why is Queen Alvina here?" Alpha Price asked, his voice like gravel. I didn't like listening to it, but I was prejudiced since this man had killed a sister I never knew, then tried to kill me.

"I'm here to remove the geas," she said simply, smiling a little.

Alpha Price paled.

"Jacky's conspiracy theory is you sent these humans to kill her, and that it ties into the unfortunate death of Liza, daughter of Hasan," Callahan explained, standing in front of Price, using himself as a shield to keep the werewolf from coming at me.

## CHAPTER THIRTY-FIVE

Everyone was silent as some of the North American werewolves I didn't know threw glances at each other.

"She shouldn't know it was me," Alpha Price said, his gravel voice dropping a few notes as he spoke in a whisper to Alpha Callahan. "Because I was innocent in the matter. Both you and Hasan verified I told no lie about the situation, yet it comes back to haunt me, this mistake of young werewolves."

"I'm not lying when I say three humans were asked by you to kill me," I said softly as I stood. "And that they needed to pretend to be human extremists, so the responsibility of the attack would fall on the BSA and the United States."

Callahan lifted his hand to me as he stared at Price. I closed my mouth, stopping anything else from spilling out in this room. While I disliked Callahan, he was a sitting member of the Tribunal, not just a werewolf Alpha I could get smart with.

"How dare you—"

Callahan moved the hand in front of Price, who also shut up before he could continue.

"Do you smell a lie?" Callahan asked. Alpha Price shook his head. "I couldn't either, and let me tell you, I wish there was one. We were already on high alert, knowing a species was currently negotiating with a human government about the exposure of their species. It doesn't matter if it's werecats, fae, or the fucking cambions and their nephilim, nagas, kitsune, nymphs, and trolls. When you add an assassination attempt to the issue, it is dealt with to the fullest extent of our power. Now, it's time to figure out what really happened, and since it's you, we have to remove the geas about Liza." Callahan sighed, looking back at Hasan and me for a moment, then turned to Alvina. "Remove it. I don't know how—"

Alvina's eyes glowed as power rushed into the room. I couldn't feel anything, but Price, Callahan, two other werewolf Alphas, and Hasan all winced. One went so far as to clutch his forehead. Then all of them sagged in relief, and Alvina's eyes stopped glowing.

"It's gone," she said, crossing her legs and relaxing, sinking into the couch. "Sorry for the discomfort. The geas was old, so it had rooted itself deep into your minds instead of staying on your tongues. That's what makes the magic so powerful. The longer a geas is on a topic or a person, the more embedded it becomes. Some of you may notice the topic is still difficult. You've been conditioned to speak of it in other ways. You'll have to work through those issues on your own."

"Thank you," Hasan said, putting a hand on his chest and bowing from his seat. I clenched my jaw. He'd told me never to thank a fae.

Alvina's eyes twinkled. "Now that the geas is down, I won't be putting it back up. You can deal with the consequences of the events that led to this day for as long as you all shall live."

Callahan nodded, but Price didn't look happy.

"Let's get to the full accusation," Hasan declared, standing. I walked around the couch to his side. We stared down the wolves, side by side. "Jacqueline, present your formal accusation."

"I accuse Alpha Price of attempted assassination and interfering with the affairs of a supernatural species, not his own." I looked around, and no one interrupted, waiting for me to explain the charges. "While I understand the last charge is normally most impactful against werecats, I believe it applies in the case of any species willfully trying to ruin negotiations of another species with humans."

"It was a malicious act, so the charge stands," Alvina confirmed. "Explain the other charge in full, please."

"Alpha Price convinced three humans that I was a threat to his pack, to all werewolves, and set them on the path to kill me. If they had succeeded, their reward was to be Changed and brought into the pack. They were instructed to make it seem as if they were fanatic humans who wanted to kill supernaturals. That would have removed blame from the pack and pinned the blame on humans and the BSA, who would have been believed to have leaked my identity to extremists in the middle of negotiations. It would have been disastrous." I rubbed my hands together. "When the humans were caught, they revealed it was Alpha Price who had sent them and exposed the deal. At the time, I didn't know the identity of the werewolf Alpha involved with my sister's death. The geas had prevented my family from telling me in so many words, but when I told them the identity of the werewolf who tried to kill me, they found a way to make it abundantly clear who it was."

"The geas itself gave it away," Alvina said softly, nodding. "The inability to confirm or deny—the problem with geas, something I warned both rulers in this room of."

I nodded. "Two plus two equals four. I had a two and a four. It wasn't hard to figure out the missing piece of the puzzle."

"So, how does your theory end?" Callahan demanded. "Start from the beginning of your theory, how her death is involved in this."

"My theory in full? I believe Price sent the young werewolves to kill Liza and covered it up neatly by using plays on words. He never told them to kill her, maybe only said she was a threat, and he hoped she would be dealt with one day. I think he then killed them himself to keep their words from getting back to someone else. When asked if he sent the werewolves to kill Liza, he could flat out deny it, and there was no one else to question because he had killed them. My family never had the opportunity to look further into the incident. Because they could smell no lie, there was nothing to be done except grieve. Now, a hundred years later and his identity protected, he wanted to strike again at the ruling werecats."

"Why you?" Alvina was curious, but not as if I was a child. She was genuinely interested in what I was saying, her eyes locked on me with that twinkle.

"I'm not the best of my family. I try to maintain the status quo, but I do what I believe is right, even if it goes against traditional ways of thinking and solving problems. That makes me dangerous. I exposed my kind because I worked too closely with a werewolf, a member of an open species." I didn't say Heath by name because it was familiar. I couldn't say Alpha Everson because he wasn't one. He had to remain unnamed and given no thought. "It makes some werewolves nervous that I'm willing to travel to Russia and help destroy that pack when it would protect my family. My *human* family. Imagine what I would do to protect my werecat family in a century. Imagine how much trouble I could cause."

"And you are the youngest and most vulnerable, for all the trouble you cause me," Hasan pointed out. I could only nod. "My youngest will get herself killed, eventually. I'm sure everyone in this room believes that. It would be all too easy to speed that process up and make it believable it was just the way things go."

"Price?" Callahan turned to his werewolf again, almost as if he expected Price to plead guilty. "How do you plead?"

"Innocent," he snarled, glaring at me.

And there was no lie. Everyone in the room was wide-eyed as they looked at Price, heads turning slowly. Hasan stepped forward, but Callahan was still between them.

*He tells no lies.*

"I think she may believe all of this, but those humans could have lied to her or been mistaken," Price clarified.

"Price, I have them," Geoffrey said softly. "They're in my custody. I could ask them right now. She wouldn't have been that bold if they were lying."

"Doesn't matter. Smell no lie on me," Price snapped. "I am innocent. I don't lie. I believe in the truth."

"What do we do now?" Alvina asked. "I've never seen this. How interesting." She leaned on an arm of the couch, bringing her feet up, looking downright cozy.

"I think this is an attempt for Jacky Leon to cover up her own bad behavior," Price growled, pronounced thanks to his already gravelly voice. "You exposed your people, you have foolishly run around, and maybe I should ask you to address the rumors of stealing werewolf magic." Price spit toward me.

"What?" Callahan snapped, turning on me.

"It's not the point, and I didn't steal anything," I fired back.

"Can you speak with telepathy in werecat form?" Callahan demanded.

"It's not the point," Hasan snarled next to me.

"It's a fucking important one!" Callahan yelled. "How did she get the magic of werewolves? What dark sorcery did you and your fucking *mother* do?"

Werewolves, who had been growling, went silent. The scents of the room varied widely—fear, anger, confusion, shock, and betrayal. There were so many, I couldn't identify who was feeling what.

*He knows about Subira.*

"It wasn't her. It was given to me by a fae," I corrected, trying to protect my family by throwing myself and Brin to the literal wolves. Alvina leaned forward, her eyes on me.

"It would take an incredibly powerful fae to gift such an ability," she said softly. "Who was it?"

"You met him...Brin from my trial." I looked at Hasan after I answered, wondering if I looked as scared as I felt.

"There's no lie," Hasan said softly to her, looking past me as he touched my shoulder. "We knew this would come up eventually, but Jacky has preferred not to speak about the meeting she had with this fae, as is her right. It was a personal moment."

Alvina nodded slowly. "We've never been able to locate him. Not terribly uncommon as many fae are very good at hiding, but if he's so powerful he can grant abilities such as this, he's someone I need to speak to... Brin." Alvina had a faraway expression as she settled back into a comfortable position, tasting the name as if it was a wine. "We'll come back to this."

"Why not deal with it now?" Callahan asked, glaring at his fellow Tribunal member.

"Because it's not why we're here," she snapped. "We're here to discuss one of your werewolves trying to assassinate her, and this..."—she smiled—"is a distraction tactic that even worked on me. Get back on topic." Her words were like a lash through the room.

Price was bold enough to speak first.

"And none of it changes the fact I am innocent," he growled.

"Maybe this is a misunderstanding, and another

werewolf pushed this. We'll help you find out who." Callahan was just as confused as the rest of us.

"I can verify the truth," Alvina offered, "if both of the participants are willing. I would search their memories and find their personal truths—what they saw, smelled, said, and heard."

"I'm willing," I declared.

"I'm not. I've never lied to another werewolf, and I won't be subjected to a test of my innocence," Price countered. "My honor won't allow me to be subjugated by another species to prove myself."

Everyone raised an eyebrow at Price, who shook his head again.

"Price, it doesn't look good for you to be against this," Harrison said blandly. "While I hate Jacky, I wouldn't want to give her any more ammunition to keep coming back with this. Just verify the truth with the fae mediator, Queen Alvina, and move on."

"I'll do it, and I'll let Alvina verify that a fae gave me my ability. Just so you can't continue bitching about that," I said, glaring at the werewolf I *knew* killed my sister and tried to kill me. "What? Too scared to back up what you believe to be the truth?"

"I expect my fellow wolves to back me up because they know *my* honor is unimpeachable," Price snapped back.

*Now the werewolves need to choose between protecting and trusting one of their own or throwing him into something he doesn't want. Good play.*

The answer was obvious—the werewolves believed in doing anything for the pack.

"Price, you don't have to. I have faith in you," Callahan said, turning his narrowed eye gaze on me. "But you are more than welcome to."

"Yes, because my daughter's honor isn't unimpeachable. We all understand the implication. Don't try to be coy. You're not good at it," Hasan said, both insulted and insulting, not finding Callahan and Price as smart as they obviously thought themselves. He was a different man than I was used to. With his children, he was patient and kind but fierce. This was cold and removed, underscored with pure confidence that he was better than them in every way. He hadn't acted this way the last time we spoke to Callahan, but I had been the troublemaker then. That was the only difference I could find, except for Corissa's absence.

"How does this work?" I asked, looking at Alvina, who rose to her feet in one graceful, unbroken movement, which seemed to be both practiced and natural.

"Simple." She reached out and placed her hands on the sides of my head, covering my ears. "Close your eyes, and don't be scared."

It felt as if the ground fell out from under my feet the moment I closed my eyes.

## 36
## CHAPTER THIRTY-SIX

Alvina's presence was like a strong wind, whipping through my mind as it found a space where it could fit. I saw memories flash as if I was reliving everything in reverse and forward at the same time.

*"I know what a lie smells like,"* Alvina whispered in my head. *"Think of the moment the humans told you about Alpha Price. Concentrate on it. Right now, I'm on a magical ride through your memories, where I know you don't want me. You have...a very dangerous romantic life for the position you're in."*

Shit. She knows about Heath.

Just like that, I went to the memory of my birthday, seeing him tell me how much he cared for me. My mind tried to go through the steps, showing how he fell in love with me, and I had barely noticed it until it was too late to come back from. I hadn't noticed until it was impossible to ignore. How he looked at me, the memories now colored in a different light, knowing where we were now. It also showed me how I fell for him, the steady rock, who had many of the same principles, always willing to fight for what was right, even if we disagreed, as we did with Gwen.

*"Concentrate, Jacqueline. This isn't my business, and I won't tell anyone. Concentrate. The longer this takes, the more likely they are to think you are hiding something or something is wrong...Alpha Price, not Alpha Everson."*

I concentrated on Alpha Price's name, thinking about the humans I caught. It was a strange way of going through my memories. It started with the first attack, then the warning on the door. After that, I tried to skip when I'd been sniped, but still had to relive it. We flowed through the hospital on fast forward as I tried so hard to get to the right point.

*Why is this so hard?*

*"Minds and memories work in funny ways. You want me to know the truth. Your subconscious believes every step is important and is forcing us to walk through each step to the inevitable reveal. Yes, before you ask, I can hear your thoughts, every single one. I'm as much a part of your mind right now as you are."*

Understanding, I let her see the theories as Heath and I tried to walk our way through the situation. I was able to shove Zuri out of the picture, not needing a third opinion. She was helpful, but my sister wasn't involved. The same was true for my conversations with my family about the BSA.

We finally reached the interrogations. Alvina already knew the smell of a lie, so she hummed in my head when the scent never came.

*"The humans believe they tell the truth. This Sam Blake*

*wanted to be healed and to be part of something great again. He was easy to manipulate by an Alpha, who could give him both of those things. He understands right and wrong, though, and eventually realized he had done something very wrong."*

*Yes.*

*"I will tell the others you speak the truth of your encounter with these humans and the truth you received. Now, for the second order of business, something I am, admittedly, very curious about."*

*Brin, the fae.*

*"Yes...I can feel his magic on you now. He made a space for it, and the gift has intertwined with your curse. Only he could possibly take it away from you. I don't know if I have the power to do it."*

*You're the Queen of the Fae.*

*"I'm the third to hold the title," she admitted. "My mother, Titania, was the first. My elder sister and the oldest daughter of Oberon and Titania was the second. There aren't many fae more powerful than me, and those who are...They're my family."*

*I don't like the sound of that.*

*"I don't either. Think of this Brin."*

I took myself back to the motel and the moment I met Brin, the Irish fae who refused to tell me his clan.

*"I remember his face, but he doesn't seem powerful,"* Alvina whispered, very apparent she was talking to herself.

I made it to the night of the full moon and his act of gift giving, feeling how uncomfortable I had been.

*"No...it cannot be."*

*Who? What don't I know?*

*"He always did like cats. He would have considered it a small thing for one of his favorite species and a woman who needed help. My dear brother, Brion, always did like cats. That's his real name, so you understand how grand a gift you were given. King Brion of the fae, firstborn of Oberon and Titania, the first of the royal family, and the first of the Sidhe. Thank you for allowing me to see this memory. You've given me a great gift. I did not think I would ever discover what happened to him."*

She left my mind, and I was left stumbling into the real world, falling against Hasan as she stood very still. My heart was pounding as her words echoed in my head.

*I'll unpack this later. Don't have the time to be thinking about that.*

"Jacqueline, daughter of Hasan, speaks the truth. My formal recommendation is as stands. Bring the humans and have them verify what they said to her and verify the identity of Alpha Price or that someone was impersonating him." Alvina spoke while staring at me with wide eyes. "As for the other, her gift is of fae magic, not that of the moon cursed. I cannot remove it or alter it in any way, and it was a gift freely given with no bargain made." She sat down and became a statue. "It is unique to her, and therefore, there is no threat to the werewolves of more werecats getting this gift." She repeated nothing of what she had said to me. "It is not the sort of gift just any fae can give, so don't think about trying to convince others to give something similar to anyone else."

"Alvina, Queen of the fae and member of the Tribunal, has spoken," Hasan declared. "Your move, wolves."

"The humans can clear this up," Alvina said again. "Callahan?"

"I'm not bringing in humans to condemn my werewolves."

"Don't play favorites. I've executed fae for less than what he is accused of doing. Don't protect a potential murderer who won't submit himself to me. He might be a werewolf, but we made a deal eight hundred years ago—in the end, they all answer to the Tribunal. I'm willing to call the other members if this can't be resolved among us. We'll make an entire trial of it." She yawned. "But I'm tired of this. Jacky has been nothing but forthcoming, while your werewolf has hidden behind the pack, playing on the idea that his honor is perfect." Smiling, her teeth weren't human, not even close. They had been earlier, but now they were more like a shark's. "And *no one* has perfect honor."

"A duel of honor, then. A common fae tradition that would do well between a werecat and a werewolf," Price said loudly, stepping forward. "Silver blades, human forms, and no magic. Whoever wins will be the accepted truth of this matter. I'll put my life on the line for it."

*No, you just found a way to kill me and get what you want anyway—the ability to walk away without any sort of repercussions.*

Hasan and I looked at each other at the same moment.

"This is up to you," he said softly. "He's an older wolf, and you're a young werecat. On a full moon, I would have the fullest confidence in you, but..."

"In human form, we're more even, which makes it

fair," I finished, nodding. I turned back to Price. "I'll also put my life on the line. A duel of honor, trial by combat... whatever you want to call it."

"Needless waste of life," Alvina muttered. "And it might not even give the truth."

"He's correct. It's a fae tradition and would suit nicely for the problem we have," Hasan said as he went to her. "I would ask a small favor. Two silver blades, if you will."

Alvina nodded and raised her hands. In a blink, each hand closed on a hilt. Both blades looked exactly the same, a matching set.

"Daggers," she decided. "If you're allowing me to set the terms. These are silver daggers worn at the waist of a fae guard. Traditionally used to fight off assassins in close quarters, every member of my guard has one made this way for their uniforms. They are not ceremonial and are kept very sharp. They have no magic on them, something each of you can verify with your noses."

Callahan crossed the room and grabbed the one offered to him without hesitation. Hasan took the other more slowly, and I saw the worry of a father as he picked up the weapon his daughter was about to fight with.

"The humans are a much better idea," Alpha Lewis muttered, shaking his head.

"Yeah, well, take that up with your other Alpha," I growled across the room. "He's the one who refuses to go with easier options. He really does want me dead."

Price glared at me.

"Once the duel of honor has begun, it cannot be stopped until one of two things happens," Alvina began as each ruler sniffed the blades, then handed them off. It was heavy in my hands. "The obvious is death. If someone dies, the duel is over. The other option is for a side to concede, admitting they were wrong, and allowing the other side to exact punishment or retribution. This can include death. Considering we're dealing with a werewolf and a werecat, I have a feeling someone is going to die, anyway." Alvina seemed annoyed. "This ritual was started by the men in my family, and I've always hated it. Alpha Price, it doesn't endear you to me that you mentioned it without understanding its history."

"I don't need your endearment," he growled, looking over the dagger Callahan gave him.

"Callahan, train your wolves better," Alvina said softly, a clear warning. "If another insults me, it'll be the last thing they say."

"I'll remind them to be respectful of the Tribunal, regardless of species."

The room was cleared of furniture in a snap of Alvina's hands, the couches, tables, and chairs disappearing. Alpha Price and I stepped forward, glaring at each other.

"No, I won't be a party to this," Alpha Lewis said sharply, making everyone look at him in surprise. "I can't abide by this. Alpha Price has only ever spoken the truth, and Jacky Leon is a good soul who has proven she's willing to put her life on the line for anyone, regardless of species. I can't abide by this foolish behavior. I like a good fight as much as the rest of us, but this isn't a good fight. Even if we decide Price or Jacky is the winner, how does that make the truth clear? How? This just needlessly kills someone. I'm bringing the humans. They'll verify if they knew Alpha Price or not."

"No!" Price snarled.

"Why the fuck not?" Geoffrey asked, throwing up his hands. "Price, please explain to me—"

"Don't turn yourself into another traitor like Everson," Price growled.

"Watch your tone," Callahan warned. "Lewis is just as much an Alpha on this council as you are, and Everson is not the discussion today."

"He's always part of the discussion now that he's one of the most powerful wolves in the world. Him and her, his little buddy who can't even stay in line for her own family." Price pointed at me with the dagger. "The fact anyone here would entertain her theories and drag me here shows me none of you are fit to rule the werewolves. Werewolves first—that's what we used to believe. I'm going to take us back to that, and dealing with this is the first of a new future for our kind."

The room went utterly silent.

"Are you challenging me?" Callahan asked softly, stepping closer to Price.

"Not yet, not if you prove yourself worthy to rule our kind," Price countered.

Callahan looked at me, then back at his werewolf. He was the ruler of the werewolves, and it was apparent to everyone he was being held by the balls—caught between his responsibilities as a member of the Tribunal, his other Alphas, and Price's claims.

"Did you try to kill Jacky Leon?" he asked softly.

"I did not. I don't lie. Ever. I can't." Price was adamant,

and there was no smell of a lie in the words, just as he had promised.

"Because you have magic that covers it, don't you?" Hasan asked from beside me. His words sent ripples through the room. "You *are* Talented. I was beginning to wonder if I was going mad. You are a liar. You lie all the time."

Alpha Price's eyes went wide.

"You...you don't know what you're talking about."

"Is that the *truth*, Price?" Callahan snarled.

Price took a step back, knowing he had been exposed.

"Grab him, wolves," Callahan commanded. "Alvina, will you go into his mind and find the truth against his will?"

"With pleasure," she purred, walking closer as the Alphas of the North American Werewolf Council grabbed their friend and forced him to his knees. Alvina was fast, grabbing hold of his head. Price screamed as his mind was violated and searched. She started to laugh, then pulled away.

"Oh, Hasan, you were always one of the smartest men I know. Such a useful ability, to lie without getting caught. He manipulates his scent." She stepped back. "And he's the one who told the human government Jacky's name. He purposefully used it when he knew they were in the room, knowing they were already curious about her. This was all a game to him, honed to a deadly edge by the hate in his heart." She smiled cruelly, those dangerous teeth showing through. "He had Liza killed, then killed the young werewolves, just as Jacky put together. Smell no lie, moon cursed."

"Jacqueline, kill him," my father ordered, his words cold. "You were his next victim. It's your right."

I walked across the room, vindicated as Price looked up in fear. His dagger was gone. He was unarmed, as all of us were when we entered the room.

He didn't try to run, knowing his scheme was over. I grabbed his hair and shoved the dagger into his throat, feeling the blood pour over my hands. I yanked it out and stabbed again in his chest, aiming for his black heart.

I didn't count how many times I stabbed him, but at that moment, I knew I hated him as much as he hated me. He had tried to destroy my life, everything I had been working toward, by revealing me. He had tried to kill me and destroy my family, as he had once before.

Hasan had to pull me off him, covered in his blood.

"Let's go home," he whispered. "Let's take you home. It's over. You did it, Jacky."

## 37

# CHAPTER THIRTY-SEVEN
## APRIL 14, 2021

I was walking into the bar when I saw them. Three agents from the BSA, one with his arm in a sling, looking more upset than the other two, who were enjoying a drink. Special Agent Collins couldn't drink while he was on the painkillers the hospital had given him, something I found both funny and sad. Instead, he spun his pack of cigarettes on the table, looking put out as Miller and an unknown woman toasted silently and drank.

As I watched the scene unfold, I heard the news on the televisions around the bar.

"Today, we're bringing you an amazing revelation that will change our country and the world. The Bureau of Supernatural Affairs has confirmed the existence of yet another supernatural species, the werecats."

It had been similar for hours since the news broke at noon. Everyone was rehashing what the BSA put out to the public over and over again.

I wasn't too worried at the moment. No one was trying to kill me, no one knew who I was, and no one knew I was the woman who spoke to the President that morning, thanking him for his respect for the deal I had come to with the BSA.

*I own a bar, and I talk to the President. What a fucking world.*

"I thought we had a deal," I finally said loudly as I walked toward the agents. Dirk was behind the bar, serving them, and groaned as I came closer. He was only there helping the other bartender because of the agents. That's how I knew they were even around. He was keeping an eye on them for me.

"We're having a drink in celebration," Special Agent Miller explained. "For...you know."

"And with this, we wanted to introduce you to someone," Special Agent Collins said, getting off the barstool and walking closer to me, making a semi-circle perimeter. "If you have a moment."

"Yeah—"

"Hey, Jacky! Did you hear about this?" Joey asked across the bar, pointing up at the screen closest to him.

"Yes, I did," I confirmed patiently.

"Have you met any?" he asked.

I smiled and knew my eyes shifted to my feline gold. "Yes, Joey, I've met a werecat or two." *Or a dozen.* "And that's the only time I'll indulge that question."

He paused, his eyes going wide. I waved and walked out the backdoor, letting the agents follow me.

"Who are you?" I asked, turning to the female agent.

"Agent Kirk, but you can call me Bethany. I'm the

agent who will be stationed here to continue working with you. I currently live in Houston, but I'm looking for a home here in Jacksonville because you're going to be my number one priority."

"I'm going to have to train another one of you?" I frowned at Collins and Miller.

"We tried warning you that we're not the people who get to stay," Collins said without any sympathy. "Agent Kirk is good, and you can trust her. We've briefed her on everything we can."

"I understand you live a very private life and will do my best to respect that."

"Yeah…" I sighed. "We'll catch up later. How's Sunday when I'm off? Tonight is a friend's birthday party, so I need to head out."

"That's fine."

"Wait," Collins said, trying to step around me to stop me from running off. "You never did tell us what happened to the men who tried to kill you."

"Oh…uh…" I tsked. "That's too bad."

"Miss Leon, anything is better than nothing."

"One of them has been given work with another pack, a clean start. The two others were a little less repentant, and that's all I know. I let the werewolves deal with it because they were the ones who sent them after me. That's how these things work." I shrugged.

"That's not—"

"They're not dead or being abused. That I can promise. Reach out to Alpha Lewis. He'll be able to give you more details."

"I'll do that," he warned.

"Alpha Lewis already knows you will. Now, I'm leaving. You're not supposed to hang out in the bar in uniform, so...fix that. Customers or not, you can't be agents drinking in my bar. That doesn't work for me." I waved them back inside. When Dirk saw me, I pointed at them behind their back. "Keep an eye on them," I mouthed.

He nodded and started chatting them up the moment they got back to the bar. He was reminding them of the same rules I had put down for them after I killed Alpha Price. Miller was trying to argue, but it wasn't flying with Dirk, who was finding comfortable confidence in his new position. He was a tough guy and didn't let people intimidate him. It worked out.

I smiled and went out to my new car, a Kia Soul...with a roll cage installed, and a number of other things that didn't come standard. It had a nice bit of space in the back, though, and it was an incredibly normal vehicle otherwise, something I thought was important. I certainly didn't need the one-hundred-thousand-dollar SUV Heath had tried to convince me to get, even if I could afford it.

I drove away from my bar, feeling normal for the first time in weeks, even with pictures of my werecat form being splashed all over the news. I tried the radio and realized it was hopeless, too. Everyone and their grandmother had something to say about the new supernatural species. Everyone was wondering how many were hiding in the world, what we could do if we were just like werewolves, and more.

The identities of my people were safe. Even if the BSA leaked me, it was just me. I knew it would get hard to hold that fragile barrier up as time went on, but it was something I could survive.

I pulled up in front of Heath's, grinning as Carey came out to greet me, her father right behind her.

I was home, and everyone was safe. Alpha Price couldn't take this away from me. I grabbed the presents I put in the new Kia the day before and handed them off to Carey after a hug. Heath wrapped his arm around my shoulders as we closed the front door.

"How do you feel?" he asked softly.

"Like we're going to enjoy a moment of peace, then something else will happen," I admitted. "I just met Agent Kirk, assigned to me by the BSA to be my permanent liaison. You know that's going to be a problem."

"Yeah, but we'll enjoy the new normal while it lasts."

"We will," I agreed. "Let's have cake and ice cream and pretend everything is fine."

He laughed and held me to his side as we entered the dining room, where Carey was watching Landon put candles on the cake. She looked up and smiled at us.

"I like this," she declared. "You two. I was mad at first, but you know, now that I've thought about it a lot, it's pretty cool."

"Well, with her approval, who would dare tell us to stop?" I laughed as I sat down. Landon even smirked, shaking his head a little.

With this odd family I had found, I felt as though I

could handle whatever was thrown at me next. We'd survived everything…so far.

Keep reading for more information about the next release, special news, and more.

# DEAR READER

Thank you for reading!

If you don't like the call to action on the previous page... Let me know? It's my first time doing it.

I want to mention a special project I have coming! You know that whole Zuri plot part of this book? THERE'S A BABY! There's also a novella coming telling her story while she's been away and how she ended up where we see her with Jacky. You can find it right in the Call of Magic Anthology! Preorder now for **only $0.99** on any platform.

**Call of Magic Anthology**
Ancient and Immortal: A Tribunal Archives Story
October 26, 2021

Now we'll talk about the book you just read.

I mean, humans know about Jacky and werecats now. And while it might not be what would realistically happen in our world if we discovered werecats, let's

*Dear Reader*

remember, this is not our world. They've known about supernaturals for more than a couple of decades now. This world is something parallel to ours in technology and culture, but it's a split from our timeline, I guess. They had werewolves come out to the public and that's changed everything, including human perspective and politics.

Meaning, it's my world and my fake United States will act however I want it to.

Now, onto the best news... WHEN IS THE NEXT BOOK?

## ROYAL PAWN
## JACKY LEON BOOK SIX
## JULY 13, 2021

If I still have you, head over to my website to get the latest updates on the next book in the series. Head over to my website and sign up for my mailing list! There are exclusive teasers for those who are signed up: Knbanet.com/newsletter

Also, I have a Patreon, where I write a monthly short story or novella. You can check that out here: Patreon.com/knbanet

And remember,

Reviews are always welcome, whether you loved or hated the book. Please consider taking a few moments to leave one and know I appreciate every second of your time and I'm thankful.

# THE TRIBUNAL ARCHIVES

The Jacky Leon series is set in the world of The Tribunal. Every series and standalone novel is written so it can be read alone.

For more information about The Tribunal Archives and the different series in it, you can go here:

tribunalarchives.com

# ACKNOWLEDGMENTS

I'm very bad at giving really public praise. I shower people in praise in private. But that's not everyone's love language and that's okay.

So this little page shall now be dedicated to everyone who helps me get these books from the concept to the release and beyond. From my PA, to my editor and my proofreader, to my wonderful friends helping me through the hardest moments. To my husband, who doesn't read my books, but loves that I write them and is willing to listen to me talk about them for hours.

And to you, the reader, for without you, I wouldn't have anyone to share these stories with. I'm a storyteller at heart and you have given me the greatest gift of listening.

I love all of you. Thank you for continuing to go on this journey with me.

# ABOUT THE AUTHOR

KNBanet.com

Living in Arizona with her husband and 5 pets (2 dogs and 3 cats), K.N. Banet is a voracious... video game player. Actually, she spends most of her time writing, and when she's not writing she's either gaming or reading.

She enjoys writing about the complexities of relationships, no matter the type. Familial, romantic, or even political. The connections between characters is what draws her into writing all of her work. The ideas of responsibility, passion, and forging one's own path all make appearances.

- facebook.com/KNBanet
- instagram.com/Knbanetauthor
- bookbub.com/authors/k-n-banet
- amazon.com/K.N.-Banet/e/B08412L9VV
- patreon.com/knbanet

## ALSO BY K.N. BANET

**The Jacky Leon Series**

Oath Sworn

Family and Honor

Broken Loyalty

Echoed Defiance

Shades of Hate

Royal Pawn

Rogue Alpha

Bitter Discord

**Volume One:** Books 1-3

**The Kaliya Sahni Series**

Bounty

Snared

Monsters

Reborn

Legends

Destiny

**Volume One:** Books 1-3

**The Everly Abbott Series**

Servant of the Blood

Blood of the Wicked

**Tribunal Archives Stories**

Ancient and Immortal (Call of Magic Anthology)

Hearts at War

Full Moon Magic (Rituals and Runes Anthology)

Made in United States
Orlando, FL
19 July 2023